Comfort and Mirth

Comfort and Mirth

Lori Joan Swick

TCU Press

Fort Worth, Texas

Library of Congress Cataloging-in-Publication Data

Swick, Lori Joan.
    Comfort and mirth / Lori Joan Swick.
        p. cm.
    ISBN 978-0-87565-394-5 (paper : alk. paper)
    1. Self-realization in women--Fiction. 2. Housewives--
Fiction. 3. Austin (Tex.)--Fiction. 4. Texas--History--
1846–1950--Fiction. I. Title.
    PS3619.W525C66 2009
    813'.6--dc22

                                        2008036399

                        TCU Press
                     P. O. Box 298300
                   Fort Worth, Texas 76129
                       817.257.7822
                    http://www.prs.tcu.edu

            To order books: 800.826.8911

        Designed by Barbara Mathews Whitehead

For Mindy

Contents

Comfort and Mirth

# Prologue

Dear Mother,

If a broken mirror brings seven years of bad luck, how long would it take the world to right itself if the sky shattered? I ask because the southwestern winds have sheared the clouds into a sheet of glass with the luster of quicksilver, and lately, I have come to understand how incredibly fragile the firmament is. I don't suppose one could catch a glimpse of what's really going on in Heaven before the future fell into crystal pieces at her feet?

It seems like a lifetime since I left you in Seattle. I was so excited about starting my new life in Texas with Brooks, I never could have foreseen myself writing you a letter like this one, but I have great news and great regrets. I'll start with the regrets, for they threaten the rest of my thoughts like a pair of open scissors in an apron pocket. First, I regret I don't write this news with the joy I'd always imagined I would—this is also the deepest edge of my guilt. Second, I regret I did not write this letter last month when it actually was news, but I have a daughter. I named her Margery Rose because she is so small, sweet, and beautiful—at least to me.

I went into labor just after midnight on the tenth of last month; it wasn't difficult, but lasted a long time. Dr. Steiger administered a sedative, and of course, that's all I remember until I awoke in a hospital room the next morning. I rang for the nurse. When she finally came in, I asked her if I'd had a girl or a boy. She told me it was a girl. When I asked to see my daughter, she didn't respond, but as she took my temperature and blood pressure, I could tell from the look on her face something was terribly wrong . . .

1. Daughters

The brakemen called to one another from above, a whistle pierced the drone of the engine, and the train slowed to pass through another station. Perhaps they would stop at this one, she thought; she longed to walk in fresh air for a moment or two and renew her perspective. A slate-frame building passed by the window before she could read the name of the town on the sign over the platform. The only break from the scenic monotony was a glimpse of a rotund station master leaning over to scratch his knee and the sound of the brass pounder furiously tapping Morse code messages onto wires reeled out over the hills. Their destination lay less than an hour away when Camille realized she had no idea of what was to happen when they arrived. They couldn't stay the night in their house; they had no furniture. Brooks snored softly beside her. She eased the watch out of his vest pocket—only half-past four in the afternoon, but the sky was so heavy with dark clouds it felt much later.

"I'm going to stretch my legs a bit," she whispered to her sleeping husband as she gently pushed his weight off her shoulder, stood up, and smoothed the creases out of her woolen skirt. She strolled toward the back of the car, trying not to look into the faces of the few weary travelers who hadn't fallen asleep.

As she neared the door to the adjoining car, a gruff voice from the rear window seat addressed her, "I wouldn't go back there, if I were you." An elderly man with masses of graying black hair around his face glared at her. "A pretty little white lady like you would never make it back in one piece."

Camille looked down at her feet; several of her shoe buttons had come unfastened. Her cheeks flushed. She strained to see through the layers of earth-beaten windows into the car behind them, but she couldn't make out the faces of the passengers. "That's the Jim Crow car." He eyed her intensely. A young woman seated next to him appeared from under a wide-brimmed black hat with a huge silk Castilian red rose spilling over the brim. The pungency of her perfume and the deep purple and black bruises around her right eye sent a quiver of nausea through the pit of Camille's stomach. The man dropped a heavy hand on the woman's arm, and she looked back into her lap. Camille nodded and quickly made her way back to her seat, hounded all the way by his guttural laughter.

"Newlyweds?" A petite woman with flaming hair and close features smiled from the seat across the aisle; a red-headed daughter napped under each arm.

"How could you tell?" Camille sighed as she rebuttoned her shoes.

The woman nodded toward Brooks. "Your husband spends much less time in the smoking car than the other men."

Camille sat back and smiled. The little girls looked like angels in their sleep. How lovely to have daughters. She imagined her own with Brooks' dark curls and her rosy complexion. They would have two—perhaps even three. "Your girls are beautiful," she said.

"And heavy," the woman answered as she shifted the weight of one. "Tess Dunning. How long you been married?"

"Not quite a week. I suppose you could say this is our honeymoon."

Tess shook her fiery locks and closed her eyes. "How romantic! I remember when Carl and I were first married. He couldn't stand to leave me when it was time for him to go out." She giggled. "Now he practically celebrates the whole day before."

"Go out?"

"He works the rail. We're on our way to Louisiana because the Southern Pacific offered him a better rate—the trips are longer. They gave us free fare, only they don't go past Houston, so Carl has to work for fare while we're still on the U.P. He's the flagman in the caboose. What's your name?"

"Camille De . . . uh—Abernathy."

Tess laughed. "What does your husband do?"

Camille sat up straighter. A thrill shot through her at the word "husband." The man who slept next to her was still so mysterious—so unknown—eight years her elder, so intelligent and so worldly. It didn't seem possible he had become a part of her life in such a way the rest of the world should notice. "He's accepted a position as professor of philosophy at the University of Texas at Austin. We're moving down from Seattle."

Tess shook her head again. "Handsome and rich. You did well."

Her words would have been flattering had they not been so presumptuous. Their financial affairs were no one's business but their own. She didn't know the extent of them herself. She turned her attention away from Tess and looked out the window where the ochre hills rolled out to the horizon stippled with bare trees stabbing at the vast gray sky without grace or form. A chill passed through her. Brooks snored louder.

"We got a little place in Houma," Tess rambled on. "It's across the street from the house where I grew up. It only has two rooms, but Carl can build on. How about you?"

"Brooks bought a home for us. I haven't seen it yet."

Tess' eyes widened. "You mean you let a man pick out a house for you?"

Camille looked back at her blankly. Brooks had traveled down a couple of months earlier by himself to select their home while she planned their wedding and tended to other matters in Seattle. Though it had concerned her to allow a man of such stern practicality to make such a vital decision, lost in his attentions and preoccupied with all the other aspects of such dramatic life changes, she had forgotten to make any specific demands about the rooms, the kitchen, or even the grounds. Since then, she worried the rooms would be too dark, she might not have adequate garden space, and the soil might be infertile or so sandy she could raise nothing but cactus and sagebrush.

Brooks moaned and rolled his head in search of support. His hat slipped from his hand, and she caught it before it dropped onto the dusty hardwood planks of the train floor. Tess' eyes followed her, so she forced a smile. "Our house has two stories and electricity."

"You have electricity? You must be rich. Does it have indoor plumbing?"

"Yes. I believe he said it does—with heated water on the lower floor. I'm sure I'll like the house if Brooks does."

"I would feel like an absolute queen in a house with electricity and an indoor toilet!"

Camille sighed as she fingered the rim of Brooks' flannel bowler. Tess pressed her, "He must be an important professor."

"He's just starting out, but he's written a book."

"He's an author?" Tess' voice shot up a half a range. Her daughters both started in their sleep. "I've never met an author before. What's his book about?"

"Well, it's very philosophical. It's called *The Dichotomy of Human Nature.*"

"Oh." Tess wrinkled a mass of freckles up into her forehead.

Camille went on, "It's been translated into five languages and is sold all over the world."

"Really? Do you think he would autograph one for me?"

"Why yes, but . . . " Brooks stopped snoring and stirred. "But, what?"

"Well, you wouldn't want to ask him right after he wakes up—and we haven't any unpacked copies."

One of the little girls awoke and started to whine. Camille watched as the woman stroked her daughter's hair and gently reassured her. "If you'll give me your address in Houma, I'll send one along to you later."

Tess dictated the information before her daughters were both completely awake. Camille put the note in her hatbox while the train whistle screeched the announcement of the next station and the rhythm of the wheels slowed to syncopated jerks. Brooks awoke and blinked madly while feeling for his hat. Camille placed it in his hands and looked out the window. Her heart sank. "Oh, this can't be Austin. It looks so forlorn."

Brooks stretched and rubbed his eyes before leaning over her and taking a look for himself. "It isn't," he said. "It's Round Rock. We're close, though."

Camille sighed and pulled her mother's shawl more closely around herself to keep the chill from seeping through the surface of her skin and settling into her soul. "Will someone be there to meet us?"

"Nothing was said." He stared at his hat in his hand. "I thought we might get a room at the Driskill tonight, or above the Pearl House Saloon. Tomorrow we'll get some furniture and hopefully spend our first night in our new home." He put his hat on, looked into her eyes, and smiled. She relaxed a little.

"All I long for right now is a proper bath," she said.

"Sounds marvelous, doesn't it?"

They rode in silence until the view suddenly came alive. Yellow lights gleamed from the windows of domiciles tucked into the hills, and the stained glass of a cathedral shone out of the glowering sky—now empurpled of an early dusk. Garlands of greenery festooned the buildings, and a huge red velvet bow hung on each gaslight. Christmas of 1910 would be unlike any other she had known. The whistle wailed for the last time, and the view stilled at last in front of a large brownstone building resembling book drawings of medieval castles. The conductor barked out their arrival in Austin. The trip had taken seven long days and nights with nine train changes—a journey too long and arduous to be endeavored again anytime soon, if ever. A thick, cold drizzle greeted them as they descended onto the platform. A Christmas tree winked from inside the busy station. Her thoughts uttered themselves aloud, "I miss my mother."

Brooks dealt her a hard look. "Don't crumble on me now, Camille!"

2. Perception

"Abernathy!" Camille's new last name resounded from within the crowd. Brooks looked around.

"Thomas! How good of you to come." A young man with a captivating smile and horn-rimmed glasses hurried over with an attractive woman on his arm. Brooks started introductions. "This is Professor Thomas Leighton. He teaches psychology at the university and occupies the office next to the one I am to have. He was gracious enough to show me around on my previous trip."

"This is my wife, Eveline," Thomas said.

Brooks nodded and tipped his bowler. "Nice to meet you, and may I introduce my bride, Camille." Camille managed a thin smile as she set her mother's gray moiré hatbox by her feet to offer a hand in greeting and rewrap her shawl. A gruff call from the platform announced the unloading of the baggage, and the men hurried over to collect the only material consolations she had left in the world.

The women stood in the middle of the platform, jostled from all directions. Eveline addressed her with a velvet smooth voice, "Thomas is so fond of your husband. He said everyone at the university is bubbling over with news of his arrival and the stunning success of his book."

Camille looked over at Brooks as he pulled her father's old carpetbag from the lading hold and placed it on a jitney. She picked up her hatbox. "Have you read it?"

The woman's long lashes twitched over her fair cheeks. "I've skimmed through it."

Camille looked into her hazel eyes. They were painted modestly, but perfectly. Her tawny hair was combed up and wrapped under the side rise of her black hat with precision, and her Wooltex dress was exquisitely tailored to her trim form. Camille sighed and pulled a damp curl out of her face. "I don't understand it either."

Eveline smiled until they broke into laughter. "I've fixed up the guestroom at our home for the two of you."

"You needn't put yourself to such trouble. Brooks says we can rent a room for tonight and. . ."

"I've done everything already," Eveline interrupted. "I've been looking forward to your arrival—especially as we are to be neighbors."

"We're neighbors?"

"Yes, Thomas told me your husband purchased the Woods' house three doors down."

The men finished loading the baggage. Thomas wrote directions for the jitney courier and Brooks paid him. Thomas helped Camille up into the backseat of his scroll spring surrey. Brooks climbed up beside her with a sly wink. As Thomas shook the reins, the two large roans clomped over the red bricks of Congress Avenue toward the capitol building. Eveline pointed out the finest shopping establishments while Thomas provided them with a more historical and architectural account of what could be seen through the darkening mist. He showed them two opera houses, four saloons, and the Littlefield Building, which, as he explained, would be the tallest skyscraper between New Orleans and San Francisco upon completion of the ninth floor—currently under construction strictly for the purpose of justifying the claim. They drove around the massive capitol building and past the northwestern corner of the university grounds where Brooks named one building after another. His voice faded as Camille's vision blurred. She closed her eyes and huddled herself against the icy fist tightening its grip within her chest.

Eveline put a hand on her shoulder. "Are you well, Camille?"

"Quite. I've just taken a chill."

"Don't take cold now," Eveline exclaimed. "Not just before Christmas. I have Irish stew on the stove, and I'll make some tea."

"We'll go by the house first," Brooks said. "I'm anxious for Camille to see it."

"No!" Camille blurted. "Not now, dear—please. I can't." She shuddered from the damp cold that seemed to originate from within her and emanate outward.

"Why not? We'll pass right by it for heaven's sake!"

Eveline reached over and took Camille's hands in her own. "Why, she's shivering. She'll take ill for sure. Please hurry, Thomas. We need to get her out of this weather."

Thomas snapped the reins, and the horses quickened their pace. "I'll pass around on Rio Grande," he said. "We'll be there in no time."

Camille looked up into Brooks' incredulous glare. "Not in this gray drizzle," she explained. "I don't want to see it for the first time like this."

"I don't understand."

"It's a matter of first impressions. Don't you carry away certain attitudes about things based on your first impressions of them?" Her teeth chattered.

"Of course not," he growled. "That would be ridiculous. Do you expect me to believe you could never come to enjoy this lovely home I've bought for you if you were to see it for the first time on an overcast day? That's preposterous, Camille!"

Thomas came to her defense. "Certain conditions can distort one's perception, you know, Brooks. I understand how she feels."

"Perception . . . yes, I suppose I do understand." His face iced over. "Two distinct theories of perception present themselves: the Realist theory, which asserts whatever is perceived exists independently of being perceived, which is to say that an educated individual automatically adjusts his perception to accommodate his ever-changing needs and sense of self-satisfaction. Then there is the theory of Naive Realism—that of the plain man, who sees things exactly the way they are and is incapable of filtering that which is perceived to meet the demands of his own human nature."

The horses' hooves beat into the soft earth. Camille's face grew white-hot despite her chill. At last they reached the Leightons' home. Eveline hurried Camille in and up the stairs to the guestroom while the men put the carriage in the shed and tended to the horses. Eveline took Camille's damp shawl and wrapped her in a pale yellow quilt with forget-me-not edging. Camille sank into the warmth like a child curling up in her mother's lap. "It was good of you to meet us at the station and bring us into your home, Mrs. Leighton."

"Please, call me Eveline. I'm sure we'll become fast friends, and such formalities will only get in the way. May I call you Camille?"

"Of course." It felt good to be fussed over, and she realized for the first time since she had left home how desperately she had been craving female companionship.

"Lie down now—make yourself comfortable and get warmed up. I'm going down to heat water for your bath. I'll send Thomas up later to make a fire for you, and I'll have

Brooks bring up your things as soon as they are delivered. Will you have a bowl of stew while you wait?"

"Thank you, no. I have no appetite."

"Maybe later. I'll make your tea. Do you like Earl Grey?"

"Yes." Camille managed a smile. "But do you by any chance have any chamomile?"

"I believe I do," Eveline answered. "Would you like a mild blend?"

"That would be wonderful." Camille took off her hat and hung it on a bedpost. "I find chamomile chases chills and soothes raw nerves better than anything else I've tried."

As Eveline left, Camille sat on the soft, high bed taking in the simple elegance of the Leightons' guestroom. She lay her head down, covered herself with the quilt, and stared at the ceiling trying to decide just what color it was—peach, ecru, salmon, pink? No, flesh, she decided. It was just a rosy flesh tone no matter how she looked at it.

She awoke well after nightfall to find her white gown and fresh bath linens on the bed next to her. On the vanity was a tray with Viola soap and talcum powder. She took everything into the adjoining bath. A hanging incandescent lamp illuminated a massive cast-iron ball-and-claw-footed tub filled with steaming rose water. She undressed slowly, watching her slender form flicker in and out of shadow in the oval glass over the washstand. She poured cool water from the Delft-blue pitcher into the bowl, splashed her porcelain-pink cheeks, and rubbed her eyelids. She stared into her own dark eyes— looking for the beautiful woman so many others seemed to see. She lowered herself into the tub and steeped until the last of the chill, which had vexed her all evening, seeped out of her pores and evaporated into the steam over her head.

When she returned to the guestroom, a small flame whispered secrets to itself in the fireplace on the far wall.

Hammered-tin tiles and polished brass accessories twinkled in the glow. Cream-colored drapes with passementerie of the same flesh tone at the hem had been drawn shut, and the bed had been remade with the quilt turned back. She sat under the covers, pulled the pins out of her dark hair, and brushed her soft curls, allowing the warmth of the room to overtake her in waves—one with every long stroke. Eveline tapped on the door. She brought in another tray with an intoxicating smell of aromatic spices, which mingled with the floral scent of the Viola toiletries still fresh on Camille's skin. Memories of home enveloped her in alternating pulses of pain and hope.

Eveline placed the tray on the nightstand and pulled a rocking chair over from a corner by the fireplace. She poured tea. "Milk? Sugar? I know you said you weren't hungry, but I made gingerbread for dessert and thought you might like a little with some warm applesauce."

"Neither in the tea, thank you, but I'd love some of your gingerbread. I recovered my appetite when the smell of all-spice came into the room." Camille accepted a cup and saucer and took a sip. "I'm sorry I've spoiled your dinner plans. I hope Thomas won't think me rude for not coming down."

"Don't be a goose. He knew you weren't feeling well. Brooks came in to check on you while you slept. The men are in Thomas' study now, smoking smelly cigars and speaking all scientifically. I'm glad you napped. You seem to have shaken your chill."

"I feel wonderful now."

"Good. We came down from Massachusetts by rail. I won't soon forget the trials and discomforts of long-distance travel."

"How long ago?"

"Three years." Eveline handed Camille a plate of gingerbread generously topped with the applesauce. "Four in April. Perhaps you would prefer to have some stew now?"

"No, really. This is heavenly."

"The stew didn't turn out especially good, anyway. I'm much better at baking than cooking. Do you like to bake?"

"Mother and I loved to bake—pies mostly—all sorts of berries grow wild in the Northwest, so we made berry pies and tarts. And when apples came over the Cascades from Washington to the market, we made apple pies and strudels, but the berry pies were always my favorite."

"Do you still have the recipes?"

"Um-hmm. We contrived most of them ourselves, but we always wrote them down and kept perfecting them. I could never part with my recipes. My mother has always been an amazing gardener, so we based our recipes on herbs and flowers we grew around our house. We sold our baked goods at market every Saturday, as well as herb plants, sachets, and herb and floral arrangements."

Eveline carefully measured three teaspoons of milk into her own cup. "How lovely! Your mother was a professional herbalist?"

"Yes, of necessity, actually. My father died when I was four. Mother had to sell the house on the island and rent a house on a half acre of land in Seattle's Belltown district. She developed her penchant for gardening and baking into a profession, which supported the two of us well enough. I always loved helping her—even when I was very young."

"You were an only child?"

"Yes."

"So was I. How was it—if you don't mind my asking—your father died?"

Camille took a bite of her gingerbread and savored it for a moment before continuing. "He was a foreman in the ship-building industry. He was taken quickly and painlessly, I was told, when an iron brace that supported the mast of a ship he had been inspecting slipped and dropped the wooden rigging onto his head."

"I'm sorry . . ."

"It was a long time ago. I have no real memories of him. I don't even know what he looked like. I try and try to remember and I just can't."

"Your mother has no photographs?"

"None. The man hated cameras and refused to stand before one. Mother said he always wore a thick beard. I have only one vague personal recollection."

"What?"

"It's silly."

"No, it isn't. It's part of your legacy. Perhaps even the largest part, if it's what you remember."

Camille set her plate down and hugged her knees. "I was sitting on his lap riding across the sound on a steamer. That's all. I can't remember his face. I can't even remember if we were on our way to Belltown or back to the island. I have no idea of anything he said or what he might have been thinking."

"Your mother doesn't remember?"

"I don't think she was with us; I never discussed it with her. I have no more of him than the one memory—just . . ."

"Just what?"

"It doesn't matter."

"Of course it matters. Please, tell me."

"Of all things, I remember how he smelled. It was a distinctively masculine smell, like none I have noticed since—

rather like the smell of a campfire made from fir kindling on a winter's night—but not exactly so, of course. As I said, it's ridiculous."

"I don't think so." Eveline sat silently for a while before pouring more tea.

"At any rate," Camille continued, "I still have lots of the recipes that Mother and I concocted, and I dare say many were so good people stood in lines for our pies and fussed and moaned when we sold out."

"Perhaps we could exchange some of our favorites," Eveline suggested. "If you don't mind sharing them."

"Oh, of course not. They aren't secrets any more. I would like your recipe for gingerbread to begin with."

"Then you shall have it," Eveline laughed softly. "It's a favorite of Thomas', especially at Christmastime."

They sipped their tea, finished their desserts, and watched as the fire snapped. "Brooks is very handsome," Eveline commented. "According to Thomas, he has already become somewhat of a legend around the university—having his first book become a best seller so quickly and all. You must be very proud of him."

Camille hesitated, her thoughts of Brooks still clouded over and thick with drizzle. "I am proud of him, but he certainly didn't display very legendary behavior on the way over from the train station, did he?"

Eveline sat back and rocked herself gently. "I'm sure he was just tired."

Camille stared into the brilliance of the fire. "How cleverly he thinks he sends his insults over my head—what with his 'plain man' quotes and theories and all—as if a twist of gender and a lengthy word or two could throw me from deciphering his intent." She stole her gaze from the hearth and looked into Eveline's eyes. "I suppose I must admit to a certain amount of the naiveté which he assigns me, but, oh Eveline, I am not a fool!"

Eveline stopped rocking and leaned forward. "Of course you aren't, Camille, and I'm sure Brooks doesn't have you figured for one. His nerves were wearing on him. That's all."

"I've a little perception philosophy for him. 'Simple creatures, whose thoughts are not taken up, like those of educated people, with the care of a great museum of dead phrases, are very quick to see the live facts which are going on around them.'"

Eveline's eyes sparkled new greens and golds. "Oliver Wendell Holmes!"

"Yes, do you read contemporary prose?"

"I do. I've taken a degree in literature up in Boston."

Camille's hand flew to her mouth. "And here I am complaining about educated people! I've already managed to insult you, and you've shown me such kindness."

"Not at all," Eveline laughed. "My bachelor's degree is so diminutive compared to Thomas' doctoral training, and I am constantly kept aware of it. I'm still in a position to appreciate a good slap in the face of scholastic snobbery—and one so strategically placed."

"Scholastic snobbery," Camille turned the phrase over in her mind. "Aptly put. When Brooks encounters any social situation he isn't quite sure how to handle, he swings right into what I have come to regard as his 'professor's defense.' He starts bellowing out his philosophically practical pomp and his scientifically stolid stuffiness and . . . How horrid I must sound!"

Eveline tipped her head back and laughed. "I know just what you mean! And a psychologist is no easier to tussle with, believe me. Every time I start to get the better of him in any argument, he falls right into his pseudo-psychoanalysis of my anomalous personality, and so, of course, any disagreement we should have is all attributable to my disordered methods of reasoning due to the scars of my pampered childhood and repressed adolescence."

"Naturally," Camille quipped, "the discord could never originate with him."

"No, not with all the paper that hangs framed in his office."

They laughed until tears filled their eyes. Camille smoothed the quilt over her lap. "I shouldn't say such things. I've just met Thomas, and he defended me so nobly."

Eveline sighed. "He is charming—especially in social gatherings. But you know how men pull out their dark shadow selves when they feel their egos have been trifled with."

"I suppose I had my initiation this evening." They looked at one another and broke out into a fresh round of laughter. "I can't help wondering, though—what is Thomas' final analysis of you?"

Eveline stifled a giggle and dramatically straightened herself. "He says I'm staid."

"Staid?"

"Yes." Eveline's shoulders began to shake again. "Could he have picked a more insensitive word?"

"I'm not sure." Camille couldn't resist teasing her along. "Is there any truth in it?"

"Well, yes, I suppose so . . ." She laughed even louder than before.

Camille's head felt light. "You mustn't think Brooks always behaves this way—in fact, this really is the first time we've had any sort of quarrel."

"Oh, I'm sure, dear."

"As you said, the trip simply got the best of us. We spent so much concentrated time together on the train, we've been tearing away at each other's nerves. I'm sure it must have hurt him when I didn't want to see the house he selected for us; that must have felt more like an ego trouncing than a trifling. Perhaps I really was cruel."

"No. I'm sure I would have felt the same way."

Camille set her cup on the tray. "Really?"

Eveline poured her more tea. "Of course. I think first impressions are crucial."

"I suppose I panicked in trying to imagine what sort of house Brooks would pick out, and I knew I couldn't muster enough poise under the circumstances to appear pleased if it was nothing like the home I'd dreamed up for myself."

"Entirely understandable—but now I have a secret to share about your new home."

"A secret?"

"Yes. Brooks didn't exactly pick out the house for you by himself. I helped."

"I thought you and Brooks had never met."

"We hadn't, but when Thomas came home from the university and told me about Brooks and how he was in from out of state looking for a home for his new bride, I insisted he show him the Woods' estate up the street. So he did, and it was the only home Brooks even looked at. He fell in love with it instantly and bought it on the spot. You own a beautiful home, Camille."

"Do I?"

"Among the finest anywhere."

"Have you seen the inside?"

"Many times. The Woodses used to host the most elegant Christmas parties. We would all go a-caroling, drink mulled wine, and dance in their parlor until after two in the morning. But don't ask me to tell you any more about it. I want you to be surprised."

"Fine. I feel so much better knowing you like it."

"I love it, and you will too."

"Do tell me one thing, though."

"No."

"Just one, it's important."

"What?"

"Has it a large lawn? One good for gardening?"

"That's two things."

"Please."

"Yes and yes. I'm certain you will be gloriously happy. And speaking of caroling—we still go every year on the evening of the twenty-third. You must come along this year. You can meet more of your neighbors."

"I'd love to, but I don't know about Brooks. He hates to sing."

"We'll leave him to Thomas."

The room was quiet, and Camille's eyes felt heavy. "I believe this is the coziest room I've ever been in. How lovely to have a fireplace in the bedroom."

"We have four fireplaces in this house—one in each of the three bedrooms as well as one in the parlor."

Camille smiled. "Your future children will never be cold in the night, and St. Nicholas will have his pick of chimneys from which to descend and delight."

Eveline stood and arranged the empty dishes on the tray. She spoke just above a whisper, "We found out recently I cannot bear children."

"Please, forgive me."

"Don't feel bad. You had no way of knowing." She lifted the tray; the cups rattled in their saucers. "Thomas swears he hasn't the temperament for raising children anyway. He says it's all just as well with him—but I've spent more than one night lying awake and wondering if he really means it or if he is just being kind." The muffled voices of the men from downstairs suddenly became audible as she opened the door. "You should get more sleep. Have you had enough to eat?"

"Yes, my favorite dinners consist of mere desserts."

Eveline smiled. "Sleep well then. I'm so glad you have come, Camille."

"So am I." Camille turned off the lamp and settled into the warmth and comfort of promising new friendship. She drifted to sleep trying to count how many changes of perception she had undergone in the course of the day. She never heard Brooks come in.

3. Tidings

December 23, 1910
Dear Mother,

Brooks insists I write to you. I've put it off for some time—I know you understand. It's hard for me to realize the only way I can communicate with you now is to pour myself out on paper, but I promised Brooks I would make the best of this situation and keep my spirits up, so here is my first attempt at long-distance love.

How I wish you could see the house Brooks bought for us. It's much grander than anything I could have dreamed. It's situated west of the center of town and is on a street named, appropriately enough, West Avenue. Unlike the other frame houses up and down the street, it's constructed all around of white stone. Brooks says it will stand until the end of time. The front entrance is grand—six stone steps up to a massive French paired door painted forest green (as are the shutters). A porch with an elegant balustrade runs the width of the front of the house on each of the two levels. The sun rises in the front of the house and sets in the back.

The rooms are spacious and full of light. Downstairs we have a huge parlor running the depth of the house on the north side of the stairway (to the right as you enter the front door—the previous owners held dances here), and on the other side is a perfectly square room big enough to serve as a formal dining area with built-in drawing room. The kitchen is situated in back of the house with doors to the dining area and a back service entrance. It's a little long and plain, but sunny and cheerful with a large window across the back and access to the screen porch on the southwest side. As soon as possible, I will have it painted light blue and hang crocheted curtains so it will feel more like our kitchen at home. We are fortunate the previous owner left a double-door oak icebox and a wood and gas burning stove with two side-warming ovens. I'll have plenty of baking capacity.

Did you know there are no basements in Texas? Isn't that odd? My first trip through the house I looked all over for a staircase going down, and Brooks just laughed at me. I'll have to store everything in the attic.

Of course, we've not much in the way of furniture yet. It broke my heart to leave so much behind in Seattle. We've purchased a mahogany bed ensemble with a wardrobe, a bureau, a nightstand, and a matching writing desk. Brooks already works away furiously scribbling out notes for his next book. I awoke late last night to find him sitting by candlelight, tapping inkblots on paper, waiting for the right thought to pop into his mind. (He receives his inspirations at the oddest times and says he must play slave to them or risk losing them forever.) At any rate, while we were there at Swann's Furniture Company, I fell in love with a velvet gray davenport, and Brooks bought it for me to put into the parlor along with a standing lamp with crystal drops around the shade. Can you believe it? (I have to pinch myself regularly.) I want to wait a month or two before selecting any more furniture, though. It's hard to know just what I will want here and about until I've had the chance to analyze each of the rooms in all their different characters—with the changing light throughout the day. Then there are the different affectations brought about by the progression of the four seasons and the many moods of the weather—and taking into consideration, of course, the nuances brought about in the ups and downs of everyday living. For instance, in a contemplative mood on a stormy day, where would be the best spot and in what type of chair would one want to curl up and watch the rain and the changing sky, read a verse or two from the Psalms, and contemplate the motives of God and nature? And on a clear spring morning, by which window and at what sort of table would one wish to sit at and savor breakfast? I never realized how many things one must consider when setting up a household. I want our home to be the happiest and most comfortable place in the world.

Brooks bought the house from a man by the name of Woods, who had it built twenty years ago. He and his wife raised seven daughters within these walls. He moved to Austin when a granite dam was built to provide enough power to the city to make it the manufacturing center of the Southwest. Woods spent his inheritance setting up a rubber plant to make tires for motorcars. Unfortunately, the dam burst, and after ten years of valiantly trying to make his floundering business thrive with insufficient energy, he gave up and moved home to Pittsburgh. Woods needed to sell the house quickly, so he offered it to Brooks at a remarkable price.

I especially wish you could walk this lawn with me. Oh, the things you could do with a lawn such as this one! The front extends twenty—maybe thirty yards to the road, and the back lawn is as wide and twice as deep. We have several established trees, mostly oak and Spanish elm. I plan to put an arched trellis in the back with climbing vines and maybe some star jasmine and lots of lavender. I'll have to research the soil and climate conditions more before making final decisions about what herbs to plant. Eveline says camellias do not do well in the Texas heat, but all kinds of roses thrive with diligent care. I have such plans!

Eveline lives a few doors down. Her husband teaches psychology at the university, and he and Brooks have become good friends. I suppose I may say the same for Eveline and myself. They're a perfectly lovely couple, and I'm glad they live so near. We went a-caroling with them this evening and had such a splendid time. We strolled up and down the street and met most of our neighbors. Oh, Mother, you would have laughed so at Brooks. I know you didn't have enough time to get to know him well, but he does so hate to sing and is so (I'm sure he wouldn't mind me saying) deplorably bad at it. Yet he sang out this evening with all his heart and the devilish side of his soul. He was in rare spirits. He is truly happy here. We sang "O Come All Ye Faithful" and "God Rest Ye Merry Gentlemen" at least a dozen times each. I'm so glad we had the opportunity to go. It's about all we have done in the way of celebrating Christmas.

We did manage to put up a small tree opposite the new daven-port in the parlor so as not to let Christmas pass us by completely. We've been so caught up in all the excitement of the wedding, Brooks' new position at the university, not to mention the sudden move and everything else, I find myself totally unprepared to plan any sort of celebration, but the clock has just turned past midnight. It's Christmas Eve. I find myself suddenly wishing I could get up in the morning and start cooking, baking, and setting up a dazzling table of holiday delights just as you and I always did; but I haven't the cookware or even the table yet, and Brooks has promised he won't feel bad about it. He quotes a philosopher by the name of Burke say-ing, "Our patience will achieve more than force," and then he launches into one of his scientifically accurate and philosophically sound campaigns and is so intent with all his worldly appraisals (and oh—so very handsome), I wouldn't dream of disagreeing with him.

Married life is good, Mother. No, the word good is not nearly good enough. Blissful—yes, my life is blissful now—except for hav-ing to pass my first Christmas without you. Pray for me. I pray for you every day and night.

> *Love—the kind that transcends time*
> *and space and sets the world aglow,*
> *Your Camille.*

4. Promises Made

She folded the papers neatly and placed them in the drawer of the nightstand. Brooks set his pen down and stretched. "Are you still awake?" he asked. "I thought you were sleeping."

"I've written a letter to Mother."

"Good for you!" He stood and eyed her as if expecting a verbal synopsis of its contents.

She held out her arms. "And, how is your next philosophical masterpiece coming along?"

He crawled into the bed beside her and pulled her into his strong embrace. "It's not, actually. I haven't discovered exactly the right angle on what I want to research and explore. I'm not technically developing a book as of yet—just contemplating on paper."

"What about?"

"You know I hate to discuss what I'm working on."

"But you're not actually working on anything. You can tell me what you're contemplating. It might even help you to refine your approach."

He grinned. "I was thinking about what we sang this evening."

She pinched his ribcage. "You were in rare form."

"Ouch! Made rather an ass of myself, did I?"

"No. You were charming, really."

He kissed her and sang out in his painfully flattened bass, "A-nd tidings of com-fort and joy, comfort and joy! A-nd ti-i-dings of co-omfort and joy!"

"You should join the Saengerrunde," she jested.

"Think they'll have me?"

"Undoubtedly."

He changed his tone as he caressed her cheek with the back of his hand. "Think about it though, Camille, the concepts of comfort and joy."

She sighed. "Must you qualify and quantify everything so?"

"Listen—honestly, I'm finding an important connection between the two. My hypothesis is—between them is a philosophical web that forms the basis for all mortal endeavors. I've been sitting at the desk trying to come up with just one human motive which does not have its foundation in either of the two, and try as I might, I can't."

"It's natural to seek happiness," she said. "Sounds like more of a psychological issue; you should discuss this with Thomas."

He ran his fingertips down her spine and tickled the small of her back. "You said you wanted to help me work this out, and you're not getting out of it now. Can you think of anything you've ever done for any essential reason other than for the comfort or joy of yourself or someone else?"

She rolled away from him and looked up into the ceiling spackling. Shapes appeared and faded like miniature ghosts in the wavering light of the lamp. "Comfort is a form of happiness, is it not? Aren't they essentially the same?"

"I thought about that, too, and I decided it's not necessarily so. He rolled on his back and put his hands under his head. "We tend to assume comfort is something we somehow just deserve. We still work for it—desperately—but it's different in character. Our desire for joy is something extraneous in our minds. It exceeds the expectation of a certain level of comfort."

Her arm tingled, still under his weight, and she struggled to pull it out from under his back. "It's hard to be joyful when you're not at least tolerably comfortable."

"True," he conceded. "But it's not impossible."

She thought for a moment. "You're right, some people have their most euphoric experiences during their greatest times of suffering."

"And many times we're comfortable and not joyful," he continued.

She watched her mother's face appear and disappear in light and shadow.

"Camille?" He turned and put his arm around her.

"Now I'm contemplating." She felt his breath on her temple. "Surely other reasons exist for all the things people do—what about good health?"

"Comfort—ultimately."

"Of course. Wealth?"

"Pursued under the assumption it will produce joy."

"I suppose that's true—home?"

"Comfort."

"Food and drink?"

"Comfort—and joy, too."

"Power," she said. "People seek power ruthlessly, and it usually brings them anything but comfort or joy."

He rolled on top of her. "No, but they still assume it will, which is the reason they do what they do."

"Love?"

His arms tightened around her. "Great joy."

"Marriage?" she teased.

"Comfort and great, great joy."

"Not joy, mirth." She kissed his neck.

"What?"

"I much prefer the term mirth to joy, especially when talking about our marriage."

"Mirth is a rather impish form of joy, is it not?"

She took a deep breath as her mind leapt from the mechanics of thought to the essence of feeling. "Yes, mirth. Mirth is even a greater joy than joy itself. It's like watching a winter sunset after sipping a glass of good champagne—or the delicious tingle of excitement you get when the first rush of autumn blows through the trees. Mirth is magical. It's not only to be enjoyed but actually savored."

He whispered into her ear. "So, what's the real distinction?"

"Joy is ephemeral whereas mirth is absolutely ethereal," she murmured. "And everyone should know mirth like this."

"You would make a splendid utilitarian."

"What?"

"Never mind," he whispered. "Mirth it is then. We will build our lives upon the promises of comfort and mirth—a good resolution to start off our first full year together. Agreed?"

"Agreed." She looped her arms around his neck. "And I'll start on the comfort first thing tomorrow. I'll make this home the most comfortable place in the world for you and for our children."

He turned the lamp off. "So then, I'll devote myself to the task of supplying the children." He kissed her with tenderness. "And the mirth."

5. Germination

Brooks started at the university in early January, and Camille spent her days bustling from room to room in her new home making decisions about future furniture design and wall and window treatments. She walked the lawn often, taking note of tree placement and the movement of shade across the yard throughout the day. In the following weeks, Camille had the kitchen painted a pale cornflower blue and purchased a large square table with four ladder-back chairs and a matching sideboard and hutch of rock maple. Set in the middle of her open kitchen, her table was her workbench for a variety of her favorite domestic projects and crafts.

On weekday mornings, she made Brooks' coffee, eggs, bacon, and baking powder biscuits and packed his favorite lunch—a cured ham sandwich, potato salad, and whatever form of cookie or dessert bar she had made on Sunday to display on the cupboard shelf for the week. She saw him off to work with a long kiss, hummed Chopin's études as she washed the dishes, and cleared off the table in preparation for her winter project of the day. On some days she sprinkled the laundry and rolled each piece before ironing; on others she cut out and hand stitched lace curtains or designed patterns for crocheted doilies. On one mild February morning, she covered her table thoroughly but sparingly with old papers from the *Statesman* and set out the large enamel trays she had selected at the hardware store the weekend before. She went out to the screen porch to drag in the first of the three gunnysacks of garden loam, when the iceman came through the gate. She let him in through the porch door, and after he placed the ice in the box, he insisted on carrying the sacks into the kitchen for her. Camille poured him a cup of coffee and served him a date bar before she saw him out.

She took a deep breath before she went upstairs and pulled her mother's hatbox out from under their bed. Dusting it off with her apron, she carried it down to the kitchen. Sitting at the table covered in newsprint, she opened the box, inspecting the stiff scrollwork of the handwritten labels as she unpacked the brown paper packets and placed each next to a tray. When the box was empty, she replaced the cover and held her head in her hands until her vision cleared, then spent another two hours arranging the packets until she felt she had them all in the proper places.

She lightly filled each of the trays with the rich black soil and pressed several indentions in each of the first three with the bottom of a juice glass. She used the bottom of a coffee cup to make carefully spaced indentions in the fourth tray. She tore strips from newsprint and started lining each of the smaller indentions, realizing halfway through the second tray that she would not have enough to finish. She phoned Eveline and asked if she had any old newspapers. Eveline was at the door within minutes. When Camille let her in, her mouth fell open. "What on earth, or I suppose I should say, what in earth are you up to?"

"I'm sowing seeds for my herb garden," Camille replied, looking down at her dirt-smudged apron and grimy hands as Eveline entered.

"In the middle of winter?" Eveline queried. "What if it freezes over? Sometimes it happens here in February."

"The almanac says it isn't likely this year," Camille answered with a grin, "but it wouldn't matter anyway. Thank you for bringing your papers. I've been working all morning, and I would hate to have to stop now." She led Eveline into the kitchen and rinsed her hands before taking the newspapers and tearing them into strips. "Will you have tea?"

Eveline looked over the trays of moist black soil on the table and the curved smudges of dirt across the floor. "Thank you, no," she replied. "What manner of planting is this?"

"I'm getting the seeds started indoors, so next month when I put them in the bed outside, they'll be well rooted and hardy enough to withstand the Texas heat. I'll have fresh herbs for cooking by late May." Camille resumed lining her soil indentions.

"What's the newsprint for?" Eveline asked.

"It makes a soft little pot to separate the seedlings as they grow. The roots can work their way through a layer or two. It makes them easier to transplant, and the noninvasive ones can be allowed to grow at their own rate," Camille answered.

Eveline pulled a chair back against the window and inspected the seat carefully before sitting down. "What kind of herbs are you planting?"

"I have several varieties from seeds Mother and I harvested from our garden in Seattle—lavender, anise, bergamot, rose geranium—take a look." She nodded toward the seed packets. "They're all labeled, but please be careful not to move them; I finally have them all in order."

Eveline stood and took a quick look, tucking her hands into the folds of her skirt. "I've never heard of some of these. You have them in order?"

"I'm planting the seeds in the trays in the same configuration I plan to put them into the garden," Camille explained as she worked. "I've designed my herb garden landscape according to size, shape, and color. Since my plot backs up to the fence, I'll plant the taller ones in back, like borage and bee balm; the smaller ones, such as sweet woodruff and clary, in the middle; and as the violets, thymes, basils and chamomile grow closer to the ground, I'll place them in front. Then," she continued as she tore another strip of paper and deftly tucked it into place, "they must be sorted according to their different properties and temperaments."

"Herbs have temperaments?" Eveline asked.

"Absolutely," Camille assured her. "Some make excellent companions, attracting cross-pollination and repelling insects from one another. For example, sweet marjoram is so good-natured it can be planted with any other combination of herbs. On the other hand, some types compete for space, sun, or soil nutrients."

"I had no idea it was so complicated," Eveline remarked.

"It's not, really," Camille replied. "I suppose if I'd had to figure it all out myself it would be, but since I worked with Mother every year, I simply learned as I grew up." She finished lining her third tray of small indentions and started tearing larger strips for the fourth tray. She wound two to three times as much newsprint around the larger indentions, with even more layers in the largest indention set off farthest from the rest.

"What will you plant in that one?" Eveline asked.

"This tray is for the invasive plants," Camille answered. "Rosemary, tansy, and mints self-sow so abundantly they must be isolated when planting or they will eventually crowd out other herbs."

"And the large hole in the corner by itself?" Eveline sat down again and pointed. "That one must have an especially bad disposition."

"My comfrey goes there," Camille smiled. "And you're right; it's a notorious bully. It spreads with tenacity and will overpower more delicate herbs with ease if not contained properly, and what's worse, it's almost impossible to get rid of once it roots itself somewhere."

Eveline wrinkled her nose. "What do you cook with comfrey?"

"Nothing!" Camille answered. "It's poisonous. I'll plant it in a separate pot when it germinates so I can move it when necessary."

"Then why plant it at all?" Eveline scowled.

Camille finished her newsprint cups, washed her hands, and dried them carefully. "Because," she answered, "for all its arrogance, nothing soothes a bruise more effectively than a skin massage with a good old-fashioned comfrey salve."

Eveline watched as Camille filled each newsprint pot three-quarters full with soil, meticulously dropped three to four tiny seeds in each, and covered them over with another quarter inch of soil. "How can you stand to have your hands so dirty?" she asked.

"I don't think of it as dirt." Camille raised her wrist and watched as the black substance dropped over a nasturtium seed. "I love having my hands in the earth," she said softly. "Though most people would find it not especially ladylike, I like it even better when I'm sitting right on the ground and I can reach my hand in and feel the depth of the dew, the exuberance of life so small—I can't even see it yet. I'm part of nature in my garden." She patted the surface of the soil with a fingertip. "Not just watching the fullness of life from a seat in some sort of grand world theater, but actually play-ing a vital role. It's as though I'm actually working with God—the two of us together making something beautiful, something meaningful happen."

She sprinkled her herbs with cool water and covered each tray with moistened cup towels. Eveline helped her carry them upstairs and place them in a dark corner of the empty bedroom on the southeastern corner of the house. After Camille washed up, they walked down to Eveline's for egg salad sandwiches and blackberry tea.

6. Probability

March 25, 1911
Dear Mother,

We've put off getting a carriage, as Brooks wants to buy a motor-car. No matter how late he gets home in the evening, he spends at least an hour after dinner studying the motor ads in the newspaper, no doubt trying to imagine which one he would look the most dashing in driving down University Avenue, waving nonchalantly to his colleagues as they pass. (Between you and me—he's somewhat of an egotist.) I've bought him one of those slouchy plaid automobile caps and a pair of driving gloves for his birthday next week. I must find something else to put with them. He gave me a Victor Victrola for my birthday with a record of my favorite Chopin Etude, op. 10, no. 3. *I've played it over so many times, Eveline says I will wear it out, but I can't help myself. The first movement is so tender—so endearing; I close my eyes and hear it crying. At any rate, I'm having a difficult time trying to find appropriate gifts for Brooks of equivalent value—not necessarily in price, but in sentiment. It's hard for me to discern his sentimental side.*

He rides to campus with Thomas every day. Eveline and I often take the electric streetcar into town. It stops just one block away over on Rio Grande Street and costs five cents each way. The first time I rode alone, I noticed people staring at me in a peculiar way, until after a mile or so a gentleman explained the Jim Crow laws were strictly enforced in Texas and I had accidentally sat in the colored section. I was embarrassed, but I forced myself to get past it, for while I don't

mind doing housework, as you know, I have no intention of spend-
ing every day at home doing nothing but. Except for the incessant
ringing of the bell, the streetcar is not an unpleasant means of trans-
portation. It passes right by the State Capitol and runs down
Congress Avenue to all the finest shops. Austin is much more cosmo-
politan than I imagined it would be. I suppose it's silly, but before,
whenever I thought of Texas, I automatically pictured cowboys and
tumbleweed. You can imagine how pleased I was to find I was wrong.

The capitol building sits at the head of Congress Avenue like a
queen on her throne opening her mantle to protect her precious
Central Texas commerce. Thomas says it's only a hundred feet lower
than the pyramids along the Nile, and it's more than a hundred feet
higher than the nation's capitol. A statue of a hideously ugly woman
stands by herself on top, bravely holding a lone star up to the heav-
ens. Her backside is turned to the university. When construction on
the main building started, controversy broke out about the univer-
sity's close proximity to all those politicians and smooth lobbyists—
the Colonial Dames were afraid it would be a bad moral example
for the students. But the capitol is an imposing structure of sunset-
red Texas granite mined by convicts southwest of town. Its lawn rolls
over a couple of square acres surrounded by an iron fence. Aside from
all the old oaks, caretakers have planted hundreds of young tree vari-
eties representative of all those that grow indigenously in the state.

Congress Avenue bustles with excitement and progress. It's as if
someone has drawn an invisible line down the center. The east side
is lined with banks, general stores, barbershops, and saloons. Some
men still wear western hats and boots (and probably still stuff pistols
in the backs of their belts by the looks of them), but while they scur-
ry down the blocks tending to their business transactions and pleas-
ures, women stroll the west side with its delicious assortment of fine
furnishing companies, ice cream parlors, drug stores, and ready-to-
wear establishments. In the last year, they've built two skyscrapers on
Congress Avenue—one of which is the most elegant department

store. I went there for the first time last month for their Austin Spring Fashion Exhibition. Eveline had promised to take me to Scarbrough and Hicks for my first time, but every time we planned to go, something came up, and that weekend she and Thomas were both down with dengue fever. I took them a pot roast and some parsley new potatoes and told poor Eveline I was sorry not to wait for her, but I'd never been to a fashion exhibition in my life. She said she understood, and after I coaxed her back to bed, I walked straight over to Rio Grande Street and hopped on the streetcar.

I wish you could have been with me. It's a lot like the Bon Marché, but about five times bigger with at least ten times more merchandise clustered into stylish departments. When you first walk into Scarbrough and Hicks, there are counters and counters of perfumes and cosmetics from France, Belgium, and even Egypt. If you show an interest in any of the perfumes at all, the salesgirls dab some right on your wrist. I was still standing at the cosmetic counter when the clerk told me if I wanted a good seat I had better hurry on up to the dress department, for the exhibition was to begin in an hour and the seats always filled up early.

The show was spectacular with live orchestra music and moving lights along the runway. Almost every item in the show was stark white. It seems white is quite the thing this season. After the show, I looked through the racks for some of the dresses that had been modeled, and when I found them, I almost blushed looking at the price tags. I made my way over to the hat department, and that is where I had the most fun of all. Mother, you've never seen such hats—ribbons, willow plumes, and flowers of velvet and silk. I think the only thing more beautiful than the hats at Scarbrough and Hicks are the boxes they come in. I must have stood in that department for over an hour admiring those hats, never entertaining a thought about trying one on.

Later that evening when Brooks came in, I told him about my excursion. He smiled and nodded, no doubt wishing I would leave him to his writing—but Eveline was sick and I had no one else to bubble over on, so after I raved about the hats for as long as he could stand it, he looked at me and asked me why I hadn't bought one for myself if I liked them so much. I told him how expensive they were and he shrugged. I was stunned. I reminded him I never carry that much money about with me, especially when traveling on the street-car, and though this is true, I wondered why I had never even con-sidered buying something a little extravagant for myself. Brooks makes good money and has never denied me anything I wanted. It occurred to me I might not ever get over the feeling such finery will always be meant for others and never for me. I don't mean to sound pitiful, Mother, and you know this is in no way meant as a reflec-tion on you or my childhood, but I just can't seem to snap into a "Lady of the Manor" mode even though it really is what I have always dreamed of. Do you know what I mean?

Brooks agreed I should not carry sums of money in town, and the next day he rode the streetcar back to Scarbrough and Hicks with me and went straight to the office and set up a charge account. Then he marched me over to the hat department and left me, as he had to teach a class at the university, but not before ordering me not to leave the store without at least two hats! I stood there feeling like a little girl at the candy counter for quite a long time before I mustered enough gumption to ask the salesgirl if I might try one on. She was so kind and accommodating; I mastered my sheepishness almost immediately. I knew from the start, of course, which one I really wanted, but as there was a second choice to make and as I was hav-ing such a marvelous time, I acted as though I were completely inde-cisive and tried and retried at least ten or twelve of them. If you had been there with me, we would have had to stifle our laughter.

I chose a white one, of course. It's made of straw, but much soft-er and lighter than any woven straw I've ever seen before. It has a large silk satin ribbon around the crown, and the brim is cocked on the right side to reveal a profusion of silk and organza roses. All I had to do was sign my name on the receipt, and the sales girl wrapped it up in white tissue and tucked it into a glossy flowered box with a blue-striped lid. I suppose I cheated in the end, for instead of selecting another hat (I couldn't even find a close second), for the same price I bought some French toilet water (it smelled nearly as good as the perfume and cost a full third less), the riding gloves and hat for Brooks, and this stationery. (I sprinkled a little of the toilet water on it for you.)

When Eveline felt better, she came over to see my new hat. She asked what dress I would wear it with, and we went through all my dresses and skirts and blouses. I really could not find one solitary frock that could do such a hat justice, so Eveline arranged for all four of us to return to town last Saturday in their carriage. The men spent the day in the barber shop getting haircuts, shaves, and playing pool while Eveline helped me pick out the most beautiful dress of embroidered white voile. I still can't believe these things are happening to me. Sometimes I feel like life is just too good to be true right now and something wicked is certainly due to occur. Is this not the severest form of pessimism? Am I putting a jinx on myself? I just can't believe everything could be so perfect. In the back of my mind a stanza of a poem by Richard Barnfield keeps repeating itself:

> *Nothing more certain than uncertainties;*
> *Fortune is full of variety:*
> *Constant in nothing but inconsistency.*

Last night I made the mistake of telling Brooks my life had become such a beautiful fairy tale that at times I felt something bad would probably happen. He has no patience with such forms of reasoning. Because of my unfortunate choice of words, he darted off on a lecture about different theories of probability and calculus and ratios and relationships between evidence and conclusions, and faith and certainty—quoting some philosopher by the name of Locke—and in the end I felt quite small for having opened my mouth about the matter at all. That's why I had to write to you—one of the reasons.

This is turning out to be quite the letter, isn't it? Before I go, though, I must bring you up to date about the house. I had the kitchen painted. I was all set to do it myself, but Brooks wouldn't hear of it. He hired a man. I found a sturdy square table for the kitchen with a sideboard hutch at Kreisle's—a wonderful furniture store, but it's disconcerting shopping there, for Mr. Kreisle is also the local undertaker and you have to step around the hearse in front to enter the furniture showroom. I made Belgian lace curtains for the parlor. I sewed each stitch by hand. It took a lot of time, but they turned out to be worth it. They are so romantic looking and so European. Soon I'll get mint green drapes to hang over them. We've added a couple of dark wood tables in the parlor and a bookcase with etched glass doors where I keep your Bible, my books of verse, and a volume of Shakespeare's plays that Eveline recommended. I keep my few beloved books on the top shelf over Brooks' collection of philosophical tomes. We've also invested in a lovely set of cherry wood dining room furniture, including a china hutch and a buffet. Brooks says we will have many occasions to entertain his colleagues throughout the years. I've decided to put up flowered wallpaper in the dining room and the parlor.

I planted the herb seeds in trays last month, and by next week, all of them should have germinated. I've picked a plot for my herb bed next to the house just opposite the screen porch where the sunlight and shade varies just right. I've not planned formal floral gardens yet, as I haven't been able to find the right trellis and I'm determined to plan the landscaping around it. Brooks says he will have one specially made for me, but he hasn't managed to get to it. He works so much. Of course, we knew it would be this way. He's usually gone well into the evenings and often has to go to the campus to tie up loose ends on the weekends. I'm not really lonely, though. I see

Eveline almost every day, and I always have so many things to attend to around the house.

I don't miss you nearly so much as I used to. I don't mean this the way it must sound. I somehow don't feel as far away from you as I did at first. Does this make sense? Of course it doesn't. I do love you more than I used to, though—with every passing day of my adulthood, I learn to appreciate you more.

> *Love—flowered, perfumed,*
> *and wrapped in beauty,*
> *Your Camille*

7. Promises Kept

March 25, 1911
Dear Tess,

Here is the book I promised at last. With the move and all the details of setting up a household, time got away from me and I didn't get this off to you nearly as soon as I had intended. But, of course, I did not forget. Brooks signed it to your name as you will see.

I hope all is going well for you in your new house. We have settled in well. Our home is a rather large two story with an enormous green lawn. I love to garden, so Brooks had a large trellis specially designed and constructed for the backyard. I am in the process of planting English ivy, tea roses, and an herb garden just outside the kitchen screen porch.

Austin is a lovely city—quite cosmopolitan. I attended a spring fashion exposition recently and charged myself a new white wardrobe complete with perfume from France and two new hats.

Brooks loves his work. He is almost as devoted to it as he is to me. Let me know what you think of his book after you have had a chance to read it. I find it quite provocative (but then I suppose I should as he is my husband).

Best wishes to Carl
and your girls,
Camille Abernathy

 # 8. Mirth

Camille watched the oranges and lavenders of the sunset flatten themselves across the western hills and understood how Austin had come to be called the violet crown. Shadows of dusk lengthened over the gold and green grass of her back lawn. Her herb garden was thriving, but another planting season had passed and still there was no trellis and no flower garden. Something almost cool wafted in the evening air after the longest, hottest summer she had ever known. She inhaled all she could of the essence of autumn from the still, humid air as she finished hanging diapers for the last time that day.

Her gardening plans would have to wait for the following spring; now she had other priorities. She sat at the table on the screen porch determined to take a moment to think, but exhaustion wouldn't allow her to focus on anything meaningful before worries about unswept floors or unfolded laundry took over. She longed to lie down next to Brooks for a nap, but baby Andrew would wake any moment for his evening feeding and probably fuss right through to his late night feeding as he had the last four nights since she had brought him home from the hospital. He would finally settle just after midnight, only to awaken again at three or four in the morning—and so her schedule went. Her breasts were so sore she almost shuddered in anticipation of his cry, but when she thought of holding his soft, small head in the cup of her hand and watching his serious little blue eyes as she sang to him, she wished he would awaken early.

She slipped in through the back door and tiptoed up the stairs, stopping to look into the dark nursery where Mother Goose characters stupidly smiled and winked at one another in deep shadows. She had worked so hard for months to furnish and decorate a nursery before bringing baby Andrew home from the hospital, and now she wouldn't consider allowing him to pass a night in a room down the hall from her for a matter of months. She had much to learn about being a mother. She closed the door on the cow still hung mid-flight over the moon and crept around the stairwell to the room she shared with her husband.

Andrew was not in his bassinet where she had left him, but sleeping like a prince next to Brooks, propped on all sides by pillows and looking so peaceful he almost glowed. She slipped off her house shoes and lay down next to her new son.

Brooks stirred. "Camille?"

"Shhh."

He lowered his voice to a whisper. "What time is it?"

"Half-past seven. I've made potato soup for you." She smiled at the angelic face of the sleeping infant and her bare-chested husband with his hair all rumpled, his face ruddy from his late afternoon nap. Andrew's complexion had the same radiant quality as his father's, and his shock of silken hair was almost as black as Brooks'.

"Potato soup?" he whined.

"I would have made something more substantial, but as you know, I've not been able to get to the market. So I worked with what I could find around the house."

"No meat at all?"

"Perhaps you could go to Hyde Park Grocery tomorrow."

"I'll drive you into town." He stretched himself and curled back up next to his infant son. "We have no food in the pantry, and we both need a good meal. We can go to the Excelsior Market and get a rump roast. We should stop in Wukasch's and get some vegetables and dry goods, too. I'll make Sunday dinner tomorrow; you can talk me through it."

"What a lovely offer, but you may have to do the marketing yourself. I'm not up to a trip into town yet, and Andrew's too young to go out."

"Nonsense," Brooks chortled. "We can try out the fancy new baby carriage with the built-in awning we just had to have. I'll bring the box camera, and we can stop by the capitol grounds and take our photographs on the bridge. The fresh air will do you both good."

"He's too young; he'll take sick."

"He's an Abernathy! He's as hale and hearty as they come. Look at him."

Camille gently put her arm around Andrew. The bow of his small, protruded upper lip trembled in his sleep. She whispered over him, "You're not going to be one of those fathers who insists on pushing his sons right through childhood into a premature and aggressive adulthood, now are you? What is the philosophy in that?"

"No, I'm not," he hissed. "And you're not going to be one of those overprotective mothers who hides her son behind her skirts at the first sign of trouble—or keeps him sheltered until he develops an inability to interact socially or build up a natural immune system, are you?"

"Of course not! But I . . ." She saw him grin through the shadows that laced them together across the child. "Oh, Brooks, I'm not up to this."

"I'm sorry. You're just so beautiful when you're self-righteous." He leaned across the baby and kissed her on the forehead. "All of a sudden I find myself saying and doing all the things my father did. I'll pick up a bottle of Scott's Emulsion for you tomorrow."

"Thank you, but I don't trust those chemical pick-me-up street show elixirs. I'll make myself an infusion of peppermint, rosemary, and geranium blossoms while you cook your blue-ribbon Sunday dinner."

The infant jerked his arm up in his sleep, stretched out his pink mouth, and let out a shrill wail before his eyes opened. Camille sat up perfunctorily, propped the pillows behind her, and took the child to her breast. Brooks watched as she winced with pain until the baby settled into position. She felt her womb tighten with every pull; she had never been so physically exhausted in her life. Her back hurt and her head ached from fatigue as she watched her son take advantage of the motherhood she gave him without reserve. "I've never been so happy."

"Nor I," he smiled.

"This is a dichotomy, isn't it Brooks? Being so happy even when I am also more miserable than I've ever been before?"

"In its truest form." He took a deep breath. "Do you know what Marcus Aurelius Antoninus said about happiness?"

"The Roman statesman?" Camille asked as he sat up and turned on the lamp.

"Actually, he was a Roman emperor and a philosopher. He said, 'No man is happy who does not think himself so.'"

"He thought happiness was nothing more than a state of mind?"

"To an extent."

"I disagree." Baby Andrew started fussing, so she moved him to her other breast.

Brooks held up a hand. "Now think about it for a minute. It seems one can always find reasons to be happy and sad at the same time. Would you agree to that? Can you think of one instance in your life when everything was completely good?"

She reflected on her childhood and her past year of adulthood. "Not offhand, but I'm sure if I wasn't so tired and really thought it over . . ."

"The elements are never pure in life unless your mind is preconditioned to see them so." He stood and took his trousers from the bedpost and pulled them on. "And no matter how bad things seem, there is always something to be thankful for."

"I can agree with that, but I still think happiness is dependent to a certain degree on circumstances and occurrences."

"Only those you're attached to."

"What?"

"Never mind." He took a comb out of his pocket and ran it through his hair. "That opens up a whole new vein of philosophic thought, and I'm much too hungry to start in with it. But suffice it to say, if someone really wants to be happy, he will find a way. And by the same token, if he really wants to be unhappy, he will succeed at that as well."

"It's a good thing," she said as her back began to ache and she struggled to move a pillow further under her shoulder without disturbing Andrew's feeding.

"Why?" he asked as he watched.

"Because then, one could certainly precondition his

mind to unattach itself from meat, go downstairs, and be delighted to heat up a bowl of potato soup and eat it for his supper."

He left the room.

9. Lunacy

Baby Andrew was three weeks old when he had his first outing; he slept through most of it. Camille dressed him in cotton leggings and swaddled him against the autumn chill in his plaid flannel hooded bunting. She felt his soft breath on her neck as Brooks carefully lined the trunk of his Cadillac with blankets before loading the carriage.

"Did you get the umbrella?" she asked.

"It's in the backseat with the picnic basket," he assured her.

"Do you think he's warm enough?"

Brooks opened the passenger door and carefully took the sleeping baby from her arms as she climbed in. "He looks perfectly snug to me." He smiled and handed him back to his mother. He cranked the car until it sputtered itself into a consistent growl. Opening and closing the door around himself in one deft movement, he landed in the driver's seat with a bounce. He took his driving cap and gloves from the dash box, checked himself in the rearview mirror, arranged the cap over his arched left brow, pulled the gloves on, and ran his hands around the steering wheel with a dexterous flourish. He expertly released the hand brake and slowly eased his new, sleek black machine backward over the pebbles of the driveway.

"I thought Wooldridge Park was the other direction," she said, looking up from the sleeping child as Brooks wrestled the steering wheel to the left and aimed the rubber wheels north down the back alley. "Where are we going?"

"The lunatic asylum," he said.

"I didn't ask you where you thought we belonged," she jested. "I asked you where we are going to picnic."

"Then I answered both questions," he chided, taking his view from the road just long enough to cast her a wry glance. "Believe it or not, according to my colleagues, the new place to be seen on a Sunday is on the western grounds of the lunatic asylum. I thought it would be fun to rumble over and see what the fuss is about." "Curious," she mused. "I've not read anything about it in the *Statesman,* though now that I think about it, Eveline mentioned she had gone to the asylum once or twice. I assumed she went to visit a patient."

"Thomas oversees internships and consults with the caretakers from time to time. He must have taken her to enjoy the scenery and society at some point."

"We should have given them a ring."

"In case you hadn't noticed," he waved a black leather hand, "we have no more room." He honked the horn and slowed to allow a family of three to pass on their mules. "Stay on the side! Damned outsiders," he mumbled as he resumed his original speed. "Besides, I thought it time we had a real Abernathy family outing."

Camille turned to watch the brown face of the mother reel toward Brooks with pain and vexation. The boy's black hair tossed every direction as he struggled to stay his burro, and the father waved a fist toward the back of the car. The short spire of Old Main passed on the right. "In the months we've been here I've never been north of the campus," she remarked.

"You've been busy." He slowed to turn right on Guadalupe and made a quick swerve back to the north on

Pearl Street. Andrew jumped, rumpled his lips, and relaxed back into a deep sleep. "The area north of the university is Hyde Park," he explained. "It was developed by the same gentleman who funded the electric streetcar—Mr. Ship, or Shipe, or something like that. He sold lots at an astounding rate by advertising that the air was more salubrious on this side of the capitol. How asinine is that?"

"You've been here before?" she asked.

"I've driven up the Speedway a short distance, but not all the way to the asylum. The neighborhoods are quaint, but not nearly so nice as ours." He watched the passing street signs closely. "Here it is," he announced as he turned right onto a wide road, then left onto a gravel drive through a dense canopy of oak branches. The engine sputtered to a stop where deep green lawns rolled backward under the trees to a stately building with three stories and a classical portico. A banner hanging between the Corinthian columns read "Fall Carnival," and a few picnic tables stood clustered by the entrance with white cloths and various festival games. Dozens of families reclined on blankets spread across the lawns near the building, and lovers were paired under the trees and along a necklace of small lakes and lily ponds linked by cedar bridges with intricate latticework. The smallest lake lay in the shadow of the institution, trickling water into successively larger ones. The largest, at least two hundred yards long and fifty feet wide, reflected the sky like a huge mirror in the southern extremity of the grounds; children rowed small boats to an island in the middle. Flowering trees and shrubs lined the streams, and the vines that laced the trees together produced the effect of a Japanese tea garden.

"It's beautiful." Camille looked around as Brooks unloaded the Cadillac. Once baby Andrew was tucked in his carriage and covered over to her satisfaction, they strolled up the lawns and picked out a spot on the lush Bermuda grass next to a small pond with lilies as large around as her hat. Brooks spread blankets and set the picnic basket in the middle. Camille felt the baby's face to make sure he was not in a draft before she sat on the ground next to her husband, carefully arranging her skirts.

"Now, isn't this lovely." Brooks looked through the crowd.

"This will never do," said Camille.

"What?" He watched as she folded blankets to make a pallet and set up the umbrella behind it.

"I can't see him at all," she said as she shot up and gently lifted the infant out of the carriage.

"He's fine. Camille, please relax. Look, there's Durwood Jones. Maybe I can show Andrew off when he wakes up."

"When he wakes up, he's going to be hungry," she said as she lay him on the blankets next to her, covered him over, and adjusted the silk umbrella against the early evening air. "And he's not fond of the bottle."

"If he's hungry enough, he'll take it. Can we eat now?"

"We probably should before the bread gets stale," she said as she started unpacking chicken sandwiches, coleslaw, and lemon bars. Brooks pried the tops off two root beers, and they ate listening to the children laugh as they played and the water as it trickled downstream. The branches above them swayed and knocked against one another in the autumn breezes. Members of a small brass ensemble appeared under the portico; they set up their chairs and music stands and sat down to warm up their instruments. The front doors of the asylum burst open, and at least fifty costumed children rushed out whooping and cheering. The children playing on the lawns and around the lakes drifted up one by one to join the outer fringes of the assembly. It took two nuns twenty minutes to get the little jack-o'-lanterns, cats, and various other hobgoblins seated on the ground around the musicians, and hushed. A brilliant moment of silence rang throughout the gardens and into the orange-gilded dusk before a quick gust of autumn threw the trombonist's sheet music straight up in the air, into a manic spin, and out across the lawn. The children roared with laughter. Once the music was retrieved and trapped with rocks produced by a child not in costume, the nuns went to work subduing the crowd again. At last the trumpet player counted to four and the horns launched into a lively round of "Put on Your Old Gray Bonnet." By the time they played "After the Ball" and "Down by the Old Mill Stream," every adult on the sloped lawn was singing along, except for Brooks, who dozed while Camille tidied up. Andrew slumbered through the noise, so she gathered a few cabbage roses from a shrub and busied herself with braiding them. The band finished their concert with a rousing rendition of "Ta-ra-ra-Boom-de-ay!" Brooks awoke on the first "boom" and watched the remainder of the festivities. The musicians folded up their seats and stands and disappeared into the building, and the children were divided up to enjoy carnival events at the separate tables. Some bobbed for apples, some tried to drop clothespins into bottles, and others walked for cakes while one of the nuns started and stopped the Victrola at odd places in nursery tunes.

Brooks watched as Camille wove soft stems together and worked the feathery green leaves into angles framing the delicate pink flowers. "Remind you of anything?" he asked as he reached into the basket and pulled out another lemon bar.

Camille blushed. "No."

He laughed. "I'll never forget the first time you looked up at me, tying those poor dead roses to that bunch of branches in the middle of the Klondike Gold Rush Fair."

"They weren't dead; they were dried, and that bunch of branches was a grapevine wreath. You never had any appreciation for my art," she teased.

"I appreciated every aesthetic detail then, as I do now." He finished the last morsel, dusted the crumbs off his hands, kissed her forehead, and looked hard into her eyes. "You're all right now, aren't you, Camille?"

"I miss some things," she replied. "I can't deny that." She finished her work and placed the pink halo on the sleeping child's bundled head. "But I'm gloriously happy here with you and Andrew."

"Look," he whispered as he pointed to the trees across the lawn. A huge October moon—full, pale golden, and almost transparent in the last apricot rays of the sun—had risen above the graying tree line. Heavy on the topmost branches, it stared down at its own ominous reflection in the large lake.

Camille caught her breath and watched in awe. A large elderly man puffing on a pipe strolled across the horizon, followed by a woman in a plain gray dress wearing an enormous hat. A cloud of silvery-green veiling flowed from under the cocked side brim and was gathered up into a tremendous bow under her chin, with the trails tossed over her shoulders to dance in the short gusts of air scrolling over the lawn. Against the fading trees she looked like the ghost of a giant Luna moth fluttering toward the firelight.

"Professor Jones!" Brooks called. Andrew awoke with a yelp. Camille felt her breasts tighten as she picked him up. She placed him in the carriage and had his diaper changed before Brooks pulled the bottle out of the basket and unwrapped the newsprint.

The gentleman advanced and held up a monocle. "Hello, young—Abernathy, isn't it?" He walked over, the sneer on his puffy red face visible behind the giant ivory carved pipe. The woman came up behind him. Camille judged her to be about her own age—in her early twenties—with a complexion so pale it almost blued in the twilight.

"Brooks Abernathy—philosophy." He stood and offered a hand.

"Of course, you're the new one." Professor Jones gave Brooks' hand a tug, inhaled, and slowly blew a trail of malodorous smoke out of each of his great nostrils. Camille held Andrew against her breast as she offered him the bottle. He nuzzled her, fussed, and chewed the bottle nipple.

"I've been here almost a year." Brooks introduced Camille and Andrew.

"Charming. I'd offer a hand, but . . ." he gestured toward Camille, eyeing her keenly before turning to introduce his wife. Morgan Jones nodded politely. Though little of her face was visible under her swabs of veiling, she seemed to be smiling at Andrew.

Howls rang out from the tree directly behind the pond where they stood. One of the older girls with a nurse's hood and cape left the carnival area, rushed across the lawn and around the pond, and pulled down a young boy covered in gray fur.

Professor Jones bit the nib of his pipe as he chuckled. "A dog? A wolf? How did that rascal get way over there?" The child never stopped howling as the girl shouldered him and carried him back to the portico and into the building.

"Lovely evening," Camille offered. Her breasts had swollen considerably; she pulled Andrew closer as he tossed and fidgeted.

"Professor Jones teaches history," Brooks explained to her.

"I'm working on an article about the history of Austin's Lunatic Asylum for a trade journal. I brought Morgan out this evening for a little fresh air when I learned the brass ensemble from the university was to play."

"Wasn't it delightful?" asked Brooks.

Andrew took the bottle, and Camille rocked him gently. "Are the costumed children residents?" she asked.

"They are the young lunatics," Professor Jones assured her.

Brooks winced at the scream of a child from across the lawn. "Do they often let them interact so freely with society at large?"

"On weekends—except for the violently insane and the idiots." Professor Jones pursed his large kidney-shaped lips, took a step into the deep shadow of the trees, and gave off another cloud of foul smoke. "In the past, those diagnosed with insanity have been immured indefinitely, whereas the modern approach is more therapeutic. With mild shock treatment, occasional ice plunges, and weekly exposure to peers in a more balanced mental state, many of the inmates can be cured of their lunacy and perhaps someday be reintegrated into society."

"And what about the violently insane and the idiots?" asked Brooks.

"Incurable," Jones answered. "They must stay in the crossroom at all times."

"Where is the crossroom?" Brooks looked around.

"I'm not sure," Jones hissed, his smoke emanating from deep shadow. "I've not been allowed to see the crossroom, though I've made several requests."

Camille watched as some of the children lost interest in their games and started to run in circles and tease one another. The older inmates organized a game of London Bridge. She drew a long breath. "'The lunatic, the lover, and the poet, are of imagination all compact.'"

"Where did that come from?" asked Brooks with a laugh.

"A Midsummer's Night's Dream," she answered as Professor Jones dropped his monocle.

"Splendid," Brooks said. "'The owl of Minerva spreads its wings only with the falling of the dusk.' That was Georg Hegel."

"Surely you're not suggesting anyone who falls in love or expresses themselves artistically is the same as these little lunatics." Professor Jones' face was suddenly caught in an amber glow as the Hyde Park tower light came on. Deep crevices in his complexion shadowed purple, and the spittle on his jutted lower lip glistened under the stump of his pipe.

"I don't know." Brooks' eyes sparkled between the setting sun, the hovering moon, and the oscillating rays of the bulbs as they warmed up. "Sophocles abstained from sex, claiming conjugal love was a 'mad and savage master,' and Alexander Pope said 'every poet is a fool.' Maybe they aren't exactly the same, but I see it as a classic dichotomy—the line between genius and lunacy is actually quite fine."

"He's doing it again! He's doing it again!" a child's voice cried from the carnival area. A masked marauder had removed his cape and shirt and was struggling to unbutton his pants. One of the nuns hurried over and appointed an older boy the task of guiding him in the process of redressing himself. She clapped her hands five times, and after a round of wails and sobs, the inmates stumbled into their assigned places. The children without costumes broke out into games of tag and kick the can as the costumed children disappeared through the front door of the institution.

"There is a line." Professor Jones replaced his monocle.

Morgan sighed. "Why must there always be a line?" Her husband turned his look on her and exhaled a puff of smoke.

She shrank further under the shadow of her hat.

Andrew's face soured, and he started fussing. Camille felt herself start to leak. She lifted the child over her shoulder and vigorously patted his back. Cymbals clashed, drums beat, and women's voices chanted from the street behind them. Everyone turned and strained to see the source of the din through the oaks and changing lights. Professor Jones took his pipe from his mouth.

"Look—here's a classic line of lunatics, now!"

"God, here we go again," wailed Brooks.

Camille turned toward the street, where the procession passed into the light of the moon lamp. Mules pulled carts decorated with red, white, and blue crepe paper carrying women with signs that read "Enfranchise Texas Women" and "Suffragists Unite." Hundreds of women and a few men walked in clusters between the carts, holding torches and chanting, "I am Elisabet Ney. I am Elisabet Ney." "Who is Elisabet Ney?" she asked.

"Town preternatural madwoman," retorted Jones. "She studied sculpture in Europe and cast the statues of Stephen F. Austin and Sam Houston for the World's Fair in Chicago."

"I've heard of her," Brooks interjected. "She's the one who did Schopenhauer's bust."

"Indeed," Jones snarled. "She married a hardworking scientist, then refused to use his name and left him in Georgia to start an art school in Austin. She squandered his money on a homely studio where she did nothing but sculpt all day and into the night. Then she slept alone on the roof in the raw elements like an uncivilized beast. She wore pants, for God's sake, rode a horse like a man, and maintained a one-way phone service so no one could call her—including her son, whom she had estranged."

"Sounds ghastly," Brooks remarked. Shouts from the

demonstrators rang from the street below the trees. "I am Elisabet Ney. I am Elisabet Ney." Children stopped running and watched as the torches snapped in the night breezes, and the parade wound east toward the heart of Hyde Park. Across the lawns men and women stood and stretched, packed up their picnics, and folded up blankets.

"You've not heard the worst," Jones continued. "It's said she cremated her own stillborn son in the fireplace."

Brooks cast a wild glance at Camille. "A regular Hansel and Gretel style witch!"

Jones pulled a pouch from his vest pocket and restoked his pipe. "She died a few years ago, and a group of presumptuous women got the inane idea to preserve her home and make it into a museum. They've apotheosized her into a sort of unchristian-like goddess of womanly rebellion. The house is up the road a few blocks." He gestured toward the moon, which had finally pulled itself up over the tree line and shrunken to the size of a shiny white dinner plate. "No doubt it's where their march will end."

"We went through this in Seattle," said Brooks.

Jones panted as he relit his pipe and took a series of long puffs. "Ney is a stunning example of the dangers of enfranchising women. As soon as they are allowed to vote, they will all neglect their housewifing duties and lose their natural feminine charms. 'Demonic frenzy, moping melancholy, and moonstruck madness.' That's Milton."

Andrew let out a tremendous burp. Everyone laughed but Jones, and Morgan stepped forward and gave him a loving pat on the back.

"Women in Washington are now voting," Camille said as she turned to Brooks. "We should get Andrew home."

10. Dichotomy

November 2, 1911
Dear Mother,

How shall I describe your grandson to you? He has lots of dark hair and the face of a cherub. He even has his own intoxicating smell, different from any other in the world. His miniature hands and feet are all wrinkled and pink, and his new red baby face is smoothing out into a wonderful ruddy–tawny Celtic glow. (I wouldn't admit this to anyone else in the world, but he looks so much more like Brooks than me.) His eyes are dark blue, but the doctor told me they could still change. His sleeping pattern is finally simmering down to a fairly predictable schedule, though he still wakes at least once during the night, and usually twice. We've named him Andrew Michael. At first, I wanted to name him after Brooks, but Brooks said it had been so frustrating for him, having such an unusual name—people always dropping the "s" or reading it as his last name; he said he had no intention of putting his son through it. I understand his point of view, so when he suggested Andrew because he liked the way it sounded with Abernathy, I agreed. Our son will carry this name forever. I find this somewhat overwhelming—assigning someone a name for life is a daunting responsibility, but I'm glad I had Brooks to help me through it. I have a lot of new forevers—I will be a mother forever. No matter how old Andrew grows, I'll always worry about his welfare and strive for his happiness. But in another way, it's like *he's always been with me. I can't understand how I lived twenty-one long years without knowing I was supposed to be missing him.*

Brooks had the week off when Andrew came. It was good to have him here, and he was helpful in his way. He's back teaching again, of course, and stays later than ever. He's well into writing his next book and says he can't concentrate at home with Andrew crying so much. I explained to him it's no small task to try and maintain such a large house and fix him three meals a day at his odd hours while breastfeeding this child around the clock, and washing and hanging diapers all day. He thought for a few minutes, went into the hall, picked up the telephone, and had those poor operators ringing around town in all directions. He discovered Hyde Park Grocery will deliver for a handsome percentage, and he deemed it well worth it under the circumstances. He told me if I ever find myself without a slab of bacon, or a good thick Porterhouse I felt I needed for his Sunday breakfast or weekday supper, all I have to do is walk to the phone, have the operator ring the store, and tell them what I want and when I want it.

He also hired a maid. Coral is a Negro. She and her husband live in Wheatville, where he tends a bar every day of the week. He brought her over in his carriage last Wednesday morning. She cleaned the whole house and asked if I needed her to fix supper. I told her I had dinner planned and underway, but she helped me skin the potatoes, dice the onions, and dredge the beef. While I was adding the potato water to the meat sizzling in the pan, Andrew woke up in his bassinet and started his ritual screaming. Her eyes lit up and she said, "Oh, Miss Camille, I do so love babies, may I?" Honestly Mother, I didn't know how he would react to her, but I also didn't know how to tell her no, so I nodded and she went over and said, "Now, now, sweet baby." He stopped crying, and when she picked him up, his eyes looked just like those big black coat buttons with the cross-hatching you kept in your tin. I had the hardest time keeping myself from laughing out loud. But while I got the meat to a steady simmer, she rocked him in her arms and sang, "Skeeters are a 'hangin' on a honeysuckle vine," in the most beautiful, deep woman's voice I've ever heard. Andrew snuggled right up to her and completely forgot he was supposed to be mean for his supper. I'm sure Coral's going to work out fine. Her husband came around for her just after six, and I was sorry to see her go.

Of course Eveline comes over often. The day after we came home from the hospital, she brought over a blue plaque with the poem, "Where did you come from my baby dear, out of the nowhere and into the here." Brooks hung it in the nursery for me. She also brought over a couple of Jane Austen novels because she had heard babies sleep all the time. I still haven't read them yet, but now, with Coral's help, I'm hopeful I'll have time to read, bake, work on the house, and maybe even do some gardening soon—the herb garden needs a good weeding, and some of the plants need to be seeded and clipped back before the first frost. It's been hectic. I thought having a baby would be so much easier. I hope I don't sound selfish—I love Andrew fiercely, but since he's been born I've had no real time even to think. For instance, I told Brooks I'm happier now than I've ever been before, while at the same time I'm more exhausted and uncomfortable than I ever imagined I could be. He told me about an ancient philosophical theory that happiness is entirely in the mind. He says one can be happy or unhappy at will, despite any circumstances. I've been vexed since, and not because of what he said, but because I want to think this over and try and understand how he could believe something that seems so impossible to me; under normal circumstances, I would have already worked it out in my mind. But now, every time I sit down and start to entertain any serious thought, Andrew cries, or its time to hang out laundry, or the telephone rings, or I'm just too tired. I love motherhood, but will I ever be able to finish a line of thought again?

Until I can isolate the problem with Brooks' theory, a certain quote runs through my mind. I can't remember where I heard or read it, but someone somewhere once said, "Happiness is no laughing matter." I used to find this amusing, but now it seems profound. Happiness is not a lonely traveler. It always seems to arrive with a healthy measure of frustration, pain, and usually both. This is one of Brooks' dichotomies. I wish I could will these nagging aches and frustrations into another realm and purely enjoy my baby with nothing but happiness, but I haven't discovered how. I miss Brooks. I wish he would at least discuss his new book with me, but he won't even tell me what it's about. He says it stunts the flow of his genius. He bought me a new collection of poetry last week. I haven't started reading it either. Before Andrew was born, I read a few verses from your Bible every day, but nothing since.

That's enough about me. I'll spend this precious time while Andrew naps telling you about him. He's taken two outings so far. Yesterday Eveline and I took him into town to shop for boy baby clothes (everything he has is green or yellow, and Brooks said he needed something that would do his sex more honor). We found some darling rompers—pin-striped like a baseball player's—and a couple pairs of long-sleeved cotton shirts and tiny breeches that button down the inseam.

Last Sunday, Brooks took us for a picnic on the grounds of the lunatic asylum. As strange as it sounds, it's a popular recreation spot in Austin as its gardens and lakes are without compare. We watched a children's carnival, and I met one of Brooks' colleagues. Andrew slept until the end of the evening, then took a bottle for the first time. He seemed as though he was enjoying the fresh air, but I'll be glad when he starts to smile so I can tell for sure. The asylum is on the northern edge of the city next to a subdivision called Hyde Park. It's the fashionable part of town, and everything of social importance that's not political or academic seems to happen there. I read in the paper that the first airplane landed in Austin last week just east of where we had our picnic, and Eveline said the State Fair was held there several years ago. A pavilion remains where they used to race horses and place bets; now it's used for political rallies and outdoor plays. The Texas militia still holds their annual encampment on the fields adjacent to the lunatic asylum. They stage battles every year. Eveline says it's amazing to watch and we should take Andrew when he's older.

A parade of suffragists passed as we were leaving. This is something else I want to think more about when I can. When they demonstrated in Seattle, I never stopped to consider that what they were working so hard for could actually pertain to me. I suppose we were always too busy to worry about such things, but I find myself wondering why women were never allowed to vote in the first place. Why shouldn't we be granted full citizenship? Are we less than human? I remember you said you had registered to vote before I was born, and voted in one primary before women were re-disenfranchised in Washington. How did that happen? I wish you could come to Austin for a visit. I dream about picking you up at the train station and bringing you back to our home. We would fix breakfast in the morning and rush Brooks off to work so we could sit on the screen porch with a pot of Earl Grey and a plate of lavender shortbreads and discuss women's rights and wrongs and high aspirations and low expectations. Here, the New Woman refers to herself as "Elisabet Ney." She was a local sculptress who got important commissions, wore pants when she wanted, and left her husband to move to Austin and fulfill her own vocation. According to one horrible story, she cremated her own stillborn child. I refuse to believe a mother could do such a thing to her beautiful infant. If it's true, her studio house must be haunted. The thought frightens me, and I will never go there.

But this Mrs. Ney certainly did a lot of things her own unique way without a care about what anyone thought. She makes me won-

der what I would do if I weren't so devoted to my family and my household and could choose a profession. I loved our herbal arts, but I'm not sure I would commit myself to it as a life vocation if I could make my choice. I never even considered having a choice. Should I have a choice? (Is this a wicked thought?) Maybe it would be fun to be a telephone operator for a while or a salesgirl at Scarbrough and Hicks. Although, if I truly had my choice, I suppose I would rather be a buyer. How grand it would be to choose the fashions for everyone else in town to select from. I could be a gentle and compassionate doctor. Probably no one would come to a woman doctor, but I could be a good one. It's fun to think about. Maybe this is what Brooks means. I've created a true state of happiness by myself, and all it took was a small measure of modern rebellion.

Why is it, Mother, we can do for others what we can't do for ourselves? How is it when I can't sort my thoughts no matter how hard I try on my own, I can somehow lay them out on paper for you? And how is it I can do four times as much in one day, with one-fourth the amount of sleep in taking constant care of baby Andrew? Isn't love an amazing thing? Isn't it the most effective form of motivation of all? I've outperformed myself more for love of this little one than I ever have out of vanity, pride, or even necessity for myself. This new love has turned my world over. Now as I am farthest from you, I feel closest to you. Through this new life I can at last see myself through your eyes. At last I can appreciate every act of love and self-sacrifice you performed for me. My heart aches in your absence.

> Love—powdered, patted,
> and pinned up with care,
> Your Camille

11. Attachment

January blew in cold and wet—not the kind of weather to take a baby strolling about in—so Camille had been confined to the house for almost two weeks. Coral was coming every weekday, and though life was completely different, their daily routine was settling back into a predictable rhythm. At last Camille found an hour or two each evening to read, crochet, or sit at the kitchen table sketching garden plots while the sun sank behind the oaks.

Baby's first Christmas had come and gone. Camille baked gingerbread men and spice cookies, and Brooks set the tree up in the parlor. On Christmas morning, Santa Claus came down the chimney and surrounded the tree with toy soldiers and Teddy bears. Camille made a Christmas ham with all the trimmings. Andrew sat amidst the commotion with a bland smile and an occasional gurgle.

For Camille's birthday, Brooks kept his promise and had a tremendous ivory latticed arched trellis delivered, which he had ordered to the exact specifications she had wished for over Christmas dinner. It sat like a princess on the screen porch next to the tea table, regally awaiting milder weather for its permanent installation four to five yards beyond the back door. Camille had her culinary herb garden design done, as well as her climbers and borders around the trellis, but she couldn't decide how she wanted to landscape the rest of the backyard. In her first sketches she had opted for two large crescent gardens by the back fence, each with a crape myrtle tree, providence roses, and filled in with star jasmine. In later sketches she thought it better to stagger the main gardens to surround the larger oaks so she could grow wisteria to hang over the roses. But this evening, she played with the possibility of digging four large gardens—one in each corner—to form a pleasant vignette for a play yard. They would have to leave plenty of room for swings, playhouses, and games of tag and croquet. It would also be wise to leave grass under the oaks for picnic tables. As the children grew, they would certainly host birthday parties and garden gatherings, and barbecues were popular in Texas.

She shaded in her final plan for the night and propped her latest sketch against her applesauce preserves on the sideboard hutch. With a last look out at the trellis, she heard a few raindrops on the tin roof joints of the screen porch. She checked Brooks' veal cutlets, rice, and carrots in the warming ovens, wondering if she should wrap them and put them in the icebox. It was already after nine, and the meat would certainly be getting tough. She closed the oven door, dropped her dishtowel on the counter, threw up her hands, and sighed. She climbed the stairs for the third time to check on Andrew, who had slept through his evening feeding. He had outgrown his bassinet and slept in his crib, which Camille had moved into their bedroom despite Brooks' objections. She admired the curve of the child's long eyelids into the dark feathery lashes that lay like goose down against his pink cheeks. A gentle rain played a soothing lullaby against the bedroom window. He looked so snug she knew he would sleep through to his next feeding around midnight. She kissed her fingertips, gently touched his forehead, and taking a quilt from the rack at the bottom of their bed, wrapped herself up and went down to the parlor to wait for Brooks.

She picked up a Jane Austen novel from the mahogany coffee table, curled herself up on the gray davenport, tucking the quilt around her legs, and stared up at the pressed tin ceiling tiles. Brooks could not be reached on the phone in this weather, and he would not come home until the rain stopped for fear it would make the interior of his Cadillac smell musty. She shook her head and opened her book to her place.

As she finished the seventh chapter, the wind whipped up against the tall windows. She peered between the lace panels to watch as the rain blew toward her in large drops. The glass was beaded with cold fog, and the only thing visible through the storm was the pale halo of the tower light on the corner of Elm and Guadalupe. Thomas had told them it was the first moon lamp erected in Austin after the dam had been constructed to churn out enough hydroelectric power to light the night sky of the whole city. A year before they bought the house, a man had fallen from the top of the lamp to his death while changing one of the carbon arc bulbs. A shiver ran through her as she closed the bobbin lace over the window and drew the velvet drape. She checked on Andrew again and went into the kitchen to look over her latest garden sketch. She smiled, nodded, and took up her place on the davenport to lose herself again in the throes of hopeless romance.

Over an hour later, something she read stopped her short: "Where people wish to attach, they should always be ignorant . . ." She placed her crocheted marker on the page and closed the book. The words played themselves over in her head. "Where people wish to attach . . ." She remembered the time she and Brooks had discussed happiness, and his insistence it was contingent on personal attachments. "Am I too attached?" Her voice sank into the soft green drapes as she realized the rain had stopped.

The familiar chug of the Cadillac grew louder as Brooks came up the gravel drive and got out to open the door of his garage. She took his dinner from the warming ovens, fixed his plate, and winced at the sound of the screen porch door before he stomped the mud off his shoes and removed them. He entered the kitchen—damp, cold, and rubbing his hands together. She leaned into his quick kiss and stepped into the parlor to grab the quilt from the davenport. As he removed his hat, driving cap, and gloves, she took them and threw the quilt over his shoulders. He warmed himself by the stove as she hung his coat over the door of the hall closet.

"Dinner smells good," he said as he sat at the table and rubbed his stocking feet together. "I had to wait on the weather."

"Of course." She poured a glass of milk and brought him a napkin and silverware. He picked up his knife. "Wash your hands," Camille scolded as he nodded and leapt up. "How's your book coming?"

He reseated himself, cut his breaded veal into large pieces, and savored his first bite before he answered, "It's coming along more slowly than I had hoped."

"Are you having trouble researching?" she asked.

"No. Well, yes." He stabbed a row of carrots with his fork and looked into her face. "It's not so much that I can't find the right sources, but I'm finding so much; I'm having trouble sorting it out and refining it into the approach I want to take."

"Tell me," she coaxed.

"I can't. I explained all that to you."

Camille looked around. "I forgot your bread."

He sighed. "I'm sorry. It's just so much harder with this book than it was with the first."

She cut a slab of potato bread and put it on his plate. "How so?"

"It's hard to explain, but essentially, I've found such a copious amount of philosophical theory on the subject already, and without a doubt so much more out there needs to be explored, evaluated, and integrated. But I have so much less time now with so many theme papers to read and exams to grade. It's frustrating."

She sat down. "Are you unhappy at the university?"

"No, I like being a professor, but sometimes it's hard to concentrate on this vein of philosophic thought with so many others coming and going through my mind. It's a matter of focus."

"I see." She stood, washed the pots, and cleaned off the stove as he finished his supper. She watched as he swabbed his plate with his bread. "Will you want poppy seed pound cake?"

"No—maybe a thin slice. I'm tired. I want to go to bed."

"Shall I start a bath for you?" She took the cake from the dome and cut a generous piece.

"I'm not up to carrying water upstairs; I'll wash up down here."

After she served his cake, Camille washed his dinner plate and put a teakettle of water on the stove. She scrubbed out the basin and filled it with warm water for his toilet. She ran upstairs and checked on Andrew before taking fresh towels from the linen closet, a nightshirt from the wardrobe, and bar soap from the bathroom. She pulled a ladder-back chair up by the basin, placing the towels on the seat, hanging his nightshirt from the back, and setting the soap on the rack in front of Brooks, who had already poured the boiling water into the lukewarm water in the basin. She stood behind him and watched as he removed his shirt and splashed himself with water, steam rising from his chest. "Do you remember when we talked about happiness just after Andrew was born?" she asked.

He laughed. "No."

"You quoted a Roman statesman who said something like, 'you can only be happy if you think you are.'"

"Marcus Aurelius Antoninus," he nodded as he soaped his neck and his shoulders. "I remember now. Could you help me with my back?"

She took the soap from him, lathered up her hands and massaged the rows of muscle around his neck, between his shoulder blades, and into the small of his back. She rinsed him with the cloth and patted him dry. "Your philosophy on happiness has really been troubling me."

He took the washcloth from her, rinsed it, and washed his stomach. "Now there's the perfect dichotomy—troubling yourself about happiness." He toweled his torso. "No man is happy who does not think himself so." He handed her the towel.

"Yes, that's the one. I've thought about it a great deal, and I can see a lot of truth in it, but do you really believe that's all there is to being happy?"

"Of course not." He unbuckled his belt, drew it through the loops, and handed it to her.

She rolled it into a coil and set it on the chair. "At the time you said . . ."

"I don't remember the whole conversation, Camille, or even all the circumstances, but I suppose I presented a simplified version of the philosophy of happiness so as not to confuse you." He unbuttoned his trousers and pulled them off. She took them, folded them in creases, and hung them over the back of the chair. "You see," Brooks continued as he soaped his thighs, "the philosophy of happiness is so broad, so diverse—you have utilitarianism, Epicurianism, consequentialism, universality, hedonism, the list goes on, and each theory is more complex than the one that preceded it—it's too massive a concept for the lay person to delve into. If I were to weigh you down with all the philosophical theories I've learned on every subject we discuss, you would go mad. Surely you understand." He offered a weak smile over his shoulder.

She took a chair on the far side of the table. "Do you remember what you said that night about being attached?"

"What?" He stopped drying his calves and looked up.

"You said something about how happiness is dependent on the things one attaches himself to. I was reading something in a book about attachment, and I was trying to remember what you said."

"Are you serious?" he scowled.

"How does a person become attached, Brooks? By blood? Through marriage?"

He twisted his face and wrung hot water out of the cloth. "Women don't need to get themselves worked up over these things. Why can't you be content to raise Andrew, fix up the house, dig in your yard—hell, do whatever you like around here, I don't care." He lifted a wet hand and dripped water across the kitchen floor. "But why must you always get so caught up thinking about philosophical concepts you could never completely understand?"

"I don't know." Her hand fell on the table. She watched with delight as he jumped. "I suppose I wonder about human nature and why things are the way they are, and why we do the things we do, just like everyone else."

"Not everyone." He stared at her.

"So, how does a person get attached?" she demanded. "Promises?"

He threw the warm, wet washcloth over his face and let it steam for a few seconds before removing it to reveal a pained expression. "No, through desire."

"Desire?"

His voice was almost inaudible. "People become attached to that which they desire most. It started as a religious philosophy—probably in the Far East. When someone desires something, it often becomes his only source of happiness. It can become his god." He finished drying himself, reached into the basin, and pulled the drain plug. The sound of the water swirling around itself and rushing down the drain filled the kitchen and lasted too long.

Camille watched his face furrow as he sank into the deep silence left by his words. "It's what your book is . . ."

"Yes," he winced.

"About desire." She stepped backward into the hutch, setting the preserve jars rattling against one another and pitching her sketchbook onto the floor. She picked it up to find her new sketch folded down at a sharp angle. She smoothed it over, closed the book, and set it behind the cake stand on the bottom shelf while she pondered the dichotomy of him spending all his time researching and writing about desire at precisely the same time he seemed to feel less of it for her than ever.

He took his nightshirt from the chair and threw it around his broad shoulders and slowly buttoned the front. "What was the quote about attachment you read?"

She stared into his dark face, into the beautiful midnight-blue eyes she had fallen in love with so instantly and completely it compelled her to leave her home forever. "It's from a book Eveline lent me." She washed out the basin and fin-

ished tidying up the kitchen. "It's about attachment and ignorance."

"Ignorance? I'm intrigued," he said as he watched her.
"I'd like to hear it."

She finished wiping the table and threw the cloth into
the sink before she went into the parlor and opened the
book. He followed her to the doorway and waited as she read
the passage, "Where people wish to attach, they should always
be ignorant. To come with a well-informed mind, is to come
with an ability of administering to the vanity of others, which
a sensible person would always wish to avoid. A woman, especially, if she have the misfortune of knowing anything, should
conceal it as well as she can."

Andrew's cry resounded from overhead. She closed the
book, set it on the table, and went upstairs. As she turned
onto the landing, she caught a glimpse of Brooks leaning over
to inspect the book.

12. Pleasantries

Camille stood in her muslin corset and petticoat, eyeing herself critically in the wardrobe mirror. She had lost the extra weight from her pregnancy, but her normal body weight had redistributed itself, and none of her clothes fit as they had before. She frantically pulled off a claret one-piece gown and threw it over the pile on the bed. Brooks came from the bathroom in his undershirt and drawers with his hair combed back, smelling of witch hazel. He charged to the wardrobe and pulled out a black flannel suit. "Aren't you dressed yet?" he scolded. "We should be there now."

Camille paced back to the wardrobe and rifled through the hangers again. "I've never been to a cocktail party before," she wailed. "What do women wear to cocktail parties?"

He shook his head as he moved the clothes on the bed to make a place to sit and pull on his stockings. "I don't know, I never thought about it. Why didn't you ask Eveline?"

"I would have, had I had a day or two notice," she cried.

"Calm down, I'll help." He sorted through the stack of silks, cottons, and laces on the bed. "Here, wear this green one. I've always liked it on you."

She shot him a desperate look. "I've already tried it. It's horrible. I'm different now; my hips are larger." She saw him looking her over in the mirror.

"And your bust as well," he teased as he pulled on his silk shirt and looked through the bureau for the gold cuff links she had given him for Christmas.

"Stop it!" She held a golden-yellow blouse up to herself and watched her complexion turn a sour green before she threw it on the heap. It was the first university social gathering she would attend. They had been invited to two events earlier in the year—the first when she was eight months pregnant and too uncomfortable to enjoy an evening out. She sent Brooks along with Thomas and Eveline and went to bed early. She also missed the faculty Christmas party, as Andrew had a sniffle and she couldn't be cajoled into leaving him with a sitter. The affair of this evening, though arranged on short notice, could not be missed by either of them. Thomas had been promoted to Assistant Dean of the Science Department, and Dean Merriweather was throwing an impromptu cocktail party at the Driskill Bar to celebrate him. Fortunately, Coral was able to stay late with Andrew, and Camille had him well fed and down for the evening.

"Put something on now or we'll miss the whole affair," Brooks barked as he folded over his ascot and tucked it into his vest. He looked long into the mirror, cocked his head to the right and the left, and set his bowler on at his preferred angle. Camille watched with a twinge of admiration mixed with envy as she pulled on the pima white blouse with Baby Irish embroidered edging she wore almost everywhere, and a charcoal serge hobble skirt and bolero vest with Frenchy strips of velvet and black soutache trim. She pinched her cheeks, brushed her hair up into a French chignon, and pinned on a Tyrolese hat with a tightly curled ostrich plume over the side brim. As she worked to fix a cameo on her blouse at her throat, she looked around the room.

Brooks turned. "You look lovely."

She clasped the cameo hasp on straight enough to suit her and took one last look into the glass. "I look like a schoolmarm. Have you seen my black *cordelière*?"

"No," he answered as he took her by the arm and led her out of the room. "And you don't need it."

She sighed and stopped for a second to kiss Andrew goodnight and give Coral a couple of last minute instructions before they pulled on their coats and Brooks hurried her out the door.

Camille had walked into the great main corridor of the Driskill Hotel once before while on a shopping trip with Eveline. The grand hotel had been built twenty-five years earlier by a wealthy cattle baron and had hosted U.S. presidents, famous actors, opera singers, and a couple of gubernatorial inaugurations. The four-story exterior covered half a city block in cream-colored limestone brick with spires, arches, inset balustrades, and the busts of three figures staring down like gargoyles over each of the entrances. The interior was rich with polished dark wood and subtly lit with giant chandeliers; it boasted numerous antiquities and Persian rugs. The first long-distance call out of Austin had been placed from its lobby, and it had its proper share of ghost stories for a gathering place of the *noblesse oblige*. Driskill himself, it was rumored by the hotel attendants, still turned bathroom lights on and off in the upper-level guestrooms and on rare occasions made his presence known by the haunting smell of his Turkish-aged cigar smoke. The ghost of a senator's four-year-old daughter, who had fallen to her death while bouncing her ball on the grand staircase, was sometimes heard by the desk clerks late at night—still laughing and bouncing her ball down the stairs.

The concierge took their coats and led them to the reception. The room was dimly lit except for the bar, which sparkled like a many-faceted diamond from the eastern wall. The tables had been moved to the perimeter of the bar in order to create standing reception space. Forty to fifty people had been served drinks and *hors d'œuvres* and broken into conversational clusters. As Camille glanced around the room at the chinchilla wraps, satins, and nodding aigrettes, she decided she was grossly underdressed for a cocktail party. A large man with a heavily bearded face hurried over to greet them. "Brooks! So glad you made it. We couldn't celebrate Thomas without you."

"Sorry we're late." Brooks cast Camille a furtive glance. "I got caught up advising a student and didn't get out of my office in time. This is my wife, Camille."

"Oscar Merriweather at your service." He tipped his hat and smiled. "Tales of your great beauty precede you." He extended a hand. Hers felt lost in his giant palm. She sensed its strength as he gently closed his fingers over hers in a congenial shake. The smell of his cologne sent a wave of nostalgia through her that made her legs feel weak. Her face flushed as she withdrew her hand. Brooks stopped looking around the room to meet her gaze with a cool smile. Dean Merriweather urged them to get a drink immediately as he was about to propose his toast.

Brooks escorted her to the massive oak bar standing in the one source of direct light in the large room. At least a thousand bottles aligned in perfect rows on shelves hung over a tremendous mirror reflecting light like prisms into a million softly tinted rays—casting an aurora borealis effect across the faces of the mingling guests. "What will you have?" he asked.

"I don't know," she stammered. "A glass of wine, I suppose."

"Try something new," Brooks suggested. "Maybe a martini or a whiskey sour." The bartender sidled up and waited for the order.

Warmth welled up in her cheeks as she heard Eveline's voice behind her. "Camille, I'm so glad to see you. I was afraid you wouldn't make it, and no celebration in Thomas' honor would be complete without you and Brooks." The bartender waited patiently as they exchanged a hug.

Brooks ordered bourbon. "What will you try then? A whiskey sour?"

She nodded as Eveline spoke up, "Order a gin and tonic, Camille. It's what all the fashionable ladies drink these days."

"Yes, I'll have a gin and tonic, please." The bartender nodded with a slight turn of his eyes, set up two short, fat glasses, grabbed up two bottles at once, and holding each of them a good foot and a half over his targets, filled the glasses to different levels, dipping each one in turn as he set it upright into its appointed place on the mirrored rack. He took up a bottle of tonic from under the bar and topped off her gin before pushing it toward her.

Brooks dropped a coin in a glass on the bar as Thomas came over, beaming and holding out his arms. "Abernathy, so glad you made it." They almost embraced, but stopped themselves just short and smacked each other on the back a few times instead. "Camille, you look stunning."

She smiled. "I'm so happy for you, Thomas."

He thanked her and looked around the room. "I'm glad there wasn't a large turnout. This is overwhelming enough."

"I'd consider this a handsome showing for such short notice." Brooks sipped his bourbon as Dean Merriweather hushed the room by striking the side of his glass with a cock-tail fork. He commended Thomas for four years of excellence as a professor and enumerated the reasons he was expected to be an exemplary assistant to the dean's office. Everyone cheered and raised their glasses. The smell of various liquors filled the room as they clinked their glasses, sloshing their drinks onto kid gloves and the Persian rug. Camille took a sip of her drink.

As several conversations started buzzing again, Eveline gave Thomas a peck on the cheek and left his side while his colleagues gathered around to offer their congratulations. She led Camille out of the commotion. "Better than a whisky sour, don't you think?" she asked with a sly grin.

"I've never had a whiskey sour."

"Are you serious? You should try one next, then."

"Oh, no," Camille laughed. "Actually, I've never had a cocktail before in my life, and I'm not sure how well I'll handle this one." She took another sip. "It is good, though—wonderfully sweet with a hint of sorcery under the surface."

"What a marvelous description. Can you guess what gin is made of?"

Camille took another small sampling and held it under her tongue. "It's so mysterious." She closed her eyes and tried to identify the essence. She wrinkled her face. "Some sort of berry?" she guessed.

"It's distilled from juniper berries with rye." Eveline's eyes sparkled as she used her free hand to check the tuck of her hair up under her toreador hat and smooth the peplum of her peacock-blue jacket into perfectly even folds. "Isn't it divine?"

"Absolutely—on the surface," Camille replied, "with a devilishly strong bite underneath."

Thomas and Brooks called them over to meet the other professors and their wives. Camille clung to Brooks' arm as he introduced one professor after another; she sipped her drink as they discussed university policy and scientific breakthroughs for at least three-quarters of an hour. Eveline shot her a long look with a faux yawn from across the circle. Thomas took their empty glasses and brought each of them a fresh drink.

A large woman with graying auburn hair bustled over— each dramatic stride emphasized by a tremendous *whoosh* of her copper-colored Dresden silk suit. A round, balding man with oversized eyeglasses followed dutifully behind. The woman stopped in front of Brooks and waved her empty brandy snifter toward Camille. In a voice deserving of such an entrance she asked, "Is this your wife, Professor Abernathy? Will you introduce us, please?"

Brooks smiled. "May I present Camille . . ."

"I just knew you would be ravishingly beautiful, since your husband is the handsomest devil on campus." She raised her jeweled lorgnette. The gentleman behind her took a large gulp of his whiskey and snorted autonomously. She turned to him. "Except for you, of course, Renfrow darling." He blinked his magnified eyes dumbfoundedly as he accepted a cocktail sausage from a passing waiter.

Brooks chuckled and introduced Jewel and Renfrow Kimbrough. "Dr. Kimbrough is professor of geology with nationally acclaimed publications in stratification of mineral and shale deposits," he explained as Kimbrough nodded his white-fringed head. "And Mrs. Kimbrough . . ."

"Is damned mad, that's what she is!" she proclaimed with a loud laugh. "What does a girl have to do to get a glass of brandy around here?" The single pheasant feather on her Napoleon hat darted in different directions as she spoke. Thomas took her glass with a grin and went to the bar. "Camille, dear," she went on, "can you guess what Eveline was telling me before you arrived? She said you've fixed up the Woods' place in a completely sumptuous manner. She tells me you have a talent for decorating one must see to appreciate. I do so love aesthetic finesse. Will you be throwing a dinner party soon?"

Camille's face flushed over again as everyone turned to hear her reply. Her muslins started to itch.

Jewel answered for her. "I just remembered, you have a new baby at home, don't you dear? You're much too busy right now."

"Andrew is almost four months old," Camille said.

"And an absolute angel," added Eveline.

"I'd love to have you over," Camille offered. "Perhaps this spring; I'll have fresh flowers and herbs, and I'll be in my entertaining element."

Eveline leaned forward. "Camille's a professional herbalist, you know."

"Don't tell me!" Jewel opened her ivory fan and cooled the beads of perspiration forming on her forehead. "I'll have to look forward to spring with twice the impatience. As for now, we'll have to conjure up some other form of decadent entertainment. Camille, have you been to the Hancock Opera House?"

"No," she replied.

Thomas returned from the bar and handed Jewel her refilled snifter. Jewel tucked her fan into her waistband and took a sip of her brandy as she threw her free arm around Thomas. "Thank you—you delightful young man. It's no wonder they advanced you over Renfrow—for a scientist you're charming, well-mannered, and have an alarming sensitivity to all the most important social graces." Thomas' cheeks colored, and his eyes crinkled behind his glasses. "Now, tell me," she pressed while she had him firmly in her grasp. "What is the extent of your psychological power? Can you read my mind?"

"Of course not," Thomas laughed.

"Don't coddle me now," she cooed. "You don't have me duped like the rest of you cohorts over there." She nodded toward her husband and the gathering of men who stopped their conversation short to watch her sport with the guest of honor. "Tell me true, Professor Leighton—what am I thinking at this very moment?"

Thomas laughed nervously, affording himself a few moments to think. "You're planning Austin's next momentous social gathering," he said.

"God of my mother's ghost! I knew you could do it; I just knew it!" She didn't wait for the chorus of laughter to end before she turned to her husband. "Renfrow, we must plan an opera evening." He nodded obediently as she continued, "Our studious Professor Abernathy has not raised his brow from his books long enough to take his charming wife to see our opulent new opera house."

"Very well, dear," Kimbrough agreed and ordered another whiskey.

"Yes, Camille," Jewel continued, "I remember the first time we met Brooks at the Barrington's dinner party last year. He said you were expecting your first child almost any day and suffering a great deal of discomfort. It's a shame you couldn't attend. Your professor kept us entertained all evening with his profound philosophical insights and paradoxes. I saw the world in a new light after listening to him expound on all those theories. I was so impressed I went out the next day and bought his book. He's promised to autograph it for me, but he hasn't yet." She wagged a finger playfully at Brooks, who diplomatically suggested she bring it by his office at her earliest convenience.

"Indeed, I shall. And I'll make all the arrangements for the opera and deliver your tickets in exchange." Brooks smiled blandly as Jewel swirled her snifter, swished over to stand just in front of her husband, and took over the men's political conversation.

Eveline whispered, "Thomas, what does she mean you were advanced over Professor Kimbrough? Do you sense resentment?"

"No," he replied, looking around as he put his arm around his wife's waist and quietly addressed her and Camille. "I'm sure it was just her style of jape. Kimbrough could have been dean years ago had he needed the extra work or income."

"Does he come from money?" Eveline asked.

"He was raised on a goat farm northwest of town," Thomas answered. "He had at least a dozen siblings, and they were dirt poor. According to the story circulating on campus, they thought Renfrow was slightly demented because he didn't talk much and couldn't be trusted to herd the goats from one pasture to another. He looked at the ground as he walked, and if he noted some unusual quality about the soil or a rock formation, he would forsake everything else, including his duties, and dig—sometimes with his bare hands if he had no tools handy. While his brothers and sisters ran through the fields trying to find the goats, he'd go to the kitchen table, set out his find, and study his rocks—inspecting every minute feature and sketching each one to different scales. His mother forbade the family to discuss his behavior in public for fear he would be placed in the lunatic asylum."

"He sounds a little irresponsible to me," commented Camille, "but not demented."

"As it turns out, you're right," Thomas said. "He's now a classic genius in the study of land formations and rock stratifications and makes a fortune on the side consulting with wildcatters."

"You're serious?" Eveline giggled.

Jewel's voice crescendoed and took over the room. "Oh, pish! As I always tell Renfrow, you can damn the prohibitionists all you like, but don't assume you will suppress the suffragists along with them. Mayor Wooldridge will set that right—you'll see."

Thomas grinned and continued, "It's commonly known he was the initiator of the drill at Spindletop and still receives handsome royalties, but he refuses to discuss it."

"Have you asked him?" Eveline queried.

"We all tease him mercilessly," he laughed. "It's become a favorite pastime before faculty meetings. He throws his hands up and tells us to mind our own mines."

Jewel cackled across all conversations, "*Whose* busts are they?"

"I believe one's Driskill's." Merriweather replied.

"My God! Such grotesques!" she ranted. "Do you mean to say he had his own head carved and displayed over the doors of his hotel like that? Who are the other two? They look over the metropolis like boars' heads on spits. It's a civic embarrassment!"

An atmospheric depression waved throughout the buzzing room. A chill passed through Camille, followed by an odor of acrid tobacco smoke and a sudden odd silence. She glanced at Eveline, who stared back—her eyelids fully retracted, her face colorless.

Professor Durwood Jones walked into the circle and took his pipe from his misshapen lips. "Professor Leighton, congratulations. I'm sorry I missed the toast." He angled his head backward toward Morgan. "We had a family matter arise that demanded immediate attention." Morgan's long lashes swept her cheek. She looked almost translucent in her dark, silvery-gray one-piece frock with an enormous floral chiffon "'tween dances" scarf wrapped around her head and shoulders. She looked up at Camille with a thin smile and stepped forward to greet her when her husband turned to her with an admonishing look. She withdrew her arm and fell back into his shadow. Jones nodded to Eveline and leered at Camille, taking so much of her in, she felt as if she was standing before him in her corset and stockings.

A waiter came by with a tray of oysters *en brochette.* Jones ordered himself a scotch and a mint julep for Morgan as he turned his attention to Brooks. "Young Abernathy, has your friend here just become your professional superior?"

Thomas intervened, "No, philosophy is a liberal art."

"Of course," Jones retorted. "And that's using the term 'liberal' quite liberally, is it not?"

Jewel placed herself between Brooks and Jones. "Have you read Professor Abernathy's book? It's absolutely brilliant."

"No," he hissed. "As a historian, I find the study of philosophy somewhat droll. I can't see that it has any real practical application, whereas history is reality no one can change to suit his whims. Only through history can we understand ourselves in context with reality, learn from our mistakes, wrestle with consequences in a reasonable manner."

"That's absurd," Jewel growled.

Brooks stepped forward and set a hand lightly on Jewel's shoulder. "I fully appreciate his point of view, Mrs. Kimbrough, don't you?" Camille recognized his mellifluous tone. He had a dichotomy of voices—one he used when talking to other men and a Caruso-style croon he used when talking to women. She remembered when he used to talk to her that way.

Jewel snatched her fan out of her sash and stepped aside to watch Brooks Abernathy work his magic. "You see," he addressed Jones, "I agree history is an invaluable tool for knowledge of self, society, and the nature of humanity in general. But for me, philosophy is the art of taking history from a temporal plane to the immortal."

Jones took out a handkerchief and muffled a deep cough. "I don't follow your line of thought, but for the sake of argument, if you could somehow philosophize history into some sort of transcendent domain, what would be the empirical value?"

Brooks listened with no change of expression. "As Georg Hegel articulated it," he answered, "'In history, we are concerned with what has been and what is; in philosophy, however, we are concerned not with what belongs, exclusively to the past or to the future, but with that which *is*, both now and eternally—in short with reason.'"

Jewel handed Kimbrough her snifter and applauded. "Bravo, Professor Abernathy, well said!"

"Hegel had some strange ideas about history," Jones retorted as he pulled his watch out of his pocket. "Still, I suppose some find it an interesting pastime—sitting around mulling over what other men have sat around and mulled over."

Camille watched Brooks nod politely and excuse himself to get another bourbon. Jones drank the rest of his scotch with a gulp and looked around for a waiter. Jewel retrieved her snifter, raised her lorgnette, and looked Morgan over.

Another glass was struck as the chemistry professor called the group's attention toward the north wall. A young woman in a stunning gold lamé dress with her yellow hair combed up into a floral spray raised her violin to her chin and struck a few dissonant chords. She tightened a couple of strings as the crowd mumbled and then hushed. Professor Williamson introduced his daughter, Lorna, who had recently placed first in the state scholastic music competition and had been gracious enough to share her winning solo with the party. She raised her bow and pulled it slowly across the strings, emitting a smooth, sonorous wail. Camille watched Brooks' face as he eyed the young girl while waiting for his drink at the bar. As Lorna played through Jules Massonet's "Meditation for Thasis," Camille's heart melted like candle wax and dripped into her womb.

After the generous round of applause, Lorna's smiling parents escorted her home. Brooks returned from the bar with a wide grin. "Renfrow, tell us again about Spindletop." The men laughed and formed a circle around Professor Kimbrough.

"I'm sure I don't know what you mean." Kimbrough blinked and bit the end off a cigar. "Has anyone a light?" he asked. Jones pulled matches from his pocket. "But I'll tell you one thing," Kimbrough continued as he lit his cigar, "the University of Texas could be the richest school in the world if the administration could be so convinced."

"You're not suggesting there's oil under Austin?" Jones asked.

Professor Kimbrough's eyes took on a strange light. "All the conditions are right." He stomped a foot. "We stand over organically rich source rock with a geological history that parallels the deposition of prehistoric plants and animals. We also have massive rifts of porous reservoir rock."

"How do you know?" Merriweather asked.

"It's so indigenous to our area, we've constructed most of the university's buildings of it."

"Limestone," Jones said.

"Limestone and thick sandstone," Kimbrough continued. "And, finally, we have the rarest and most important feature for storage of crude oil of all."

"Geological pressure," Merriweather guessed. "We have so much pressure here."

"Pressure helped to create it, but it's not the essential condition," Kimbrough answered.

"Salt domes," Jones suggested. "I read they were instrumental in the decision to drill at Spindletop."

"We do have salt domes," Kimbrough answered. "But they aren't the condition, only an effect." He spent a few moments enjoying his cigar and the atmosphere of suspense he had created.

"Tell us please, Renfrow darling," Jewel pleaded. "What is the third condition?"

"Entrapment," he yelled. Morgan jumped. Kimbrough went on, "Millions of years ago the earth's crust broke, shifted, and created the Balcones Fault."

"We may be rich because of a fault?" Brooks winked at Jewel.

"Actually, no." Kimbrough's eyes darted ominously behind the lenses until the laughter subsided. "I said the conditions were right, but the spring activity around the fault indicates the rocks and hills under our fair city are filled with nothing but air and water."

Merriweather's head twisted sharper than an owl's. "So, how do you suppose the university will cash in on the oil boom?"

"The state endowment in West Texas," Kimbrough barked. "I got a feeling it's saturated in black gold. I've been trying to get the last two school presidents to let me go out there and run some tests."

"Of course," Merriweather mused. "What did they say?"

Kimbrough grunted. "They say they'll look into it, and then let my reports die on their desks." He rolled his magnified eyes and reverted his attention to his drink, his cigar, and watching for the *hors d'œuvres* tray.

Thomas turned to Jewel. "Professor Jones may be able to answer your questions about the busts," he suggested.

"Tell us, please, Durwood," she demanded dryly. "Does your vast historical expertise include any facts about this hotel?"

Jones filled his chest with an inhalation of his pipe. "I have been writing a series of articles on Austin's history for the *National Historical Association Journal*. I submitted one last year on the Driskill and the Littlefield Building."

"Is that Driskill himself carved out of the stone lintels outside the hotel?" Jewel asked.

"Indeed," he assured her. "With his two sons—one on either side."

"How abominably arrogant!" she wailed. "Did his wife pass away when the boys were young?"

"Why no," Jones scowled. "She outlived him by several years."

"So why was she not included in the macabre family portrait?" Jewel held her empty snifter in front of Thomas, who took it immediately but didn't move toward the bar.

Jones took a long drag on his pipe and exhaled into the midst of his audience. "Madam, surely you know it would be in bad taste for a man of his stature. Demands of social propriety would not allow him to consider exposing his wife or daughters so publicly."

Jewel snapped her fan open as her face flushed purple. "He had daughters?"

"Four, I believe." Jones took his monocle from his right eye and polished it with his handkerchief. Kimbrough wiped his brow and shuffled his weight between his feet.

"Professor Jones," Jewel faced him squarely. "I would agree with you he saved his wife and daughters from a horrid public display, and I suppose we should be grateful to him on their behalf in that respect. But, given the fact he obviously saw it as a heroic memorial to himself and his heirs to have them set out over the horizon in such a permanent fashion, don't you find it at all hypocritical that he should have excluded the woman who raised his sons—as well as his daughters—cooked his meals, washed his drawers, and no doubt triumphed and suffered through all his business conquests right along with him?"

Jones replaced his monocle. "Mrs. Kimbrough, you don't seem to . . ."

"And," Jewel continued, "do you mean to defend the fact he apparently saw fit to immortalize his sons and not his daughters?"

Jones clasped his pipe in his stained teeth as he spoke, "Madam, you miss the point." A look of terror fell across Morgan's face; she looked down at her feet before she whispered something to Jones and disappeared into the crowd.

"No, Professor Jones, I did not miss the point." Jewel threw her shoulders back. "I took it straight through the heart, as I have all my life—over and over again—as all women have been conditioned to take the stabs of self-abnegation from men like Driskill, from men like you, with such self-serving, imperious attitudes."

Jones stood mute, his temples bulging, his fists clenched.

The bar lights flickered. "What was that?" asked Eveline.

"Power surge," Thomas answered.

Jones looked at Jewel blankly. "Madam, you are a hysterical madwoman." He tipped his hat and walked to the bar.

Brooks took a sip of his bourbon. "What does he stoke

that thing with, anyway?"

"Camel dung, I've heard tell," Thomas replied as he turned to Jewel. "I'll get your drink. Eveline, Camille, anyone ready for another?"

"No," they answered in unison.

As the men busied themselves placating Jewel, who shook with rage as she fanned herself, Camille noticed the bar lights had blurred over, casting a shimmering effect over the room that vibrated new intensity. "My satin pumps are making my feet throb," she told Eveline.

"I'm tired, too," Eveline answered. "I wish things would break up so the guest of honor could take me home."

Camille giggled. "Can you keep a secret?"

"What?" Eveline smiled.

"I think I'm tipsy."

"I'll get Brooks to take you home," Eveline said as she started toward the men.

"No," Camille gasped as she took Eveline by the arm. "I'm going to find the ladies' lounge and sit for a minute. Please tell Brooks for me."

"I should come with you," Eveline said as her smile faded.

"I'll be fine," Camille assured her. Eveline nodded and joined Thomas as Camille made her way slowly through lights which had started to dip and spin. She concentrated on maintaining her balance for fear of leaning into a stranger. When she found the ladies' room, she dabbed water on her face and neck and looked into the mirror. She thought for a moment she really was beautiful, though her eyes looked dull. On her way back through the lounge, she found Morgan sitting in a chair sponging her shoulder with a bathroom towel. "Did you run into something?" Camille asked as she sat on a satin chair next to her.

Morgan quickly pulled her scarf up around her head and smiled. "Yes." She wiped her eye with the back of her hand. "It's nothing, really. Isn't this a nice tribute to Thomas?"

"Quite," Camille answered. "Are you enjoying yourself?"

"Oh, yes!" A shrill lilt animated Morgan's voice. "I'm having a wonderful time."

13. The Trellis

Herbs have a variety of temperaments, and flowers have distinctive characters. Camille had learned this as a young child and made careful allowances for it in planning the formal gardens for the backyard. According to the 1912 *Farmer's Almanac*, all danger of frost would be over in the southern states by March twelfth, so Brooks had hired men to dig up and cultivate gardens according to her specifications and set the trellis in the ground by the tenth. On the morning of the twelfth, Camille bounded out of bed, pulled on a broadcloth skirt and cotton blouse, and fixed Brooks' coffee and eggs. She let Coral in to make the beds and tidy up the bathroom while she fed Andrew, fixed Brooks' lunch, and sent him on his way. Andrew chewed on his toys and gurgled in his play crib on the screen porch while she got started. She stopped on the porch to pull on her gardening smock and gloves and step into her green garden shoes before she entered the raw wonder of her back lawn. A hundred wonderful scents from her herb garden greeted her as she stepped out onto the flagstone pathway. This morning the French tarragon, dill, and chives smelled especially fresh, but she resisted the temptation to get a bowl from the kitchen and harvest fresh leaves and buds for dinner, and walked instead through her cream-colored arched trellis. She'd had it placed fifteen feet from the back service entrance to the house, midway between the screen porch and the herb garden, opening up to the wonders of the lush oak-lined lawn where Andrew and his future sisters and brothers would grow up playing. She smiled as she rolled up her sleeves.

Her plan was wonderfully simple. First, she planted the showy, opulent Madame George Staechelin large-flowered climbers—one on each side of the arched trellis—with a soil compound specially formulated for roses. She made an indented mound of soil around the base of each plant and gently coaxed the trailers in and out of the latticework, braiding them in the style of a Renaissance convolvulus and tying them securely in place with twine. Around each embedded rose plant, she put in a thick row of French lavender seedlings, even though she had plenty of lavender blooming in her herb garden. As far as Camille was concerned, one could never have too much lavender. She found its heady clean aroma, worldly charm, and dashing presence irresistible. It could be used in a wide variety of recipes, infusions, tinctures, potpourris, and floral arrangements and made a soothing yet sensuous addition to a sachet, a cake of soap, or a steaming bath. Camille patted the black floral compound in place around the sprouts and wondered why, according to herb catalogs, it was often associated with mistrust. Around the lavender seedlings she planted a lacy white border of sweet alyssum, which despite its frivolous appearance, would grow back every year into larger white clouds and work its way among the flagstones. She would have to trim it back every season, but it would edge her trellis treatment with grace and balance the deep royal purples of the lavenders and rich pinks of the roses. She liked the way it spilled out over the deep green St. Augustine grass. She wheeled over the bar-row she'd had the hired men fill with mulch and covered the soil between all her plants.

Andrew started fussing as the mid-morning sun topped the house and warmed Camille's back. As she quickly finished smoothing the bark chips over the loam, she heard Coral's foot on the stair. "I've got him," Camille called as she pulled off her gloves.

Coral came through the kitchen. "Shall I make some lemonade, Miss Camille?"

"Please," she answered as she lifted Andrew and kissed the folds of his fat little neck. She sat at the tea table bouncing him on her lap and playing peek-a-boo until Coral came out with a tray, served Andrew juice in his special cup with Melba toast, and poured Camille and herself their ritual morning lemonade.

"I got the upstairs and the bathroom done," Coral said as she sat down, "and I'll start on the downstairs, unless you want me to watch baby while you work instead."

"No," Camille said as she sipped her lemonade and looked out over the back lawn. "It's getting too hot. I'm happy to have the trellis garden in, and I'll have to ask Brooks to take me back to the hardware store before I can put in the other gardens."

Coral nodded as she looked around. "Looks nice." She pointed to the empty back plots. "What are you going to put there?"

"Roses, mostly," Camille sighed. "I love roses." She had decided on making two large crescent gardens in the back corners of the lot, each of which encompassed three well-established oak trees, with a smaller round garden in the center by the back fence. "In one curved garden I'll plant providence roses," she continued. "They have the most heavenly scent. I wouldn't consider making a potpourri without some providence petals. And in the other I'll set in a Kathryn Morley English Rose—they're prim, pale pink, and so ladylike—and some Gallica bushes for sure; they look so much like camellias it's startling. Some are a stunning shade of magenta. I'll get one of those and perhaps a red and a white one."

"Um-hmm." Coral looked out into the yard as if she could also see the roses blooming.

"I'll edge the gardens with lamb's ears," Camille went on. "Its leaves are a soft sterling-green and work into wreaths particularly well. Jasmine creepers will connect the rose bushes with lush green leaves and a starry sparkly effect, and wisteria vines will run up the tree trunks and hang over the roses in long, silvery lavender sweeps."

"Ah," sighed Coral. "In Kentucky, one of the mansions in town had wisteria growing from a big old oak tree. I watched for it to blossom every spring; it didn't bloom for very long, and I always thought it was sad it couldn't stand up on its own, but I just loved the way it looked—to me it was like a lady crying just because everything was so beautiful."

Camille sat back in her chair and smiled as Andrew reached out for Coral, who looked for Camille's approval before taking him into her lap for a gentle gallop. "This is the way the city folks ride, nice and slow and easy." Andrew broke into an infectious laugh.

"What part of Kentucky are you from?" Camille asked.

Coral finished her rhyme with a broad smile. "Bumpity, bumpity, bumpity bump! I grew up outside of Louisville," she said. "My parents were both freed slaves, and we had a little house on the back of the land owned by my father's master. My father was lucky. His master was kind and treated him like a man with some dignity. He didn't want to see him leave, so he set him up right there on his property. It was a little teeny place, but there were lots of trees and clear streams, and I loved to walk around and listen to the trees whisper secrets to one another. Sometimes, I thought I could tell what they were saying."

"Does your family still live there?" Camille asked.

"Daddy does," Coral's smile faded. "With my youngest brother. My other brother works on the riverboats and hardly ever goes home."

"What made you and Samuel decide to move to Austin?" Camille asked.

"We came down here a couple of years ago when the Buckhorn Bar where Samuel worked in Louisville closed down. Lots of his friends moved to Austin because word got out manufacturing jobs were opening up. Samuel worked on a line making engine parts until the dam broke and the factory had to close. Most of his friends had to move back home or down to San Antonio to look for work, but Samuel got a job mixing drinks and ringing sales at the colored bar in Wheatville."

"Samuel likes to tend a bar?" Camille stood and slipped off her garden shoes and her smock.

"Not particularly," Coral answered. "But it's pretty good money right now, with the baby coming and everything."

Camille spun around. "Coral! You didn't tell me you were expecting."

Coral's eyes shone as she continued to jostle Andrew on her knees. "It's a little early to be talking about it, but the baby's due in early November."

"Are you feeling well?"

"I've been a little sick, but not too bad."

Camille sat down and took another sip of her lemonade. She stared at the beads of cold perspiration on her glass and held it momentarily against her forehead. "What about your mother?"

Coral looked out at the herb garden. "She took cholera when it passed through a few years back. We buried her the year before I met Samuel."

Bees buzzed over the bergamot and a dragonfly snapped. "I'm so sorry," Camille said.

"Thank you, Miss Camille," Coral replied with a rasp in her voice, "but it all happened pretty fast, and her fever only lasted a couple of days, so she didn't suffer as much as a lot of other folks did. I always figured it's just what the Lord had planned for her."

A blue jay landed on the top of the trellis and trilled a fast aria before flying up over the house. Camille drummed the rhythm of the bird's song on the tabletop. "Have you seen a doctor?"

Andrew laughed and threw his Teddy bear on the ground. "Yes, ma'am." Coral leaned over to retrieve the toy; she handed it to the child, who took it, rubbed his face on it, and grinned as he threw it down again.

"He's getting unreasonable. I'll take him," Camille said.

"I don't mind, really." Coral picked up the bear again and held it at an arm's length as the child reached for it and whined. She gave it to him and stroked his dark hair.

"What were the trees whispering?" Camille asked.

Coral grinned thoughtfully as she watched Andrew hit himself in the head with his bear. "Different things at different times. Sometimes they shared general forest secrets, like 'Brace yourself, a north-easterly's blowing through with lots of clouds,' or 'Look here at this hollow of baby chipmunks— but don't touch, they're still too little.'" Andrew looked up into Coral's eyes and made a cooing sound. "Other times," she continued, "it seemed they were trying to explain things to me, like . . ." her voice diminished.

"Like . . .?" Camille asked softly.

Coral took a deep breath and looked around the yard into the oaks. "Like why my mother whipped me for tearing a hole in my blue dress, even when she knew I could sew it right up." Coral took a slow sip of lemonade. "Or for things she knew my brothers did and blamed on me."

The cicadas stopped rattling. Camille leaned forward. "Odd, isn't it?" she said as she wiped her neck with her napkin. "I never heard those insects buzzing until they quieted down." A soft spring breeze blew scents of rosemary and sweet cicely through the porch and rustled the oak branches. "What did the trees say about your mother?"

Coral's face went blank. "They said it was because she was beaten so much when she was young. It's the only way she knew how to raise a little girl."

"She wasn't so lucky," Camille remarked.

"No, I guess she wasn't lucky at all. Daddy told us she never knew her mother—she was probably taken from her when she was a baby. All she could remember was being a servant in the kitchen on the plantation. If she dropped a cup or burned a sauce, she was caned. She had welts all over her backside."

Andrew grew restless, and Coral placed him over her shoulder and hummed. Camille looked out at her trellis standing naked in the middle of the yard with a few green and white sprouts entwined at its base. She had seen it in her mind every day for the last two years—but as it would be in future summers, covered over with greenery and laden with color and fragrance. She took the last sip of her ice-diluted lemonade and felt it run cold through her veins.

Andrew calmed to the sound of Coral's voice and looked around the porch with wide eyes. "What goes in the back?" Coral asked quietly between stanzas.

Camille took the mint sprig from her empty glass and chewed on it for a moment to sweeten the bitter taste in her mouth. "Lady Banks roses and a Japanese honeysuckle will brighten up the back fence and attract butterflies and hummingbirds for Andrew to watch." She looked over at her son, now deep in his morning nap on Coral's narrow shoulder.

"And what about the little round plot in the center?" Coral asked.

Camille peered through the web of screen at another little dream she would soon work hard to make come true. "I'll plant a crape myrtle bush with something bright around the edge. Perhaps some verbena, or . . ." she turned, "some Coralbells. Of course, Coralbells should go in there."

"Oh, Miss Camille," Coral's face broke out into a wide grin. "You don't have to do that on my account."

"I won't," answered Camille. "I'll do it for myself. I'll look out there and see those bright, colorful florets on their dainty stocks, and I'll think of someone I've become very fond of. It will give me cheer on my darkest day. I'll propagate some for you, and you can plant them around your house as well."

"We don't have much of a yard," Coral said. "But I'd like to have one or two to put on the table from time to time."

"We'll grow lots of Coralbells," Camille said, "and you can take home as many as you like."

Coral let out a deep breath. "I better put this little one in his crib and get back to work."

14. Seedlings

March 21, 1912
Dear Mother,

I've finally finished putting in gardens in the back lawn. It doesn't look like much now, save the herb garden, which produces new delights daily, but in a couple of months I should have lots of roses, and by fall the beds should be filling in. Coral helped a great deal. She comes over every weekday around eight and stays until just after noon when her husband can come for her in his boss's wagon. It would be so much easier for her to ride the trolley, but she refuses to succumb to the Jim Crow segregation arrangement, and I love her all the more for her obstinacy. Brooks would be livid if he ever found out, but I help her clean the house every day after the sun tops the roof so we can spend the cooler part of the morning planting the rose bushes and other assorted seedlings. You would love Coral. She has a rare wisdom of the ways and balances of nature. She's had a hard life and lost her mother before she moved to Texas, but instead of becoming bitter, she has learned to nurture herself from the generous hand of Mother Nature—and for this, I also admire her. She's about to become a mother herself this fall, and I have resolved in my own mind to support her in any way I can. I would miss her terribly if it prevented her from coming every day. I'm sure Providence will see us both through this.

Andrew has grown into a healthy, round baby. He sits up stoutly and creeps everywhere. He propels himself across the floors so much more quickly than I ever would have suspected possible. It's getting harder and harder to stay a step ahead of him and keep him safe. I must keep careful watch to block the stairway at both ends; on the top I've set large boxes of Brooks' discarded clothes and at the bottom I am constantly hauling the coffee table back and forth. He'll soon learn to scramble over that, and I'll have to find another roadblock. He's cunning. For a six-month-old, it's amazing how he's already learned to play on my sympathies and devotions. He works me with those big blue eyes so well; I know what he wants before he starts fussing. He reminds me of Brooks more every day. Thank God, he still takes a short morning nap and a longer one after his lunch.

Eveline often comes over for tea in the middle of the afternoon. Sometimes she brings freshly baked sweet potato scones or orange pecan muffins, and we sip my latest concoction of herbal tea, read and discuss poetry, and gossip a little. I savor these times. You would also like Eveline. She's soft-spoken and quite refined. She's taken a degree in literature from a women's college in Boston and always knows what novels and poetry I'd like to read. She would never dream of rooting around in garden dirt the way we do, and I'm not at all sure what she thinks of me for it, but she does admire my gardens—especially the herb garden as it is in its full glory. She's especially in awe of my herb drying racks in the extra bedroom on the southeastern corner of the house. I've already amassed enough bundles to fill the rafters with color and a rich floral scent. Sometimes we talk or she reads as I wind herb wreaths and garlands, but she won't try her hand at it no matter how hard I coax. She does, however, help brew herbal vinegars and oils. She especially likes the tarragon–chive vinegar, fennel, and oregano oils. She always takes at least a couple of bottles home and obviously uses them according to my instructions on salads and meats she serves Thomas, for whenever I see him, he always has a word of thanks or praise about his last evening's dinner.

At any rate, on afternoons when Andrew is well rested and in relatively sweet spirits, we take the trolley into town to lunch at the Cactus Tea Room or the Driskill and shop for dresses or toddling clothes for Andrew. Last week we stopped in William Fink and Co., a marvelous store with all sorts of domestic and imported yard goods. Eveline and I looked through the bolts and decided we would each need one of those new electric sewing machines. We both sew by hand and crochet so well, we feel sure we can learn the craft readily enough. I found some soft cotton lawn, so I bought a couple of yards, and when Brooks came home late that evening, I explained the many domestic values of owning a new electric sewing machine. He told me to go to Wheeler and Wilson's and ask for demonstrations on each of the new models, and when I was sure which one would best suit my needs, he would go round and purchase it for me on the next Saturday afternoon when he went to the banking saloon. Eveline decided she would wait until I've had mine for a while to decide which one she would get. She loves the traditional women's arts as much as I do, but sometimes needs a little more encouragement. I don't mind. I don't think her mother did any of these things with her, so she lacks a little self-confidence. (Did I tell you she cannot bear children? I often wonder if it affects her psychologically in this manner.) But I have great plans with my new machine—a paper pattern is featured every day in the Statesman, *a couple of which I'm dying to try. I will make all sorts of rompers for Andrew and blouses and skirts for myself, not to mention the table linens and curtains I'll be able to turn out in a fraction of the time it takes to whip stitch the edges by hand.*

Eveline and I spend even more time together lately as Thomas has received a promotion at the university and works almost as much as Brooks does. We attended a reception in his honor. I met the most fascinating woman. Her name is Jewel, and her behavior is so outrageous she frightens and delights me at the same time. She said she would arrange for all of us to attend the opera, and she did. Brooks brought home the tickets last evening. We will see the English hit, H.M.S. Pinafore, in a couple of weeks. Eveline and I will have fun shopping for evening attire. I'm looking forward to the production, and I hope Brooks is as well, although if he wanted to take me for a formal evening out, it seems he would have done it before without Jewel's insistence.

But to get back to Eveline—I treasure our friendship; she's won-derfully patient with Andrew and a great source of intellectual stim-ulation. Still, certain things dear to my heart cannot be shared with her—not that she can't be trusted, of course, but our husbands are so close that some matters are best just shared with you. Every evening after Andrew's eaten his ground fruit and rice for dinner, I carry him through the back lawn to see the new blossoms and smell the fresh herbs, and while he crawls the flagstones under the trellis, I talk to you. We talk about our summer outings on the beach at the sound, the brooding of Mount Rainier, and all sorts of things no one here knows anything about, save Brooks, who never seems to miss any of them at all. He never talks about Seattle or even about the orchard in Tacoma. We've received a couple of letters from his mother, but if he has answered, he must have done it from his office, for I have never seen him post a letter from home. I suppose men just aren't as sen-timental about these things. His mind is too full of philosophy for anything else lately. I try to talk to him, to share this important aspect of his life, but his knowledge of theories and command of quotes is so vast, he gets impatient and refuses to respond. He's par-ticularly vexed with me lately because I've guessed what his new book is about. You're the only one in the world I can share this with—he writes about desire! Can you imagine what he reads and thinks about all day and into the night while he stays late and coun-sels those young coeds in his office until well after dark? What wor-ries me most, Mother, is that he studies desirous motives and activi-ty as if it were some sort of science to be experimented with and worked over—and except for a rare evening of after dinner-amuse-

ment, these days he doesn't speak to me any more than he absolutely has to—to get his supper and land himself clean and snug in bed. With no more than a peck on my cheek and a pat on Andrew's back, he rolls over and falls into a deep sleep until his alarm calls him up to shave, slather himself with witch hazel, dress himself impeccably, eat, and dash off to his wonderful work life again. Do you think it possible for a man to spend so much time thinking and writing about desire and not have more of an outlet for it? Neither do I. Tuck this one into your heart.

This thought haunts me as I move through my house, my garden, as I rock our beautiful son to sleep in the evening. I had to write to you. My sanity hinges on these letters. Writing each one is like painting a self-portrait and standing back to look at it. Today I don't like what I see.

Love—forgiving and just,
Your Camille

15. The Opera

Camille and Eveline spent the afternoon at the beauty parlor the day of the opera. Eveline had purchased a dark blue frock with a narrow lace yoke and bands of shirring, while Camille had selected a champagne-pink Marquisette gown with ivory lace and a matching ostrich-plumed hat. Brooks washed and waxed his Cadillac for the occasion, and the two couples drank a glass of port at the Leightons' home before Brooks drove them all downtown.

The Hancock Opera House lay just west of Congress on Pecan Street. Many of Austin's noteworthy politicians and socialites had already arrived. The Bremonds had ordered drinks and were inquiring about their seats, while Governor Colquitt and his wife climbed the stairs to their box in the mezzanine. Brooks ordered scotch for himself and Thomas and gin and tonics for Camille and Eveline before they entered the theater and showed the usher their tickets. He directed them to the center of the auditorium in the seventh row, where Camille and Eveline took seats together. Camille gasped as she looked around. Bas-reliefs of flora and fauna covered the walls, and the three-tiered stage curtain was a spectacle in itself—hand-painted with a variety of pastoral and celestial scenes. Muses danced in clouds on either side of the stage, and cherub faces complacently glared down from their frames of golden scrollwork. The orchestra played a Chopin étude softly from the pit. Camille and Eveline admired the intricacies of the decor and commented on the attire of the other women while Brooks and Thomas stood on the aisle exchanging greetings with colleagues and acquaintances. Camille was amazed how many people Brooks knew.

Eveline pointed out local dignitaries. "In that box," she nodded toward the mezzanine, "that's Mayor Wooldridge and his wife, and look," she motioned toward the left wall, "that's Colonel Edward House, President Wilson's closest political advisor and confidant."

"Here in Austin?" Camille asked.

"It's said Wilson doesn't do anything without consulting him first." Eveline looked around. Her tone changed. "Who's that?"

"Doctor Abernathy!" A young blonde woman in a red satin frock with Spanish black lace approached Brooks. Her décolletage was unavoidable and the look in her eyes, unmistakable. Camille watched as he politely nodded and crooned a greeting with a backward glance at her and Eveline. He didn't introduce them.

"Have you ever seen her before?" Eveline asked.

"No," Camille replied and took a large sip of her gin.

"Here we are!" Jewel's alto could be heard well before she appeared on the aisle aglow in a chocolate-brown satin dress with a gold lamé jacket and a small cap with a pheasant feather rising like an exclamation point above her head. "Let's see, we're all here except for Merriweather and Alicia. Camille, Eveline, hello." Camille and Eveline rose to join the circle in the aisle as Brooks' blonde friend excused herself and made her way to her seat. Jewel gave them each a perfunctory hug and praises for their attire. Professor Kimbrough stopped next to the men without a word and downed half his whiskey. "I've made reservations at the Driskill for a late dinner," Jewel announced. Kimbrough wrinkled his brow. "Or an early breakfast," she wagged a finger toward her husband. "It's the fashionable thing to do after the theater."

"Sounds lovely," Eveline remarked.

"It will be, dear," Jewel assured her. "And we can discuss the artistic merit and depth of metaphor in the show."

"I need a cigar," Kimbrough declared. "Anyone else?"

"I have an announcement!" Jewel interjected. "This week I've officially joined the suffragists." She turned to Camille and Eveline. "And I'll shamelessly work to enlist your talents as well." Brooks' eyes spun up toward the ceiling as he raised his elbow and took a sip of his scotch. "I saw that, Professor Abernathy," Jewel scolded. "Surely you would encourage your wife in this manner. We have an important moral duty to raise the status of women above that of mere children. I've been raving about your modern philosophical views all over town, and I know we can count on your support."

Brooks straightened his ascot. "I would consider such activity an imperfect moral duty."

Jewel frowned. "I like you, Dr. Abernathy. I find your work intense, but intelligent and *avant garde*, so tell me in terms I can readily digest. What do you mean by 'imperfect'?"

He grinned. "According to Immanuel Kant, there are two types of moral duty—perfect and imperfect."

"The difference, Professor?" Jewel asked as she raised her lorgnette.

"A perfect duty is absolute," Brooks answered, "and cannot be put off or avoided."

"And an imperfect duty?" Jewel glowered.

"An imperfect duty is one that can be neglected by more pressing duties or obligations."

Jewel's mouth tightened around her words. "And what duties and obligations would you deem more pressing?"

"Ah, here's Dean Merriweather." Brooks extended a hand as the dean came down the aisle and greeted them. He introduced Camille and Eveline to his wide-eyed wife, Alicia, who giggled as he spoke her name.

"Will Morgan Jones be joining us?" Camille asked Jewel.

"I would love to have included dear Morgan," Jewel answered, "if there were any way possible to do so while excluding that loathsome husband of hers. But, I'm hoping Ida Plimpton and some of the other suffragists will attend." She looked around as the lights flickered. "There's our curtain call," she said. "We should find our seats."

"I should have gotten a cigar," Kimbrough whined. "I've been thinking about smoking a good cigar all day."

Brooks laughed. "You know, Kimbrough, according to an eastern philosopher, 'A man is what he thinks about all day.'"

"Really, professor?" Jewel resounded. "So tell me, please, what is a woman? What she has been cooking for supper all day?" Brooks lost his grin while Kimbrough downed the rest of his drink. "No wonder I feel so much like a fricasseed chicken!" Jewel shrieked and pulled her hands up into her armpits, flapping and clucking so loud the seated patrons had difficulty stifling their laughter.

"I want a cigar," Kimbrough announced. "But now I suppose it would be prudent to wait until after the first act."

Jewel stopped flapping. "What do you know of prudence?" she moaned. Kimbrough nodded and strode up the aisle. Brooks gave Camille a desperate glance and followed. Everyone else found their seats just before the orchestra stopped playing its soft background music and a man stepped onto center stage and announced Gilbert and Sullivan's blockbuster hit in London and New York, *H.M.S. Pinafore.* The audience thundered its applause as the lights dimmed and the orchestra launched into the overture. The last panel of the curtain rose to reveal the sailors assiduously scrubbing the quarterdeck of Her Majesty's Ship, *Pinafore*, before the arrival of the First Admiral.

Brooks slipped into his seat beside Camille. She gently waved off his cigar smoke to clear her line of vision. "That woman is impossible!" Brooks whispered in her ear as the red, round, and rosy bumboat woman, Little Buttercup, climbed aboard and solicited the sailors with her stock of "snuff and tobaccy and excellent jacky."

It was after eleven o'clock by the time they were all seated in the grand dining saloon. Camille sat between Brooks and Oscar Merriweather. Brooks' witch hazel mixed with Merriweather's mysterious masculine smell made her head feel light and sent a tingling wave of weakness down her back and into her lower extremities. It thrilled her almost more than it frightened her. Jewel ordered champagne for everyone and watched judiciously as the glasses were poured. She nudged Kimbrough until he raised his glass. Camille kept her hand on her glass and her smile fixed for him, though it was impossible to tell who he actually looked at through his tremendous lenses. "To friends!" he declared. His eyes glazed over and he fell silent. Jewel's lashes twitched as she leaned over and whispered into his ear. "And fart lovers!" he added.

"No!" Jewel cried, amidst the laughter and clinking of glasses. "I said *art* lovers!"

"So sorry, dear," Kimbrough said without a change of expression and held his glass out to the waiter for a refill.

"You're incorrigible," she growled. "You'll be fricasseeing your own chickens from now on." She whisked her ivory fan out of her sash as she ordered the waiter to refill the glasses.

"Now, for a real toast." She looked around the table. "Professor Leighton, I'm sure you're up to the task."

Thomas colored slightly and winked amicably at Jewel. His eyes darted up into the chandelier and stayed until the glasses were all refilled and everyone's eyes were on him. He raised his glass. "So give three cheers and one cheer more . . ."

"He *is* an Englishman!" They all sang out together and turned back and forth tapping glasses three or four times each before their laughter subsided enough to consummate their toast. As they reseated themselves, Camille felt Merriweather's chair inch closer to hers. Alicia could not stop giggling while the waiter brought salted almonds, queen olives, and cheese straws to the table and presented the dinner menus.

Jewel leaned over hers and looked at the olives before spearing one with the relish fork. "Camille, what did you think of the operetta?"

"It was delightful," Camille replied. "In fact, it's left me in such a seafaring spirit, I believe I'll order the halibut steak . . ."

"*Maître d'hôtel with pommes à la duchesse,*" Brooks finished for her. "That's the special with whipped potatoes."

"Excellent choice," Jewel exclaimed. "I'll have the same," she told the waiter as she handed him her menu. "And open four bottles of wine," she told him as he nodded. "Two of your best whites and a bordeaux?" she asked as she looked around the table. Brooks nodded. "Two bordeaux then. You might bring them now," she added. "We'll open them and let them breathe. And you, Eveline," she leaned forward to look across Thomas, "what did you think?"

"It was splendid," she answered. "I'll never get those tunes out of my head." Jewel snorted a laugh, and Alicia started giggling again. "But," Eveline continued, "are the English really so rigid about marriage across social class lines?"

"I'm sure that aspect was meant to be satirical," Brooks answered and ordered the tenderloin of beef with mushrooms. "No one's that biased. Not even in England."

Camille watched him as he snatched up a handful of almonds and sat back in his chair—his black hair so perfectly combed back and angled into a rift that ended in a half curl over his temple, his profile so sharp and sure against the red velvet-satin-striped wallpaper. "Something confuses me," she said.

"What?" Jewel asked as she fanned herself and prompted Kimbrough to pour her more champagne.

"Did I misunderstand something or did the captain end up marrying the woman who had nursed him as a baby?" Dean Merriweather's forearm brushed against hers as he turned in his chair to look directly at her. "An interesting Freudian twist," he smiled. "I can't believe I never made the connection." Something in his eyes startled her.

"No, no, you see . . ." Jewel stopped fanning herself as she stared across the table. "My God," she murmured, "I believe you're right."

"Little Buttercup had been his foster mother," Alicia said. "No one said she had actually nursed him, did they?"

"Still," Eveline said, "it's rather unsettling." Alicia giggled.

Brooks looked down at the almonds in his hand. "It's downright ghastly," he remarked with a high-pitched laugh. "So, Captain Corcoran had an Oedipus complex or Gilbert or Sullivan did."

Thomas raised his glass and looked through his champagne at Camille. He slowly pulled the glass closer to his face. Camille watched as his eye grew hideously large through the amber bubbles; she blurted a laugh and covered her mouth. Thomas smiled and lowered his glass. "Eye of Horus," he said.

"What?" Camille couldn't stop giggling, and for the first time that evening, Alicia had stopped.

"I've been reading a remarkable new book by a psychologist named Jung," Thomas answered as he looked at Brooks. "You would be interested, Abernathy. He introduces a dichotomy of thinking—directed and dreamlike."

"I've heard of him," Brooks said. "He's a Freudian, is he not?"

"He was." Thomas watched as the waiter set his soup in front of him and nodded his thanks. "But he seems to have made a dramatic break with this study. He agrees in theory with Freud's concept of male—mother lust, but disagrees the attraction is completely sexual."

"Back up," Brooks said. "What does he mean by dreamlike thought?"

"Thought that's not directed by language," Thomas said as he watched the waiter open the wines. "Basically, before language was refined, people thought in clusters of schematic images, much like we do in dreams. Mythology is essentially the dream—thought of a culture or society."

"What about an operetta?" Jewel asked.

"Probably a combination of both," Thomas answered. "But Captain Corcoran's marriage to Little Buttercup makes sense in his conception of how the male psyche works."

Jewel set her soup spoon down. "You have us all intrigued," she assured him with a lusty undertone. Alicia started giggling again. Eveline smoothed her napkin over her lap and fingered the back of her French chignon for loose ends. "How *does* the male psyche work?" Jewel pressed.

"In order to understand his concept, it's important to keep in mind the ultimate goal of the human psyche." Thomas paused.

"In philosophy we would call that a core value," Brooks said. "And it would have to be happiness—all sorts of moral philosophical systems are based on measures of happiness."

"It goes much deeper," Thomas said. "What would give us the greatest happiness of all?"

"Order," Eveline said as she looked across the table strewn with plates, cups, trays and dishes. "We need order in our lives."

Thomas placed his hand over hers. "You're on the right track, dear, but what is it we most urgently need to feel we can order and never really can?" The waiter passed salads around the table and collected the soup bowls. He lifted a wine bottle and looked for Jewel's nod before he asked each diner his preference and poured a small amount of wine in each glass. He went back to the kitchen with his tray of bowls. No one lifted a fork or glass.

"Fear," Jewel shouted. "It has to be fear. If we could just order our fears, we could live our lives in absolute freedom and fulfillment." Thomas grinned as Merriweather leaned toward Camille to take up his glass of bordeaux. She felt his breath on her arm, and the smell of his cologne overtook all other scents for an instant. It was a fresh but acrid essence, like fir kindling smoldering on a cold night.

"Immortality," Camille stated flatly as she took up her own glass of white wine. "We fear death more than anything and subconsciously strive to work out our own assurance of eternal life in some form or another." Thomas' grin widened into a surprised smile. Everyone looked at her. She blushed and set her wineglass down.

Jewel's mouth fell open. "Camille, I must introduce you to Ida Plimpton. Your wisdom is sorely needed on the front." Brooks scowled, snatched up a cheese straw, and started in on his salad.

"You're right, Camille," continued Thomas. "Immortality is the ultimate goal of the subconscious mind, and for a man, the only way one can be reinitiated into an eternal life after an eminent natural death is to re-enter the mother's womb and be reborn. This is where the concept of the libido comes into play."

"That being the unconscious creative force," added Merriweather. Alicia's giggling took on a new intensity.

Brooks looked up from his plate. "It's desire pure and simple—appetite in its natural state. The libido is impulse unchecked by any kind of authority, moral or otherwise."

"Exactly," said Thomas. "So the whole Oedipus 'sexual activity to re-impregnate the mother' Freudian ideal lies deep in the libidinal unconscious of the male psyche. But, and here's where Jung takes Freudian psychology to a new level, the conscious activity of the psyche is repulsed by such tabooed sexual behavior and, in repressing the libido in this respect, makes it work to create other more socially acceptable ways to re-enter the mother and effect rebirth. This manifests itself in a variety of ways in mythology. Immortal sons are conceived by a natural mother impregnated by the wind of spirit, shooting stars, auspicious dreams, and all sorts of means."

"Brilliant!" Jewel exclaimed. "I must read this book."

"I'll send a copy home with Dr. Kimbrough," Thomas answered.

Renfrow finished his salad and swabbed his plate with a roll. "What did I order?" he asked.

"The *kirschenwasser* omelet," Jewel reminded him with a gentle nudge.

"Good, good," he nodded.

Brooks looked at Thomas intently. "Do you really think Captain Corcoran's marriage to Little Buttercup was meant to convey a sort of tabooed male rebirth through a conjugal relationship with his foster mother?"

"Yes and no," answered Thomas. "On a purely cognitive level, probably not, but on a subconscious level, I think the dream–thinking function kicked in when the play was conceived, and Corcoran, who would otherwise be left without a real life of any sort, was given a sort of rebirth through a woman who had mothered him to an extent in the first place, without him having to cross over the taboo of possibly impregnating the same womb he had originally sprung from."

"Which is what he really wanted deep in his libido?" Camille asked, suddenly aware of the effects of mixing champagne and wine with a gin and tonic, and choosing to focus on the joys of her new sense of freedom of voice over the horrors of possible impropriety.

Thomas raised a brow. "Yes," he admitted.

"That explains a great many things," Camille said before she bit into a cocktail tomato and enjoyed the taste of the bittersweet pulp as it ran over her tongue and tingled the sides. "Underneath it all, men really just want their wives to be sexy mothers."

Brooks turned on her. "Camille!" he scolded. Merriweather's back arched. Alicia stared into space. Jewel's face lit up. Kimbrough jerked his head to the left and kept eating. Eveline set her fork on her bread plate with care, and Thomas' eyes darted back and forth.

Jewel stood up and pointed across the table. "She's right! You know she's absolutely right, so don't even try to deny it. And now, thanks to our Thomas, we have professional proof."

Camille took a cheese straw and savored the smooth, buttery cheddar essence. "How surprisingly perfect," she remarked, "a touch of cayenne."

Jewel sat down, shaking her head with a smile. "What I'd like to know, then, is why this mother–lover figure was named 'Little Buttercup' of all things. She certainly wasn't little and was much too old for us to believe she had never been deflowered." Kimbrough cast his eyes up into the ceiling vault and poured himself more wine.

"Jung says the struggle between the libido and consciousness to resolve this mother image dilemma causes an actual split in the form of the mother in the male psyche. On one hand, reintegration with the mother is the supreme goal, and on the other, the mother is the most frightful danger and takes on the dark crone characteristics. In some way, the buttercup imagery must play in, but I'm not sure what a buttercup is." He looked around the table.

"It's a small bright yellow flower," Camille explained. "In some areas it's called 'crowfoot' because its petals are shaped as such."

"There," said Jewel. "There's your crone imagery."

"It would seem so," agreed Thomas.

Camille continued, "It's poisonous if taken internally, but its extracts are used to soothe hemorrhoids."

Kimbrough raised his wineglass. "And to really big fart lovers!" he cried. They all raised their glasses and sang, "He *is* an Englishman!"

"You naughty, naughty man." Jewel smacked him on the shoulder with her closed fan, Alicia's giggles overtook the room, and Eveline laughed so hard that tears formed in the corners of her eyes.

The entrées were served and more wine poured. Brooks attacked his tenderloins with his knife, sighing loud enough for Camille alone to hear. Merriweather slathered his saddle of venison with jelly, and Camille enjoyed her halibut.

Jewel tested her dinner and raved its perfection for the

waiter to convey to the chef. She turned back to Thomas. "Now then," she continued, "I can appreciate that in the male psyche one half of the mother image split is this dark, shadowy old crone with crow's feet whom he wants to impregnate with himself, but the thought of actually having sex with her is completely poisonous to him, despite the fact she is the one who can soothe him in distress and save his ass . . ." She stole another bite of her pommes de la Duchesse while the group roared laughter over her synopsis. "But," she continued, "what is the other half of the mother image split?"

"Her polar opposite," Thomas answered coolly. "The psyche always strives for balance, so any split made by the unconscious would have its counterpart idealized in his conscious. So she would be a bright, white, young mother image without blemish whom he would love to have sex with but could not jeopardize the treasure of her virginity."

"Ah!" replied Jewel. "The Virgin Mary mother image, of course—sweet Josephine in her white gown in our operetta. So, this is where the classic double standard has its psychological root."

"Yes," nodded Thomas. "The idealized, unsullied mother of lore."

"But," Jewel angled her fork at him, "can she soothe and save him from himself?"

Thomas shook his head as he chuckled, and the conversation broke up into private chats as they finished dinner. Fresh strawberries and cream were served with coffee for dessert. Jewel and Kimbrough ordered brandies, and Kimbrough passed out the rest of the cigars he had purchased at the theater.

"I wonder," Camille said as she sat back in her chair, "if the mother image split is the way the male psyche struggles to work out its immortality, how does it work for a woman?"

Thomas looked back at her blankly. "I never even considered it," he answered.

Eveline set her coffee cup in the saucer. "According to ancient writings, the feminine psychic quest is the journey through the underworld to face a demonic dark force and come back up, but with conditions and strict time constraints. For example, Hades took Psyche into the underworld and let her back up in springtime to re-fertilize the earth, but made her return and serve as his wife during the winter months."

"So," mused Camille, "she does go back into the womb, but with a more cosmic sense of mother as nature or earth, and when she is rebirthed, she takes part in the natural regeneration process of the world."

"Yes," Jewel answered as she swirled her brandy round and round in her snifter. "She soothes and saves everyone, over and over again." She stopped for a second to savor the essence of the brandy. "However, she's still split into dark and light halves." Brooks put out his cigar and stretched himself out in his chair.

Camille sighed. "So is that really her own psychic quest, or a male conception of what the female psychic quest should be?"

Alicia yawned. "You lost me," she said.

Jewel checked Kimbrough's pocket watch with her lorgnette. She looked up at Camille. "Either way, she seeks eternity without having to draw a line down the center of maleness and demand all mortal men stay on one side or the other." She called the waiter over and asked for the check.

"I don't know," Brooks commented as he looked sideways at Camille. "I feel as if I've been made out to be somewhat of a devil this evening."

Camille took one last sip of coffee. "So being cast as the devil would be the unconscious polar opposite of what other aspect of your conscious sense of being?"

Brooks looked confused. Merriweather cast her an admiring look. Jewel had Kimbrough settle the bill, and after offering gracious thanks and many congenial hugs, Camille and Eveline had much to talk about on the way home.

16. Sunsets

April 8, 1912
Dear Tess,

Another daughter! How delightful! Now you have a trio of angels. It was so good of you to remember me with an announcement, and it leaves me feeling somewhat foolish, for I had a son last October and never thought to mail cards. Andrew is seven months old and looks like a miniature Brooks. He's strong and stubborn and crawls around the house at a speed that keeps me dizzy in pursuit. I would have gone mad by now had Brooks not hired a maid for me. She comes in every morning and tends to the housework while I play with Andrew and work in my gardens.

Easter was lovely. The bunny hid colored eggs among the honeysuckle and wisteria sweeps, and a basket for Andrew in the star jasmine. Brooks recently bought me a new electric sewing machine, so I had whipped up a lavender linen suit for myself and a navy blue outfit for Andrew. We attended Mass at St. Mary's Cathedral downtown and had our neighbors come for dinner. I served a clove-studded ham with cherry port glaze and scalloped sage potatoes. (I still have everyone guessing my secret ingredient, which gave the glaze such an exotic aroma and flavor and lent the whole meal a wonderful mysterious quality. I'll share it with you alone—a teaspoon and a half of finely ground cardamom seed.) I baked a rosemary lemon pound cake for dessert with a sprinkling of crushed lavender blossoms. It was a lot of work, but the weather was clear and not terribly hot, and we all had a splendid time.

I love entertaining. I've also been busy planning a dinner party for the professors' wives. I'm trying to decide between scallops and shrimp St. Jacques style or a roasted chicken with a blend of herbes de provence. I've planned a variegated rose centerpiece for the table and garlands for the hallways. This week I'm hemming lace for a tablecloth with a shell stitch and brewing fresh tarragon vinegar for deviled eggs. Next week I'll start baking. I shook some fresh caraway from the garden, so I'll start with a light rye bread and serve a lemon tart or raspberry soufflé for dessert—maybe both.

Brooks and I have developed a penchant for the opera. This month we saw Gilbert and Sullivan's H.M.S. Pinafore, *which had a certain mundane level of classical charm. We always dine afterwards at the Driskill Hotel Grand Dining Saloon, where we meet with other professors, authors, actors, and a few politicians to discuss the aesthetic merits of the performance and intricacies of the plot until the early morning hours. It's so thoughtful of Brooks. He's always looking for new ways to balance the rigors of my domestic life with these social and cultural outings.*

Marriage is such a blessing. As hard as Brooks works, he goes out of his way to spend as much time as possible with Andrew and me. Over dinner every evening we share a laugh about the antics of one or another of his students and discuss theories for his book chapters. We play with Andrew until he gets fussy, and after Brooks reads Jack and the Beanstalk *or* Rumpelstiltskin *to him, I tuck him into his crib, and Brooks and I steal an hour or two on the back porch sipping French wine and watching the sun melt itself into the far hills. In the spring it lays itself across the horizon in pearly pink-gold tones that sink into a violet so deep—it makes you ache from the inside out.*

Fondest Regards to you, Carl, and all
three of your beautiful girls,
Camille Abernathy

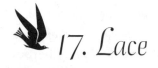# 17. Lace

Coral arranged to stay late the day of the dinner party. She had the house sparkling clean by noon and spent the afternoon keeping Andrew content and helping Camille hang her herbal garlands and watch the oven. As the sun started its slant behind the trellis, Eveline came through the back porch door with a bottle of port in each hand, exclaiming over the wondrous symphony of smells emanating from the kitchen and echoing through the rooms. She bent over to give Andrew a kiss on his forehead as he hammered pegs into a board in his play crib. Camille was too busy to accept the accolades. "Eveline, how good of you to bring the wine. I knew you would choose the right one."

"I love port," Eveline replied. "It has such a full, fruity bouquet, it will go well with your scrumptious looking lemon dessert." She stopped to inhale the essence of the tart Camille took from the oven. "It would be prudent to bring it out late in the evening as it has a higher alcohol content than other wines."

"Perfect," said Camille as she placed the tart in a warming oven. "We can serve it with the coffee. I'm going to assemble the soufflé next, but I'll bake the croutons first. Let's see," her eyes darted around the kitchen.

"Can't you adjust the oven temperature to bake them at the same time?" Eveline asked as she set the port on the counter and tied on an apron.

"Oh, no," Camille cried as she carefully cracked an egg and poured the yolk back and forth between the shell halves, allowing the whites to fall in viscous drops into a glass bowl. "The croutons will be ready to take out in twenty minutes, and if I open the oven, the soufflé will fall." Coral adjusted the oven temperature and stood by with the pan of freshly cut crouton dough nests for Camille's scallops and shrimp.

"I see," Eveline sighed as she took the empty eggshells from Camille. "Calm down, now, you have plenty of help, and with your command of the traditional women's arts, this dinner party will be the talk of the town for months. What will you have me do next? Is the table set?"

"No," Camille gasped. "I started to set it and got as far as ironing the cloths before the timer went off and I got waylaid snipping dill and deviling eggs." She wiped her hands.

"I'll get them," Eveline said as she started up the stairs to get the cloths off a rack in the herb drying room. Camille nodded as she wiped her brow with her apron and swabbed her wire whisk with the dishcloth before she went to work on the egg whites.

Eveline returned with two cloths. "Which one?" she asked.

"Both," Camille answered as she tried to blow a wisp of hair out of her eye while furiously beating the whites into frothy peaks. "The mint green one first, with the ivory Venetian lace on top."

"What a marvelous idea," Eveline said as she started for the dining room, calling over her shoulder, "Isn't this the lace you bought downtown last month? I love your scalloped edging."

"Yes," Camille sighed as she placed the bowl on the table and shook her arm. "I finished it yesterday."

Eveline called from the dining room as she opened the silver chest. "How many places shall I set?"

"Eight," Camille cried, "seven—no eight. I don't know. I haven't heard from Morgan, so I don't know if she'll be coming or not."

Andrew started throwing pegs out of the crib.

"He's getting bored," Coral said as she placed the pan of croutons in the oven, set the timer, waited as Camille lifted Andrew, and took him into the parlor to let him crawl around on the floor for some exercise.

Camille took her saucepan of raspberry syrup from the stove and poured it into the egg whites in a thin stream while folding it in with a spatula. She took a deep breath before pouring it slowly into a prepared soufflé dish. "Good," she said as she went into the dining room.

Eveline had straightened the cloths over the table, placed china for eight settings, and had busied herself arranging the silverware. "Will we need soup plates and spoons?" she asked.

"Yes," Camille answered. "I made a simple broth with a little roasted chicken, carrots, celery, and a special blend of French herbs."

"Sounds delightful." Eveline turned for the spoons while Camille took out the crystal water and wine glasses and placed them carefully. "She probably never even saw the invitation," Eveline said.

"Who?" asked Camille as she went into the kitchen and returned with a crystal bowl with huge burgundy providence roses, delicate pink Madame George Staechelins, and ivory tree roses with blushing edges floating in full bloom amid their dark green jagged leaves.

"Morgan," said Eveline as she stopped to admire the rose arrangement Camille gently placed in the center of the table and moved slightly several times. "I'll bet her spitty, snotty old professor screens all her mail and never lets her go anywhere he can't lead her and stand over her like a vulture. I made a place for her all the same. We'll look more gracious taking away a setting than we will having to add one at the last minute." She stooped to smell the roses. "Heavenly," she said. "They fill the whole room."

"My providence potpourri helps," Camille said as she pointed out the bowls placed strategically on side tables throughout the drawing room and in the salon where Coral romped with Andrew. Camille smiled and took the crystal candleholders from the hutch and set them on the table on either side of the roses. She placed in each an elegant, long ivory taper, which matched the roses in the lacework as well as those in the centerpiece perfectly.

"Exquisite!" Eveline whispered. They stood back to check everything for proper spacing. "Should we make place cards?" Eveline asked.

"Oh, yes," Camille nodded as she turned. "I did." She took them from the buffet drawer as the timer chimed from the kitchen. Eveline took the cards and began setting them strategically in the soup plates as Camille rushed in and took the croutons out of the oven and put the soufflé in. She set the timer again as the telephone rang.

Eveline set out two or three of the cards and shook her head. She picked them up and walked around the table three times before Camille returned.

"That was Brooks," Camille told her. "He said to tell you he and Thomas are going into town after their faculty meeting to get a steak and play some billiards. They promised not to be home in time to interrupt our dinner."

Eveline looked up from her cards, her eyes reflecting a strange shade of cobalt. "How thoughtful," she remarked as she started another revolution around the table. "You should sit at the head near the kitchen, as you will be getting up and down to serve," she said. "At first I planned to put myself next to you to help, but maybe I should sit at the other side of the table next to Alicia so we can keep conversation flowing from either end."

Camille stopped to picture the placement of personalities. "You don't really want to sit next to that goose, do you? Put Faye next to her, they're friendly, aren't they? And for God's sake, we'll have Jewel to keep the conversation alive."

Coral carried Andrew through the dining room. "Miss Camille, what shall I give him for dinner?"

Camille followed them into the kitchen and heated the chicken and carrots she had ground earlier. She checked her breads and her tart in the warming ovens and rejoined Eveline in the dining room. "I'll make the St. Jacques sauce after I dress; otherwise, I think I have everything ready."

Eveline had placed herself to the left of Camille and Jewel to the right. "Shall I put Morgan next to Jewel?"

"Let's put her at the other end. If she doesn't show, it won't leave such a noticeable gap."

"Of course," Eveline agreed as she laid out the cards and walked around the table examining the settings and making minor adjustments where necessary. "Should we light the candles?"

"It's a little early," said Camille as she stood back and admired the effect. She smiled as she looked up at her friend, noticing the perfect sweep of her soft dark golden curls and the graceful drape of her white eyelet waist and hobble skirt with a cornflower-blue under-frock. "Eveline, you look stunning—I'm sorry I didn't say so before. Is your skirt cut on the bias?"

"Thank you, dear," Eveline answered as she untied her apron, turned around, and looked down. "I don't know how it's cut, but Thomas said it made me look elegant, so I bought it."

"Thomas is right, as usual," Camille sighed. "I should get myself dressed. Will you help me with my hair?"

"Of course," Eveline agreed. Camille reminded Coral to watch the soufflé as she went upstairs and sat at the dressing table while Eveline combed her hair up into a chignon and anchored it with a mother of pearl comb wired with fresh rosebuds and lavender. At the sound of the timer, they both ran downstairs to find Coral pulling a perfectly round, pink soufflé out of the oven. Eveline helped Camille steam the shrimp and scallops and make the St. Jacques sauce. She stirred the broth as the flour thickened, while Camille heated water to carry upstairs for a quick wash up. She doused herself with talcum powder and sprinkled her neck and wrists with rose water. She dressed in the lavender linen frock she had bought for the occasion and pulled on the ivory baby doll shoes she had worn to Mass at Easter. She looked herself over in the mirror with satisfaction and, glancing at the clock on the bed stand, hurried downstairs to attend to last-minute details.

Coral finished cleaning Andrew's dinner dishes and lifted him out of his chair for Camille's goodnight kiss. She carried him upstairs to rock him to sleep. Eveline stood at the table cutting butter squares. "You look radiant," she said.

The doorbell rang. "Is it seven thirty already?" Camille asked as she surveyed the contents of the kitchen table.

"Not quite," Eveline answered with a gentle smile, "but it's show time anyway."

Camille walked toward the front door, grimacing at the hollow pounding noises her shoes made on the hardwood floors. She wondered why she hadn't noticed it at Easter. Eveline rinsed her hands and followed.

"Joy! Joy! Good clean fun with a dash of larceny! I love a gathering of wily women more than just about anything.

Camille, your home is simply stunning!" Jewel bustled through the door in a plum shantung dress with a Chantilly overlay cinched under her bust with a spill of silver frills. Her hair was tucked up under a pert plum-colored hat with two willow plumes and one pheasant feather. She hurried in the door hunched over a large carpetbag. "Forgive me for showing up early, but I dropped poor dear Renfrow off at his stuffy old fellow's meeting and had intended to putter up and down the speedway a few times to while away the extra quarter of an hour, before it occurred to me how imprudent it was to race around with this." She hoisted her bag up on the hall table and took out two bottles of wine. "Madeira." She nodded to Camille. "It's Portugese—the new aristocratic dinner rage."

"What a lovely gesture," Camille smiled against the wide-eyed glare Eveline shot over Jewel's shoulder.

"You *drive*?" Eveline exclaimed.

"Of course I drive, don't you?" Jewel demanded as her eyes scanned the contents of the parlor and the drawing room.

"No, I . . ." Eveline looked at Camille. "I thought it was unladylike."

"Oh, pish! Not unless it's considered ladylike to be helpless. I haven't time to wait around the house for Renfrow to decide to take me into town or on my rounds. I taught myself to drive the day I decided to join the Austin Women's Suffragist Association. It's easy. I'll teach you, too."

Camille smiled. "Is Madeira served at room temperature?" she asked.

"Usually, but I like to put it on ice for just a few minutes before I open it. Renfrow laughs at me, but I think a bit of a chill accentuates the thrill." She laughed with her hostess. "And for some reason, it isn't as apt to give me indigestion."

"I'll ice it now," said Camille.

"Oh, that's not all," Jewel continued. "I brought a few of my favorite recordings—Falkenstein and Caruso for dinner—you have heard Caruso, haven't you?" she moaned. "His tenor is so rich, it makes an old heart melt. I brought his performance in Giuseppe Verdi's *Rigoletto*; his libretto is chocolate, I tell you, pure bittersweet chocolate." Jewel took the recordings out of her bag and set them on the entry table. "And here," she thumped a record jacket cover, "here is a collection of the best of Joplin's ragtime tunes for the sake of sheer merriment. You do have a Victrola?"

"Yes," Camille stammered. "I hadn't even thought to bring it down."

"God of my mother's ghost!" Jewel exclaimed as she took another look around. "This home is a vision of grace and enchantment. This mirror!" She turned her gaze on the rococo-style mirror over the table. "And the flowers, did you arrange them?"

Camille beamed as Eveline answered, "That's one of her herbal garlands. You'll find them tucked about here and there throughout the house." She pointed out the lavender, rosemary, and stephanotis buds as Jewel sighed. "You should see her herb room upstairs," Eveline added.

"I would love to." Jewel opened her bag again. "But first, let's break out my favorite hostess gift." She pulled a final bottle halfway out as she whispered, "It's just for us early girls— a sort of pre-party ticklish favor—a six-year-old French *Jaunay*, already chilled to perfection." She paused to savor their reactions. "It's the champagne Napoleon drank to celebrate his conquests. Come, let's open it now."

They hurried into the kitchen, and as Camille rearranged the contents of the icebox in order to wedge in the Madeira, Eveline produced a clean dishtowel for Jewel, who treated them to a dramatic display of the art and excitement of opening a bottle of French champagne. Camille took wine glasses from the table, and they sipped the sparkling smooth essence as Camille checked the contents of her ovens again. Jewel looked over her shoulder and inhaled deeply. "Dinner smells simply marvelous!"

Eveline giggled, "I can't believe we're drinking French champagne before dinner." She took a surreptitious sip. "Oh, Jewel, could you really teach me to drive?"

"Of course!" she sang as she led them back into the entry. "Now, where is that Victrola?"

"It's upstairs in my herb drying room," Camille answered. "I like to listen to Chopin as I work."

"Ah, Chopin," Jewel repeated. "I knew you were a woman of refined taste. Let's bring that recording down, too. Look at that magnificent staircase." She took her lorgnette from her sash. "One could easily imagine angels ascending and descending a stairway such as that."

Coral rounded the top banister and plumped down the stairs. Jewel took such a start that she spilled a drop or two of her champagne. "Baby's asleep," Coral announced. "Samuel will be along in a few minutes. If you want me to stay and serve, we can ring him before he leaves the bar."

"Thank you, Coral," answered Camille, "but you've been here all day and I'm sure I can get it from here."

As long as Jewel's lorgnette was out, she gave Coral a good looking over while Camille did introductions. "Will you have some champagne?" Jewel offered with a grin.

"Thank you, ma'am," Coral answered with wide eyes, "but I shouldn't be drinking."

"I'll go up and get the Victrola," Eveline said as she went up the stair.

"I'll help." Coral started up behind her.

"No," Camille intervened, "not in your condition. I'll go."

Coral eased a wary look at Jewel. "Miss Camille, shall I fix up the bread baskets before I go?"

"Yes," Camille answered, as she hesitated. "I forgot about the bread linens and baskets."

"You attend to things in the kitchen," Jewel patted Camille's shoulder, "and I'll help Eveline with the Victrola. I'll steal a peek at your herb room while I'm at it, and we'll all be well employed." She set her champagne glass on the hall table next to a crystal dish of providence potpourri and, stealing a nod at herself in the mirror, deftly took a foot-long diamond-studded pin from her hat, cocked the hat an inch forward, and reskewered it on either side of her wound-up graying hair, securing the pin with a deft twist of her wrist. She took the stairs with determination, while Camille followed Coral into the kitchen, sipping her champagne and worrying about whether the bread linens were completely dry on the line out back. Coral took the china baskets from the hutch as Camille slipped out the back and pulled fresh, dry linens down. She passed back through the kitchen door to find Coral slicing the steaming dill braid and the rye loaf. Camille folded a sharp pleat down the center of each napkin, tucked the ends under, and snapped them smart into a bread envelope. Coral placed the bread in the baskets. Camille rewarded herself with another sip of champagne and stopped short. "The French beans!" She whirled around. "I'm afraid I'm losing my mind. I can't believe I forgot the vegetable." She rushed to the cupboard and pulled out a saucepan. "For heaven's sake, Coral, don't tell anyone. They'll have me committed to the lunatic asylum."

Coral set the nestled breads on the sideboard and turned to the icebox. "I got it, Miss. Don't you worry. You attend to your guests, and I'll have them snipped and simmering in your tarragon vinegar with a pinch of brown sugar before they get down here with your music box."

Camille nodded and drew an inch of water into the small saucepan. Coral took it and waved her off as she rinsed the green beans and heated the burner. "I suppose everything's all right," Camille said as she took a final peek in the warming ovens. She heard thumping overhead. "I hope they don't wake Andrew."

"He's out sound," Coral said as she flavored the water and trimmed the beans. "Stop worrying," she scolded. "This is your night."

Camille stood in the middle of the kitchen for a moment before she pulled her shoulders back and gave Coral a hug. Coral shrugged with a grin and bent to rummage through the cupboard for a strainer. They both froze as a tremendous dull thud resounded from the top of the stair. They looked at one another in the ensuing silence and bolted for the entry hall as a soft giggle grew into a chorus of wheezing laughter. Eveline stood near the top of the staircase straining to hold the horn of the Victrola up against the weight of Jewel, who had lost her footing and fallen into the wall on the parlor side of the stair under the weight of the machine. Jewel's shoulders were shaking so hard, she couldn't steady herself, but stood folded over, balancing herself with her right elbow and hip. Camille stifled a giggle and resisted a look at Coral as they both rushed up the stairs. Coral steadied the Victrola as Camille helped Jewel guide her foot back into her silver shoe and gently led the party safely to the foot of the stair and into the parlor. She cleared off the side table. Once the Victrola was down, Coral rushed back into the kitchen, and Jewel and Eveline recounted the story of the fall between giggles. Jewel raved about the aromas and visions in the herb room. "I also convinced Eveline to let me into the nursery for a peek at your little angel." Jewel retrieved her champagne and records.

"I told you he was precious," Eveline said as she darted into the kitchen.

"He's a little Brooks." Jewel opened the jacket of the Joplin record and placed it on the turntable. "A little professor, indeed, with those ruddy cheeks and that wonderful hair." Eveline returned with a cloth, dusted the Victrola, and gave the table a couple of strokes. Jewel vigorously cranked the arm until the machine was fully wound and, once the record was spinning evenly, set the needle on the outer edge of the record. After the initial scratches, "The Maple Leaf Rag" animated the parlor, and none of them could keep their feet still.

"Isn't it just magical?" Jewel howled over the tinkling of the piano keys. Eveline's shoulders swayed with the beat, and Camille danced into the kitchen to check on the beans. "Bring the champagne on your way back," Jewel called after her. When Camille returned, Jewel was demonstrating the latest dance craze out of New York, the *Maxixe*. Camille and Eveline stood behind her and tried to match her step for swirl, with little success.

"Your feet move so fast, I can't see them, much less follow," Eveline laughed.

Jewel's feet didn't miss a step as she poured around more champagne and took Eveline's hands. "It's easy, look." She led Eveline one step at a time, until she and Eveline were dancing circles around the parlor. Eveline fell on the arm of the divan to catch her breath while the tempo changed into the "Stoptime Rag."

"When Renfrow and I were in New York last year," Jewel explained as she two-stepped, "we attended a performance of Irene and Vernon Castle. They did the Castle Rag, which went like this." She stepped back and to the side with sprightly hip sachets while Camille followed. "And, oh yes," Jewel panted, "the animal dances were all the rage. Let's see." She looked down at her feet. "They did the Turkey Trot." she thrust her knees forward and took a few steps with sharp neck thrusts. Eveline clapped her hands together, and Camille laughed so hard she had to set her glass down. "And, of course, the Bunny Hug." Jewel threw her arms wide and took side hops while jerking her chin to the left and then the right. Eveline stomped her feet. "The Chicken Scratch." Jewel did her chicken moves. "And the Grizzly Bear—come Camille, you can do this one."

"Oh, no," Camille laughed. "That doesn't sound safe."

Coral rushed in from the kitchen, wiping her hands on a dishtowel. "Didn't you hear the door?" she cried.

"Oh!" Jewel exclaimed as she turned the volume down on the Victrola. "Another guest." Eveline stood, fluffed out her waist, and smoothed down her skirt. Camille swung the door open to find Samuel filling the frame, his broad-rimmed hat in his hand.

"Sorry I was knocking so hard," he said. "I've been sitting out here for quite a while." Coral stood on her tiptoes to kiss his cheek. "I'm sorry, baby, I was busy helping Miss Camille with her dinner."

Camille's cheeks flushed. "Samuel, we had the music too loud. Please, come in."

Samuel glanced back at the street. "Just for minute. I've got the horses tied up."

"I'll be ready in a second," Coral said as she rushed back into the kitchen.

"Champagne?" Jewel asked Samuel as she raised the bottle.

"No, oh no," Samuel grinned. "It looks like you ladies are having fun, but I just got through pouring drinks at the bar, and I'm ready to go home and drink a big glass of milk. I like your music, though. I've always been a Joplin fan."

"Then surely you know how to do the Maxixe." Jewel held out her arms.

"Yes, ma'am, I do," Samuel said as he grinned and took her hands lightly in his. He matched her step for step once around the parlor.

"You're a master," raved Jewel. "Why, if you could teach Renfrow to dance like that, I'd be the happiest woman in Central Texas."

"You gotta feel it here," Samuel pounded his chest.

Coral came in from the kitchen with a tray of cheese wafers and assorted canapés. She set it on the coffee table. "The French beans are warming on the stove, the breads are on the sideboard, and the candles in the dining room are lit." She watched her husband as he put his hat on. "Were you dancing?" she asked with a grin.

"Hey, did you show them that dance we learned at the bar in Louisville?" He turned to Jewel. "The Negroes from Virginia were teaching all of us this new dance, and no one could do it like Corrie, here. Show them a step or two."

"Please!" Jewel urged. "I love to learn new dances."

Coral gave Samuel a playful glower and slipped her leather shoes off.

"Now, be careful," Camille warned.

"I'll be fine," Coral assured her as her arms flew in both directions. She stepped back with her left foot, then in front with her right. Her whole body swayed with so much rhythm, Jewel turned the volume back up on the "Rose Leaf Rag," kicked off her shoes, and tried to imitate the steps.

When the song ended, Coral put her shoes back on while Jewel pleaded for more. "I gotta get my boy home," Coral said.

"I never can remember the name of that dance." Samuel shook his head.

"The Charleston." Coral took him by the hand. "Let's get."

Camille thanked her and waved as the couple went down the walk and Samuel helped her up into the wagon. Jewel turned up the volume on "The Entertainer" as a car pulled up to the front of the house. A willowy figure flowed out of the passenger door, and the car sped off almost as soon as her feet touched the ground. The sun had fallen behind the back of the house, leaving the world in shadow except for the glowing pink treetops swaying to the rhythm of the rag. Camille couldn't decide if the nearing silhouette looked more like a ghost or a moving statue of the Virgin from St. Mary's Cathedral.

Eveline came up behind her. "Who is it?" she asked.

"I think it's Morgan," Camille whispered. They waited as she came up to the door with slow, measured steps. Camille held out her hands. "I'm so glad you could come." As Morgan took her hand, a surge of strength seemed to pass through Camille's palm and into the woman draped in silver scarving from head to toe. "You look elegant."

"Thank you for inviting me," Morgan said. "Durwood says it's customary to take a bottle of wine to a dinner party, but I thought you might like this." She handed Camille a delicate linen handkerchief with crocheted lace edging, folded up and tied with a pink satin ribbon in the shape of a delicate rose. "It's from France," she added.

"It's lovely," Camille sighed as Jewel Charlestoned over to greet Morgan and urged her to try the new steps.

"I don't dance," Morgan forced a winsome smile. "Ragtime—how gay. Just like they play in Guy . . ." she hesitated.

"In Guy Town?" Jewel spun around in time to see Morgan drop into a chair and put a hand to her forehead. Jewel stopped dancing and slipped her shoes back on. "Let's listen to Chopin," she said as she changed the record and rewound the Victrola. She asked for another glass and poured out the last of the champagne for Morgan.

Alicia and Faye arrived together, both with silk frocks, kid gloves, lots of heavy jewelry, and each with a bottle of white wine. The women broke into small groups to chatter while Camille went into the kitchen to heat the soup and put the breadbaskets on the table. Maribel arrived in a stunning taupe frock with a dramatic orange tabard and metallic lace trim, and seconds later Edna made her entrance in an ecru needle-run lace tea dress. Jewel opened the burgundy and made sure everyone had a glass while they picked at the *hors d'œuvres*. Faye and Alicia discussed their husbands' latest works and achievements while Jewel batted her eyes and fanned her flushed face. "Isn't that a prelude?" Faye asked as she pointed a slender satin finger toward the Victrola, her pearl and diamond bracelets jangling against one another.

"It's Chopin's fifteenth," Camille answered. "The Raindrop Prelude."

"Of course," Faye chanted. "I love the sound of the piano. I must learn to play. I told Adolph we simply must purchase a piano. Everyone in Hyde Park has one, you know." She removed a glove, picked up an olive toast, examined it closely, and set it down on the edge of the tray.

"I want my children to learn," Alicia said as she watched Eveline brush a loose hair off the divan.

"You don't have any children!" Faye's laugh reminded Camille of the sound of breaking glass.

"Well, I will," Alicia blurted before she started in with her giggling. "Oscar says he wants at least four boys."

"And you think your boys will all want to sit around and play classical music on the piano while the other boys are out breaking windows with their baseballs?" Faye carefully worked her other glove from under her bracelets before she peeled it from her hand and placed the pair in her beaded bag. Alicia's back arched as she pierced a square of Edam with a toothpick. Sitting next to Faye in the lamplight, Camille noticed for the first time how coarse her features were.

Jewel plopped herself down in an armchair. "They might play some Chopin, or Mozart, or perhaps even some ragtime like Joplin."

Faye tilted her head back and trilled like ice clinking across a hardwood floor. "Of course, Alicia's boys would keep the family dancing the rag. I can see you with at least a couple of little Joplins, and maybe even a couple of Jolsons."

Alicia's lower lip trembled as she giggled. Camille told Edna how much she had enjoyed her daughter's violin solo at Thomas' cocktail party. Jewel and Eveline agreed, and while Edna recounted the expenses, trials, and triumphs of Lorna's musical training, Camille led everyone into the dining room. As they stood at their places, Eveline filled the water glasses and Camille poured the soup into the tureen. Maribel asked if she might lead them in prayer before dinner was served and extended a hand to Eveline on her right and Edna on her left. The rest joined hands and waited while Maribel closed her eyes and gathered her spiritual thoughts. She waited until Faye's bracelets stopped jingling and began, "Dear Father in Heaven, we thank Thee for this fellowship, this food, and for our loving husbands, without whom we would not enjoy such bounty; in fact, if it were not for them, we would never have come together at this table at all." She stopped and breathed hard through her nostrils while Camille wondered if they were supposed to keep holding hands. Jewel burped and excused herself under her breath. After Alicia's giggling stopped, Maribel went on, "We thank Thee for your grace and guidance. Please help us enjoy this repast in the spirit of love and friendship, and help us live our lives humbly and with modest dignity. In Jesus' name we pray." Eveline and Jewel squeezed Camille's hand as they said, "Amen."

"That was lovely," Camille commented. She ladled soup from the tureen as Eveline started the bread around.

"I need more wine," Jewel howled. As Camille turned to open another bottle, Jewel placed a hand on her forearm. "Sit down, my dear, I'll get it." Camille nodded and took her seat.

"Do you attend Mass at the Cathedral?" Edna asked Maribel.

"No, we are members at First Methodist." Maribel beamed as she buttered a triangle of dill bread. "Charles' family has always been Methodist."

Jewel came from the kitchen with both bottles of Madeira and filled empty glasses before she set them down on either side of the tapers. "And what was your family?" she asked with a side glance at Maribel as she sat down to her soup.

"My mother was Catholic," Maribel mused as she sipped from the edge of her spoon. "But my father didn't believe in God and wouldn't let her go to church." Her lips pursed.

"Marvelous soup, Camille." Edna offered a thin smile.

"What a wondrous blend of spices!" Jewel mused as she set down her spoon and glared at Maribel. "So your mother gave up her faith because your father had none?"

"Not completely." Maribel wiped the corner of her mouth with her napkin. "She used to keep her beads in her apron pocket. And when he was at work or in another room, she would put her hand in her pocket and pray like crazy." Faye sniggered and Alicia giggled. "She must have said a thousand Hail Marys a day," Maribel laughed. "Of course, in our church, we focus on the Our Fathers."

The women broke into different conversations concerning their churches and religious upbringing, while Camille watched Morgan rewrap her scarf around her head so it wouldn't slip over a shoulder as she spooned her soup. Morgan looked up in time to see Camille watching her and looked away, her cheeks flushed scarlet. Chopin's étude played softly from the parlor. Alicia turned to Jewel. "Aren't you Episcopalian?" she asked. "And how does one pray in your church?"

"I don't know what they're mumbling in the churches." Jewel reached for a slice of rye. "The last time I went, I counted as the minister invoked the higher powers in two hundred and eighteen different male nouns and pronouns, without ever considering the fact that a divine spirit could take on female attributes just as readily." She watched Maribel's face fall and poured her more Madeira. "It's been at least three years," she added. Alicia reached for the bottle as Jewel set it down. They all listened to the sound of the wine trickling into the glass until the soothing passages of the first movement of the étude jerked into a series of dissonant chords. Alicia raised the glass to her mouth and set it down without taking a sip.

Faye set her butter knife carefully on the edge of the bread plate. "Surely you don't think God could be a woman?"

Maribel let her spoon drop in her soup, and Edna reached

over and patted her arm. Eveline brushed a couple of bread-crumbs off the lace cloth and folded her hands. "Morgan," Jewel blurted, "wouldn't you be more comfortable without that wrap?"

Morgan pulled her wrap around her neck and sat back in her chair. "Sometimes," she said, her voice so low they all leaned in, "sometimes at night when Durwood is snoring—you know in that eerie time before you're really asleep, but you're not awake either . . ." Faye's bracelets jangled as a lily-white hand rose to support her chin. Morgan's lashes swept her cheeks as she continued, "Sometimes I think I hear God calling my name in a voice that is certainly more female than male."

"What does it sound like?" Edna whispered.

Morgan's flush deepened. "Oh, I don't know."

The étude shifted back into the romantic mellifluous *andante* of the first movement. Camille remembered why she had asked Brooks for the recording for her birthday two long years before. "Wisdom is a woman," she said as she deftly wiped a tear from her eye and stood to serve the next course. Eveline rose to help.

"What do you mean?" Maribel turned as Camille took her bowl.

"In the Bible," Camille explained. "All through the Book of Wisdom. Wisdom is a characteristic of God and is described in unmistakably feminine terms." She floated into the kitchen with Eveline right behind her. The voices in the dining room steadily rose into a fervent buzz.

"Brilliant!" Eveline smirked as they took the damp towels from the salad trays and returned to the dining room.

"Boston butter lettuce with mandarin orange and raspberry currant dressing," Eveline announced. "It's Camille's signature salad."

After everyone was served, Camille and Eveline took their seats. The chattering stopped as Maribel picked up her salad fork and looked hard at Camille. "We were just discussing," her voiced thinned and stopped. She looked down at her salad and speared an orange.

Jewel refilled Camille's glass with Madeira. "The salad is ungodly good," she sang, "and while you were in the kitchen, we were debating about the Book of Wisdom. You see, Maribel here says there's no Book of Wisdom in the Bible."

"I'm sorry, Camille," Maribel threw her shoulders back, "But, I've read both Testaments through and I've never seen a book called 'Wisdom.'"

"It's the Wisdom of Solomon," Camille countered, "right after the Song of Solomon."

"No dear," Maribel forced a smile. "The Book of Isaiah is right after the Song of Solomon."

Camille set her napkin by her plate and went into the parlor to take her mother's Bible from the bookcase. She thumbed through it until she found her place, sat down, and read,

> For in her is a spirit,
> intelligent, holy, unique,
> Manifold, subtle, agile,
> clear, unstained, certain,
> Not baneful, loving the good, keen,
> unhampered, beneficent, kindly,
> Firm, secure, tranquil,
> all-powerful, all-seeing,
> And pervading all spirits,
> though they be intelligent, pure, and very
> subtle.

For Wisdom is mobile beyond all motion,
and she penetrates and pervades all things
by reason of her purity.
For she is an aura of the might of God
and a pure effusion of the glory of the
Almighty.

"Wisdom, chapter seven, verses twenty-two through twenty-five," Camille said as she watched Maribel's eyebrows fold in over the bridge of her nose.

"I can't believe it. May I see?" Maribel held out a hand, and Camille passed over the open book. Maribel looked at the verse and started flipping the pages forward and backward. "I don't understand," she mumbled.

"It's marvelous!" Jewel cried. "Maribel, read it again!" Maribel's face darkened as she shot Jewel a reproving glance over the turning leaves of the book. Edna leaned in to help her figure out the mystery.

"Camille," Jewel cried, "you simply must join the cause. I dare say Wisdom is a woman, and her name could well be Camille Abernathy. Your quiet strength, your shrewd analysis is sorely needed on the front. You'd be a stunning suffragette. I can't wait to introduce you to Ida and the girls."

Maribel's hands trembled as she perused the table of contents. "This is impossible. I tell you there is no book called the Wisdom of Solomon in the Bible!"

Eveline leaned in. "But, you see it there, Maribel dear. You must have just missed it before."

"Please, girls," Jewel wailed and took out her lorgnette. "Eveline, you read again, I must hear it again."

"No," Maribel bleated, "I know the Bible like my own children, I . . ."

Morgan raised her glass slowly and spoke into her wine, "Is it a Catholic Bible?" The question floated mid-table and dropped into the rose bowl. Camille put a hand to her ear and shook her head.

"She wants to know if it's a Catholic Bible," Alicia yelled over the commotion as Faye set her salad fork on her plate, leaned back in her chair, and winced.

"Oh, I suppose so," Camille said. "It was my mother's Bible. We usually just went to church on Christmas and at Easter, but we would always go to the Catholic Church."

Morgan mouthed a response, but stopped when she realized she couldn't be heard. Jewel held up her hands. "Hush now, Morgan can solve your debate, and then we can read it again. I want to enlighten the girls with this before our rounds on Tuesday evening."

The women stopped arguing and turned to Morgan, who shrank back into her veiling. "The Catholic Bible has more books than the Protestant Bibles. Durwood said some of the early reformers thought some of the books, like the Wisdom Book, were not inspired, so they took them out."

"Inspired by whom?" Faye asked with a sneer.

"Why, the Holy Ghost, of course," Maribel countered as she snapped the tome shut.

"Hand it back over to Camille," Jewel ordered. "I like the way she reads it."

Maribel passed the book back to Camille and tossed a side glance at Edna. Camille read the passage again while Jewel looked up into the chandelier and drummed her cheek with her fingertips. "Subtle," she stated as Camille stood and set the Bible on the China cabinet. "Wisdom is indeed a womanly manifestation of God with all those marvelous attributes—love, power. Oh my, it's just incredibly true to life, but the passage refers to Wisdom as being subtle two times."

Her eyes swung down and over to Camille. "Why do you think that is?"

"I never thought about it," Camille stammered.

The étude ended and Jewel jumped up. "Now is the time for Caruso," she declared, nodding on the sorority as if bestowing a benediction before she rustled into the parlor to change the record.

Alicia poured around the last of the Madeira as Camille and Eveline gathered the salad plates and took them into the kitchen. Eveline scraped plates while Camille spooned the scallops and shrimp St. Jacques over the croutons. "I didn't know you had such a deep appreciation of sacred scripture," Eveline commented with a wink.

"I didn't either," Camille quipped. "I guess more of it stuck than I realized." Caruso's rich tenor filled the parlor.

"Camille darling," Faye called from the dining room, "will you open the white?"

Eveline raised her nose and silently mimicked the plea while she pulled the bottle from a bowl of ice and took up a paring knife. "Jewel's working hard to enlist you in the suffragist movement," she whispered. "Will you do it?" She scored the foil wrap on the white burgundy.

Camille turned off the hot water and patted a stray hair back into her chignon with her moist hands. "Brooks would lose his mind," she grinned.

"Would you do it?" Eveline repeated as she pulled the cork out of the bottle with a neat "plop."

Camille set a sprig of thyme across each entrée. "I don't know . . . maybe." She looked up at Eveline with a wry smile. "Only if you will, too." She lifted the tray.

"It wouldn't be as fun for me," Eveline said as she took a sip out of the wine bottle. "Thomas would understand."

Camille set the tray on the edge of the table just in time

before she doubled over. "I can't believe you did that!" She laughed until Jewel came into the kitchen.

"Girls, what havoc have you wrought in here?" She looked around.

Eveline raised the bottle and smiled, while Camille regained her composure. "We were sharing a trifle or two about our dear professors," she said. "And you were right about Caruso, his voice is pure chocolate. Do you think he'll hold out until dessert?"

Jewel laughed heartily, opened her eyes so wide her lids twitched, and whisked out her ivory fan. "If not, we will wind him back up."

The entrées were served and savored while Jewel interpreted Italian phrases from Caruso's aria. "He's the Duke, you know. Listen! He's telling his retainer how he plans to finish his conquest of a young girl he's admired at church every Sunday for the last three months."

"Oh, he goes to church every Sunday!" Alicia giggled.

"To ogle young women!" Edna clucked her tongue.

"There," Jewel moved her fork in tight circles in the air, "that note he holds forever—ah! He says he's found out where she lives and watches her house every night."

"A peeping Tom, this Duke," Eveline laughed as she sipped her burgundy. "Doesn't he have a duchess or anything better to do in his palace?" Camille jumped up. "Did I say something?" Eveline asked with a start.

"What? No," Camille said as she went into the kitchen. "I just remembered the deviled eggs." She came back with a chilled plate and passed them around. Caruso's tenor evened out into a low moan before it swelled into mellow exclamation.

"He's admiring the women attending his ball." A candle flickered with the force of Jewel's whisper.

"How fickle," Faye pushed her plate back. "He's a pig."

"He's a man," Edna added, flaking the side of her crouton with her fork.

Jewel gazed over the table as her shoulders slowly swayed. "He especially admires the elegant beauty of the wife of Count Ceprano." Morgan's eyes flared gold as she stared into the dancing flame.

Alicia's voice cracked, "Wasn't Cinderella invited to the ball?"

Jewel interrupted her reverie to cast Alicia a look of disgust as Caruso broke into a rousing new rhythm. "His famous libretto, *Questa o Quella!*" she shivered and sighed.

"What does that mean?" Maribel looked up from her plate and raised her hands to her head. "Oh my, please, don't anyone tell Charles how much wine I've had."

Alicia giggled, and Jewel snapped her fingers. "This part," she glanced around the table. "This is my favorite." She closed her eyes as he launched a golden ring of a vowel spinning slowly up from the parlor, over the staircase, and down into the dining room, landing like a halo around Jewel's beaming countenance. After the sighs abated, Jewel answered, "Loosely translated, it means 'either she or her.' Women are all the same to the Duke of Mantua."

Morgan tore her stare from the candle and looked down into her lap. Edna sat back in her chair, her face cast green in Maribel's shadow. "A typical man," she said. "No man is ever satisfied with one woman—no matter how beautiful or brilliant she is." Caruso's voice faded after the coda, and the record scratched round and round.

"Who will drink coffee with dessert?" Camille stood and collected the dinner plates. Morgan drifted into the parlor, put on Faulkenstein, and turned the volume down. Jewel smiled, still rapt in the afterglow of the aria, while Edna and Maribel raised their hands for coffee and Faye and Alicia reviled the Duke's ignoble behavior. Camille put the coffee on the stove while Eveline opened the port and poured cream into the pitcher. "I forgot to ask who wants what," Camille said as she unmolded the soufflé.

Eveline nodded and bustled back into the parlor. "Camille has a lovely raspberry soufflé with Chambord sauce, or a lemon tart citron."

"Oh, God," Jewel squealed. "Who could make a decision like that? Why don't you just put it all out on the table, deal the plates around, and let us sample it all with no pretense. We're past all that, aren't we girls?"

Camille smiled and brought the desserts in. Eveline took down the cordial glasses and poured around the port. Camille hesitated before she sat down. "I should check on Andrew."

"Allow me," Jewel shouted as she sprang up. She wove her steps toward the staircase as Eveline shot Camille a concerned glance. Camille shrugged and sat down, watching with pride as the women enjoyed helping themselves to large portions of her culinary gifts. Jewel made her way down the stairs. Stumbling over the rug in the entry, she made an awkward recovery and roared with laughter as she made her way back to her seat and reached for the silver pie server. "I smell coffee," she sang. "Better get me grounded before I aim Renfrow's Buick back toward the Bremond block. Pray I can drive better than I can walk."

Eveline shot into the kitchen and came back with the pot and the cream. "You really do think you can teach me to drive?"

"Of course!" Jewel took a large swig of her port.

"I don't mean today, of course." Eveline poured coffee for Edna, Maribel, and herself before she took her seat.

"I'll tell you what," Jewel slapped a hand on the lace beside her plate, "next Saturday we'll take a spin out to Formosa to see Ney's gorgeous rendering of Prometheus, and you can drive home."

"I don't know." Eveline looked over at Camille. "Maybe if Camille will come, too."

"Formosa?" Camille poured herself more port. Morgan shifted in her chair.

"Why not?" Jewel demanded. "We'll bask in the powerful juices of Elisabet's art, and Eveline will drive us back to Woolridge Park for the AWSA rally. It will be grand. By then we'll be so full of feminine indignation, Camille can drive us through Guy Town while we jeer every whore and her john out of their houses!"

Edna raised a fist and cheered as Alicia let out a howl. Eveline smiled and leaned toward Camille. "Let's do it!" she urged. "Imagine Brooks' and Thomas' faces when we nonchalantly volunteer to drive on our next outing. It's too delicious."

"What's Guy Town?" Camille asked. The cheering and laughing stopped.

Jewel leaned in and put a hand on Camille's arm. "You've been in Austin how long?" she asked.

"Over a year." Eveline responded.

"And you've never heard of Guy Town?" The resonance of Jewel's last syllable left all the women staring at Camille. Tallow melted over the side of a taper and fell into a large glob on the crystal holder. Jewel glanced at Eveline.

Eveline shrugged her shoulders. "I suppose it's not one of my favorite subjects."

Morgan drew a deep breath. Across the table and through the flickering light, her face seemed to pulsate from the inside to the outside of her veiling and back; she looked like pictures Camille had seen of ancient virgin martyrs.

"Guy Town is the red light district," Edna informed her. "If you walk three blocks south of Scarbrough and Hicks on Congress, and take one block west, you'll be standing right across from Blanche Dumont's bawdy house."

Camille felt warmth rise in her temples. "That's practically in the shadow of the state capitol. Isn't prostitution illegal?"

"Of course it's illegal," Jewel raved. "But our esteemed congressmen act as though no one really knows what's going on down there."

"Maybe they don't," Camille offered. Morgan glowered at the far wall, and Alicia's giggles cut through the room like a buzz saw.

Jewel let out a sarcastic cackle. "It's well known when the legislature is in session, Blanche hires extra soiled doves from surrounding towns to handle the business."

"I wonder if Brooks knows." As Camille rubbed her temples, the heat receded into a dull headache.

"Oh, he knows!" Faye smiled wryly and nudged Alicia.

Maribel whispered, "In church last week, the minister said one man told him over a hundred University of Texas students could be counted there on any given night."

"But, not the professors." Camille shook her head until the centerpiece started to spin. "They could never risk being seen in a place like that. Surely it would jeopardize their careers."

Morgan stood. "Where is the powder room?"

As Camille rose to show her the way, her hand caught her glass of port. She watched the rich red liquid flow across the lines of the lace and seep into the rose motifs in hideous blotches.

Eveline gasped and sprang out of her chair. "I'll get a towel."

"Don't trouble yourself," Camille sighed. "It will never come out."

18. Propagation

Texas was abloom in May. Bluebonnets, black-eyed Susans, and Indian paintbrushes covered the fields and roadsides, and Camille's herbs thrived in a splendid array of color and aroma. On Eveline's last visit, she told Camille she would like to put in a small herb garden off her own back porch, so Camille and Coral worked side by side propagating some of Eveline's favorites in hopes to produce a healthy set of seedlings in time for fall. Coral took cuttings of lavender, rosemary, tarragon, and nasturtium, placing each gently in her apron as she moved about the garden. Andrew was practicing pulling himself up to his feet in his play yard and howling at the birds that landed on the trellis. Coral looked over at him and smiled. "He'll be too big for that play crib soon."

Camille loosened a long strand of oregano from the bush and gently pulled off the middle leaves. "I'm afraid you're right," she sighed as she watched a blackbird fly up into the air and scold Andrew back. She used a hand spade to dig a shallow hole and, laying the bare part of the stem into the ground, spread the dark loam over it and molded a rift of soil to support the underside of the stem end. "We can divide some Coralbell stems now," she said as she leveled a stem of dill. "We'll plant them in pots for you to take home."

Coral's eyes shone. Andrew plopped down on his bottom and pulled himself up again. He shook the play yard poles and growled. "Shall I get him?" she asked.

"He's fine. He's just practicing his inborn sense of male dominion," Camille assured her with a short laugh.

"I guess there's no stopping that." Coral stood and arranged the contents of her apron. "I'll go in and put these in water."

Camille leveled sprouts of parsley, caraway, and dill before she heard a high-pitched scream from the play yard. As she spun around, she saw Coral run from the kitchen shouting, "Hold it there! Hold on, I got you!" Andrew had worked himself over the side of the play yard and hung teetering on his belly, his head falling toward the cement porch.

Camille screamed as Coral bent to catch the sobbing child, who had fallen below her knee level. She heaved him up into her arms and held him to her breast. By the time Camille got to the screen porch and took him in her arms, she realized how weak her knees were. She collapsed into a chair and rocked the child furiously. Coral gave him a nervous pat on the head. "I'll get us something cold to drink," she said as she went back into the kitchen.

Camille pulled off her gloves and smoothed tears from Andrew's red cheeks. "There, there, now. What am I going to do if you won't stay in your play crib?" Coral returned with a pitcher of ice water and poured a drink for Andrew. Camille held the cup to his mouth. "I can't think what might have happened had you not been here, Coral." As Camille took up her glass, she noticed a thin stream of blood behind Coral across the porch floor. "Oh, dear," she whispered.

"What is it?" Coral recognized the new horror on Camille's face and turned to follow her stare. "Oh, Lord!" she gasped and sank into a chair.

Camille stood. "All right. We will remain calm."

"Oh, my dear, dear Lord!" Coral's face went blank.

"Calm." Camille forced a steady syllable. "We will get you

into the divan." Holding Andrew with one arm, she helped Coral to her feet with the other and slowly led her inside.

"Oh, my sweet Lord, please . . ." Coral wailed as Camille helped her through the kitchen. She stopped short and let out a wail of pain; her knees sagged under her.

"To the divan," Camille repeated. "Just a little farther."

"Maybe the divan isn't such a good idea," Coral wailed. "Maybe I better see if I can get up to the bathroom."

"No, we need your feet off the floor." With her resolve, Camille sensed a rush of renewed strength. She led her to the parlor and, setting Andrew down, helped Coral onto the divan. "Stay here," she ordered. "I'm going to get help." She looked around the room, scooped Andrew up, and ran upstairs to get a quilt from the rack in her room and towels from the bath. When she came down, Coral's wails had softened into horrible low moans, and her bleeding had intensified. Camille ran into the hall and, rocking Andrew back on her hip, clicked the phone until the operator answered. "I need an ambulance," she said.

"Hold for the hospital," the operator replied.

Andrew fussed and threw his weight against her balance. She set him on the floor. "Stay right here next to Mama, Andrew," she said.

After a succession of clicks and one long ring, the voice of an elderly woman greeted her. "City County Hospital."

"I'm Camille Abernathy. We need an ambulance at 910 West Avenue. My housekeeper is with child and she's bleeding."

"Your housekeeper?"

"Yes," Camille tried to keep her thoughts clear as Andrew crept around the corner into the kitchen. "She's in pain, and she's bleeding a lot. An awful lot."

"Your colored housekeeper?" the woman asked.

"Why, yes . . ." Camille paused.

"Please hold."

Camille sighed and set the receiver down while she lifted Andrew from the kitchen floor and flew into the parlor to check on Coral, who tossed and moaned, her face wet with fever. "Hold on," Camille said as she wiped her face with a towel. "I've got the hospital on the phone." She grabbed Andrew's favorite tin fire engine from the corner and rushed back into the hall to pick up the phone. "Hello?"

In a moment the woman returned. "I'm sorry, Mrs. Abernathy, is it? Our ambulance is out on a call. Please leave your exchange with the operator, and we will notify you when it returns."

"There's no time!" Camille wailed as the woman hung up. She set Andrew down with the fire engine and, after leaving the operator the number, asked for a connection with the Wheatville Bar.

"Let's see . . ." the operator mused. "Do you know the exchange?"

"No . . . I," Camille wailed, "hold on a minute. Coral! Can you tell me Samuel's exchange?" Coral did not reply.

"Oh, here it is," the operator said. "Please hold."

The phone at the Wheatville Bar rang seven times before Samuel answered.

"Samuel, thank God it's you," Camille gasped.

"Miss Camille?"

"It's Coral," Camille continued. "She's, well, she's on the divan; she's losing blood."

"Oh, no," Samuel whispered.

"I've called for an ambulance. The woman at the hospital said it was out, but she would call when it came back."

"She won't be calling back," Samuel's voice faded. "I'll be there fast as I can."

"I'll try Brooks," Camille said. "If he's in his office, I'll have him bring the car."

She hung up and picked Andrew off the floor. "Such a good boy." She kissed him on the forehead. Coral's bleeding had not abated, and she gasped for air between moans. Camille wiped her forehead again and patted her hand. "Samuel's on his way. I'm going to see if I can catch Brooks to bring the car."

She carried Andrew back into the hall and had the operator ring Brooks' office.

"Professor Abernathy," he answered.

"Brooks! I'm so glad you're not in class!"

"What is it? Is Andrew all right?"

"Yes, he's right here. It's Coral. I'm afraid she might be having a miscarriage."

"Where is she?" Brooks sighed.

"On the divan," Camille answered. "Can you please come and take her to the hospital? I called for an ambulance and it's not available."

"In my Cadillac?"

Camille drew a sharp breath. "She's in pain, Brooks. She takes care of our child, and now her own is in jeopardy."

"I have a meeting I can't get out of," Brooks stammered. "A disciplinary issue with two deans and three students. Everyone is counting on me."

"Brooks!"

"I'll get out of it as soon as I can."

Camille stared at the humming receiver. Andrew started to cry. She changed his diaper on the floor in the parlor as she watched Coral toss on the divan. She rushed into the kitchen for milk and toast for Andrew and a cool cloth to wipe the sweat from Coral's neck and face. The mantle clock seemed to stop. Camille struggled to keep Andrew content with his midmorning snack, which she served on the parlor floor while she continued to try and keep Coral cool and wondered what else she should be doing for her. By the time Samuel arrived, Coral was curled up around her cramping womb, softly sobbing.

Camille flew to the door. "I don't know what else to do," she moaned.

Samuel lunged for the divan. "Oh, Corrie," he crooned as he rubbed her brow and leaned over to kiss her slightly swollen belly. "Everything's gonna be fine." He wrapped his arms around her and gently gathered her up off the divan. He turned to Camille with a tear in his eye. "I'll pay for your sofa, Miss Camille."

Andrew looked up at Samuel and, taking a start, began fussing. "Please, Samuel," Camille picked Andrew up, "just take care of Coral and don't worry about anything else."

Samuel nodded and hesitated, looking deep into Camille's eyes.

Camille rubbed Andrew's back; he stopped fussing and, twisting himself around in her embrace, regarded Samuel with wonder. "Brooks couldn't seem to get away," she said as she opened the door for him.

Samuel nodded and carried Coral through the door and down the walk. He stopped in front of the wagon, looked down at Coral, and eyed up the buckboard seat and wooden wagon bed. He took a deep breath, heaved Coral over the side of the bed, and laid her as gently as he could into the corner behind the seat. Coral let out a high-pitched scream and went silent. Andrew started to cry. Camille raised a hand to her mouth. "I'll get pillows," she shouted.

"No time," Samuel replied. "The doctor's waiting for us."

He tipped his hat. "Thank you, Miss Camille," he said as he untied the horses, swung himself up into the seat, and with a backward glance at Coral, snapped the reins and led the horses down West Avenue.

Andrew rubbed his wet face before he held out a hand. "Dada!" he blurted.

"Your first word." Camille wiped her cheek with the back of her hand. "Your father will be so proud."

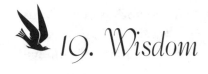

19. Wisdom

May 27, 1912
Dear Mother,

Before dad died, did you ever wake up in the morning with the feeling your husband had somehow disappeared through the window during the night and a man who looked like him had taken his place? I scrubbed the floors until well after midnight, mostly because I did not want to lie next to the stranger in my bed.

Coral had a miscarriage. I will never forget the look on her face as she stood on the screen porch and realized what was happening. I didn't know what to do. I'm afraid I might have neglected something that may have made a difference. I kept trying to imagine some subtle blend of herbs brewed into an infusion that might stop her contractions and ease her pain, but my mind went white. Since, I've looked my herbal companion backward and forward and now wonder if I should have tried some fennel or anise. Goldenseal and shepherd's purse are noted for stopping heavy bleeding, but I grow neither, and both tend to stimulate contractions. Raspberry is sometimes used, but only in the last month of pregnancy, and of course, it is too early for raspberries. I still feel helpless. I don't know if she will ever come back to work again. I couldn't blame her if she didn't. Andrew would miss her singing, and I would miss working with her in the garden. You would appreciate her style of gardening. I don't know if I can explain it, but the way she digs up the soil with such wonder in her dark eyes is a sheer delight to watch. She so earnestly expects to find magic in the raw earth that she inevitably always does. She has me watching the seizing and stretching of earthworms with so much empathy I almost relive the whole nine months of pregnancy and childbirth with each soil-infused breath I take. When she makes cuttings, she subtly lays each of them in her apron—arranging such an artistic treasure that would surely inspire Monet to mix a new palette. She pulls weeds and prunes wilted roses with such a solemn air of respect and serenity, I sometimes find myself watching her with an inexplicable sense of envy.

It looks as if it might rain today. I hope it does. The past couple of weeks have been incredibly hot and dry, and I'm tired of lugging the watering can through the yard. Truthfully, I'm getting sick of the way the sun beats relentlessly down on everything. It's so oppressive and utterly inescapable. My days will be especially limited without Coral, because it's intolerable to be out after ten in the morning or before seven in the evening, and those are the times when Brooks expects his meals. This summer I will be a prisoner to this house. I won't even be able to enjoy shopping along Congress Avenue any more. The only shade there backs up insultingly close to the purveyors of finery and the ice cream parlors.

All of a sudden, this city feels sticky and dirty. Sometimes I just want to come home. But I know things could never be the same, and Brooks would never leave Texas. He's taken to wearing a black western hat from time to time. He thinks he looks like some sort of mysteriously intellectual outlaw, but I think he looks ridiculous. I couldn't bring the baby up to Seattle by myself, for the trip would be too arduous for him and he would miss his father terribly. He adores Brooks. Yesterday, he spoke his first word. Of course, he said, "Dada." That's typical, isn't it? Maybe it was cruel of me, but I didn't tell Brooks when he finally got home. His only concern was whether or not Samuel would sue us. I told him even though he probably should, I felt sure he would not. Then I didn't feel like talking any more.

I also didn't tell him I have decided to learn to drive. And, if Coral ever comes back to help me with Andrew, I'm going to join the suffragist movement. I hope to attend a rally in Wooldridge Park next weekend with Eveline and some of the other women who attended my dinner party. I want to vote in the upcoming elections. I'm interested in a lot of the local issues.

Brooks had the divan removed this morning before he left for work. He told me to pick out another one today, but I haven't the heart to shop, and no matter how much furniture I might buy and have delivered, the new empty space in my home could never be filled.

Love, Mother—
Writhing alive and doubly subtle,
Your Camille

20. Tinctures

Brooks brought his typewriter home in June to work on his book. He set up a study corner in the guestroom and worked for an hour or two every afternoon. After dinner most evenings, he went back in, shut the door, and didn't come back out until after Andrew and Camille were asleep. On Saturday mornings, he took Camille into town to do her shopping, and after a long afternoon of work, he went into town to unwind with his colleagues at the faculty club or at the Crystal Saloon. He and Thomas had taken to playing golf on Sunday afternoons, and on Sunday evenings, he ate his dinner, belched his gratitude, and shrank back into what Camille had come to call his "cave."

One Saturday morning, Andrew slept until almost 8:00 A.M. and woke up fussier than usual. As she made breakfast, he coughed while he pushed his fire engine around the kitchen floor. Before she and Andrew had finished their breakfast, Brooks appeared in the kitchen door.

Camille peered at him over her coffee. "You're up early."

He grimaced. "Had a bad night. Nagging headache." Camille finished her coffee and wiped Andrew's face and hands. "What's for breakfast?" he mumbled.

"Soft boiled eggs and toast," she answered as she wiped the tray of the highchair and set the fire engine on it for Andrew.

"No bacon?" Brooks yawned and held his head.

"No, but I have fresh cantaloupe, and if you'll keep an eye on Andrew for a few moments, I'll make your eggs."

He shrugged and sat down next to Andrew. "How does the fire engine go?" he sang as he rolled the toy back forth across the tray.

"Woo-oo!" Andrew shrieked until he coughed. Brooks winced. "Why is he coughing?"

"He woke up with some chest congestion."

"Have you given him anything?"

"Not yet." Camille took out a loaf of buttermilk bread and sliced off two thick pieces. "I wanted to feed him first."

Brooks lifted Andrew out of his chair and held him on his lap. "What's the matter, big boy, did you get a cold?" He turned and watched as Camille buttered his bread and put it in the oven. "Do we have any Fletcher's Castoria?"

"No," Camille laughed as she lifted his eggs out of boiling water with a fork. "And I wouldn't give my baby any of that street show olio if I did."

Brooks frowned. "Will Dr. Steiger come out on a Saturday?"

Camille poured his coffee and checked the toast in the oven. "It's just a touch of catarrh," she said. "I'll have him feeling better in an hour or two."

Andrew started fussing. Camille served Brooks his breakfast and took the child. Brooks cracked an egg open and spooned it into his mouth. "I guess you won't be going into town today," he said as he looked around. "Where's the cantaloupe?"

"No, but I need for you to pick up some things for me, please." Camille hummed and patted Andrew on the back until he relaxed over her shoulder. She got the cantaloupe from the icebox.

"I don't know if I should do anything with this throbbing in my head," he whined as he finished his toast.

"You have egg on your cheek," she nodded as she walked out through the screen porch. She returned with the child draped over her shoulder and a handful of fresh hyssop and lavender.

Brooks pushed his plate aside and sat back with his coffee. "What do you need from town?"

"A fifth of vodka," she answered as she handed Andrew back to him.

"You're not serious!" he snapped.

Camille put the teakettle on and rinsed the herbs. "I need a fifth of vodka—at least a hundred proof—and some beeswax."

"What in the hell do you need vodka for? You don't drink vodka." Andrew started coughing and rubbed his face.

"I have an important project I need to do today," she answered as she bruised the herbs in a tea towel, separated them carefully, and placed each in an enamel bowl. Brooks started to argue, but put a hand to his forehead instead. "Has your work got you vexed or do you think you have sinus pressure?" she asked as steam whistled from the kettle. She poured boiling water over each of the herbs and stirred them gently as they steeped.

"A little of both, I suppose," he sipped his coffee.

She strained the hyssop into a cup first and set it in the icebox to cool. "Oh, I also need a couple of those dark blue stoppered bottles from the hardware store."

"What are you up to?" he growled as he repositioned Andrew.

"Dada!" Andrew blurted and started to fuss again.

"Did you hear that?" Brooks wailed. "He said dada! His first word!"

"What do you know?" Camille smiled as she poured the lavender infusion onto a clean dishtowel and folded it over.

"Be sure and write it on the calendar," Brooks exclaimed.

"Oh, I won't forget the day he said his first word." Camille checked the temperature of the hyssop infusion, tasted it, and poured in a glass of cold water. She placed it back into the icebox and took Andrew in her arms. "Here." She held out the compress for Brooks. "Put this on your forehead and lie down for a half hour or so; you'll feel much better."

Brooks wrinkled his forehead, but took the compress. "I'll try anything at this point. Maybe my son will take a nap with me."

"I'll give him his infusion, and then I'll bring him up." After the infusion cooled, Camille mixed it with more cold water and apple juice and poured eight ounces into Andrew's cup. After he drank it, she rocked him to sleep, carried him upstairs, and laid him next to Brooks, who snored softly with the compress still on his forehead. She smiled before she turned and hurried downstairs.

She washed the breakfast dishes and looked around the kitchen as she dried her hands. She took two clean bowls—one large and one small—from the cupboard. In the screen porch, she put on her gardening gear and rummaged through the extra clay pots until she found her snippers. The sun beat down on her though it was not yet midmorning, but she smiled as she watched a hummingbird flirt with a cluster of bergamot and wished Andrew had not gone back to sleep so soon. She tiptoed through her herb garden, harvesting several of the heartiest stems of thyme and summer savory leaves and placing them in the large bowl. She snipped about twenty marigold stems in full blossom and a handful each of betony and feverfew, also placing them carefully in her bowl. The scent of the sweet marjoram gave her such delight that she harvested several clusters for a centerpiece. She stopped to watch the hummingbird as it thrust its beak into a red floweret, unruffled by her presence. The whirr of its tiny wings filled the air around her until a grackle landed on the rooftop with a hiss and a squawk. Camille scowled at the black bird shining purple in the heat. It turned its head, and its eye bore through her with such an evil glint, she caught her breath and took a step backward into a row of angelica. "Shoo!" she scolded until it flew up over the fence.

Her comfrey pot was on the far side of the house where she could keep it from invading the other herbs and flowers. The single sprout she had planted in February of the previous year had reproduced itself into over a dozen thick bile-green stalks with drooping racemes of delicate pink teardrops. Camille pulled five of the stalks up by their roots and placed them in her smaller bowl. With a last look around for the hummingbird, she sighed and pruned a few fresh roses growing on the trellis before returning to the kitchen.

She rinsed the cuttings and set them in rows on dishtowels to dry. Taking her favorite crystal bowl from the dining room hutch, she made a floating centerpiece with the roses and marjoram. She sat down at the table and made her lists. As she rose to check her herbs, Brooks bounded down the stairs. "Is Andrew still asleep?" she asked.

"Yes, I put him in his crib."

"Good." She turned a few of the stems over. "How's your headache?"

Brooks cocked his head to the right. "Gone, actually. Any more coffee?"

Camille nodded and pointed to the pot on the stove. "Where's the compress?"

"I must have left it upstairs." Brooks poured himself a cup of coffee and looked up at the clock. "I'll go into town now.

I'd like to get back and work a few hours before the billiards tournament tonight."

"Billiards tournament?" Camille sighed as she picked up the list she had made out for Brooks. "Here's what I need."

Brooks looked over the list as he took his hat from the hall hook. "Really, Camille," he turned. "I'll not buy you distilled spirits unless you tell me what you want it for."

"Why not?" Camille spread out a dry dishtowel and turned the rest of her herbs onto it. "I'm an adult, and we have no prohibition law."

"Camille," Brooks thundered.

She turned to look into his dark eyes and stood suddenly mesmerized again by the drone of the hummingbird. She felt the sinister stare of the grackle through her heart. She resisted a dark urge to wrap her fingers around his neck. She wanted to strangle him for being so dastardly handsome, so self-assured, so free—so unconcerned. "I'm going to make some tinctures with it," she said as she straightened her apron.

"What's a tincture?" Brooks sat down.

"An infusion of herbal leaves or buds with alcohol, which, after a few weeks of careful distillation, will relieve a headache like nothing else." She gently pulled betony leaves off the stems.

"How much do you have to drink?" Brooks asked.

Camille smiled. "You place a few drops under the tongue."

"And it makes a headache go away?" He sneered and finished his coffee. "What's the beeswax for?"

"Salves," she answered. "I'm making a marigold salve for minor burns and sunburn, a thyme and summer savory salve for insect bites, and a comfrey salve for wounds and bruises."

Brooks placed his cup in the sink. "Why don't you make

some nice jams and jellies instead?" He looked at her the way adults look at their children.

Camille felt her fists tighten. "Because the laws of nature won't allow it."

"What?" He twisted his face. "Natural law has nothing to do with jelly. I can assure you of that."

"That's next month's project." Camille mentally worked to keep her shoulders relaxed. "Fruits and flowers for jellies bloom in mid- to late summer. Now is the season for medicinal herbs. Besides, it's prudent to have the right tinctures and salves on hand in case of an emergency. You never know what might . . ."

"None of the other professors' wives make kitchen concoction remedies. Why can't you just . . ." He waved an arm in the air.

Camille drew a deep breath. "Look, Brooks, you express yourself through your writing. My gifts are in my herbal arts. Surely you wouldn't deny me that?"

He shook his head. "Of course not. Vodka for the little lady it is." He pulled his keys out of his pocket and started for the door.

"And tomorrow evening," Camille kept her voice level, "I'll be going to the suffragist rally with Eveline and Jewel."

He stopped and reeled around. His mouth fell open. "Why . . . um." He scratched his head.

Camille pulled her garden gloves on and started chopping the comfrey roots. "We'll leave before you get home from your golf, so I'll ring Coral. Samuel says she's ready to come back, and I'm sure she won't mind keeping Andrew for a couple of hours or so."

"Actually," Brooks looked at his shoes, "I was thinking we might take a family drive out to the lake. They're building a new dam, you know, and I thought it might be fun to take Andrew up there for a picnic." He looked up and offered a weak smile. "Maybe Thomas and Eveline would like to come, too."

"Why didn't you mention it before?" Camille asked.

"I guess I hadn't thought it through. But how about it?"

She crushed the chopped roots with the side of her knife. "We couldn't take Andrew for a picnic with a cough," she replied and turned to face him squarely. "And as I just told you, I have plans tomorrow evening."

His face soured as he shuffled his feet in the hallway. "All right, then. But you don't have to call Coral. I'll stay with Andrew."

"But your golf?" Camille grinned.

"I'll see if Thomas can go earlier," he answered. "I'll be home before five."

"I don't know." Camille took off her gloves and rinsed her hands. "He's not easy to keep up with these days. He can crawl out of anything, and you can't take your eyes off him for a minute."

Brooks crimped his forehead. "Camille, I think I can take care of my own son for an hour or two," he snapped.

"Very well." Camille walked into the hallway and gave him a peck on the cheek. "If you promise to be home by five."

"Damn!" Brooks grabbed his ears. "My headache's back." He gave her a desperate last look and left.

21. The Gazebo

Camille had dinner on the table by the time Brooks got home from golf. Andrew's cough had eased considerably, and he ate all his chicken and dumplings. She had the kitchen clean in record time, and as she pulled on a mint green cotton blouse and a lightweight forest green skirt with a back kick pleat, she recited a litany of instructions and precautions. Brooks carried Andrew from room to room listening in silence until the sound of a car horn blared from the street. Camille gave them each a quick kiss before she ran out to find Jewel and Eveline waiting in a midnight-blue Ford Model T Touring Car. "Jewel actually owns this car!" Eveline exclaimed.

"Oh, Jewel." Camille eyed the sleek lines of the automobile as she stepped onto the running board and opened the door to the backseat. "I can't believe Renfrow bought you your own car." She stifled a giggle as Jewel turned in her goggles and aviator's helmet.

"Renfrow would never deny me anything, bless his petrified heart," she said. "He loves me because I'm the only thing he can no longer read with a Geiger counter." The engine sputtered, and Jewel gave a pedal a few jabs with her left foot until it growled fiercely and fell into a steady idle. "No, my dears," she continued, "in Renfrow's world, I am a full-blown gusher, and unfortunately for him, capping and refining are out of his field of expertise. Eveline, are you ready to drive?"

"Oh, no." Eveline's face paled. "Brooks might be looking out the window, and I don't want him or Thomas to know just yet. I have a plan. Next time we all go for a drive into town, I'll nonchalantly say, 'Camille, do you feel like driving, or shall I?' I can't wait to see their faces!"

"Very well, then." Jewel released the brake, and her saffron chiffon driving scarf flared up behind her in the wind. "I'll drive to the rally, and you can drive home."

Eveline shot an anxious look back at Camille as Jewel went on, "Sorry again, girls, that my day spun out of control and we couldn't do Formosa as we'd planned. But you simply must see it. Ney's work is a noble testament to the power of the female spirit. We'll make a full day of it. This morning one of the university regents phoned to tell Renfrow they had decided to send him to West Texas to run some geological tests. He was wild to leave this morning before anyone on the board had a chance to change his mind. I spent all morning packing him up and drove him to the train station, which left me barely enough time to help the girls get the park ready and collect the flyers from the printer for the rally. This one's going to be especially grand. Mayor Wooldridge is coming to address us. It seems he has every intention of supporting Austin women in their struggle for full enfranchisement. You're joining the cause at a particularly auspicious time." Jewel expounded the details of the rally agenda and the full contents of the flyers as she sped down West Avenue and turned onto Ash Street.

Wooldridge Square consisted of a square of lawn lined by old oak trees dipping gracefully down into a bowl-shaped esplanade. In the center stood a stark white gazebo built in classical revival style with star-spangled blue banners softening each of the upper corners and a huge red-and-white-striped bunting draped across the front of the raised stage.

Members of a small band were setting up to the left of the structure. "Ah, everything is shaping up nicely," Jewel sighed. "Mayor Wooldridge had the square cleared and the gazebo built a couple of years ago." She pulled the hand brake, and the car jerked to a stop.

"Cleared of what?" Camille asked.

"Landfill," Jewel said flatly as they watched a steady stream of attendees make their way to the benches around the gazebo. "Before that it was just a big hole in the ground where everyone threw their trash."

Eveline stood and shielded her eyes. The sun hung on the tops of the trees on the western side of the park. "I see Alicia and Faye," she reported as she pointed to the right.

"How splendid." Jewel took her goggles and helmet off, plumped her hair with her fingers, and secured it with several hairpins. "I'm so glad they decided to come. We'll sit with the veteran sisters over on the left." Camille and Eveline exchanged a glance. "This park," Jewel continued, "along with several others currently being surveyed, is part of the mayor's master plan for a more moral, healthful, and physically attractive urban environment. He's also declared his intentions to pave all the main streets in town, to improve street lighting, and to construct a sewer system to serve Austin residents clear out to East Avenue." She firmly placed a maroon felt hat with a single pheasant feather on her head and secured it with a topaz pin.

"That's wonderful," Eveline remarked as she climbed out of the car. "I hope it won't take too long."

"And I'll tell you girls a secret," Jewel lowered her voice as she pulled on her ecru gloves, "if you promise not to share it with anyone." Camille and Eveline nodded. "We have cooked up a most delicious plan. The other AWSA officers and I have decided that after the mayor offers his support this evening, we will invite him and Mrs. Wooldridge to a sumptuous luncheon in their honor and then drop a few well-planned hints that Guy Town be eliminated for good—as part of his campaign for a moral society, of course." Jewel slid across the front seat toward the door on the passenger side.

"Why not just ask him this evening?" Camille asked.

Jewel stopped mid-seat. "Well, you see, dear, how shall I put this . . . In the four years our group has been active, we've discovered it necessary to be somewhat reserved in order to escape criticism and ridicule."

"I see," Camille said. Jewel led them to the benches on the left side of the park nearest the bandstand, where she hurriedly introduced them to the other AWSA officers as they flew about attending to last minute details. Camille and Eveline selected seats in the back row, as they were already in shade. Jewel and three other officers took their places on-stage while members handed out the flyers. Camille and Eveline glanced around the benches as they filled, waving to acquaintances and pointing out the civic notorieties they recognized. The cry of a bugle pierced the sultry evening air, and a hush fell over the crowd. As the band struck up a march, people milling around took their seats or looked for shady places to stand. Once everyone was situated, the band died out and Jewel stepped forward with a megaphone. "Welcome sister suffragettes!" As the cheers abated, she added, "And a few brothers, as well, I see. Thank you. Thank you all for coming." She gleamed as she waited for the applause to subside. "As vice president of the Austin Woman Suffrage Association, it is my pleasure to introduce our esteemed chapter president, Mrs. Ida Plimpton."

President Plimpton took the megaphone and smiled graciously until the crowd settled down, then went over the pressing issues listed on the flyers before she started her speech. "As the only woman's suffragist association in the great state of Texas to date, we have a daunting, yet pressing duty. We've been raising social consciousness in the Austin area for four years now, and it's time we come a little further into the foreground. Jewel, here, will be passing around sections of a petition that I hope all of you will sign." Jewel held up a stack of clipboards with dangling pencils. Mrs. Plimpton continued, "We are determined to lobby the state legislature to support a women's suffrage amendment to the state constitution." The crowd went wild as Jewel took the steps from the bandstand and handed out petitions to the first woman seated in each row. "Before I introduce our special guest," Mrs. Plimpton paused, "I have a couple of important announcements. First, we've been invited to march in this year's Fourth of July parade." After the new round of cheers, she urged all registered members who wished to march to sign up with any of the officers and take a paper with instructions for parade dress and marching alignment. "Next," Mrs. Plimpton continued, "I wish to remind the suffragettes that our meeting next month will be at the home of Jewel Kimbrough." Jewel nodded over her shoulder. "The address is on the flyer," Mrs. Plimpton added. "Mrs. Leida Winn, the president of the suffrage movement in Georgia, will be in town and has agreed to share a lecture from her article entitled 'Separation of Issues for Southern Suffragists.' And now," she cleared her throat, "it is my privilege to present to you the honorable mayor of the city of Austin, Mr. A. P. Wooldridge."

As the suffragists applauded and shouted their appreciation, an impeccably groomed man with a stern face and a fine white film of hair on his round head took the steps up to the gazebo in the town square that bore his name. He shook hands with each of the officers and waved to silence the crowd before he took the megaphone from Mrs. Plimpton and delivered his speech amid periodic outbursts of applause. "Dear fellow Austinites, welcome to the Progressive Era in the heart of Texas. At this critical time in American history, we are challenged with the task of promoting true justice and insuring the constitutional ideals our forefathers have ordained. Consequently, the question of conferring suffrage on women should be uppermost in the minds of the people. In fact," he smiled until the noise subsided, "in fact, it is my hope that the great state of Texas take the lead among southern states in giving women the vote."

Camille jumped off the bench with the rest of the crowd and clapped until her hands throbbed. As the cheering abated, a voice from the back of the crowd called out, "What about Negro women, Mr. Mayor?"

A. P. Wooldridge coolly lifted the mouthpiece. "Now, as you all know, here in the South we have a distinct color line—mutually conceded. Just as segregation is a positive measure that serves the interests of both races, this rally for the enfranchisement of white women cannot tolerate any idea of social equity for reasons I hardly need to explain at this point." His face lit up in a wide smile as the applause thundered and the base drummer pounded out a slow common time rhythm. The chapter members held hands and sang the "Suffrage Song" to the tune of "America."

Camille stopped clapping and sat down. "What's the matter?" Eveline asked.

"Nothing." Camille shook her head. "The noise and heat just made me feel faint for a moment. I'll be fine." Eveline gave her arm a squeeze. The mayor took a plumed pen from Mrs. Plimpton, signed the first page of the petition, and passed the pen back to the chapter president. Each of the officers ceremoniously added her name to the list, and at the end of the song, they all held it up while the secretary led them in the chant "Enfranchise Texas women."

Jewel stepped forward. "Thank you, Mr. Mayor, for your generous support." She waved until she had the crowd hushed. "And now, as a modest gesture of our deep appreciation, the other officers of the Austin Woman Suffrage Association and I would like to invite you and Mrs. Wooldridge to a luncheon in your honor in the Cactus Room next Saturday."

The mayor nodded courteously, waved to the crowd, and marched down the stairs as the band played "Deep in the Heart of Texas." He walked quickly to the edge of the park and climbed into a waiting car, speeding away. Mrs. Plimpton read off a long list of facts concerning the triumphs of other suffrage groups across the country, and Jewel closed the rally by collecting the petitions as everyone sang the National Anthem. The band continued to play as the crowd milled about and visited until the oaks cast deep auburn shadows across the lawn. As the musicians packed up their instruments, Camille and Eveline helped to gather the bunting from the gazebo, fold it neatly, and place it in the trunk of Jewel's car.

Jewel pranced across the lawn rifling through the petitions. "I say—that was absolutely the most inspiring rally to date. Did you see all those people? We must have over three hundred signatures—not to mention a legal endorsement from the mayor himself." She tucked the petitions between the folds of the bunting and, with a final pat, closed the trunk. "We should celebrate!" she sang as Eveline opened the door to the backseat. "Not so fast, young lady," she scolded. "You're driving."

"Oh, not now," Eveline demurred. "Let Camille go first."

Camille climbed into the backseat. "No, this is all part of your plan."

Eveline bit her lower lip as she pulled herself up into the front seat and scooted herself over to sit behind the steering wheel. "This is scarier than I thought it would be."

"Oh, pish!" Jewel clucked her tongue. "It's only as scary as you allow it to be. If Thomas can drive, you certainly can, too."

"All right then." Eveline put a hand on each side of the wheel. "What are these gadgets?"

Camille watched as Jewel pointed out the starter and speedometer on the dashboard and explained how each worked. Then she told Eveline how to work the pedals and the hand brake. Eveline repeated the instructions back four times before Jewel asked Mr. Plimpton to give the car a crank while Ida put her megaphone into their Buick. Eveline kept the Model T idling until the Plimptons were gone and Jewel gave her the go-ahead nod.

"Release the brake," Jewel barked. Eveline let the brake off as the engine faltered. "Low gear," Jewel called. "Press the pedal on the left—softly, mind you." Eveline's hands flew to her face as she looked at her feet and finally pressed her left foot down until the engine groaned and evened out and the car started rolling. "Good," Jewel straightened her waist. "Now, turn the steering wheel to the left." Eveline worked furiously to turn the wheel as she inched the car off the edge of the lawn and onto the road gravel. Shooting a quick grin back at Camille, the car swerved hard left. "Easy," Jewel cried, "to the right . . . a little more, now straighten out . . . splendid." She pulled her fan out of her belt.

"I'm sorry," Eveline said. "It's tricky."

"It just takes a little while to get the feel," Jewel assured her. "You're doing fine. Let's turn here on San Antonio Street." Jewel took the bottom of the steering wheel and guided Eveline through the turn. "Good, carry on while Camille and I devise the perfect after-rally revelry. Shall we go to the Driskill for dessert?"

"I don't think I can do Congress Avenue just yet," Eveline said as her hands tightened on the wheel and she glanced quickly into the rearview mirror. "Cars go up to twelve miles an hour over there, and I might get nervous and run into a streetcar or a mule cart." Eveline drove several blocks before she jerked the wheel to the right to avoid a pothole. A dark-haired man and woman walking on the side of the road jumped onto the curb.

"Don't hit the outsiders!" Jewel shrieked and grabbed the wheel again. "No telling what kind of lawsuit would come out of that."

Eveline drew her shoulders together. "I couldn't see them in the shadow of the building. Maybe I should pull over."

"You're not giving up now," Jewel said as she fanned herself. "Besides, it's not your fault. It's getting dark, and I should have told you to turn the lights on before we left the park." Jewel pulled a switch on the dashboard, and the gas headlights illumined the road immediately in front of them; side and rear kerosene lanterns cast a dim opal glow across the tufted leather seats.

"What are outsiders?" Camille asked.

"Vagrants who come and go over the border from Mexico," Jewel explained. "They walk the streets looking for work. Oh, I know! We said we would take a run through Guy Town—remember? What marvelous sport for us on this wonderful summer evening."

"I don't know," Camille said.

"Come, come," Jewel coaxed. "We'll miss the traffic. Surely by now all the trollops will be thrashing about with their clients in their rooms, and I'm so intoxicated from the rally, I'm longing to do something deliciously devilish."

"If there won't be any traffic, I say we go," Eveline said. "I always wondered what really does go on down there at night." Jewel turned to Camille with a faux pout on her round face.

"All right," Camille smiled, "but don't tell Brooks, whatever you do."

"Why would we do a thing like that?" Jewel laughed.

"Where do I go?" Eveline asked.

"Let's see." Jewel looked around. "We need to turn left." Eveline slowed almost to a stop before she made a turn onto Pecan Street.

"How was that?" she asked with a lilt in her voice.

"Perfect turn, just perfect," Jewel commented. "Oh, yes, and take the next right at Lavaca."

Eveline made another neat turn. "You're a marvelous driver," Camille said. "Look, the moon's almost full."

"Thank you. Now which way?"

"Straight ahead." Jewel pointed. "It starts here at Cedar Street." Camille sat back and cradled her head in her hands. "Are you all right, dear?" Jewel strained to check her color.

"She had a weak spell during the rally," Eveline told Jewel. "Maybe we should go home."

"I'm fine," Camille assured them. "I don't want to go home yet. Let's invade Guy Town."

"Tally-ho!" Jewel yelled. "That's the spirit." Jewel commandeered them up and down a couple of dark streets past saloons and a Negro gambling establishment.

"How can you tell which one is a house of ill repute?" Camille asked.

"Most of them are in the bigger houses that have saloons," Jewel answered. "On the maps they mark them 'Female Boarding.' Isn't that preposterous? Listen!" Jewel put a glove to her ear. "Hear that piano? I'm pretty sure it's coming from Frankie's Place. She has quite an operation. It's rumored she services a true cross-section of the community—university students, businessmen, politicians, laborers, artisans, gamblers, visiting cattlemen, and the state militiamen who attend the summer encampments at Camp Mabry. Let's see . . . oh, yes, it's that one." She pointed to a large frame home with Victorian trim on the left side of the street as the piano tinkling grew louder.

"Morgan was right," Camille said under her breath.

"What?" Jewel whispered.

"They play ragtime."

"Yes," Jewel said. "It's probably one of those pianos that plays reels by itself." As Eveline inched by the front of the house, warm light, rowdy laughter, and raucous voices poured from the windows of the bottom floors. "Sounds like quite a party," Jewel remarked. On the side of the house stood a dark yard with wire fencing and the sounds of chickens clucking. Eveline slowed at the corner of Cypress Street. "Stop here," Jewel said as Eveline pulled the hand brake. "I don't think there's anything worth seeing up this way."

"What do you think they're doing in there?" Camille asked.

"Oh," Jewel sighed. "The ones waiting for a turn upstairs are drinking, flirting, and playing poker. Let's turn around and go back; this time, just as we pass, we'll honk the horn."

"I'll be arrested!" Eveline exclaimed.

"For what?" Jewel laughed. "Horn blowing isn't against the law. We can't leave without doing *something.*"

"All right," Eveline conceded, "but only after we've passed." Jewel coached Eveline through the U-turn as Camille moved over to the right side of the seat to get a better look.

"Did you see any actual prostitutes?" she asked.

"Not yet," Jewel answered. "Maybe this round. Let's go."

Eveline slowly drove halfway past the house. "Now!" Jewel whispered. "Squeeze the horn now."

"Not yet," Eveline wailed. Jewel reached over her and gave the horn a quick succession of toots. She and Camille laughed so hard they didn't notice Jewel's elbow had banged Eveline in the right ear as she retracted her arm. As Eveline recoiled from the blow, her feet pushed both pedals to the floor, sending the car into high gear and reverse all at once.

Camille and Jewel screamed in unison as the car spun backward and dove into a shallow ditch at the side of the road. After a few seconds of shock, Camille saw Eveline hunched over the steering wheel holding her ear.

"Eveline, are you all right?" Camille cried.

"Jewel's elbow," Eveline gasped. "I'm sorry, I . . ."

"Who's there?" A woman with curls piled high on her head stepped out of the house and onto the sidewalk.

"Is that Frankie?" Camille whispered.

"Great god of my mother's ghost!" Jewel screamed as she looked into the ditch. They sat in silence before Eveline started giggling, and within seconds, they all laughed hysterically.

A man in boots and a cowboy hat came out behind the woman. "Do you know them?" he asked the woman.

"I think she said she's one of the girl's mothers," she answered.

"Heavens!" Jewel ranted under her breath. "As if any daughter of mine would ever . . . Put it in reverse, Eveline."

"You drive," Eveline whimpered.

"Do you need help?" the woman called as two girls in white petticoats came out behind her to watch.

"No!" Jewel yelled back as she opened her car door. It hit the side of the ditch at an angle she couldn't squeeze through. "We're fine. Really. Just got a little lost. Please, go on back to your debauchery. We'll be on our way."

"Well, I never," the woman swore. "Did you hear what she said?"

Fear couldn't quell their laughter. "I can't get out," Jewel told Eveline. "Quick, turn the wheel hard right and drive forward." Eveline did as she was instructed.

"Who in blazes are you, and what are you doing here?" the man yelled as he walked toward the car.

"Now," Jewel shouted, "turn left and push the accelerator." Eveline tugged on the wheel with all her strength and hit the gear pedal with such force that gravel sprayed in every direction as the car pulled out of the ditch and started up Lavaca. The man cursed and waved his fist in the moonlight behind them.

"That was close," Eveline sighed. "Will you take the wheel now? My knees are so weak, I don't think I can make it home."

"That was marvelous!" Jewel howled. "I don't know when I've had such fun. Take two more blocks first; I don't think our new friend will come this far for us, but I want to be sure."

"He looked pretty mad," Camille laughed. "If Brooks ever found out, he'd have me tarred and feathered."

"Thomas would never believe it." Eveline stopped under a street light at the corner of Lavaca and Pecan, set the brake, and ran around the car to inspect the side that had been lodged in the ditch. "No dents or scratches, thank goodness. I would have felt terrible."

"It would have been worth it either way," Jewel raved. "It's been a priceless evening from start to finish. Camille, why don't you drive us by Blanche Dumont's house? It's twice the size of Frankie's and three times as fancy."

"I couldn't possibly," Camille yawned. "My nerves snapped somewhere between Cypress and Cedar Streets."

When Camille got home, Andrew was asleep in his crib and Brooks was working in his room with the door closed. She washed up in the kitchen and curled up on the new divan to read poetry, but she couldn't concentrate. She took out her violet stationery and started a letter to her mother. Halfway through the first page, the tears came. They washed her words into swirls of blue nonsense, so she tore it up and went to bed.

 22. *Power*

As registered suffragists, Camille and Eveline had been encouraged to march in the Fourth of July parade. But Camille wanted to watch the parade with Andrew, and Eveline didn't want to march without Camille, so the Abernathys and the Leightons attended the parade together. By the time they got there, such a dense crowd had gathered along both sides of Congress Avenue, Brooks had to hold Andrew on his shoulders so he could see the passing ponies, bicycles, and fire engines. When his back started to ache, Andrew was transferred onto Thomas' shoulders. He shouted with glee and smacked Thomas soundly on the top of his head several times when the university band marched by playing "The Eyes of Texas." Thomas laughed until tears glistened in the corners of his eyes under his glasses. After Mayor Wooldridge rode by dressed as Uncle Sam in a float fitted out with red, white, and blue crepe paper, the broom brigade followed, sweeping the rubble from the streets.

Thomas handed Andrew over to Camille. "What shall we do now?" he asked. "It won't be dark enough to shoot our fireworks until at least eight this evening."

"Let's have a picnic," Eveline suggested as she smoothed the wrinkles out of Thomas' shirt.

"Sounds fun," Camille agreed. "I've made a custard so we can crank ice cream." Andrew started to pitch in her arms. The sidewalk had cleared, so she set him on his feet and held his hands while he stretched his legs.

"We could drive up into the hills and picnic on the river," Brooks said. "I've been curious to see the new dam Wooldridge is having built. Maybe we can get a look at the generator."

"I'd like to see that, too," Thomas agreed. "The first dam broke before we got here, but I've heard the lake formed out of the river was a grand place for all sorts of recreational sport. People came from all over the country for sailboat regattas, and a fleet of boats could be rented—including a steamboat for moonlight excursions."

"Wouldn't that be wonderful?" Eveline smiled at Camille. After much discussion, they decided to return to their respective homes to prepare a picnic before driving out to the dam. Then they would return to the Abernathys' to make ice cream and shoot fireworks. Thomas said he would help Eveline fry chicken and boil corn on the cob, so Camille volunteered to make potato salad and coleslaw.

Brooks and Andrew napped while Camille boiled potatoes and shredded cabbages. She snipped some fresh dill and chives from her garden and had both salads mixed and well chilled by noon. When Brooks awoke, he helped her pack a basket and went out to the garage to find something in which to ice down his beer. Camille fixed a snack for Andrew and got him ready as Brooks came in with a tin pail and checked his watch. "They're late," he said. "I'll give them a ring."

Camille checked through the basket to make sure Brooks packed everything she had laid out, then sat down at the kitchen table to watch Andrew as he played with his fire truck on the floor. Brooks hung up the receiver and came into the kitchen with a puzzled frown. "That was odd," he said as he chipped ice from the block in the icebox.

"Are they all right?" Camille asked.

"I think so," his voice trailed. "Thomas said they were running behind but they're just about ready."

"It takes time to fry chicken," Camille remarked.

"He sounded upset." Brooks packed ice around the bottles in his pail and went into the hall to get his black western hat. "I told him we'd pick them up. I'll put everything in the car."

Camille gathered a few of Andrew's smaller toys and tucked them into a bag with his diapers; she put on her straw boater, grabbed up a couple of summer parasols and, balancing Andrew on her hip, followed Brooks out to the car. "Maybe they're arguing," she said. "Why don't we give them a few more minutes?"

"I'm starving now," Brooks answered. "Whatever it is, I'm sure they'll rise above it. Let's go."

When Brooks squeezed the horn outside the Leightons' home, Thomas hurried out to the car with a basket and Eveline followed with pale cheeks, red eyes, and a weak smile. Brooks and Thomas discussed the last faculty meeting as the Cadillac chugged up the steep green hills, while Camille and Eveline pointed out passing goats, cows, and an occasional truck for Andrew. After an hour of driving, sparkling glimpses of the river passed through the trees on the left side of road. "It won't be long now," Brooks announced. He drove up the winding trail beside the river until they came to a large clearing where the river widened considerably. "There it is," Brooks announced as he pointed to where the water lapped against a low wall.

"That's the dam?" Camille asked.

"I'm pretty sure that's a temporary retaining wall," Thomas replied.

As Brooks drove alongside the structure, they saw another wall holding back the river on the other side, and between them was a trench the width of the river dug so deep, they could not see the bottom. "I had hoped they would be further along," Brooks said. "It would've been fun to visit the powerhouse and see how big those generators are. They would have to be huge to light up a whole city."

"Boat!" Andrew blurted and pointed at the river. An abandoned steamboat was docked on the far side.

"There she sits," Thomas sighed, "the mighty Ben Hur." He winced as the sun came out from behind a cloud. "Kind of sad, isn't it?"

"It's beautiful," Camille said, "and almost as big as the steamers that cross the sound."

"They used to do exclusive dinner cruises," Thomas explained, "and dances. If you listen closely, you can still hear the sound of the saxophone, and on silent, starry evenings, they say you can also hear the sound of tinkling glasses and the laughter of the ghosts of snooty old women who got too drunk."

"You're hilarious," Eveline groaned.

They stopped at a grassy place on the side of the road with a view of the upper river and the dam. The men spread blankets and popped open a couple of Pabsts while the women took out plates, linens, and forks, and set out the food. "Want a beer?" Brooks asked Eveline.

"No, thank you," she answered as she wiped her hands on a dishtowel. "I brought a bottle of port for Camille and me."

"I'll get it," Thomas said as he pulled the bottle from the basket and dug around for the opener. "But I hope the sound of your laughter doesn't carry back over the water to the old bachelors still standing at the bar."

Camille giggled as she opened a parasol and propped it up to shade Andrew from the sun as he played with his trucks in the sand. Thomas handed Camille a paper cup of port.

When she finished setting up the picnic, she sat back and wiped her forehead and neck with a napkin. "It's really too hot for a picnic," she said as she took a sip of port. It tasted thicker and sweeter than the port Eveline had brought to her dinner party; it burned in her throat and sat on her stomach like an iron hand.

Brooks looked up at the sky and pointed eastward. "See that big white cloud over there? It's going to be in front of the sun in a few minutes and you'll be fine."

"I hope you're right," Camille answered as she loosened Andrew's collar. The men ate quickly and reclined on a blanket while they finished their beers and discussed the benefits the dam would bring upon completion. Eventually, the cloud did overtake the sun, and Camille relaxed as she fed Andrew.

"You're not eating much," she said to Eveline, who had gathered her skirts closely around herself and sat on the corner of a blanket sipping her wine with her meal at her feet.

"Neither are you." Eveline pointed to Camille's plate. "Don't you like our chicken?"

"It's wonderful," Camille answered. "I'm a little queasy from the drive."

Eveline poured herself more port. "Drink up so I can pour you another glass."

"I can't," Camille said as she finished wiping Andrew's face. "I don't know if it's the heat or the excitement, but it's not agreeing with me today."

Thomas turned and smiled. "The dam could generate enough power to put streetlights on every corner of Austin." Eveline turned her face toward the hills.

Camille shook her head. "I don't understand how a big wall in the middle of a river can generate electricity."

"It's simple," Brooks replied. "The dam will back the river up here into a reservoir lake. In fact, where we sit now will be the bottom of the lake in a year or two." He waved his arm. "See how the land rises behind us? The water from this lake will rush down into an intake valve cut into the wall under the surface. From there it will pulse down a long, thin canal inside the dam until it reaches a gate. It forces the gate open and flows down into a hollow space and powers the turbine down inside to spin.

"What's a turbine?" asked Eveline.

"A turbine is essentially a large windmill lying on its back." Brooks opened another Pabst. "A shaft from the spinning turbine makes the generator turn and create friction at an enormous rate. It stores up this energy in a powerhouse until it amasses into units of power called amperes. And there you have it—electricity is born and sent out to all parts of the city on a network of power lines."

"'The awful shadow of some unseen Power floats though unseen among us,'" Camille whispered.

"What?" Brooks' head spun around. Eveline cast her a sharp glance.

"Shelley," Camille reported as she stood and held Andrew's hands until he pulled himself to his feet.

"We thought we'd hike down and take a look into the great dam hole and see what's going on," Thomas said. "Want to come?"

"No, thank you," Eveline replied.

"I'll stay with Eveline," Camille said. "I'm exhausted from just sitting in the sun today."

Brooks held out his hands for Andrew. "Come on, Sport; let's see if we can get a closer look at that boat."

After the men walked down the hill, Camille took out the cloths and paper sacks she'd brought for cleanup and started gathering the plates. Eveline eyed her wordlessly and began to help. After all the dishes and bowls had been wiped and packed back in the baskets, they sat under their parasols and looked down the hill toward the dam, until they saw Thomas lead the way to the edge of the hole and Brooks, holding Andrew on his back, following close behind. "I thought you might volunteer to drive," Camille said.

"Not today," Eveline replied while tightly wrapping her cobalt blue skirt back up around herself and checking her white linen waist for picnic stains or debris. She folded her hands and looked out across the river.

Camille yawned and lay down on her side as she watched Brooks peer into the massive hole. He was careful to keep Andrew away from the edge, so she closed her eyes. "You're not going to sleep, are you?" Eveline whimpered.

"No," Camille propped herself up on her elbows, "just resting my eyes."

"Oh," Eveline looked down into her lap and her shoulders began to twitch.

Camille sat up and put an arm around her. "What is it, Eveline?"

Eveline pulled a handkerchief from her skirt pocket and patted the corners of her eyes. "When we got home from the parade, Thomas asked me how I'd feel about driving up north of town next week to St. John's Orphanage to talk to someone about adopting a child." New tears appeared on her cheeks.

"Maybe," Camille glanced up at the hills behind Eveline, "maybe it would bring you both a great deal of joy."

"That's easy for you to say," Eveline snapped. "You can bear children. But I can't, and now that Thomas has suggested adoption, I know he really does want to be a father, and unless I agree to adopt, he'll leave me." She buried her face in her knees.

Camille stroked Eveline's hair as she sobbed. "You're overreacting. Thomas loves you madly. He'll never leave you."

Eveline didn't look up. Camille shrugged her shoulders. "If you don't want to raise children, I'm sure he'll understand."

"It's not that." Eveline jerked her head up, and her whole body shook. "I just don't think I could ever love anyone else's child like my own." Her eyes searched Camille's face.

"Perhaps you're selling yourself short," Camille said. "You might surprise yourself if you give it a chance. After all, you love Andrew, don't you?"

"Yes," Eveline stammered, "but that's different."

"How?" Camille asked.

Eveline felt her kerchief for a dry spot as she thought. "I love you and Brooks, so naturally I love your son. But to go somewhere and pick out my own baby like one would go to the Excelsior Market and pick out a Christmas ham, oh Camille, surely even you could never do that."

Camille offered Eveline her own handkerchief and kept her arm around her until the men came up the hill. Eveline dabbed her eyes, put the handkerchiefs in her pocket, and pulled her shoulders back. Brooks set Andrew on the blanket and opened another beer. Camille smiled. "Did you see the generator?"

"It's not in yet, but she's really something." Brooks sat down to catch his breath.

"She?" Camille asked.

"The hole," Brooks arched an eyebrow. "It's a line—at least a hundred yards deep clear across the river—and the well is cored out even deeper for the turbine."

Camille moved a parasol to shade Andrew. "Why is a big hole in the ground a 'she'?"

Brooks' eyes shot toward the sun as he sipped his beer. "Honestly, Camille. It's just an expression."

Andrew crawled into her lap and whimpered. She handed

him his cup, and after a few sips of milk, he curled up for a nap. "I wonder," she mused, "what would be the 'he' in this case—the turbine, the generator? Surely it must be what creates the power."

Brooks twisted his mouth into a face she'd never seen before. "What's gotten into you?"

"Water." Thomas said as he sat down next to Eveline and put a hand on her knee. "Water is the actual source of power, and psychologically speaking, water usually carries a feminine connotation, but in this case . . ." Thomas looked back down the hill. "Considering the function of the dam, the water would symbolize the male fertilizing aspect of the power system."

Brooks turned to eye Thomas. "You're kidding, right?"

"No," Thomas replied. He smiled as Eveline laid her head on his shoulder. "Humans naturally think in gender symbolism. Most languages differentiate all nouns with male and female articles. The fact you called the hole a 'she' instead of a 'he' or an 'it' shows you have subconsciously assigned it a gender."

"Is this another Freudian analysis?" Brooks quipped.

Thomas hesitated as he stared at the horizon. "Now that you mention it, yes," he answered. "Especially if you analyze the biological symbolism."

"You've lost me." Brooks fell backward on the ground and put his hands behind his head. "But," he crossed one leg over the other and bounced a foot in the air before he sat up, "according to Locke, there are two kinds of power."

"Of course," Camille grinned. "Male and female?"

"In a way," he answered. "The example he used is if you put a spoonful of sugar into water, the sugar dissolves because the water has the active power to dissolve the sugar and the

sugar has the passive power to be dissolved. So the two different kinds of power—active and passive—work together in
order to get the job done."

Camille stroked Andrew's hair as he napped on her lap.
"So, let me guess, the active power is male, and the passive
power is female."

"Well, naturally." He glared at her. "One suffragist rally
has certainly had a powerful effect on you."

"It has nothing to do with the rally." Camille arched her
back. "I don't understand why everything has to be so black
and white for you."

"It's not," Brooks protested. "But before you take offense
for the sake of your gender, as Thomas says, consider the biological implications. Think about it—if the sugar did not have
the passive power to be acted upon, the water could not
actively dissolve it. Both powers are essential."

Camille shook her head and looked at her child in her
lap. "I can't settle for passive power," she said.

Eveline lifted her head. "What time is it?" she asked.

Brooks took out his watch. "Four forty-five."

"Maybe we should start back." Eveline stretched her arms
over her head. "I'd like to get freshened up before we make
ice cream and shoot fireworks."

The men loaded the car, and they started for home.
Camille took another look down into the darkness of the
massive pit as Brooks drove by the dam line. The bittersweet
taste of the port stung on the back of her tongue. Her arms
sweated under Andrew's weight as he slept, and she struggled
to reposition him without waking him. As they rode silently
back through the trees, Eveline grinned at Camille when
they heard Thomas snore softly from the front seat. Camille
watched the oak and cedar trees pass in front of the amethyst-
blue river, golden-gilt in the late afternoon sun. As they rode

down the hills toward town, she spied a familiar thicket of brush. "Brooks, stop!" she cried.

Brooks slowed and wheeled around. "What's the matter?"

"I saw a bramble of blackberries back there." She pointed.

Brooks narrowed his glare. "Blackberries? You want to stop and pick blackberries?"

"Yes," Camille sighed. "I haven't seen any blackberries in the markets or in the wilds since I left Seattle."

"We're all tired." Brooks nodded toward Thomas, curled against the door sleeping. "Is this wave of nostalgia really that important?"

"I suppose not," Camille said as Brooks glanced skyward and pushed the high gear pedal. "I was just thinking," Camille continued, "how good a blackberry streusel pie would be with home-cranked ice cream."

Brooks pulled the brake. The car lurched. Andrew awoke with a piercing scream, and Thomas' head hit the door. Brooks put the car in reverse. "Do you have anything to put them in?" he asked.

Camille thought quickly as she soothed Andrew and leaned forward to see if Thomas was all right. "I have a couple of brown paper bags." She showed Brooks where to stop and set Andrew on the seat beside her. She took Andrew's cup out of her bag and found the paper sacks. Brooks pulled the brake and turned to watch her as she started out of the car. "If you were to help, it would take half the time," she remarked. Thomas stopped rubbing his head and sprang out of the car. Brooks looked back at Eveline.

"I'll sit here with Andrew," Eveline said as she smoothed her skirt over her knees and took him into her lap. Brooks turned the engine off and followed Camille and Thomas into the brambles.

The bushes were dense, but the berries were huge and perfectly ripe. "These are dewberries," Thomas said as he stepped into the middle of the cluster and started harvesting.

Camille rolled up the sleeves of the sailor blouse she had made and reached into the brush carefully to keep from staining her navy skirt. "I've probably picked over a million blackberries in my life and made everything out of them from jam, to pie, to blackberry and bee balm tea, and I assure you, these are blackberries."

"That may be true," Thomas winked, "but in Boston, this is what we call a dewberry." They filled two bags with the fruit in less than fifteen minutes and hurried back to the car. Andrew had fallen back to sleep with his head on Eveline's lap. Thomas ran around front to crank the engine, and they rode back through the hill country toward West Avenue as the sun flattened behind them.

Camille held up a fat berry to show Eveline. "Thomas says these are called dewberries in Boston."

Eveline nodded. "I think it's an Old English word. Shakespeare used the term in one of his sonnets."

Camille turned the berry over in her hand. "That's interesting," she mused. "Whoever named them probably saw them for the first time shining in morning dew."

"Or thought they were plumped up with dew," Eveline said and shrugged her shoulders. "Who knows?"

When they got home, Camille put a pound of butter in a tub of ice and checked to make sure she had all the ingredients for her pie. While Thomas and Eveline went to their house to wash up, she gave Andrew a quick sponge bath by the kitchen sink and set out the custard and rock salt for the ice cream. Brooks came in from the garage with a box of fireworks and a red, white, and blue pinwheel for Andrew. He spent ten minutes showing Andrew how to blow on it, until he got a headache, and finally took him out to the front porch to hold it in the evening breeze while they waited for the Leightons to return. Camille set the men to churning the ice cream on the front porch, while she cut the cold butter into flour with two knives. Eveline washed and dried the blackberries, sprinkled them with sugar and grated lemon rind, and heated them with sour cream as per Camille's specifications. Camille deftly molded the crust into a pie plate, and Eveline poured in the filling. While Camille cut the streusel topping, Eveline made coffee and went out to check on the ice cream and help Andrew find the right wind angle with his pinwheel.

By the time the sun had completely set behind the house, they sat on the front steps savoring their dessert and coffee and watching fireworks fill the sky. After their second helpings, Brooks and Thomas popped a black cat or two. Camille ran in to rummage through the coat closet for Andrew's earmuffs before they fired up several more. Camille's stomach soured as they started in on the bottle rockets. Her temples flashed hot as she watched a flare shoot up into the black night, and her head felt suddenly light. "Eveline, please," she wailed, "take Andrew." As the plume of light opened up into a fountain of red and silver spangles, gray clouds swirled over them. Camille closed her eyes to clear her vision and fell into the black.

23. Dewberries

July 5, 1912
Dear Mother,

I'm ten weeks pregnant. This one is so different from the first. I suffer with more nausea than I did with Andrew, and I have weak spells. Brooks called the doctor over last night after I fainted on the front steps. Eveline brought me to with smelling salts, and when Dr. Steiger got here, he ordered me straight to bed and told me to stay here for a week. Brooks had to go into his office today, but before he went, he drove to the drug store to pick up prescriptions for the dizziness and nausea even though I assured him I wouldn't take them. I tried to explain to him how much more effective and safe a few ginger infusions would be, but he said I was not allowed out of bed and he was not about to make them for me. He scolded me for thinking I could know what I needed better than a trained medical professional. Coral is here. I know she would do it if I asked, but I also know she is half scared of Brooks, and I don't want to put her in the middle. I'll call Eveline and ask her to bake some of her wonderful gingerbread. A slice of it each day should do the trick.

I'm excited about the baby. I know it will be difficult with Andrew still toddling about the house at the speed of sound, but I'm glad my children will be close in age. I'm sure you remember how I yearned for a brother or sister when I was growing up. I hope my children will be lifelong companions. Wouldn't it be delicious if this one were a girl? Perhaps that's a wicked thing to write; I couldn't have experienced more joy with any child than I have with Andrew, so another little boy would surely be a blessing. I've had a girl's name picked out since before Andrew was born, but I can't tell you what it is yet because I'm afraid I'll jinx it. I'd have to think about a boy's name. Brooks and I agonized over finding the right name for Andrew, and if there's one thing I've learned for sure, the right name is crucial.

For instance, yesterday Brooks and I took Andrew on a picnic with Eveline and Thomas, and on the way home, I found a bramble of blackberries. As we picked some for pie, Thomas said in Boston they call them "dewberries." Then, when Coral got here this morning and brought a dish up with my breakfast, she referred to them as "gooseberries." I told her they were blackberries, and she assured me in Kentucky she had never heard them called anything but gooseberries.

I began to wonder if Shakespeare was right. Would a rose smell as sweet as a rose were it not called a rose? Would a blackberry taste as sweet as a blackberry were it called a dewberry or a gooseberry? So, I decided to conduct my own blackberry experiment. I closed my eyes, cleared my mind as well as I could, and recited the word "dewberry" a hundred times before I popped one in my mouth, and I kept repeating the word in my mind as I ate it. It tasted like wet grass. Then I did the same thing with the "gooseberry." It tasted like damp earth but tingled on the sides of my tongue, and believe it or not, my arms broke out in goose pimples. Of course, I repeated the process reciting the word "blackberry." It tasted more like I thought a black-berry should, but more bittersweet than sweet. And as I swallowed the last tiny seed, I experienced a strange flash of visions that includ-ed the seats in Jewel's new car, a grackle that scolded me in my back-yard last month, my friend Morgan's eyes, the feel of the sun on my shoulders, and the sting of the brush on my ankles as we gathered berries in the meadow down the lane. I was shocked that these images passed through my mind before I remembered the pies and

*cobblers we used to bake and the jams we put up every summer—
for these are the blackberry memories dearest to my heart and the
ones that prompted me to ask Brooks to stop the car in the first place.
How complex this bumpy little black and purple bubble of juice is in
my mind. The power of granting a name is a tremendous responsibility.*

*I almost forgot to tell you, I attended my first suffragist rally last
week. The mayor of the city of Austin spoke. He's quite popular with
the citizens, for he's setting up systems of parks, sewage, and electric
power, and he wholeheartedly supports women's rights to vote and
participate in civic improvements and policy-making. Or rather I
should say he supports white women's rights. When questioned by
someone in the crowd about Negroes' rights to vote—I don't remember his exact words—but he was adamant about the fact Negroes
should not expect to hold the same civic rights as whites for their good
as well as ours. I thought about Coral crying on the divan as she lost
her child because the hospital would not send an ambulance for a colored woman, and I could not follow his line of reasoning.*

*Love—like an arrow
that pierces through all other powers,
Your Camille*

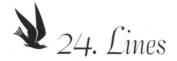# 24. Lines

Brooks took his typewriter back to his office in late July so he could write in between his frequent meetings and preparations for the fall semester. Every Monday morning, Eveline baked fresh gingerbread and brought a pan over to Camille right after Brooks and Thomas left for work. Camille kept the medicine Dr. Steiger prescribed in a pitcher on the top shelf of a kitchen cupboard and went about her daily gardening, cooking, and chasing Andrew around the house.

Coral came over one Thursday morning, washed the floors, dusted the furniture, and started squeezing lemons before she told Camille her news. "I don't think I can work for you after next month."

Camille looked up from the herbal wreath she was making at the kitchen table. "Is it Brooks?"

"Oh, no, ma'am." Coral shook her head. "The Wheatville Bar is going out of business, so Samuel has been looking around and was offered a tending job at Charles Maroney's saloon on the east side of town. We talked about it for a long time last night, and we decided to move out that way so Samuel can go to school while he works. But he won't be able to use his boss's wagon any more, so I don't see how I could get across town every day."

"I didn't know Samuel wanted to go to school. Maybe Brooks could . . ." Camille caught the baleful look in Coral's glance as she measured the sugar. She snipped the ends off a handful of lavender at a slant and worked the stems into her arrangement. "Of course," she sighed. "Where will he go?"

"He's going to apply to Tillotson College," Coral answered. "They have a degree for teachers, and he's always wanted to teach high school history."

"Samuel will make a fine history teacher." Camille surveyed the dried flowers strewn across the table. Coral set a glass of lemonade and a slice of gingerbread next to her. "I seem to have left my dried Kathryn Morley's upstairs," Camille said as she pushed her chair back.

"I'll get them." Coral started up the stairs. Camille shaped stems of lamb's ears under the lavender and trimmed shoots of tansy until Coral brought down the delicate pink dried rosebuds. Coral examined the wreath. "It's beautiful," she commented. "I like the colors."

"It's for Eveline," Camille explained, "to thank her for all the gingerbread."

Coral nodded. "How's her herb garden coming along?"

Camille worked lamb's ears behind a rosebud. "She said her cuttings died out despite her best efforts, but between you and me," she lowered her voice, "I don't think she could tend them without occasionally getting her hands in the soil and her apron smudged, so she gave up."

Coral grinned. "Do you want me to start lunch?"

"I don't think so," Camille answered. "I'll make sandwiches when I'm through. But if you would slice and bake the lavender shortbreads, I would be grateful. I want to take them to Jewel's meeting tonight, and this project is taking longer than I had thought." Coral found the cookie rolls in the icebox, while Camille worked the Queen Anne's lace in. "Why did Samuel's boss decide to close the Wheatville Bar?" she asked.

"He didn't," Coral replied as she lit the stove. "The city

passed an ordinance that made it impossible for him to keep it."

"What kind of an ordinance?" Camille asked.

"I don't know exactly. Something about zoning, but Samuel said it's because it's so close to Hyde Park. When those homes were sold, they told people it would be a totally white neighborhood. And now that it's spreading up toward the university, it runs right up next to the bar. I guess the houses in that part are harder to sell because of it."

Camille wiped her hands, sipped her lemonade, and stared out the window. "That doesn't sound fair."

Coral sliced the cookie dough into thin rounds and spaced them on the cookie sheet. "It isn't. But after a while, you realize there's not much you can do about it, so you just go with it. The owner said he was too old to start over, so he's going to retire a little earlier than he had planned."

Camille sighed and went back to her work. "Well, I guess it's time I learned to drive."

"You're going to learn to drive?" Coral cried.

Camille smiled. "If it's the only way I can get you over here during the day, then I suppose I'll have to." Coral's face lit up as she stooped to help Andrew push his cars through a cracker canister tunnel.

Eveline phoned to say she'd be over at six forty-five and to ask Camille to watch for her so they wouldn't have to crank the engine again. Coral had the cookies baked, made dinner, and left before Brooks got home. Camille caught him before he came in from the porch. "Watch your shoes; Coral mopped today."

Brooks wiped his feet on the mat. "What's for dinner?"

"Lamb chops," Camille answered. "They're in the warming oven; help yourself." She bounded up the stairs.

"Good. Where's Andrew?" he called after her.

"He's taking a nap. You'll have to get him up soon or he won't go down for you this evening," she called back. She dressed in an ivory lace waist with her navy linen skirt, pulled her hair up into a twist, and adorned it with some of the left-over dried Queen Anne's lace and a fresh Gallica rose.

As she came down the stairs, Brooks stood on the landing picking his teeth with a scowl on his face. "I forgot you were going out tonight."

"Have you made plans?" she asked. "Maybe Coral could . . ."

"No, it's all right. Do I have time to wash up before you leave?"

"Eveline said she'd be here at six forty-five," she said.

Brooks pulled his watch out of his pocket and nodded. He started up the stairs and stopped. "Are you walking?"

"Of course not; it's at least a mile away, and we're wearing heels." Camille pointed to her shoes before she rechecked her hair in the hall mirror.

"So, you're going on a streetcar."

"No, we're going in Thomas' car." She turned around. "And you'd better hurry, because I promised her I'd be in the front and ready to go on time."

Brooks stepped back down the stairs. "Thomas didn't say anything about driving you two to your meeting."

"He isn't." Camille repressed a grin. "Eveline is."

He grabbed the newel post. "Thomas taught Eveline to drive?"

"Actually, Jewel did."

"I knew that woman was trouble," he groaned.

Camille started for the kitchen. "But Thomas has encouraged her and ridden with her several times. I'm going to learn, too. Do you want to teach me, or shall I learn from Jewel or Eveline?"

He followed her. "What on earth do you need to learn to drive for?"

"I have a hundred good reasons," Camille replied as she got his plate from the table and carried it to the sink. "I've all sorts of errands to run."

"The streetcar goes straight into town," Brooks argued.

Camille wheeled around. "Yes, but it's two streets over, which with one small child seems like two miles and with another baby will be impossible." She paused to search Brooks' face. "And Coral's moving across town. Samuel's changing jobs and won't be able to bring her over in the wagon."

"Coral can ride the streetcar," he fumed.

"She won't, and you know it." Camille stamped a foot.

"Then we'll find another maid." Brooks unbuttoned his shirt and stretched his neck.

"I don't want another maid," Camille wailed. "I want Coral. She knows what I need even before I say anything, and Andrew will never take to anyone else like he has to her."

Brooks paced the floor. "Did you know the police have the power to arrest agitators who dissuade colored people from riding the streetcars? If you were to drive out to east Austin to pick up our domestic help, I could be fined." He stopped and glared at her. "Besides, Camille, how could you pick her up without a car?"

"I'll get up early and take the Cadillac," she answered as she arranged the cookies on a plate. "You'll be here with Andrew, and I'll be back in plenty of time for you to get to work."

He pinched the bridge of his nose. "You're being unreasonable, and I don't have time for such a ridiculous discussion. I'm going to get cleaned up."

Eveline parked behind a line of other cars at the corner of Rio Grande and Bois d'Arc. The Victorian Tudor style mansion with a wraparound porch was situated on half a city block. "It looks like a damned castle," Eveline whispered as she pulled the brake.

Camille scanned the gabled roof with its variegated tiles, the high arched windows, round tower corners, and intricate ironwork. "Did you expect anything less?"

"I suppose not," Eveline sighed. "Who would guess that crazy old coot could make more money than anyone else in town?"

Jewel greeted them at the door in a red and white ruffled shirt, a navy blue skirt, and a trim navy blue riding hat with a red plume and a pheasant feather. She cradled a Scottish terrier on one arm and stroked its back with another. "Welcome, welcome girls," she called. "I'm so glad the professors' wives could make it this evening. She gratefully accepted Camille's lavender shortbreads and Eveline's cheese wafers, calling one of the waiters to take them and giving strict instructions on their placement on the hostess tables.

"Your home," Eveline exclaimed as she turned a full circle in the reception hall, "it's incredible."

"You're too kind," Jewel pursed her lips. "While Ida has everything under control in the back, I can give you a quick tour if you like."

They nodded while she whisked them into the sitting room with plum-colored striped wallpaper and apricot satin couches. In the corner round stood an ivory grand piano draped with a purple and gold floral silk shawl and covered with portraits. "This is my daughter, Esmerelda." She stopped to finger the frame. "She and her husband and two daughters live in Manhattan. And this," she picked up a portrait of a young man in a black suit, "this is our son, Stewart. He's a banker in St. Louis when he's not a rancher in Montana, if you know what I mean." She threw her eyes at them and chuckled. She led them upstairs to see her bedrooms—each designed in a different cultural theme with treasures they had sent back from different places they had visited. One guestroom was adorned in an African bush theme with a zebra-striped bedspread, cheetah-skinned pillows, jaguar chairs, and glass tables with elephant tusks for legs. Another was done in the spirit of the Japanese kabuki theater with coral and jade silk linens, gilded paper parasols hanging from the ceiling, and a midnight-blue and silver kabuki gown hanging framed on the wall. Her daughter's room was decorated in French provincial style with white Louis XIV furnishings, fleur-de-lis imprinted wallpaper, French blue trimmings, and a painting by Renoir. Jewel's son's room had tanned leather wall coverings and a cowhide canopy. "He's always been a cowboy at heart," Jewel exhaled deeply as she closed the double doors and showed them to her own room, painted in a glossy shade of tomato and furnished in English oak. On the far wall stood a massive Elizabethan four poster bed lavished with olive and ivory satin linens and accented with two Gainsborough portraits and a landscape of the English countryside.

Before they were through examining the intricate woodwork on the bedposts, Jewel ushered them up a small spiral staircase to a turret room on a third story. "You must take a peek at Renfrow's rock room," she wheezed as she took the final step.

They moved into a dark room lined with lighted shelves. "I'd turn on the overhead light," she stopped to catch her breath, "but they show better without it." Camille and

Eveline walked the perimeter of the room, taking in the stunning beauty of the rocks, gems, and minerals Renfrow had collected from all corners of the world. Jewel explained how she had sorted and strategically placed each one according to its geological classification and geographical origin, and she expounded on the rigors of perfecting lighting to show off their various natural characteristics. Camille longed to stay a little longer and look into the amethyst geodes, but Jewel motioned toward the stairway. "Now let's take a quick look at my collection," she said.

They followed her down to the first story and into the back of the manse to a formal dining room papered in a dark green fern-frond relief. Jewel led them around the huge mahogany dining table with a scrolling candelabra centerpiece to a lighted china cabinet that spanned the west wall of the room. "Here is my salt and pepper shaker collection," she announced as the dog on her arm let out a short bark. "Yes, yes, dear," Jewel rubbed his head, "we know how much you like mama's salt and pepper collection. It all started after we visited Buckingham Palace in London," she explained. "At a china shop around the corner, I found this pair in Royal Doulton." She pointed to the miniature likenesses of Queen Victoria and Prince Albert with intricately handpainted accoutrements and gilt detail.

"They're stunning!" Eveline exclaimed. "Do you use them?"

"Interesting you should inquire." Jewel held up her lorgnette and smiled as she leaned in to admire them. "This is the only set we use at all, and only on rare occasions when Renfrow and I get the doldrums and need a little cheering up. Then I order in a beef Wellington and uncork a bottle of rare red wine, and I dust off the little queen and her prince and set them between us on the table. We reminisce about our summer in London and usually end up planning our next trip." She turned and grinned. "Our miniature royalties were invited out last week, and this spring, we are going to Peru." Jewel pointed out the German silver-plated shakers and the Chinese gold porcelains when her dog barked again. "Of course, McAllister," she crooned. "Here are our salt and pepper Scotty dogs." A bell sounded from the hall, and Jewel excused herself to answer the door.

Camille and Eveline inspected the hundreds of salt and pepper sets Jewel had amassed from all parts of the globe. She had arranged them in groupings of contrasting color, size, and style, and had orchestrated the lighting with as much care as Renfrow's geological display. Eveline fell in love with an English floral bone china set, and Camille pointed out the cast-iron engine and caboose. They laughed over Mr. and Mrs. Santa Claus and Little Boy Blue and Bo-Peep. "Do you think those paintings are originals?" Eveline whispered as Camille pointed to a set of Sealtest milk bottles in a green porcelain base.

"I don't know." Camille pulled her hand back. "Surely not. Do you think they could be?"

Eveline shook her head. "It wouldn't surprise me."

Jewel breezed by the dining room, ushering guests through the hall. She set the dog down on an easy chair, where it curled up into a ball and closed its eyes. "We're in the back, girls. Come on out and try some wine from the Rhineland." Camille and Eveline followed them out to the backyard, where chairs had been set up in the grass facing a makeshift dais under a canopy of established oaks hung with hundreds of lighted red and gold paper lanterns. As they found seats, waiters bustled by with trays of white wine, Danish cheeses, and strawberries tipped with Belgian chocolate.

"This is more fun than a wedding," Eveline remarked as Camille asked the waiter for a glass of punch.

Maribel and Edna arrived together. "I'm so glad you came," Camille said as they exchanged informal hugs and took adjacent seats.

"We were afraid not to," Edna giggled. "Milton and Charles said Jewel came by the faculty offices three times last week to be sure they reminded us of the importance of our civic sorority and our duty as women of the capitol city of Texas to bear the standard of suffrage for the state."

"In other words," Maribel forced a grin, "be here, or our husbands would suffer interminably in the future."

"Since the time he arrived home yesterday evening," Edna cupped a hand to her cheek, "Milton has practically been begging me to come."

"Jewel can be persuasive." Eveline waved to Faye Rittenhauer sitting across the lawn. "Who's she sitting with?" she asked as she turned.

"I don't know any of those women," Edna said. "I'm surprised Alicia isn't with her."

A deafening trill pierced the air, drawing everyone's attention to the dais where Jewel dropped a police whistle to dangle by a cord around her neck. She nodded to Ida Plimpton, who, after taking her fingers out of her ears, called the meeting to order. The minutes from the last meeting were read, various items of old business discussed, and Jewel passed around the petition for anyone who had missed signing it at the rally. Many of the seated women were yawning and staring into space by the time Mrs. Plimpton introduced the guest lecturer.

Leida Winn took over the dais and waited for the applause to die down before she started her speech. "As you know, the struggle for equal enfranchisement for women in the South has its own distinct character. In Georgia, we've learned the hard way how important it is to separate certain issues in order to move forward. First of all, we must resist the temptation to collate the temperance movement with our demands for suffrage." She paused as some women in the crowd mumbled.

Jewel stepped forward and held up her hands. "Now, listen, please. As a relatively young coalition, we have much to learn from our sisters who have been campaigning for several years."

Mrs. Winn nodded her thanks. "I know how you feel about drunken revelry and carousing," she continued, "but as one of our founding mothers, Elizabeth Cady Stanton, so shrewdly noted, when abolition is associated with suffrage, women tend to lose suffrage elections because men are convinced that if women vote, the saloons will dry up."

Maribel inched her gloved hand into the air. When Mrs. Winn recognized her, she stood up and drew her shoulders in. "But, in the Good Book, the Lord himself warns against drunkenness."

Jewel tossed her eyes up into the trees and rushed forward. "God of my mother's ghost!" she exclaimed as Maribel's face went white. "Jesus changed water into wine and referred to himself as a wineskin."

"That, that was because . . ." Maribel stammered.

Jewel went on, "And you and I have shared more than one glass on more than one occasion."

"It's not that I'm against a social drink," Maribel's eyes went wild, "it's the other problem of depravity it tends to lead to in this town."

"Oh, that!" Jewel beamed as Mrs. Winn placed her elbow on the lectern to support her chin. "I don't think you're going to have to worry about that much longer. You see, at our luncheon with the mayor and his wife last week, the other officers and I had an interesting discussion about *those* drinking establishments, and while it's too early to celebrate, I think we'll be seeing some drastic changes in the months to come."

Maribel's face bloomed into a pink flush as she nodded and sat down. The women applauded the news, and Jewel left the dais back to Mrs. Winn. "Very well, then." Leida straightened herself and delivered her second line of contention. "It's also vital to our cause that we separate the issue of women's suffrage from that of Negro suffrage." An eerie hush fell over the congregation. "It's a national disgrace," Leida raised a fist, "that the Fifteenth Amendment rendered such an injustice to the refined white women of America in making them political inferiors to former slaves. Since the rights issued to the states in the Fourteenth Amendment allowed for Negroes' disenfranchisement in the South, many female suffragists have chosen to take up their cause for full re-enfranchisement." Mrs. Winn scanned her audience. "As brave and loyal as this may seem, it is detrimental to our cause. The stability of the government depends on the rule of the intelligent portion of the population, so decreasing the political power of unfit groups will increase our own." She raised her voice over those who had started to applaud her words. "Our cause cannot support theirs." She gratefully took a sip of the water offered by Jewel while the fifty or more women in attendance thundered their appreciation.

"Do you think it matters that they were former slaves?" Camille whispered to Eveline.

"Of course," Eveline replied as she clapped. "Doesn't it bother you that colored men were awarded the vote before us?"

One of the women sitting with Faye stood and waved a

fist in the air. "Amen!" she cheered. "And imagine how hard it will be to control our domestic help if they have the same political rights as we do."

Camille watched the woman sit down with satisfaction as the other women rallied behind her. Faye's smug face started her stomach turning. "It bothers me on both accounts," she whispered to Eveline. "After all, didn't white men bring the Negroes here and force slavery upon them in the first place?"

Leida Winn motioned for silence unsuccessfully, so Jewel gave her whistle another toot. "Statistics have proven," Leida cast Jewel a pained glance, "there are more white women in the South than Negro men and women combined. Thus, the enfranchisement of women would greatly increase the white majority in the electorate and insure white supremacy."

Camille's hands felt clammy as she clapped. Edna leaned over Eveline to address her. "Listen, Camille, I don't like the idea of racial supremacy any more than you do, but think of it this way. If we win the vote, we can use it to further their cause if we so choose. Since one will not pass with the other, separating the issues is the only way to move forward on either front."

When Mrs. Winn finished her lecture, Ida called for new business. Their voices faded and seemed to float up over the trees. Camille lowered her head and missed the whole discussion. Eveline put a hand on Camille's forehead. "You're breaking a sweat," she said. "Are you dizzy? Look at me! Camille?"

"A little," Camille replied as she looked up and tried to focus on Eveline's eyes.

Eveline shot out of her chair. "Help me," she shouted, "she's going to faint."

Edna and Maribel each took one of Camille's arms while Jewel flew down the aisle pulling her fan from her pocket.

"Hold on, dear," she yelped as she furiously fanned Camille's face. Camille's eyelids grew heavy and Eveline's face darkened over. "Quick," Jewel looked around for a waiter. "Some water over here! What's wrong with her?" she wailed.

"She's pregnant," Eveline cried as she loosened the top buttons of Camille's blouse and cradled her head until the waiter hurried over and handed her a glass of water. Camille took a sip and her eyelashes fluttered.

"Let's get her inside," Jewel ordered. Edna, Maribel, and Jewel supported Camille as she stumbled to the couch in the parlor. When she was fully revived, they all delighted in bringing her punch and plates of sweets and fruits while Jewel professed her congratulations and joy. After most of the women had left, Jewel helped Eveline guide Camille out to the car, gave it a hearty crank, and waved until they were well down the road.

"Can you believe Maribel had the nerve to interrupt the lecture and give us a sermon on what Jesus said about drinking?" Eveline asked as she drove north on Rio Grande Street.

Camille watched the moon tower on the corner of the Bremond block flicker through the oaks. "Actually," she replied, "I admired her for finding the courage to make a stand for what she felt was right and true."

25. Sons

February 3, 1913
Dear Tess,

As you see, I followed your lead and sent out announcements this time. Alexander is a beautiful baby—much fairer than Andrew and a full pound heavier in birth weight. Though it's only been sixteen months since Andrew was born, I'd forgotten just how small an infant feels in my arms and how heavy my heart beats in my breast when I look at him. My mother is coming down from Seattle to see her grandsons and help me while I regain my strength. I haven't seen her since we came to Austin over two years ago, and I'm beside myself with joy.

This pregnancy was difficult. I spent most of the first six months in bed, as I had severe nausea and fainting spells. Every morning Brooks measured my medicine and watched as I took it before he went to work. I would not have survived without my housekeeper. I was afraid I was going to lose her when she and her husband moved across town, and I was in no shape to drive so far and pick her up. But the Negroes in east Austin organized a hack service so they wouldn't have to subject themselves to the humility of riding backward in the rear seats on the streetcar. I'm delighted to pay the fare. A runner brings her over every morning. She takes sweet care of Andrew, keeps the house sparkling clean, and cooks all our meals. Then in late afternoon, a runner comes back and she climbs up in the back of the hack and rides through town to her house. When

Alexander is a little older, I'll drive her back and forth in the Cadillac.

Brooks scolds me for having allowed myself to grow so fond of our maid, but she has been such a blessing to me in so many ways. When I came to Austin, I was shocked to find the Jim Crow laws still in effect. I thought this was the only city in the world that time forgot, but I discovered this seems to be the standard throughout the South. Here they are also not allowed to vote in spite of the Fourteenth Amendment. Is this true in Houma? I wonder about New Orleans—do you know? I learned this is the case in Georgia, because a guest speaker at one of our suffrage meetings last summer said it was of utmost importance to separate the issues of women's suffrage from that of the Negroes' suffrage in order to maintain white supremacy. I was so outraged I stood right up and declared to everyone that human beings are human beings. I made a lot of women mad, but I didn't care. Then I said that justice is justice, and to draw a line through it at any angle would make it into an injustice. It's the last meeting I attended before the doctor ordered me to bed to stay, and since I've had plenty of time to contemplate the issues, I've decided not to abandon the cause for full enfranchisement of Texas women. As a friend of mine pointed out, if women win the vote, we can better help change the status of those who still can't. When Alexander is old enough to be away from me for a few hours, I plan to attend all the suffrage rallies and meetings and even do weekly rounds campaigning from door to door with another one of my friends, Jewel, who is also the chapter vice president. Still, I won't relent on my position that all adult citizens are entitled to full suffrage regardless of race or gender, and I'll not hesitate to exercise my opinion until I win the other girls over. I've promised myself I'll raise my sons to respect women as well as men and to treat Negroes and Outsiders the same way they treat their white friends.

I intended to write a friendly note and not a political statement! I'll stop myself here to say how much I enjoyed receiving your Christmas greeting and send my hopes that you and Carl and all three of your daughters are in good health and spirits.

Best Wishes,
Camille Abernathy

26. The Trolley

The University of Texas faculty held its year-end picnic at Deep Eddy Recreation Area on the Colorado River. Camille was reluctant to take four-month-old Alexander out in the mid-May sun, but Brooks insisted they make an appearance and promised they would only stay for an hour or two. Camille nursed Alexander before they left and tried on her bathing suit. It lay uncomfortably snug across her bust and still swollen belly, and with one glance in the mirror, she moaned and searched through the wardrobe for a soft cotton sundress.

They arrived in the middle of the afternoon, after the festivities were well underway. Dean Merriweather greeted them and directed them to the buffet, where they made plates of barbeque brisket, pinto beans, and banana pudding. Brooks found Thomas and Eveline and lay a blanket on the ground next to theirs beneath a canopy of oaks. They ate as they watched bathers take turns splashing into the water from a giant slide. Most of the faculty members and their spouses stood lined up on the stairs waiting to take their turn on a platform built at least thirty feet high. "Look!" Brooks pointed as two women in black swim skirts soared out over the river screaming. He laughed as they both let go of the overhead cable at the same time and smacked the surface of the river, splashing water high into the air.

Andrew jumped up and down, clapping his hands as the men on the platform pulled on the trolley wires to bring the cable handles back. "That's too deep for you," Camille told him as she turned to Brooks. "Could you take him on the slide?"

Brooks watched the bathers sliding into the water on the other side of the trolley platform. "It looks pretty deep; I don't think I could keep him from going under. I'll take him for a splash over here where it's shallower as soon as I finish my beer." Thomas and Eveline left to try the trolley line as Brooks finished his Pabst and walked Andrew down the grassy slope to play in the water. One by one, all the professors came over to admire the new baby as he slept in his carriage. Camille spent the next half hour smiling as acquaintances peeked under the carriage hood, cooing and gurgling how adorable he was. She taxed herself thinking up various small talk topics and watching Andrew out of the corner of her eye. When Andrew grew hot and tired, Brooks brought him back. "I'm going to get another Blue Ribbon," he announced. "Do you want anything?"

"Maybe some more lemonade for Andrew," she replied as she toweled her son down and settled him next to her in the shade. Eveline and Thomas finally reached the front of the line for the trolley run. Camille smiled as Eveline turned back toward the ladder. Thomas put an arm around her and led her back to the edge of the platform. Camille pointed them out to Andrew, who grunted a belly laugh. They each took hold of a handle and swung out on the line over the shimmering turquoise river.

Eveline curled herself up under Thomas' free arm until he yelled, "Let go!" They dropped twenty feet into the middle of the river. Andrew watched closely until their heads popped up between the waves they had made, and he started chuckling again. Camille stroked his dark hair as Thomas and Eveline hurried up the slope for their towels.

"What are you giggling about?" Thomas tickled Andrew.

"He watched your maiden flight," Camille replied. "He can't stop laughing. Was it fun?"

"It was terrifying!" Eveline moaned as she unfolded her towel and dried herself off. "I'll never let him talk me into anything like that again."

Brooks returned with the drinks, and Thomas hurried him off for a turn on the trolley line. Eveline wrapped her towel around herself, sat down, and winced as she caught sight of Alicia Merriweather trouncing over. "I've heard how precious your son is," Alicia giggled. "I had to see for myself." She peered into the carriage at the sleeping baby and plopped herself down on the blanket. "I can't wait to have a baby," she exclaimed, "but Oscar wants to wait another year or so."

Eveline turned her face away as she combed out her hair.

"Why?" Camille stopped and shook her head. "Forgive me for being so impolite. Of course it's none of my business."

"It's all right," Alicia sighed and giggled. "He says he wants to wait until his workload slows down so he can enjoy the baby." Her face fell as she watched a couple soar out on the trolley line and laugh wildly as they fell into the river. "I've been waiting seven years now." Camille had exhausted her ability to conjure up appropriate things to say, so she watched a lacy cloud float over the trees on the far shore. "Let's take a turn on the slide," Alicia suggested.

"Not me," Eveline groaned. "Thomas did me in on the trolley line."

Camille shrugged her shoulders. "I didn't even bring a suit. I knew I would be too busy with the boys to swim."

"Swim," Andrew repeated and pointed to the slide.

"It's too big for you," Camille said. "When Daddy gets back, he'll take you swimming again."

Oscar Merriweather walked over and handed Alicia a beer. "Would you ladies like a beer?" he asked as he eyed Camille and Eveline. When they refused, Alicia urged him to join them, so he nodded and took a seat.

"Swim," Andrew said.

"In a minute," Camille replied. "Let's watch Daddy jump into the river." They waited until Brooks and Thomas took their turn on the trolley and swam to shore.

"That was invigorating!" Brooks called as he came up the hill and sat on a towel next to Oscar. Thomas winked at Eveline and opened a Pabst.

"Andrew would like to get wet again," Camille told Brooks.

"Sure," he answered. "Give me just a minute to catch my breath." The men drank their beers and discussed different theories about Renfrow Kimbrough's latest wildcatting consultation.

"Where are Jewel and Renfrow?" Eveline looked around.

"Somewhere in South America," Oscar replied.

"And what about Professor Jones and his wife?" Camille asked. "I was hoping Morgan would be here. I haven't seen her since my dinner party last year."

"Jones would never bring her to a social gathering where men and women bare their ankles," Brooks sneered and shot up the hill for another beer.

Andrew watched him leave and started to cry. "Here, Andrew," Thomas held out his arms, "let's you and I go down and take a dip." Andrew smiled and let Thomas carry him down to the water.

"I want to try the slide," Alicia whined.

"I need a rest," Oscar replied. Eveline stood with a weak smile and followed Thomas down the hill. "Come on, Oscar, just one slide," Alicia coaxed.

"You go ahead." He tapped her knee. "I'll sit here until Brooks gets back." Faye Rittenhauer surprised them from behind.

"Where have you been?" Alicia squealed and giggled.

"We just got here," she answered. "Adolph kept saying he didn't want to come, but changed his mind at the last minute."

"Where is Adolph?" Oscar asked.

"Brooks commandeered him to the trolley line," she answered as she nodded toward the platform. Camille shielded her eyes against the late afternoon sun and found Brooks standing in line with his Pabst, laughing with the other bathers on the stairs. Alicia and Faye went to the slide while Camille and Oscar watched Thomas swing Andrew around, making motorboat sounds near the bank.

Oscar propped himself on an elbow. "You're a rich woman." He looked at Camille.

"What do you mean?" Camille drew her dress closer around her as she felt her cheeks flush.

"Your sons," Oscar continued. "So handsome and healthy." He exhaled deeply, and Camille momentarily felt herself sitting in her father's lap on the streetcar in Seattle. "I long to have sons," he sighed as he turned his gaze to the sky. "And a daughter or two, of course."

"Then I'm sure you will," Camille remarked. "When the time is right."

"Oh, the time is right," he replied with a quick look toward the slide, "just not the circumstances."

Camille looked for Brooks on the platform. He and Adolph had reached the front of the line, where the bathers were joking and laughing so loud that their voices carried across the water. Adolph grabbed the trolley handle and lost his footing as Brooks was reaching for it. He flew out over the water alone and plopped into the lake like a terrible dead fish. The bathers roared with laughter while Camille held her breath until he came up and rolled onto his back to float to shore. Brooks helped reel the cable board back in with the hand that wasn't still clutching his beer. He took hold of the handle and bent his knees deeper with each shout as his comrades on the platform counted. On three, a hand slipped into the other handle, and Brooks leapt from the platform and flew out over the water chest to chest with a blonde woman, her limbs flailing over the river. He fell in first, and she landed almost on top of him.

Oscar sat up straight. Camille's heart felt like wax melting into her lungs. Her throat tightened, and for a few moments she couldn't breathe. Oscar gave her a long look and cleared his throat. "I was in Seattle once," he said and colored over as he watched the corners of her eyes glisten. "But it was a long time ago, and I really don't remember much." Camille watched as Brooks walked out of the water, the woman running to catch up with him. He turned to speak to her, and it was evident from their postures that he had scolded her and they were arguing. Oscar stood up. "Perhaps you'd like a beer now?"

"No," Camille found her voice. "No, thank you."

"A cold root beer then?" he stammered.

"A root beer." Camille nodded and turned her face away. After Oscar left, Eveline quietly stole up beside her.

"I guess you saw that," she whispered.

"I guess everyone saw that," Camille replied as she blinked back her tears. She checked on Alexander as he stirred in his carriage. "Eveline, do you think. . . ." She hesitated.

"Think what?" Eveline asked.

Camille pulled her spine up into an arch. "Do you think that was the young woman at the opera?"

"I don't know," Eveline replied. "I didn't get a good enough look either time, but I'll ask Thomas later."

"No, please." Camille swiped her eye with her ring finger. "I won't stoop to that."

Thomas carried a smiling Andrew up the hill and set him next to his mother. "We played motorboat," he reported with a half smile and searching eyes.

"I saw that," Camille sniffed. "It looked like you were having fun."

Brooks walked up slowly, his arms hanging loose. For an instant he reminded Camille of pictures she had seen of ancient primates. "Everyone here having fun?" He pulled his mouth into a cavalier grin. When no one answered, he nodded awkwardly, picked up a towel, and sat next to Andrew. "Ready for that swim, Sport?"

"Thomas took him," Camille answered evenly. Oscar brought the root beer and, with a cursory nod at Brooks, excused himself.

"Well then," Brooks vigorously toweled his hair, "what shall we do next?" Eveline and Thomas looked at one another.

"It seems we've had a full day," Camille replied. "I'd like to get home before Alexander wakes for his evening feeding."

All the way home, Andrew repeated the motorboat sound Thomas had made. As he turned onto Guadalupe Street, Brooks glanced at Camille. "I suppose you think I made rather an ass of myself today."

Camille looked down at Alexander still sleeping soundly in her arms. "I suppose what really matters is whether or not you feel like you made an ass of yourself today."

"What do you mean?" Brooks swerved and honked at another car. "Andrew," he snapped, "could you stop that blubbering for a minute?" Andrew stopped buzzing. His lower lip trembled as he said, "Motorboat."

Camille put an arm around Andrew and looked out the window. "I'm surprised Thomas and Eveline haven't adopted a child yet. Thomas would make such a marvelous father."

"What brought that on?" Brooks scowled.

"I don't know." Camille watched faces flash by in a passing streetcar. "I just remember how difficult it was growing up without a father around, and I'm sure thousands of children feel the same way; yet here is Thomas with such a natural propensity for delighting little ones while he and Eveline remain childless."

Brooks licked his lips and reached for her hand. "I suppose we should count our blessings," he said.

She drew her hand back to rub Andrew's shoulder as he huddled himself into her side. "Yes," she said. "I suppose we should."

27. Formosa

Jewel telephoned early one morning in October. "I'm calling everyone!" she shouted. "Have you read the *Statesman*?"

"Not yet," Camille replied. "I just saw Brooks off to work, and the boys are finishing breakfast."

"You won't believe it. We did it! We actually did it."

"Did what?"

"Mayor Wooldridge has officially closed down the red light district," she sang. "He told the press at a conference yesterday afternoon, and the bawdy houses have until the end of the month to get their affairs in order and close their doors for good."

"That's wonderful, Jewel."

"Renfrow and I are hosting a victory party at our home this Saturday evening. I'm counting on you and Brooks to attend for *hors d'œuvres* and cocktails."

"Of course," Camille grinned.

"Come around seven. Poor Renfrow doesn't know about the party yet, but he'll dress up for me at least a couple of times a year—especially for auspicious occasions such as this one. And bring the babies," Jewel continued. "I'll have my girls here plan some festivities for them."

"We'll be delighted," Camille answered. "Should we bring a bottle of wine?"

"Just yourselves," Jewel said. "I've ordered champagne

from the Loire Valley. But I tell you, Camille, I'm so excited I can't wait. I need to raise a little celebratory larceny right now. What shall we do?"

"Oh, I don't know," Camille looked over the breakfast mess in her kitchen. "Would you like to come over for tea? I'll invite Eveline and we can . . . "

"Tea! What a splendid idea." Jewel went silent.

"Hello?" Camille looked at the receiver.

"I was just ruminating," Jewel said. "We never took our excursion out to Formosa. Wouldn't it be wonderful to call an impromptu social tea on the grounds just the way Elisabet Ney used to? Do you know what I learned recently?"

"No." Camille shot a desperate look at Coral, who pulled Alexander out of his high chair and carried him into the parlor to play with Andrew.

"Years ago, Caruso performed in Austin and visited Formosa to take tea with Ney. Can you believe it? She also entertained all sorts of celebrities and dignitaries, including the last four Texas governors. What a perfect place for us to regale in our triumphs."

"That's extraordinary," Camille replied.

"Ella Dibrill owns Formosa now," Jewel chirped. "I'll call her. She'll let us in. Can you get away about eleven?"

"I don't know." Camille closed her eyes.

"We can bring your little ones over to stay with my maids," Jewel offered.

"It's not that," Camille sighed. "Coral's here for the day, but I don't know about Formosa."

"Why not?" Jewel demanded.

"I've heard," Camille leaned her head against the side of the telephone, "Mrs. Ney was somewhat eccentric."

"Well, of course, she was," bantered Jewel. "That's what made her so remarkable."

"I mean," Camille tapped her forehead against the wood, "someone once told me she cremated her own stillborn infant in the fireplace."

"Great god of my mother's ghost!" Jewel ranted. "Who on earth told you such a thing?"

Camille shrugged her shoulders. "Actually, it was Professor Jones."

"Oh, pish! You're an intelligent woman, Camille Abernathy; you of all people should know better than to put your confidence into Durwood's twisted histories."

"I suppose you're right." Camille took a deep breath and shook her head. "I have fresh bee balm for tea, and I made some Scotch brownies yesterday."

"Marvelous," Jewel replied. "We can make it a potluck. I'll call Ida and the other veterans if you'll call Eveline."

Jewel insisted Camille drive to Hyde Park. Since she had watched closely while Eveline learned, she mastered the skills quickly and pulled up in front of the Greek classical limestone studio having suffered only a couple close calls on the way. Ella Dibrill had opened the building and waited for them on the sidewalk under elm trees swaying in the first northern front of the season.

"It looks like a fortress," Eveline commented as she surveyed the stark square architecture, flat roof, and central tower. Jewel did introductions, and they chatted about the news while they waited for Ida and the other AWSA officers. Within a few minutes, everyone arrived and Ella started her guided tour of Elisabet Ney's sculpture studio. They entered through massive wooden double doors into an open room with sun streaming in through a ten-paned window that ran the width of the far wall. Several statues stood on wooden platforms throughout the center of the untreated hardwood floor, and tables laden with portrait busts stood in the corners.

"This is the studio," Ella explained. "Elisabet did most of her work in this room." She turned a full circle in the middle of the room. "Most of these are plaster studies that were later carved in marble."

"Where are the marble statues?" Eveline asked.

"In possession of those who commissioned them," Ella answered. "For example, King Ludwig II here is in the gardens of his palace in Linderhoff. And after multifarious political disputes, which the Daughters of the Republic of Texas and I worked diligently to help straighten out, Stephen F. Austin and Samuel Houston testify to the glorious history of the state of Texas within the south entrance to the state capitol, though Mr. Houston was originally shown at the Columbian World Fair in Chicago in 1893. Elisabet did marble replicas of each for the national capitol as well."

Jewel hurried over to a tremendous figure lying on his back, his powerful limbs curled up into a defensive posture. The midday sun streaming in from behind lent him a heavenly luster. "This one wasn't commissioned. She did this one to suit herself, and it is my absolute favorite." She took her lorgnette out of her pocket and studied the torso of the Greek god chained to a rough-hewn base. "Can you imagine rendering such strength of muscle tone? The woman was a genius."

"Yes," Ella said, "*Prometheus Bound* is an example of the neoclassical style of sculpting she learned from Master Rausch at the Berlin Academy of Art. Note the strict attention to detail."

Jewel leaned in and closely inspected the muscular indentions worked around the figure's thigh. "Breathtaking," she sighed.

"The story of how Prometheus stole light from the gods to illumine humankind was a theme Elisabet treasured." Ella's face shone white as the plaster in the midday glare. "For her, it symbolized who she had become through her work—a spirit of artistic revolution."

"Where does Prometheus stand in marble?" Jewel asked. "I'll have Renfrow take me to see it next year."

"Unfortunately, she was never able to purchase the marble to finish it. She only used the best, you know. She selected her own cuts from a quarry in Seravezza, Italy, and since it was not commissioned, time and economic restraints prevented her from sculpting him as she'd planned."

"It would have taken an awfully large block." Jewel took out her fan. "Had I only known."

"This one looks like marble." Ida led them to a sculpture of two robust young boys with angelic faces walking arm in arm up an incline. One carried a torch and the other a key. "Were these her children?"

"No," Ella replied. "She did this sculpture in Germany shortly before she married her husband, Dr. Edmund Montgomery. It is marble, purchased while she was doing the portraits of European noblemen and patriots. She called it *Genii of Mankind,* or *Sursum,* which is Latin for 'uplift your heart.' Coincidentally, she did later give birth to two sons."

Ella showed them the elevated modeling room and pointed out a narrow wooden staircase that led to the roof. "There's a small table, two chairs, and a hammock up there," she explained. "Elisabet always said she liked to sleep under a canopy of stars." Ella looked thoughtful for a moment. "She loved every aspect of nature. Once when Colonel Mabry had his encampment up the road, he gave her a tent to sleep in while her house was being built. She set it up on the back lawn and fitted it out with European rugs and furnishings. She much preferred to be outside than inside. In fact, I don't think she would have come inside at all if it had been possible for her to sculpt out in the elements."

Ella pointed out the busts of the German philosopher Schopenhauer, the great Italian patriot Garibaldi, and the German statesman Otto von Bismarck as she led them into an adjoining room. "This was the salon where Elisabet did most of her entertaining." They examined the larger than life bust of Jesus and a miniature plaster of St. Sebastian. Camille stepped over to the shallow fireplace in the corner. "That's a bust of her younger son, Lorne," Ella explained as she pointed to the figure on the mantle. The handsome youth's eyes were cast downward with a title plate that read *The Head of a Young Violinist*. She watched Camille's face, took a deep breath, and lowered her voice. "She was somewhat estranged from him for several years. He turned out to be quite the tippler and gambler."

Camille nodded and, taking a step backward, bumped into a statue draped in a white cloth. Jewel bustled through the group. "What's this? I don't believe I've seen this one before."

"It's been covered since she passed," Ella's voice failed. "Please excuse me, she was a dear friend of mine." She walked to the draped figure and put a hand to her cheek. "This is the last marble masterpiece she sculpted, and she put so much of herself into it, she referred to it as her 'best legacy to posterity.'"

"Well?" Jewel exclaimed. "Let's have a look."

"I don't know." Ella took a handkerchief out of her pocket. "I've been hesitant to unveil her—as if I'm invading her privacy in some odd manner."

"She wouldn't have sculpted it if she didn't want it to be seen," Jewel coaxed. "And what would honor her revolutionary spirit more than sharing it with such a group of pioneering women?"

"I suppose you're right." Ella blew her nose and stuffed her kerchief back into her pocket. "I don't know what's gotten into me today. I'm experiencing a late wave of nostalgia, I suppose." She nodded toward Jewel. "I might need help." Jewel stepped up and helped her gently pull the soft drape from the figure. All the women caught their breath at once, and the pure silence of awe filled the room.

"It's Lady Macbeth," Ella said as her eyes welled again. Camille's heart raced as she looked up into the partially opened eyes of the sleepwalking figure. The milky luster of her face was at peace, but her posture was twisted in bitter lament. Her loose gown fell over her left shoulder, exposing her august womanhood, and her delicate hands wound themselves into an eternal writhing. On the base, Mrs. Ney had carved the words, "Oh, oh, oh!"

Eveline stole up beside Camille and put a hand on her arm. "She's stunning," she whispered.

"'Fair is foul, and foul is fair,'" Camille said into her ear.

"What?" Eveline turned.

"You know," Camille said, "Shakespeare—the witches' portent to Macbeth before Lady Macbeth perpetrated the murder of King Duncan and confessed in her sleep."

"Of course." Eveline took another look at the tortured icon with the heavenly face. "She rubbed and rubbed and could never get her hands clean."

"How much?" Jewel gasped.

"She's been sold," Ella replied. "She's to be installed in the Smithsonian Institute in Washington. It took the other officers of the Art Institute and me years to arrange it, and my soul will surely suffer more tortures until she's safely delivered. But they assured us they would pick her up within the next few weeks."

"She'll haunt me forever," Ida said as she and Jewel helped Ella replace the drape. After they had climbed the steps of the tower to see the view of Hyde Park, Ella showed them to the downstairs living rooms. Camille heated water for tea in the small corner kitchen while several of the other women helped Ella move tables and chairs from the storeroom out to the western slopes of the lawn. They set up their picnic on a flagstone patio under a copse of twisted oaks and gnarled cedars. As the tea steeped, they passed around the assortment of sandwiches and desserts they had brought and shared stories they had heard about Elisabet Ney. "It's been said," Ida spoke barely loud enough to be heard over the leaves flailing in the wind, "gossip forced them to leave Prussia for America because of the scandal over her living with Edmund for years before they married."

"And at their plantation in Hempstead," another woman spoke up, "people said she was mad because she would never take her husband's last name."

"I heard she didn't dress like other women," Eveline said. "When she worked, she wore a black veil and a velvet skirt that barely covered her knees, and on the plantation, she rode a horse around in trousers, doing the work while her husband stayed in the house all day."

"Edmund was sick," Ella replied, "and times were hard. Elisabet loved to be outdoors, and she did what she had to do for her family."

"I can't believe she slept on the roof and on the back lawn," another woman said. "I would be scared sleeping outside in Hyde Park; up until just a few years ago, Comanche warriors camped up and down Waller Creek and made frequent raids."

"I'd be even more frightened to sleep in the house," Eveline's shoulders quivered, "with all those statues looming in the dark."

"Tell them," Jewel pointed her cheese knife toward Camille, "tell them what stuffy old Durwood Jones said to you about her."

Camille's cheeks flushed as she felt everyone's eyes turn toward her. "He said she left her husband to move to Austin." She took the strainer from the pot and poured tea around. "And, he said she had a phone which she could call out on, but no one could call in—including her own son."

As she poured tea for Ella, she watched as her eyelashes fluttered and fell over her pale cheeks.

"Go on," Jewel urged. "Tell them what you told me this morning."

Camille's throat tightened. "He also said she cremated her own infant in the fireplace." A couple of the women gasped.

"I've heard that, too!" Ida cried.

"Do you believe such nonsense?" Jewel glared at Ella.

"That can't be true," Eveline wailed.

Ella blew on her tea and took a cautious sip. The cup danced over the surface of the saucer as she replaced it. "A thousand fantastic stories about Elisabet have circulated around town since her death." She cleared her throat. "It's not quite true," she said as she set her tea on the table and looked around at the women's faces. "Actually, her oldest son died of diphtheria when he was two years old. The doctor ordered his remains be cremated immediately to keep from infecting the community, and since Edmund was away, she was forced to take care of it herself." Ella wiped her face, excused herself, and passed through the side screen door into the building.

Camille looked up into the oak branches and spied a giant cobweb glistening between the yellowing leaves. "I feel terrible," she whispered.

"It's not your fault," Jewel assured her. "We'll give her a couple of moments, and then we'll cheer her up with a chocolate truffle and a sip of champagne." She winked as she pulled a bottle out of her bag. "I told you Elisabet Ney was no madwoman, but a woman of great independence and courage. Now drink up, girls. I didn't bring glasses, so I'll pour a little in your teacup when you're ready—just a sip or two since it's so early in the day."

Ella returned in a few minutes with a forced smile. Camille apologized while Jewel offered her consolations. When the women had all finished toasting the mayor and their own part in working for the closure of the red light district, they sipped their champagne, wiped off the tables, put everything back into the storeroom, and strolled down the flagstone path to stand on the footbridge over Waller Creek. Tadpoles made circular ripples in the water, and the wind blew a fresh benediction. Camille closed her eyes to savor the feel of the sun's brilliance through the rush and imagined God rifling great flowing skirts through the trees. She experienced a spasm of rapture within her heart that faded as quickly as it had come. When she opened her eyes, she noticed the roots of the trees scrambling over the ground like black snakes writhing for after-kill nourishment. On the bank, an ashen oak bent over backward, its midsection once maimed by lightning and forever scarred. As she walked toward the car, she took a last look at the back facade of

Formosa. Through the raised studio window, the only thing visible was the huge head of Prometheus lifted in wait for the eagle en route to peck out his vital organs—his resolve shaped almost as clean as his despair.

28. Fall Annuals

October 25, 1913
Dear Mother,

I love autumn. The oaks are fading golden with an occasional exclamation of orange, and after such long hot summers, the cool breezes are especially exhilarating. I've had a spectacular late blooming with my roses, and the backyard is a wonderland of burgundy and yellow. This week Coral and I spent our mornings enjoying the fresh air as we worked in the yard. We trimmed the scraggly ends off the sweet alyssum around the trellis and planted some nasturtiums, snapdragons, and pot marigolds to add a little color in the front. Brooks brought home a large pumpkin last night. We set it on the porch banister so it can be seen from the road. Andrew can hardly wait until next week to carve it.

Brooks and Thomas took Andrew to a football game today. The university is playing against Notre Dame, which Brooks said should be an especially good contest. I'm happy for Andrew as he was so excited to be going on an outing with his father. Alexander and I are spending a quiet day at home. He sleeps much more than Andrew did. I made pumpkin raisin bread this morning—mostly because I love the way it makes the house smell like cinnamon and cloves. I started a pot roast simmering and worked on the boys' Halloween costumes for a couple of hours. Andrew wants to be a cowboy "like Daddy," so I'm stitching up chaps for him and a little leather Indian suit for Alexander.

The big news is that I have learned to drive. My friend Jewel taught me. It's really not so difficult once you get the feel of the pedals and the timing of the hand brake. I told Brooks I'm going to need a car of my own, and he flatly refused to consider it, saying driving isn't "ladylike" and raving about how humiliating it would be for him if people were to see me driving around town. What he really means is that independence is not ladylike. How marvelous for a man to have the world at his disposal, while his wife's whole world is his home. As much as I love taking care of my sons, my house, and gardens, I sometimes resent his inability to see me in any other light.

Last week I visited the home studio of a marvelously independent woman. I wrote to you about her before. Elisabet Ney passed away a few years ago. I wish I could explain the wonderful, yet eerie feeling that pervaded her studio and the surrounding grounds. Her sculpture is extraordinarily powerful and fragile at the same time. One particular statue tore at my soul in a way I'll never forget, and I'm glad I had the opportunity to see it when I did, for it is to be moved to its permanent home in the Smithsonian Institute within the month. Ney did a full-length marble statue of Lady Macbeth walking in her sleep and trying to wring her hands clean. Mother, as I looked into the slits of her eyes, I'm sure my heart stopped for a few moments. In her, Ney somehow cut out and polished the depth of womanhood—driven by love and tortured by guilt—her form so nobly beautiful, yet so cruelly twisted by fate. I have dreamed about her every night since, and I wake up feeling the full range of her tragic guilt. Then I ask myself, what do I have to feel guilty about? Why do I always feel guilty when I've done nothing but look after the comfort and happiness of Brooks and the boys? I reread Macbeth *that evening, and while according to the story, Lady Macbeth did have good reason to suffer guilt until it drove her out a third-story window with grief, I have searched my soul and come to the conclusion that I do not. Then again, this epic poem was written by a man, so Lady Macbeth is actually a male depiction of a woman in a position of power. Macbeth committed the murder, but only because his wife drove him to it. He was Adam seduced by Eve over again.*

I sometimes feel like Brooks funnels his guilt into me. I'm still not sure how this works, and I'm certain not even he knows he does it, but somehow it happens. And as it happens, lately I am more and more sure he has plenty of it. Is it my imagination, or do men displace their guilt into their women? Where is it written that women must carry all the moral responsibility for all of humanity? Brooks seems to feel he's exempt from any rules of social propriety or religious affirmation, yet when I step outside the boundary of established culture or custom even a little, he scolds me and lets me know how sorely I embarrass him. By the same token, if his friends find me attractive and appropriately meek at a gathering, he beams with pride, and only on those nights does he seem happy to share a bed with me. And what I find most puzzling of all is that he never considers picking up the Bible and reading it, but if he sees that I have, he takes up a faux sanctimonious air, as if my spiritual development had somehow seeped into his soul. It's as if my goodness becomes his, while his guilt becomes mine.

Mrs. Ney must have suffered from a severe nagging guilt in order to carve Lady Macbeth with such emotional intensity, but after considering the details of her life as they have been described to me, I don't think she deserved her guilt either. Several rumors have circulated in this city since her death. Many call her a madwoman or even a witch because she came to Austin to pursue a commission to carve two Texas heroes, leaving her husband on their plantation some hundred or so miles east of Austin. At this point in my own life, this not only sounds completely sane, but exceedingly peaceful. I wrote to you before of the disturbing gossip I'd heard concerning Ney's eldest son; the present owner of the studio told us the rest of the story. When he was about the same age as Andrew is now, he died of diphtheria. The doctor said his remains must be cremated immediately so the town would not be infected, and since her husband was gone, she did it her-self in the fireplace. I've tried to imagine whether or not I could find the courage to do the same thing if I had to, and I really don't believe I could. But this tremendous act of courage and selflessness would haunt any mother to her own grave—deserved or not. And it is her great maternal courage and independent spirit that has earned her the title of "madwoman" in many sectors of this community.

Where is the line between courageous motherhood and notorious madwoman? I'm convinced it was drawn centuries ago to differenti-ate between women who followed their hearts and those who followed the expectations of a predominantly man-fashioned society—and it has been etched deeper into stone with each succeeding generation.

Love, Mother—fierce, free, and
enduring from season to season,
Your Camille

29. Security

July 4, 1917
Dear Mother,

This year's Independence Day parade was quite a bit different from those we've seen before. Only a war could bring out such stunning examples of civic patriotism. Texans are especially determined to aid the allies in winning the war since the news has leaked that Germany sent a secret telegram to Mexico proposing an armed alliance last year, and the Mexican border is only about a day's cavalry ride away from Austin. Striped banners hung from every inch of pole or wire strung over the avenue, and no less than eleven different military organizations marched. The sound of their boots hitting the bricks in unison thrilled the boys to the same extent it sent terror through me. Some of them beat drums, and the formation from Camp Mabry sang "Over There" over and over again.

We left early. Brooks hurried us away before the politicians' cars drove through. He said he couldn't stomach the sight of Governor Ferguson, so we walked three blocks to the back street where he parked the Cadillac. The truth is, he didn't want the governor to see him—especially in his top of the line luxury car. He's been home more than usual this summer with the car hidden in the garage. I have to laugh at myself when I remember how many days and evenings I spent wishing with all my heart that Brooks would spend more time at home with us, and now as he skulks from room to room like an angry ghost, I wish with all my heart he had somewhere else *to go. He hardly ever writes—he just paces the floors looking over my shoulder as I bake pies and put up jellies, and he fusses at the boys to keep still and quiet. I finally told him to build the boys a fort and swing set in the backyard, so he worried over the project for a couple of weeks, ordered in wood and a blueprint from the hardware store, and after another couple of weeks of moving boards around by the back fence, he hired a team of men to come over and get the job done.*

I couldn't imagine what was going on with him until Eveline found out from Thomas that the governor has declared his own war on the University of Texas. I've been watching the Statesman *since and have learned Governor Ferguson has promised the university president the biggest bear fight in the history of the state if certain professors he found personally objectionable weren't fired immediately. He accuses the university of being an elitist institution that takes money away from the country boys and gives it to lazy freeloading professors. When the president asked for specific reasons, Mr. Ferguson answered that as the governor, he didn't have to give them. I've never seen the list of professors he's trying to get rid of, but it's obvious Brooks thinks he's on it.*

What would happen to us if Brooks got fired? I've put so much of myself into making this house a home, I would be heartbroken if we were to lose it. I suppose Brooks would have to find another teaching position somewhere else, and we could end up moving anywhere. Help me pray it doesn't come to that. I don't have the energy to start over again, and I would miss Eveline, Coral, Jewel, and some of the other suffragettes sorely.

Speaking of Coral—I can send good news on her account. She's given birth to a beautiful baby girl. Eveline drove me over to see her, and Mother, she looks like a teeny little Coral, lying there in her own lap. She's the cutest thing. Seeing her and Samuel so incredibly happy brought tears to my eyes. Samuel is finishing his teaching degree and is doing an internship in a history class at L. C. Anderson High School. In the fall he will take the place of the teacher who is train-

ing him, and he's so excited that his eyes shine when he talks about the students and his lesson plans. Their home is small, but completely charming. Coral has planted some of our cuttings and started herself a nice little flower garden across the front of her house and a quaint herb garden outside her kitchen door.

I miss having Coral here during the day, but while Brooks is suffering through his "house arrest," I take advantage of the childcare relief and spend lots of time campaigning for voting rights and supporting the war effort with the suffragettes. At present, we are officially "Potato Patriots." Since wheat is sorely needed in Europe right now, I've taken the wheatless pledge on behalf of my family. Brooks was furious at first, but has calmed down. I'm sure if I were to check the trunk of the Cadillac, I'd find at least a loaf or two of thick-sliced buttermilk bread from the bakery in town, but I learned long ago to let him wrestle with his own conscience—it's too big a task for me.

The schoolmaster's wife has become the president of the Austin Woman's Suffrage Association, which we've recently renamed the "Texas Equal Suffrage Association" as our efforts in the capitol city have come to establish the tempo for the suffrage movement within the state. Jane McCallum is not scared of anyone or anything. She lobbies, speaks all over the state, and writes columns for the newspapers, which is a daunting task considering the fact our governor is even less fond of suffragists than he is of the university professors. We've launched a whirlwind door-to-door campaign to canvas the city. Jewel is still the vice president and has pressed me into service as the secretary. The social responsibility has been good for me. I like to think I played at least a small part in the name change. Though it's taken me years to muster the courage to speak up in our meetings, I've not relented on the belief that voting is a right that should be held by all adult citizens regardless of gender or race. While I have no glorious moments of revelatory influence to report, the group has softened its stance against the Negroes in gentle waves, and without a whimper or complaint, the voting to change the title from that of "woman's suffrage" to "equal suffrage" carried almost unanimously. I've helped to organize bake sales to raise hundreds of dollars for our cause, and we've attracted dozens of new members. We've taken an active stance on combating immoral conditions in the Texas military camps and have sold thousands of dollars in Liberty Loans. I've also organized a bazaar to raise funds for the Red Cross. I can't tell you how many wreaths and sachets I've made and sold. I've picked my rose bushes almost clean, but I feel so good about the sacrifice, I still see and smell a heavenly garden paradise as I walk through the trellis.

Andrew will start school in a couple of months. He's excited and scared, and I am, too. I suppose I can't keep my little chickens under my wings forever. He's smart and naturally social, so I'm sure he'll be happy once he gets used to it. They grow so fast. It was five years ago today when I found out I was pregnant with Alexander. We took that picnic out at the lake because Brooks wanted to see the dam being built. He and Thomas were so excited about the power it would generate for the city. The dam has since flooded, destroying the spillway gates. The Statesman *showed a picture of a house being washed over the edge of the great wall. Workers spent a year trying to rebuild the dam, but finally gave up because our civic resources have been exhausted by this war.*

I pray the world is at peace soon. I can't imagine watching my sons sign up for selective service and standing at the dock as they salute me and drift away over a murky blue sea—not knowing whether or not I will ever see them again.

I love you—forever,
Your Camille

30. Suffrage

The state of Texas was to start impeachment proceedings against Governor Ferguson in early September of 1917 following an investigation of allegations that he had achieved his political aspirations through bribery and embezzlement. He resigned on the twenty-fifth of August. Brooks relaxed and enjoyed his preferred lifestyle of working well into the evening and playing pool and golf on the weekends. Camille took down and washed all the curtains in the house, hung all the rugs on the line, and gave them a good beating. She and Eveline took the boys into town almost daily to make sure Andrew was properly supplied and attired to start school.

On the last weekend of the summer, Brooks was pressed into hosting a philosophy conference at the university. Eveline's mother came down from Boston for a visit, so Thomas offered to take Andrew and Alexander for pony rides through Pease Park in order to get out of the house for a couple of hours. Besides making their rounds on Tuesday evenings, Camille, Jewel, and Eveline had added a late Saturday afternoon round to help get the city canvassed in time to win the right for women to vote in the state primary elections. This week Camille and Jewel set out with their flyers to visit the homes in the well-to-do neighborhood just north of the capitol and south of the university campus. They rehearsed the adjustments in their usual presentation to make up for Eveline's absence as she took the day off to enjoy her mother's company. Jewel rang the bell. If a woman answered the door, they asked if her husband was home, too, and if a man answered the door, they asked to speak to his wife. If a child answered, Jewel handed her a rainbow twist lollipop and sent her skipping to fetch mummy and daddy. They had discovered the importance of speaking to husband and wife together when possible, for the wife must understand the importance of the autonomy a vote would afford her, and the husband would actually have to cast the ballot in order for her to get it. If the wife came to the door first, Jewel handed her a flyer and asked her if she wished to remain handicapped for the rest of her life or not. If the husband appeared first, Camille smiled sweetly and, slowly closing and opening her eyes, handed him a flyer and asked him if he intended to keep his wife handicapped for the rest of her life. As soon as one or the other objected, they pointed to the flyer where it said, "The vote is a weapon; without it, woman is defenseless, exploited, handicapped." By the time Jewel and Camille had read two or three of the other statements, the couple would be engaged in a heated, yet pleasantly camouflaged argument about her handicapped rights and responsibilities while they invited Camille and Jewel into the parlor to discuss the issues further over tea. They politely declined and excused themselves to prompt domestic discord at the next house.

They worked the better part of three blocks as the sun began to set, and Camille wondered whether Thomas might be waiting for her with the boys. "Two more houses and we'll have this block finished," Jewel said as she took the steps to a Tudor style mansion almost completely covered in vines. They entered through a front-screened porch, and Jewel gasped as a cat sat up in a wicker rocking chair, arched its back, hissed, and disappeared around the corner of the house.

"Damned thing startled me." She straightened her hat and nodded at Camille as she pulled the bell. They waited a minute or two before Jewel pulled it again.

"They must be out." Camille peered at the glow emanating from the front window through a part in the curtains.

Jewel sidestepped to glance in. "Who would go out at night and leave the candelabra lit? They didn't hear the bell." She gave the cord a quick succession of tugs, and they heard slow footsteps on the stair. "There." Jewel took out her fan and cooled the beads of sweat forming on her face.

The front door opened a crack. "Who's there?" The woman's voice rasped with almost the same tonal quality as the hiss of the cat. Camille tilted her head to one side. She had heard that voice before.

Jewel launched into the routine. "Is your husband home, dear?"

"No, and I don't know when to expect him." The dark figure started to close the door.

"Wait," Jewel urged. "We just wondered if you plan to stay handicapped for the rest of your life or if you're ready to do something about it." The door widened an inch, and the silence gaped like an empty well.

Camille folded a flyer in half and angled it to fit through the space between the door and the jamb as she heard a soft sob and drew her hand back. "Morgan?"

"Camille," she panted. "You know I'm not handicapped."

Jewel's eyes glowed like an owl's in the twilight that filtered through the shadows of the trees and clawed at the front door. "Oh, dear! It was strictly a rhetorical question. I didn't mean you!"

"Morgan, please open the door," Camille moaned. "We never meant to insult you; we're just campaigning for women's rights. Look at the flyer. It's part of our delivery."

The door opened a little further, and Camille strained to see Morgan's unshrouded figure for the first time. A sour odor emanated from the inside. "You should go," Morgan warned. "Durwood could come back at any minute, and he's going to be even madder if he sees you're here talking to me."

"Madder than what?" Jewel asked as she pushed the door gently. A finger of light illumined Morgan's white face, framed by long, thick, almost black hair with an auburn tinge. She stood hunched over, holding a washcloth to her temple. The side of her neck was deeply bruised. "What has he done to you?" Jewel screeched.

"Really," Morgan insisted. "You need to leave."

"Absolutely not!" Jewel roared as she shoved the door fully open. Camille reached out, put a hand on Morgan's shoulder, and felt her melt at her touch. She put her arms around her as Morgan collapsed into her embrace and wept. Camille led her to the divan in a lushly furnished parlor while Jewel turned on a crystal table lamp and began looking Morgan over. She had suffered several blows to the left side of her head and her neck. Camille asked where the kitchen was and rushed to get ice and fresh linens. "I'll drive you to the hospital at once," Jewel ordered.

"No!" Morgan wailed. "He'll kill me!"

"My God," Jewel exclaimed and took out her lorgnette to examine the open wound at the top of her forehead more closely. "I knew the man was an ass, but I had no idea! We couldn't possibly leave you here in this condition." She shot Camille a helpless look.

"Tell me," Camille dabbed the gash in Morgan's head with a cold compress, "what else hurts?"

Morgan shrugged and looked down at her lap. "I have bruises on my thighs," her shoulders shook, "and my head—

I wish the throbbing would stop. It hurts so bad it feels like it will explode."

"How long has this been going on?" Jewel asked.

"I don't know," Morgan said. "He started about a month after we married."

"I don't mean to pry, dear," Jewel took Morgan's chin in her hand, "but you're so young and beautiful. Why on earth did you ever marry such a beast?" Morgan's silence frustrated Jewel even further. "And what in heaven's name could prompt a man to pummel a woman like this?"

Morgan lowered her eyes as Camille tenderly wiped the bruises on her neck. "It's his idea of good sex," she whispered.

"Great god of my mother's ghost!" Jewel's eyes narrowed. "I'll see he's drawn and quartered for this."

"You can't!" Morgan cried and clutched either side of her head. "If anyone finds out, it will be worse. You can't tell anyone. Not anyone! And thank you for your concern, but you really should go before he gets back."

"Where is he?" Jewel demanded.

"I don't know," Morgan answered. "He got in his car and drove off right after . . . He might have gone for more tobacco or driven out of town for scotch. Sometimes he comes back in twenty minutes, and sometimes on weekends he doesn't come back all night, but you can never know for sure, so you should go now."

"We can't leave you like this," Jewel repeated. "I will never forgive myself if I don't take you into the hospital right now. I'll call the mayor in the morning. We'll have him arrested before he gets another chance."

Morgan swallowed hard and leaned back. "The mayor won't arrest him. Durwood's written too many well-worded local histories for him."

"Then I'll send the chief of police around for him. If we show him your face and neck, he'll surely . . ."

"No," Morgan wailed. "You can't call the police no matter what. You can't know the extent of Durwood's influence in this town. He will accuse me of adultery or something else just as evil, and the officials will say they have no right to interfere with a man's right to control his own wife."

Jewel started to object and caught herself. She glanced at Camille. "What on earth shall we do?"

"I could at least stop your headache pain and soothe your cuts and bruises with some of my herbal remedies," Camille offered.

"Very well." Jewel straightened herself. "Here's what we will do for now. Camille and I will go to her house, pick up her herbs, and come right back."

"But Durwood might . . ." Morgan interrupted.

Jewel held up a hand. "If we see his car, we won't come in."

"Sometimes he puts it in the garage," Morgan said.

"Listen," Camille interjected. "If he gets home, turn the porch light off. If it's still on, we'll come in and get you fixed up as quickly as possible."

"All right," Morgan agreed. "But, don't tell your husbands, whatever you do. If Durwood thinks his colleagues know, heaven only knows what he'll do to me or perhaps even to you."

Jewel and Camille promised to keep Morgan's secret for the time being. Jewel also swore that she wouldn't rest until a more permanent remedy had been administered, but agreed it prudent to wait until they could contrive a foolproof plan. She drove Camille home to fetch her feverfew tincture and comfrey salve. They found Andrew and Alexander at the Leightons' home, where Thomas had treated them to chili dogs and ice cream after their pony rides. Eveline's mother was enjoying watching them play charades with Thomas. After explaining to Eveline that they had encountered an emergency during their rounds, she assured them the boys would be fine until they returned. Jewel sped back to Morgan's house, where they were relieved to find the porch light still on.

Morgan opened the door quickly and smiled at Camille as they entered. "We should hurry," she said. As soon as Camille had Morgan relaxed on the divan and had started to administer the bitter-smelling comfrey salve to her wounds, they heard a car in the drive.

"Oh, God!" Morgan looked up in horror. "It's like he instinctively knows if I go so far as to open the front door."

Jewel paced toward the sound of the engine as it sputtered and stopped; she lowered her shoulders and set her jaw. "Stay put and don't you worry," she said. "I'll handle this."

They heard Durwood Jones enter through the kitchen door. He bristled into the parlor puffing on his pipe and squared himself in front of Jewel, who waited for him with her hands on her hips. "Madam," he seethed, "I didn't know Morgan was expecting company." He glanced at Morgan reclining on the divan with Camille sitting next to her, smoothing salve across her cheek and neck.

"She wasn't," Jewel assured him. "Camille and I were making our rounds for the Texas Equal Suffrage Association, and it seems we arrived right after Morgan fell on the stairs. Look," Jewel pointed. "She's pretty well banged up."

Professor Jones twisted his face. "How unfortunate." He walked toward the divan and leered at Camille as she treated Morgan's forehead. "Morgan, darling, how many times have I warned you to watch your footing on the landing?" He blew a cloud of smoke around her and Camille as he turned his attention back to Jewel. "As soon as you ladies leave, I'll go to the drug store and get her some cream and a couple of bandages."

"As you can see," Jewel continued, "Camille is treating her wounds, but she needs to be taken to the hospital."

Jones placed his monocle in his eye socket and took another look at Morgan. "Nothing appears to be broken, does it now, Morgan, dear?"

"I don't think so," Morgan stammered.

"Well then," he spun to address Jewel, "I'm sure all she needs now is to heal in her own bed."

"You can't be serious," Jewel scolded. "She has an open gash in her forehead, she is badly bruised, and she has chronic head pain."

"Madam," Jones snorted. "I assure you I can take care of my wife. I'm thankful you and Mrs. Abernathy happened upon her and administered to her immediate distress, but your officious attentions are no longer necessary. I'll assess her needs and tend to them."

Camille took out a small blue bottle and a medicine dropper. She told Morgan to open her mouth as she pulled the cork from the bottle and filled the dropper. As she felt Jones move in behind her, she deftly squeezed eight drops under Morgan's tongue. "What in God's name are you giving her?" Jones huffed.

"It's a tincture," Camille responded as she twisted the cork in tight and wiped off the dropper. "It will make her head stop hurting."

"A tincture of what?" Jones demanded.

Camille looked up into his sharp black eyes. "Feverfew— an herb which has been known to ease severe headaches for centuries—steeped in alcohol, which accelerates the absorption of the feverfew into the bloodstream. It should take effect within the next few minutes."

"You gave alcohol to a woman with a pounding headache?" His monocle popped off his cheek, and he drew hard on his pipe as he glared at her.

"Eight drops," Camille repeated as she gave Morgan a loving look and set the bottle and the dropper on the side table next to the comfrey salve. "I'll leave this with you. Use the salve liberally as needed, and put eight drops of the tincture under your tongue every six hours."

Jones exhaled his smoke, took his pipe from his mouth, and waved it in the air. "You can take your potions and old wives' concoctions with you," he bellowed. "As I told you, I will make sure she gets what she needs from a trained professional apothecary."

Camille watched Morgan's face as she sucked in her lower lip and nodded. Camille gathered her bottles, put them back into her bag, and patted Morgan's hand. "Call me if there's anything I can do."

"She'll be taken care of," Jones barked as he paced to the front door and opened it wide. The cat stuck its pale yellow head around the doorjamb before it slunk into the entry. Jones drew his shoulders up to his ears and kicked it down the steps. Camille and Jewel took a last look at Morgan lying in pain on the divan and walked to the door.

"Rest well, Morgan," Jewel said as she turned her glare to Jones. "I'll be keeping an eye out for you."

31. Parades

Camille and Jewel confided only in Eveline concerning Morgan's plight, and in the following months after each of their rounds, they spent at least an hour discussing ways they could help to rescue her; every conversation ended in a renewed sense of frustration and defeat. They stopped by the Jones' manse on several occasions to check on her, but no one came to the door. Camille lay awake at night imagining what might happen if she or Jewel were to take Morgan in and notify the police, but she could never think the scenario through to any other conclusion than Jones winning in a nasty court battle and taking Morgan home to a thrashing more violent than the ones she had been receiving. What haunted her even more was the thought of living with herself if Morgan suffered more permanent damages in the interim, while she had done nothing at all.

After Labor Day, Camille stood on the front lawn every morning and every afternoon to watch as Andrew walked the two blocks to and from Pease Elementary School. He looked more than ever like a little Brooks in his tweed breeches and woven cardigans. He left the house with a wide smile, and in time, Camille surmised he had developed a crush on his teacher. The revelation was disconcerting in one respect, but a relief in another, as he was doing sums and writing words on his slate well before Christmas break.

Coral came back just before the holidays. She brought her baby over twice a week, and Camille made sure all the housework was done before she came so they could work in the yard during Daisy's naps and bake cookies, tea breads, and pies while she was awake. Alexander loved to hold her and pretend he read her picture books, so they kept each other satisfied for an hour or two in the mornings. Samuel had started his first year as a full-time teacher at the high school, and later that year, Coral swore the Lord had blessed them in the timing, for in January the men of Austin voted by a slim margin to make Austin a dry city. All the saloons and bars in town were scheduled to close before the spring.

In a later election in May, they granted women the right to vote in the state primaries, and in the summer of 1918, Camille and all the other suffragettes spent a long, hot day at the courthouse getting registered. After a discreet celebration at Jewel's house with champagne sent over from France in the drawers of a sixteenth-century bureau, the Texas Equal Suffrage Association held a lively monthly meeting discussing lobbying strategies to win full suffrage and get the temperance law back on the ballot.

Another summer melted into another autumn, and before Camille knew it, Andrew entered the second grade. One Monday in early November, Brooks called from work to tell her President Wilson had signed the Armistice and the war was officially over. He said he had two afternoon classes and an important meeting, but he would come home as soon as possible. Things started happening quickly. Within minutes Eveline had come over to share the tidings, and soon Jewel was knocking at the door. "Jane just called," she cried. "The mayor has arranged for an impromptu parade at five this evening, and the suffragists have been invited to march." She pulled out her fan and cooled her neck as she continued, "As officers, we can ride in a car behind the marchers, just before the mayor's and governor's cars." She gave each of them a hearty hug and tousled Alexander's hair as he ran by. "We have so much to do!"

"Brooks doesn't know when he'll get away," Camille said as she scolded Alexander for running in the house. "I may have the boys."

"Thomas is on his way home," Eveline replied. "Classes have been canceled for the rest of the day, and if Brooks doesn't get home in time, I'm sure he'd be thrilled to take them to the parade."

"All right then," Camille took off her apron and turned to Jewel. "What shall we do first?"

"Decorate my car for the parade," Jewel exclaimed. "I have the Old Glory bunting in the trunk, and I think we should make at least a couple of signs, don't you?"

"Absolutely," Camille agreed. "I have some card stock in my herb room upstairs, and the Fourth of July flags are in the garage, but I don't know if I have any paint."

"I do," Eveline offered. "I'll run up and get it. Call if you think of anything else before I get back." By the time Andrew got home from school, they had the hood, trunk, and sides of Jewel's car draped in stars and stripes and had made a large sign for each side of the car that read "Happy Armistice Day from the Texas Equal Suffrage Association." Jewel and Eveline hurried home to dress for the parade, and Camille bathed and donned a white blouse with bobbin lace trim and a navy blue suit. She worked a red, white, and blue striped ribbon behind the plume of her navy riding hat and smiled at herself in the mirror. She telephoned Brooks' office before she helped the boys dress, and as he didn't answer, she walked them down to the Leightons' home to wait with Thomas. Jewel picked Camille and Eveline up at a quarter to four and drove them down to the northern lot of the capitol to find their place in the motorcade.

"Watch for the other officers," Jewel ordered. "Jane said they would meet us here."

They surveyed the pandemonium across the capitol lawns, walks, and drives. Several different senators, city council members, military officers, and women's club presidents had appointed themselves parade coordinators. Jewel had been directed to line her car up in three different places before she stood up, pulled her whistle out of the glove box, and taking in an enormous breath, pierced through the din. When she had the attention of the majority of state and local dignitaries, the University of Texas band, and the various civic groups, she declared Mayor Wooldridge official parade manager and sat down behind the wheel to await his instructions.

Camille watched as the mayor surveyed the assorted groups and started assigning them places in the line. "Curious, isn't it?" she remarked.

"What?" Jewel turned her beaming face.

"Parades in general," Camille answered as a round of fire-poppers filled the air.

Eveline took her fingers out of her ears. "What do you mean?"

"Well," Camille sighed as she looked around, "I can't help but wonder why the news has filled us all with such an urgency to line ourselves up and process down the avenue."

"It's a victory march," Jewel replied.

"Yes," Camille agreed. "I suppose we've felt stuck in our lives in the past year, and now that we feel we can move forward, we have to act it out in all haste."

"What on earth are you talking about?" Eveline asked as she took off her gloves, removed her hat, and repinned her hair.

"Look," Camille waved. "The mayor has left the clowns, jugglers, and bicyclists riding in first, followed by the high school band. Now he's ushering in the women's clubs, followed by the marching cadets and business owners—staggered for good measure. And we'll no doubt be next, followed by the city politicians, the university band, and then the state politicians."

"So?" Jewel's eyes narrowed. "What's wrong with that?"

"Nothing," Camille retorted. "Except it's obvious we're being ordered in a least to highest social hierarchy—and so the parade itself reflects how different members of the community are esteemed."

"Oh, pish!" Jewel cried. "The mayor is simply trying to keep the venue interesting. It's a celebration of our triumph over freedom, nothing more."

"Freedom," Camille repeated as she watched Sampson and Henrick's car rumble into place behind the Daughters of the Republic of Texas. "It seems we're being lined up in accordance with the amount of freedom we are actually afforded."

Eveline looked up the line forming in front of them. "I don't know, Jewel," she said. "I think she might be right."

"Mayor Wooldridge is no bigot!" Jewel whispered as he neared the car and motioned for her to pull up behind the corps of cadets from Leon Springs, instructing her to leave room for the Scarbroughs' car and the marching suffragists.

"Of course he's not," Camille answered as she watched him pass the car and beckon the vehicles of the city councilmen. "I don't think he means to rank us. It's just something that goes on somewhere in the backs of our heads."

A car full of University of Texas regents came up the drive, and the president of the university waved to the mayor. Wooldridge turned a full circle and scratched his head. He had the city councilmen back up their motorcade and waved the regents in behind Jewel's car. "If I were to agree it's true," Jewel's left eye twitched, "I would have to say he gave our organization a rather high ranking—after the businessmen and the troops and before the regents and politicians—so he must hold us in at least fairly high esteem."

"Or it could be," Camille smiled as a handful of suffragists waved and took their marching places before the car, "we're of particular interest at the present time in light of our new ability to cast a ballot."

"Great god of . . ." Jewel's face went white. "We're being mollycoddled." Her head turned round as she watched the University of Texas band fill into their ranks behind the mayor's car. "So why is the marching band almost at the rear, and how in heaven's name did you know it would be?"

"They send chills down the spine as they pass with their precision moves and steps, and the drums are the heartbeat of the parade. The politicians would no doubt arrange themselves around it."

Jewel clucked her tongue. "Camille, sometimes your insight is so keen it's rather like a run-through with a silver rapier."

"I didn't mean it like that." Camille's face flushed. "The important thing is world peace and victory over tyranny; we should celebrate the day without reservation. Look," she pointed through a crowd of women amassing on the northeastern lawn, "isn't that Jane?"

Jewel stood and yelled to the other TESA officers and motioned them over to the car. As the state leaders were still being ordered into line, the mayor checked his watch and

sent a member of the city council to the front of the line to
tell them to start the parade. The high school band struck up
its rendition of the National Anthem, and despite a few
missed beats and clarinet squeaks, a prevailing feeling of joy
rose from the lawn and into the November dusk with the
music. Suffragists kept arriving with signs and finding places
to march within their formation as Camille and the other
officers practiced their parade smiles and flag-waving skills
for one another. After three-quarters of an hour of inching
through the capitol grounds, their turn came to enter the
avenue, and a thrill of accomplishment rose in Camille's heart
as she smiled, waved, and searched through the crowd for
Brooks and her sons.

Congress Avenue had been decorated in such a haphaz-
ard manner, Camille laughed as her eye followed banners
looped from streetlight to streetlight. Spectators milled about
the edges of the streets instead of watching from the sidewalk,
and hundreds of balloons rose through the air, floating toward
the sunset. Older children ran through the crowd setting off
fireworks from street corners.

Camille stood and waved as they passed Thomas and the
boys. Andrew and Alexander applauded and yelled to their
mother as Eveline shouted to Thomas to meet them at the
bridge where the parade was to end. Jewel squealed as they
rolled past Renfrow and a few of the other professors, but
Camille saw no sign of Brooks.

When they reached the Congress Street Bridge, Jewel
turned onto First Street and parked with the other parade
vehicles on the banks of Town Lake. The women hugged one
another before the other officers left to find their families.
Camille and Eveline offered to help take the signs and
bunting off Jewel's car. "I wouldn't hear of it," Jewel cried. "I'll
leave it for now, and maybe the glow of this day will remain

through at least another day or two." They walked north on Congress Avenue to meet Renfrow, Thomas, and the boys and watch the remainder of the parade.

They found them between Cypress and Cedar streets, where Andrew and Alexander ran to hug Camille and exclaim over the clowns and marching troops. "Your father missed the whole parade?" Camille asked. The boys nodded and turned as the band marched by. They clapped and sang "The Eyes of Texas Are Upon You" as the sun set and Governor Hobby's car rolled by in the dark, followed by that of Colonel House. The fireworks abated, and the crowd started to thin.

"I'm exhausted," Eveline sighed and turned to Thomas. "Where's the car?"

"Back on Pecan . . ." He stopped and pointed back up toward the capitol. "What's that?"

An eerie line of firelight moved slowly toward them through the dark, and a hush fell over the dwindling crowd. "A candlelight vigil for those who perished in the war?" Jewel speculated. "It's a nice gesture, but couldn't it have been saved for another day?"

"I don't think so," Thomas said as the horizontal line of flames condensed into a roaring blaze, split up into a vertical line, and floated noiselessly down the street. Camille was struck with a chill as piercing as the one she had experienced on the night they arrived in Austin. Only this time, the air was bone dry.

Renfrow cursed under his breath and spit a cigar nub on the street. "It's the Klan."

"They wouldn't!" Jewel gasped and waited as the torches neared and the outlines of white hooded figures drifted toward them through the smoke. "Don't just stand there, Renfrow, do something!"

"What?" he asked as the procession passed in front of them in single file. The flames roared over the silence like a pall. Camille pulled the boys into her skirts and stood transfixed by the spectacle. Each figure held a different sign. The first read "White Supremacy," followed by others saying "All Native Born," "Outsiders Go Home," "Good Negroes Have No Reason to Fear," "Austin Must Be Clean," and "Witch Woman, This is Your Last Warning."

"What is it, Mama?" Alexander asked.

"Just some people who think they can tell everyone what to do." She looked down into the fear in his face and took his cheeks in her hands. "Don't worry, they can't hurt you. I would never let anyone so ignorant anywhere near you."

Jewel whispered in her ear, "I'll bet Durwood Jones isn't home tonight."

Camille nodded and watched until the last of the Klan members disappeared over the bridge. "I didn't know they had invaded Austin," she said.

Thomas' eyes softened. "They've been around," he answered, "but they've never been very active."

Jewel shook her head. "I've never witnessed such an act of pure, vicious audacity in all my years. How dare they assign themselves a finale of oppression on this day of freedom?"

Thomas took off his glasses and wiped the lenses with a handkerchief. "Certain individuals have trouble sharing their freedoms." He put his glasses back on and winked at the boys. "Let's go to your house and see if your mother will let us have one of her famous cookies before bed."

Camille served lemon shortbread cookies and milk, saw Thomas and Eveline off, and had the boys bathed before

Brooks got home. He stole in quietly through the back door and took the first step as the boys rushed down the stairs in their pajamas. "Daddy!" Andrew bounded down into his father's arms, and Alexander followed.

"You missed the parade," Alexander said.

"I'm sorry." Brooks gave each of them a hug. "I had too much work to do. Why are you still up?"

"Thomas and Eveline just left," Camille answered as she came down the stairs in her gown. "Since Thomas took the boys to the parade and they brought us home, I felt obliged to ask them in for a bedtime snack."

"Thomas took them?" Brooks furrowed his brow.

"Yes. I rode in Jewel's car with the other TESA officers. I phoned for you, but you didn't answer."

"I'm sorry I missed that." Brooks grinned and asked the boys what they liked the best about the parade.

"I liked the soldiers," Andrew shouted.

"I liked the soldiers," Alexander echoed, "and the clowns. But I didn't like those ghosts with the fire."

"What?" Brooks glanced at Camille as she took Alexander by the hand.

"I didn't like them either," she said. "But they're long gone. We're safe at home, and it's time for bed." She led them upstairs and read from the Mother Goose book until they were both asleep. She went downstairs to clean the kitchen and lock up. Brooks sat at the table with his head in his hands. "Another headache?" she asked.

"Yes." He looked up and offered a weak smile. "It's been a long day, but isn't it wonderful the war is over?"

"It is," she said as she took the tincture from the cabinet and measured the right amount into the dropper. She handed it to Brooks and waited as he took it and handed the dropper back. "I kept expecting to see you at the parade," she remarked. "Thomas said the university classes were canceled."

"My second class was," he replied, "but I had a late afternoon meeting that lasted forever, and I'd made appointments to meet with students about their papers. I couldn't know for sure they wouldn't come because of the news, so I had to wait."

"I see." She washed the dropper and several glasses before she wiped off the table and locked the back door.

"Do you think I wanted to miss going to the parade with the boys?" Brooks pushed his chair back against the wall and stood.

"Of course not." She went into the entry hall to check the front door. "I'm just surprised you haven't asked about Alexander's ghosts."

He hesitated in the kitchen for a few moments before he followed her. "What ghosts?"

"The Klan marched after the parade," she replied. "It frightened the boys, and I found it rather unsettling myself."

"The Ku Klux Klan?" Brooks blinked and scratched his neck. "In Austin?"

"Apparently so," she faced him squarely.

"I thought they had backed off on the Negroes." He returned her stare.

"According to their signs, 'good' Negroes have no reason to be afraid. What do you think they mean by 'good' Negroes, Brooks?"

"How should I know?" he winced.

"And they seem particularly peeved about the presence of Mexicans in Austin," Camille continued. "Maybe the whole German–Mexican agreement has them worried. Do you think that could be it?"

He frowned and backed up a step. "I haven't the faintest idea."

"And just who would you guess are the witch women, Brooks?" Camille took a step forward. "The women who fight for a voice in civic matters? Women who aren't happy to just shut up and cook and clean all day?"

Brooks' face flared red, and he clenched his fists. "How the hell should I know?" he shouted.

"Don't wake the boys," she said as she started up the stairs.

"But while we're on the subject," he took her by the wrist, "Durwood Jones said you were at his house politicking last year after Morgan suffered a fall."

"Let go of me."

He relaxed his grip and glowered at her. "He said you gave Morgan one of your herbal concoctions and it sent her into a state of hallucinatory hysteria."

"Why, that's impossible," Camille whispered.

"He warned me never to allow you to come near her again or he would have us both arrested."

"Have me arrested?" she repeated. "Morgan had deep bruises and a severe headache. I treated her with the same tincture you just took. You and the boys have been taking my tinctures for years. You know they never . . ."

"Jones swears he had to take Morgan to the hospital because of you."

"Jones certainly should have taken Morgan to the hospital, but not because of what I gave her." Camille felt her temples burn and her stomach tighten. "Really, Brooks. You despise Professor Jones, yet you would take his word over mine?"

"Camille," his tone softened, "can't you imagine how it felt to have to hear this from a colleague at work? You know the word's getting around that you . . ."

"That I what?" She shook her head. "No, you're not going to shift your guilt onto me again, and neither is Durwood Jones."

A red ball bounced down the stairs. "Why aren't you in bed?" Brooks shouted.

Andrew peeked through the banister rails. "I can't sleep."

Camille gave Brooks a last look of disgust and went upstairs to soothe Andrew. After she had him resettled, her stomach started to wrench. She ran to the bathroom and vomited. After she'd cleaned herself up and put on a fresh gown, she climbed into bed next to Brooks.

"If you're sick, maybe I should sleep in the other room," he said.

"I'm not sick," she answered. "I'm pregnant."

He rolled over. "Have you gone to the doctor?"

"No."

"Then how do you know you're pregnant?"

"I just know," she said and fell asleep saying her prayers.

32. Mirrors

September 18, 1919
Dear Mother,

If a broken mirror brings seven years of bad luck, how long would it take the world to right itself if the sky shattered? I ask because the southwestern winds have sheared the clouds into a sheet of glass with the luster of quicksilver, and lately, I have come to understand how incredibly fragile the firmament is. I don't suppose one could catch a glimpse of what's really going on in Heaven before the future fell into crystal pieces at her feet?

It seems like a lifetime since I left you in Seattle. I was so excited about starting my new life in Texas with Brooks, I never could have foreseen myself writing you a letter like this one, but I have great news and great regrets. I'll start with the regrets, for they threaten the rest of my thoughts like a pair of open scissors in an apron pocket. First, I regret I don't write this news with the joy I'd always imagined I would—this is also the deepest edge of my guilt. Second, I regret I did not write this letter last month when it actually was news, but I have a daughter. I named her Margery Rose because she is so small, sweet, and beautiful—at least to me.

I went into labor just after midnight on the tenth of last month; it wasn't difficult, but lasted a long time. Dr. Steiger administered a sedative, and of course, that's all I remember until I awoke in a hospital room the next morning. I rang for the nurse. When she finally came in, I asked her if I'd had a girl or a boy. She told me it was a girl. When I asked to see my daughter, she didn't respond, but as she took my temperature and blood pressure, I could tell from the look on her face something was terribly wrong. As she left the room, she said she would call for the doctor.

I waited for an eternity before Brooks rushed in with red and white roses; he spilled water all over the floor as he set the vase on the window ledge. "Where's our daughter?" I asked.

He glowered at me. "Now, Camille," he started, and I knew my initial fears were about to be confirmed. He looked around the room, put a clammy hand on mine, and told me our daughter was a mongoloid idiot. I had never heard of such a thing before.

Dr. Steiger came in and stood by the bed with a long white face. I asked him if I could hold my baby. He and Brooks stared at one another for a long time before he said he strongly advised against it. He told me in such severe cases, it's best to take them straight to the lunatic asylum, where they are equipped to handle their violent tendencies and care for them properly, and it would be easier for me if I didn't have the chance to become attached. I insisted on seeing her at once, and despite their various pleas and attempts to sedate me, I would not take their pills or words in exchange for firsthand knowledge of my own daughter. At last Brooks nodded, and the doctor called the nurse to bring her in.

I can't describe the montage of feelings that overcame me as I held my baby girl. She weighed less than six pounds and felt so small and light in my arms—it was like holding a little cloud. From the start it was obvious she did not look like other babies, and no amount of mother love could look past this fact; her coloring was yellow, and she had folds around her eyes that made them look as if they slanted outward and upward. Dr. Steiger said this is how they came to be called "mongoloids," because their eyes look like those of the eastern Mongols. Naturally, I counted fingers and toes, and she had them all, but her hands and feet were shaped differently from those of other babies.

But Mother, I still loved her instantly with all my heart, and in light of her defects and the ferocity with which Brooks and the doctor insisted on having her immediately institutionalized, my maternal instincts hit me hard. Dr. Steiger had to call in three nurses to get Margery Rose out of my arms.

When the doctor released me from the hospital, no one brought Margery Rose into my room so I could dress her until Brooks came in and said it would be all right. He hadn't bought her any little girl clothes, so I had him bring in one of the boys' infant gowns. It was so tragically sad the way it hung on her, I took it off and put the hospital shirt back on. Brooks led us to the car, started the engine, and left the hospital parking lot. He didn't drive home.

I couldn't make words. I stared down into my daughter's little face and realized I had never heard her cry. She just looked up into the sky with an expression of complete peace and never uttered a sound. When Brooks drove up to the iron fence of the asylum, the groundskeeper opened the gates and waved us through. I must have been crying out loud, for Brooks stopped the car in the middle of the drive to plead with me to hold myself together. We entered through the front door, and a nun smiled and nodded at Margery Rose in my arms. She led us to the nursery, where two rows of cribs with yellow sheets lined the walls. All but a couple at the end were filled with babies—most of them crying. "It's time for their lunch," she said, and she led us into a larger room. Toddlers drooled all over themselves as they wandered around. One child was hitting another, and an attendant hurried over to put things right.

Brooks asked the nun how long our daughter would remain in this room, and the nun said she could stay until she became too violent to contain. I looked at my miniature infant sleeping peacefully in my arms and gave up trying not to cry in front of the asylum staff. The nun patted me on the shoulder as she assured Brooks that idiots always eventually turn stubborn and aggressive. Brooks asked her where she would go when that happened.

"Idiots end up in the crossroom," she said. Brooks asked her to take us there, but she refused, saying for security reasons, no one was ever allowed into the crossroom except those who had been committed; when the time came, we might be able to visit on Sundays and holidays if the attendants could handle her. She and Brooks stared at me, but I couldn't stop crying long enough to say anything. I did overhear something I wish I hadn't; the nun whispered to Brooks that she shouldn't be in the crossroom too long, for idiots with cases as severe as our daughter's didn't tend to live past the age of ten. She said a lot of other things about the condition in medical terms I didn't understand, except for one point she addressed directly to me—mongoloid idiots require such intensive care, it isn't fair to the other children in the family if they are not institutionalized from the start.

She led us back to the lobby and showed me to a seat on the divan. Brooks went into the business office to sign papers. My head was light from crying, and all at once the room went white. The sounds of the asylum faded into a deep silence. I felt I was suspended in time and space holding a little lost angel, and the world, as I had known it, started slipping away. In the next few minutes, all I was conscious of was the hollow sound the floor made under my shoes. It grew louder and duller as the front door neared. I looked down and realized how tightly I clutched Margery Rose, but she still didn't cry. I made myself loosen my hold as I floated down the walk and got back into the car.

By the time Brooks came out, his face was so red I almost didn't recognize him. He marched to the car and reached in to take Margery Rose out of my arms. After a nasty struggle, I slapped his face hard. He stopped cold. I've never seen Brooks look so lost before. It startled me. He stood on the walk for a long time before he shed a tear of his own and walked back into the asylum. After a quarter of an hour or so, he came back out and drove us home.

I don't know what happened in there, but I know Margery Rose has not been back and will never go back as long as I am alive. Brooks hasn't spoken to me since. I can't decide if he thinks his silent treatment will make me want my daughter any less, or if his pride has been bruised so sorely by her presence in the family that he is withdrawing himself from it by any desperate means possible. All in all, he has been doing this from the start, but his refusal to acknowledge me is not nearly as painful as his gross neglect of his own daughter. I've never heard him say her name. He won't even look at her. Andrew and Alexander sense his uneasiness with her, and they don't know what to think. They hold her from time to time, but at three months, she's still fairly unresponsive, so they play together and largely ignore her presence in the house.

Margery Rose has not manifested any of the negative characteristics everyone described to us. I was worried I'd have trouble giving the boys the attention they deserve, but so far it hasn't been a problem. Alexander started school this year, which makes it easier; while it's somewhat pathetic, the boys experience more of their father's attention than ever before, because on the rare occasions when he is home, they are the only ones he relates to. He's taken a mild interest in their schoolwork and sometimes takes them to ball games on the weekends.

The nun at the asylum was completely wrong about Margery Rose's temperament. She's not at all aggressive. If fact, she's quite passive. She's content to lie wherever she's placed and watch the world go by. At twelve weeks she doesn't grab for a rattle yet and shows no extra interest in stuffed animals or small toys. The biggest challenge I've had is in feeding her. She dribbles milk everywhere and often falls asleep at my breast. I work and work to be sure she gets enough to sustain her, but she doesn't seem to care. After three months she still rarely cries. I heard Brooks mumble once that she never gets the chance, and maybe he's forgotten how much the boys cried when they were infants no matter how hard and fast I ran up and down the stairs, but I haven't.

I'm compelled to confide the other sharp edge of my new guilt that keeps me awake at night even when I'm not trying to coax some nourishment into my baby. How could two fairly intelligent people like Brooks and me produce an infant with such defects? I can't help but wonder if it was something I did or didn't do during my pregnancy that has blighted and shortened my daughter's life—and this is the biggest mystery of all, for aside from some normal initial nausea, this pregnancy was so much easier than that of either of the boys. I was so faint while I carried Alexander that I was bedridden, yet he's so full of rambunctious energy, solid in stature, and robust of complexion, no one would guess I had such a difficult time carrying him to term. I've thought and thought back over the nine months before she was born, and I can't remember eating any food or using any herb or medication I didn't use before. I had no suspicious falls or other physical mishaps and suffered no real illness or unusual amount of stress.

I wish you were here. I know you'd know how to console me, and you are the only person in the world who would look at Margery Rose without your face falling into a sudden look of shock. You alone could love her as I do, and you would know what to say to give me strength.

I've had no time to socialize, and I'm losing my friends one by one. Since the Texas legislature ratified the federal suffrage amendment in June, the Texas Equal Suffrage Association has had little to do save plan social activities and decide whether to merge with the Daughters of the Republic of Texas or join the Federation of Texas Women's Clubs. I quit attending a couple of months before Margery Rose came, and in the meantime, it seems I've become a favorite subject of discussion at the meetings. Jewel came by when the baby was about a month old. She brought no card or gift, but smiled at me con-

descendingly and tried in her best grandmotherly voice to convince me how much better it would be for all concerned if I took Margery Rose back to the asylum. I haven't seen her since. Of course, Eveline still comes over, but not nearly as often as she used to, and while she talks to Margery Rose and makes big eyes at her, I can't help but notice she has never touched her. Not once.

I hold my daughter all day and try to keep her fed. While we're not working at that, we sit out back and watch the sky. I used to feel awe only in the sunrise or sunset, but now I find wonder in a milky blue noon or the advance of distant thunderheads. As I watch Margery Rose's half-open eyes, she seems so peaceful, it strikes me to the core. It's as if the sky is really a mirror God holds opposite her soul, and every flash of light or patch of color is a secret she shares with me alone. I may have gone as crazy as everyone thinks, but these conversations are among the most profound I've ever shared.

Please pray for Margery Rose and me,
Your Camille

33. Salves

Camille's days were long through the fall of 1919. As she spent hour after hour trying to nurse Margery Rose, she had plenty of time to think. At six months Margery Rose still refused to eat mashed fruits or even drink from a bottle, and Camille had a terrible time getting enough breast milk into her to sustain her. She couldn't stop trying long enough to take a trip into town, so she kept up with the events of the world at large through the daily newspaper. Over tea every day, she watched as the women she used to campaign with voted on current issues, planned Christmas socials, and posed with their perfectly healthy daughters in velvet dresses and starched white pinafores—themselves modeling the new styles of the modern woman with waistlines sinking lower and skirts inching shorter every month.

It worried her that Margery Rose had not tried to sit up on her own, so Camille spread a blanket on the floor every morning and propped her up with pillows for short intervals while she tried to get work done between feedings. Coral's presence on Tuesdays and Thursdays became the highlight of her week. Daisy bustled around the house and played with her toys while Margery Rose watched. On pleasant days, Daisy played in the yard while Camille and Coral took turns holding Margery Rose and weeding the gardens.

Because of her time constraints, Camille couldn't get nearly as much baked for the holidays as usual, so Coral brought Daisy over one Saturday to help make and decorate spice cookies and gingerbread men with the boys. The following Monday morning, Camille resolved she would find a way to get the house decorated and, after a great deal of trial and error, mastered the ability to string cranberries and bay leaves into garlands while she nursed. The sound of the doorbell startled her. Eveline hardly came over any more, and Camille had not ordered any deliveries. She quickly set her garland aside and pulled Margery Rose from her breast. She covered herself with her free hand as she carried her daughter to the door and opened it a crack.

"Morgan!" Camille flung the door open and pulled Morgan Jones inside.

"I'm sorry," Morgan blurted. "I would've called, but Durwood had the phone taken out."

"I'm so glad to see you," Camille smiled. "Let me take your hat and scarf."

Morgan's shoulders tightened as she looked into Camille's face and down at Margery Rose falling asleep in her arms. She hesitated before she removed her cloche hat and knit scarf and set them on the entry table. She had new bruises on her neck, and Camille noticed a slight limp as she led her to the divan. "I'll make tea," she said as she bent to rearrange the pillows on the floor before she set Margery Rose down for a nap.

Morgan leaned forward. "May I hold her?" she asked.

"Of course." Camille gently laid Margery Rose in her arms and watched as Morgan's lips tightened. A tear sparkled on her cheek.

"She's so beautiful," Morgan whispered, "like a little China doll."

Camille hurried into the kitchen, brewed some chamomile tea, and put some spice cookies on a plate. When she returned to the parlor, Morgan was still gazing intently at Margery Rose in her arms and rocking her gently. "You can set her down when your arms grow tired," Camille offered as she placed the tray on the coffee table.

"I love holding her," Morgan responded as she looked up.

"I've had you on my mind," Camille said. "I've been so worried about you. We stopped by a couple of times and then . . ."

"I was home when you came," Morgan interrupted, "but I couldn't open the door. Durwood said he'd have you arrested if you ever stepped foot in his house again. I couldn't risk him harming you in any way. That's why I had to come today."

"Did someone drop you off?" Camille asked.

"No." Morgan's face flushed as she shook her head. "I walked. He's gotten worse. He can't know I came."

Camille touched her hand. "I promise I won't tell, but I can't believe you walked so far. It must be five miles or more to your house."

"I had to warn you," Morgan continued. "Ever since you happened by a couple of years ago, he's been suspicious that you and Jewel know too much. He's been spreading rumors. He's telling everyone Jewel is a mentally imbalanced madwoman, and you're a . . ." Morgan turned her head away.

"A witch," Camille finished her sentence for her as she checked the tea to see if it had steeped long enough. She removed the strainer and filled the cups. "He told Brooks my tincture sent you into a state of hallucinatory mania, or something of that sort."

"That's a lie," Morgan replied.

"I supposed as much." Camille grinned. "I've administered my feverfew tincture and comfrey salve too many times to believe they induce any state but relief."

"After you left," Morgan carefully held her teacup away from the sleeping child as she took a sip, "I thought about what you and Jewel said. It gave me courage. It was the first time I told Durwood what I really thought of him."

Camille bit her lower lip. "What did he do?"

"He beat me again, of course." Morgan helped herself to a cookie.

Camille sighed. "I'm so sorry."

"Don't be," Morgan answered. "It wasn't your fault, and it was worth it. Your herbs helped ease the pain a great deal."

"I have more." Camille sprang up and brought the comfrey salve from the kitchen. "Here, take it with you."

"I don't dare," Morgan said. "I'm afraid Durwood will find it, and he'll know you gave it to me."

"Use some while you're here, at least," Camille said as she sat down.

"I will," Morgan agreed as she went on. "Durwood let up on you for a while when he couldn't get anyone to agree with him, but now the word's out about your baby girl."

"What about Margery Rose?" Camille straightened her back. "What's he saying about my daughter?"

Morgan took a deep breath. "It's rumored the doctor told you to take her to the lunatic asylum and you refused."

"That's absolutely true," Camille bristled.

"Don't misunderstand me, Camille." Morgan glanced deep into Camille's eyes before she looked back down at the child. "To me, you are the bravest woman in the world. I would like to believe I could have stood up to everyone the way you did, but I'm not as strong as you are."

Camille unclenched her hands and looked into her lap. "Thank you for saying so. But I didn't feel brave. I haven't felt anything but numb for the last six months. But I will tell you this. Even though Brooks isn't through torturing me,

I'm not afraid of him any more. I'm not afraid of what the doctor thinks, or the nun at the asylum, or anyone else for that matter. And I'll do whatever I can to help you out of this intolerable situation, for Durwood Jones doesn't scare me, either."

"Oh, he should," Morgan said as her eyes flashed upward. "He's a powerful man. He inherited a fortune, and he's helped finance the campaigns of most of the Texas politicians, as well as the chief of police. He's paid the price in order to write history the way he wants it. He's still stunned that women in Texas have won the right to vote, and he won't rest until he's punished everyone associated with the suffrage movement he can." Morgan's eyes spilled over. "You're the only person who has ever shown me true friendship, and if Durwood finds a way to hurt you because you helped me, I'll never forgive myself."

"First of all," Camille sat back, "if Durwood did do anything to me, it would not be your fault. It's not your fault he's mean and violent, and it's not my fault my daughter was born different from other babies. We will stop blaming ourselves." Morgan nodded, and Margery Rose stirred. Morgan struggled to reposition the baby as she turned in her arms. Camille stood, gently took up the sleeping child, and laid her between the pillows on her pallet.

Morgan's eyes followed Margery Rose. "There's something else you should know," she whispered.

"What?" Camille handed the salve to Morgan.

Morgan applied the salve to her neck. "Ah, that's heavenly. A couple of months ago, I discovered I was pregnant."

"Oh, Morgan," Camille sighed.

"In some ways I was so happy, but thoughts of how Durwood would treat a baby wouldn't quit haunting me, and I knew I had to do something."

Camille nodded as Morgan administered the salve down her throat, just under the neckline of her dress. Without all her wrappings, she looked much younger and, aside from the bruises, was actually quite beautiful. She looked up suddenly. "Have you ever heard of an herb called ergot?"

"Oh, dear God," Camille breathed. "I've heard of it, but it's not an herb. It's a fungus which grows on certain grains— usually rye. Its extract will cause contractions, but it can also cause severe spasms or even convulsions. Where on earth did you learn about it and please tell me you haven't already . . ."

"I remembered Mrs. Dumont always kept some in her pantry, just in case." Morgan's voice faltered as she stole another glance at Margery Rose.

"Blanche Dumont?" Camille cried. "You mean the infamous owner of the bawdy house in the red light district?"

"Perhaps I should start at the beginning." Morgan took a deep breath and looked up at the ceiling for a few moments. "I never knew anything about my father. My mother loved me as well as she could, I suppose. At least it seemed like she did when I was young. But she went from lover to lover trying to find someone to take care of her, and when she finally found the man she wanted, he made it clear he didn't want to father someone else's daughter. So we went to stay with my grandmother for a while, and one morning when I woke up, my mother was gone." Morgan winced as she stood, stretched, and sat back down, tucking a leg under her left hip. "My grandmother wasn't fond of children, but kept me for a few years until she died, because she didn't know what else to do with me. When she was gone, I stayed at her house until a man came and said he owned it and I would have to leave."

"How old were you?" Camille asked.

"Fifteen," she replied as she sipped her tea. "I wandered around looking for work and sleeping under trees for a week or so until someone directed me to Mrs. Dumont's house."

Camille waited silently while Morgan stopped to steady her voice. "Madame Dumont was nicer to me than anyone else I had met in a long time. She let me do housework for room and board for a couple of years, and then she taught me what she liked to call the 'woman's magic.' After that I turned at least one trick a night and usually two or three on weekends."

Camille's hand flew to her mouth. "You were so young."

"Durwood was one of my regulars." Morgan's eyes narrowed. "He came a couple of times a week for over a year before he proposed." She covered her eyes with her hands. "I hated him. I've always hated him, but I knew it was the only way I'd survive outside of lifelong prostitution, so I agreed and left Mrs. Dumont's house that night. She had a fit. She screamed about the investment she said she'd made in me, so Durwood gave her money and took me to his smelly old house on the hill."

She sobbed softly, and Camille excused herself. She ran upstairs and returned with the handkerchief rose. "You don't have to . . ."

"No. I want to," Morgan sniffed and tossed her head. She took the handkerchief from Camille, and her face softened into a sad smile as she turned it over in her hands. "Anyway, he made me swear I'd never tell anyone where we met. I picked out a trousseau from catalogs, and he ordered everything. Within a month he had a minister come to the house, and before I knew it, I was Mrs. Durwood Jones."

"Was he violent from the start?" Camille asked.

"He's always been rough." Morgan's voice cracked, and she dabbed her cheek with the kerchief. "But he didn't actually start hurting me until a month or so after we were married. It's gotten progressively worse throughout the years. Anyway, when I had accepted the fact a baby would never be safe in the home of Durwood Jones, I walked to Mrs. Dumont's house and asked her if she still had some ergot extract. Since her operation has been closed down, she's quite pressed for money, and I won't tell you how much I had to wheedle from Durwood in order to procure it, but I finally got a small bottle from her and hid it in the pocket of a dress in the back of the closet for several days while I worked out my plan."

Camille realized she was holding her breath and made herself exhale.

"I decided on a day and a time I thought Durwood was least likely to come home early," Morgan continued. "After he left for work, I took out the extract and set it on the nightstand. I measured the right amount in the dropper according to Mrs. Dumont's instructions, but I couldn't make myself take it. I don't know how long I cried before I started praying, but at some point I made the fatal mistake of falling to sleep."

"And that's how Durwood found you," Camille sighed.

"Of course he knew what ergot is and what it's used for," Morgan wailed. "He didn't bother to wake me up before he started beating me. I miscarried, and he dislocated my hip."

"I'm so sorry."

Morgan tore her face from the handkerchief. "He blames you for giving me the ergot extract. I've told him over and over again I didn't get it from you and I never took it, but of course, he doesn't believe me, and he's determined to ruin you."

Camille moved next to Morgan and put an arm around her. "We have to get you out of there," she said.

Morgan hung her head. "I've thought up a million escape plans, but none of them could ever work. No matter how far I ran, he would always be able to find me, and then he would hurt me worse."

Morgan stayed for lunch. Camille had to awaken Margery Rose to try and finish her morning feeding. She told Morgan all about the trip to the lunatic asylum and Brooks' silent treatment since. Morgan helped her string cranberries and bay leaves until Camille carried her daughter out to the front lawn to watch for the boys. It broke her heart to watch Morgan take off limping down the road.

34. Patterns

In time Camille began to observe certain patterns in Margery Rose's development. It took about twice as long for her to master motor skills as it had for either of the boys. While Andrew and Alexander sat up by themselves and started to crawl between six to nine months, Margery Rose was not able to sit up without pillow props until she was eighteen months and didn't start to crawl until after her second birthday. She pulled herself to her feet in her play yard at about two and a half years, but didn't start walking until she was nearly three.

Camille had a difficult time getting her weaned, as she was always reluctant to try new foods. By the time she was eight months old, Camille was desperate to get her off the breast. At first she practically had to force-feed her, but by her first birthday, Camille had her taking milk from a cup and was able to spoon-feed her mashed bananas, fruit sauces, and whipped carrots and potatoes. Camille tricked a little ground chicken and beef into her by mixing it in with her vegetables, but Margery Rose adamantly refused to eat anything else.

She exhibited differing levels of mental and emotional ability, which came over her in unpredictable waves. For a week or two, she would learn new skills readily, speak clearly, and relate with a sparkle in her eyes; the following week, she would be content to sit in a corner with a vacant stare and her mouth hung open.

By the time she turned four, she developed some discernible social characteristics. She was incredibly loving and affectionate—always ready with a hug for Daisy or her brothers and rubbing Camille's hair when she was held. On good days she ran and played in the yard with Daisy. She learned to dance a form of the teapot, London Bridge, and other children's songs and games under Daisy's patient instruction.

But more than anything, she loved to help Camille work in the gardens. By the spring of her fourth year, she took delight in smoothing damp earth around new flower shoots as Camille planted, and she harvested caraway and angelica seeds every bit as well as Camille could herself. Coral taught her to pinch the dry ends off the lavender shoots, and when she ran out of other tasks, she spent endless hours intent on this mission. She loved to spend mornings outside, and the only time Camille experienced any trouble with her at all was when it was time to go in for lunch.

Camille's life finally settled into a fairly predictable routine, and with Coral's help, she had time to pursue her herbal arts and other interests. She brewed a fresh array of herbal oils and vinegars and made a wreath of fresh lavender, rosemary, Queen Anne's lace, and a variety of roses for the front door. Margery Rose expressed interest in all of these tasks, so they spent their days at home in relative contentment. It was still difficult for her to shop, so Camille made extensive shopping lists for Brooks. Every Saturday he went into town and made the rounds for her before he joined his friends for golf or took the boys for a sporting event.

Camille made Margery Rose a silk seashell-pink dress for Easter, and after sending Brooks in twice for organdy for a pinafore, he had returned with a form of organza that was entirely too soft for the crisp look Camille had envisioned.

When Coral came the next Tuesday, Camille planned a trip into town to get the organdy herself. She asked Coral to mind Margery Rose while she was away.

Coral answered as she swept the kitchen, "Miss Camille, you know you don't have to ask; Daisy and I are always happy to stay with Margery Rose." She set the broom in the corner. "But don't you think the outing would do her good? She never gets out of the yard."

"Yes," Camille agreed as she sank into a chair at the table and rubbed her forehead. "It's just so hard for me to manage by myself."

"Let's all go." Coral untied her apron and put a hand on Camille's shoulder. "It will be fun. If we go early, we will practically have the stores to ourselves."

Camille looked up. "You won't ride the streetcar," she remarked.

"Maybe just this once." Coral watched as Daisy carried her breakfast dishes and rinsed them off. Margery Rose followed close behind her.

Camille sighed. "I appreciate what you're trying to do, but I'm not sure I can handle the stares and sneers, and I can't ask you to compromise your principles on my account."

"You didn't ask," Coral answered with a stern look. "I volunteered. Besides, I'm not doing it for you, I'm doing it for Margery Rose." Camille's face paled. "Look," Coral scolded, "people are going to think what they're going to think, and some of them are even going to be mean enough to say hurtful things, but as long as you let it keep you from doing what you would otherwise, you're letting them decide for you what your life is going to be like." She pointed a finger at Margery Rose, who bounded after Daisy into the parlor to play. "And your daughter's."

Camille crossed her arms and looked down into the tight weave of the tablecloth. "You're right," she said, "but I also have to consider how much stamina I actually have."

"I've never known a stronger woman than you," Coral whispered. "You've always stood up for me, for women's rights, for your children." Her voice swelled. "So sooner or later, you're going to have to start standing up for yourself."

Camille nodded and rose. "I'll dress Margery Rose." She hugged Coral and went upstairs.

Margery Rose held hands with Camille and Daisy as they walked to the corner of West Avenue and Rio Grande. "I'll sit with you," Camille told Coral.

"You can't," Coral responded. "You'll be fined."

"Even if I sit in back by choice?" Camille cried.

"Either way." Coral held her hat on her head as a breeze rushed over them. "As Samuel says, the laws are reciprocal— which means color separation in Texas is nonnegotiable."

Camille helped Margery Rose climb up the curb, while Daisy pointed down the street at the approaching electric cable car. When the car stopped, Camille carried Margery Rose up the steps, paid the fare, and looked down the aisle. The seats were empty except for an elderly gentleman near the front and two young women chatting side by side in the middle. Coral took Daisy's hand and led her to the back of the car, where the seats were turned to face backward. Camille followed and sat in the seat in front of her, facing forward. Margery Rose held out a hand for Daisy and whined the entire quarter of an hour it took to get to the corner of Congress Avenue and Pecan Street. Camille smiled at the driver as they got off. He removed his hat, wiped off the top of his balding head, and did not smile back.

Coral helped Daisy down the steps behind her before the streetcar rattled away from them. "There. We did it. We're here and none the worse for the wear."

Camille nodded and waited as Margery Rose took Daisy's hand again and laughed as she looked up and down the avenue. They walked past the new Queen Movie Theater, and Camille nodded at the young woman in the box office. The woman looked her and Coral over and turned her head. "Let's try William Fink and Company," Camille said as they turned into the yard goods store. Camille led them back to the table of sheer fabrics and looked through the bolts.

A prim, graying woman walked around Coral and advanced toward Camille. "May I help you?" she asked.

"I'm looking for organdy," Camille answered. Margery Rose started running in circles around her, so Camille took her into her arms and watched the woman's face fall while she took a closer look at her daughter.

"I'm afraid we're all out," she said as she forced an odd smile and went back to her perch behind the register.

Camille walked to the other side of the table and found three full bolts of crisp, new organdy. She nudged Coral and raised her hand to hail the saleswoman. Coral leaned in and gave her a reproving look. Camille sighed, lowered her arm, and carried Margery Rose back toward the door. "It's too bad," she said with a sugary smile. "I needed a whole bolt and several yards of silk, but I'll try Scarbrough and Hicks."

The woman looked up and paled. "We might have some in the back," she shouted. "And we have lots of silk."

Camille and Coral continued out the door and didn't stop walking until they reached the corner of Pine Street.

"Maybe we should sit down somewhere and get an early lunch," Camille said. "I need to steady my legs."

"You were brilliant," Coral answered before her smile faded. "But if you think it was awkward in the streetcar and the fabric shop, you won't want to enter an eating establishment with a colored woman and her daughter."

"I see what you mean," Camille sighed. "I've had my fill of arrogance for one day. Let's just get the organdy and get back home." They crossed the avenue and entered the front door of Scarbrough and Hicks. Coral had been right. Relatively few shoppers milled up and down the aisles. Camille took a deep breath and exhaled slowly as she led Coral and the girls toward the center of the store. "The yard goods are downstairs," she reported. The store basement was practically deserted, so they browsed leisurely through the bolts of fabric until they found the perfect organdy and miniature pearl buttons for Margery Rose's pinafore. Camille had the clerk measure out two-and-a-half yards as she watched Daisy reach out to touch a bolt of orchid sateen with embroidered forget-me-nots. Camille took the bolt from the table and had six yards cut.

"What will you make out of that?" Daisy asked as she pointed to the sateen.

"I was thinking about making matching sun dresses for you and Margery Rose," Camille answered as she watched Daisy's face broaden into a wide grin. "Will you help me look through the patterns to find the prettiest one?" Coral shook her head with a smile and took a stool at the pattern counter. She held Margery Rose in her lap as Camille and Daisy perused the girls' dress section of the pattern catalogue.

Camille heard a familiar voice from the other side of the fabric tables. "Where did they go?"

"They must have left," another familiar voice replied.

Camille began to rise and greet Alicia and Faye, but froze as she heard Faye continue, "Can you believe she traipses around town with her domestic servant and that pitiful child?"

"I can't believe she thought she could control her better than the experts at the asylum," Alicia giggled. "Did you see how squinched up her eyes were? And how her mouth hung open? How about this jacquard?"

Camille felt her stomach tighten. Her hands felt clammy, so she nodded to Daisy to turn the pages. She glanced at Coral to find her staring back—her lips pursed and eyes narrowed. Camille put a finger to her lips.

"Too bright," Faye replied. "I prefer something a little more understated. This beige is classier."

"Ooh, look at the price," Alicia laughed.

"I don't care," Faye replied. "I'm going to be the most elegant woman in the room at that reception. I plan to make Adolph insanely jealous while every other man on the faculty drools over me the way Camille's little idiot drooled all over those buttons."

The sound of Alicia's laughter cut through Camille's heart like a paring knife. She felt Coral set Margery Rose in her lap and held her so tight she was scarcely aware that Coral had left the counter and walked around the tables of fabrics. "Look at this one!" Daisy exclaimed and pointed, then hesitated at the sound of her mother's voice from behind her.

"You were guests in Miss Camille's home!" Coral scolded. Camille stood in time to catch Alicia's dumbfounded expression and Faye's acid sneer. Coral raised a fist. "You should be ashamed of yourselves talking about her and her sweet little girl like that." Coral started back, but stopped and turned. "If anyone ever cared to find out for sure, they'd know Miss Margery Rose just needs to be loved and never needed to be 'controlled' like you two vipers obviously do."

Alicia shot Camille a nervous look.

"I never!" Faye shouted and hailed the clerk. "Excuse me, don't you hear this colored woman screaming at us? I'll sue for harassment!"

Camille looked down into Daisy's eyes. "We'll get the pattern later," she said as she watched the clerk disappear into a back room. Within seconds an elderly man approached Camille.

"Excuse me." He gestured toward Coral. "Is this your maid?"

Camille strained to see his eyes through the reflection of the ceiling lights off his glasses. Coral stepped up behind him, took Daisy by the shoulders, and looked down at her shoes. "This is my friend," Camille answered.

He cleared his throat before he continued. "I'm going to have to ask you to take her and leave the store. She's upsetting the customers."

Coral stamped a foot and tossed her head. "Miss Camille's your customer, too," she said as she pointed to the large bag of goods on the floor near the pattern counter.

"Let's go," Camille said as she set Margery Rose down, took her by the hand, and picked up the bag. She fought back her tears as she watched Faye prance up to the cutting table and purchase her beige silk jacquard.

She didn't remember the walk back up the stairs, out to the street, or down to the corner, but she was never to forget the ride home, for all the way—sitting in front of Coral and Daisy, counting Margery Rose's short breaths as she slept sound and limp on her shoulder—her heart continued to bleed.

35. Subtleties

March 21, 1923

Dear Mother,

I am a colored woman. I have seen the postwar South from the underside, and it is an ugly place in which to be imprisoned. I'm much like Coral—but not entirely. Coral's so dark brown it seems she has somehow become invisible. People walk by her as if she's not there. They turn her around so they don't have to face her. They push her to the backs of their minds—like one sweeps dirt under a rug. And after the dust from their feet has made the rug too dingy to ignore, they whisk it out of the house, hang it on a line, and beat it until it is clean enough to walk on again.

I have been colored black. I'm like a nasty hole burnt through the fibers of the rug and into the woodwork of the floor. I've disfigured the fabric of society past the point where a good sweeping or even a beating will restore its appearance. A ruined rug is a big disappointment, but a rug can be thrown out and replaced. However, a gouge as deep and dark as the one I've become in the baseboards of this community is much too costly to repair—even for the Kimbroughs, the Rittenhauers, and especially for Professor Jones. He has a tough enough time trying to keep his own black goddess whitewashed for the world.

It's too bad for them I have been so well woven into the tapestry of their lives and laid so sound into the pattern of their middle-

to upper-class patriarchy. For, since I have chosen to trust in my own experience and instincts, they find themselves having to excise as much of me as possible without taking too much of themselves in the process. This is tricky, and no matter how delicately they proceed, I'm sure they realize by now they will be left with an unsightly permanent scar.

Jewel's indifference has hurt. We worked together for years to win independence for women, and it's too cruelly ironic that at the time of our final victory, I was ostracized from all civic activity and sentenced to what has essentially become a house arrest. But Eveline's silence has been the raw edge of this wound that will not heal. She had become a sister to me. We did everything together. How could she turn on me like this?

However, being black has some austere advantages. As I cannot be completely ignored, I have become a macabre curiosity. Even Brooks developed an odd new respect for me once he finally accepted he could never break me to the point where I would abandon my daughter to the system. His discovery of my power of resolution has grown into a form of awe. And while it is not the relationship I have always dreamed of sharing with my husband, it has purchased me dominion within our household. He no longer challenges my wishes or decisions. He speaks to me out of necessity only—to procure his meals and coordinate his activities with the boys. He has come to regard Margery Rose with a strained civility. Their relationship is awkward at best, but better than before.

Brooks is particularly worried right now. It seems he's finished his book, and it has been published. The university faculty has planned a reception for him, and the social situation has forced him into a dilemma. Would it be less embarrassing for him to go with his witch wife or without her? In the end, I suppose he decided it would be too big a personal concession to have to leave his spouse in complete shadow, so at the last minute, he informed me it's politic for me to accompany him. At first, I refused. I thought it apt he should have to attend his own celebration womanless or with one of his extramarital consorts, but after further consideration, I've decided it the strongest show of character not to allow the circle to believe their fear of me is reciprocated.

For this is the most powerful aspect of my social death and resurrection of all: I'm so black, I'm terrifying. While they have done their best to scrape me out of themselves and bury their feelings for me, they cannot completely cover the hole. So, they look at me as if they are peering into their own graves. They need me to rise—witch black and otherworldly. They don't know why they need me. But I do. I have become their Little Buttercup. Their Lady Macbeth. They need me for balance. It's impossible to be so pure white all the time— someone must bear the black for everyone.

Love,
—still Your Camille

36. Desire

Camille's evening dresses were hopelessly out of date, and she had no time or desire to shop. While looking through her wardrobe and fabric reserve and checking the trends as reported on the society page of the *Statesman*, she devised a plan. She pegged the sides of an old black crepe skirt until it followed the line of her leg, hemmed it up six inches, and opened a vent at the bottom of the back seam. She fashioned a quick loose-fitting tunic out of several yards of plum and black print voile she had purchased before Margery Rose was born and cut a length of the fabric on the bias to fashion a sash. The evening of the reception, she wore a black camisole with the skirt, pulled on the tunic, wrapped the sash over her hipline in front, and tied it into a huge bow in the back. She pulled the tunic up over the sash into a soft blouson. She called Coral upstairs for her opinion, and after turning in front of the mirror several times, Coral helped her untie the sash, pull it into soft pleats, and wrap it around her hipline in back, forming the bow in front just left of center. Coral stood back. "Stunning!" she reported.

Camille sighed as she pulled on her black kid gloves and rummaged through the wardrobe for her evening purse. "I just hope I make it through the night," she said.

"Miss Camille," Coral answered as she reached up and smoothed a loose strand of hair back under her comb, "you have more class than those stuffy old professors and all of their wives put together."

Camille's shoulders fell. "I wish I could make myself believe that. It's going to be brutal."

The reception was held in the faculty club dining room, where couples were taking places at round tables throughout a dimly lit room carpeted in a burnt-orange pattern that made Camille dizzy if she looked down. Oscar Merriweather greeted them at the door and led them to the table at the head of the room and nearest the lectern. Alicia was already seated. Her face flushed as she watched her husband pull out a chair across from hers for Camille. He seated Brooks to Camille's right and took his own place between his wife and the guest of honor as he briefed Brooks on the events of the evening.

Alicia's eyes darted around the room before she excused herself to the ladies' room. Camille ordered a gin and tonic from the waiter and busied herself analyzing other details of the hideous decor. Thomas led Eveline to their table and, after congratulating Brooks, gave Camille a warm smile and courteous hug. Eveline's hazel eyes widened as she nodded to Camille and took the seat next to Alicia's empty chair. "You look lovely," she remarked.

"Thank you," Camille replied as the waiter brought her gin and tonic and Brooks' bourbon. Thomas ordered bourbon as well, and Eveline's eyelashes fluttered as she asked the waiter if the bartender could make a Sazerac. The waiter left to find out.

"What's a Sazerac?" Thomas asked.

"The new rage drink out of New Orleans," Eveline explained.

Thomas winked at Camille. "What's in it?"

"I don't know," Eveline whined, "but I've been dying to try one."

Oscar finished giving Brooks directives as Alicia came back from the ladies' room and exchanged hugs with Eveline.

"Brooks." Thomas leaned forward in his chair. "Do you know what a Sazerac is?"

"Whisky with bitters," Brooks retorted. "One of those back bayou sickening sweet and sour drinks. Nasty stuff." The waiter returned with Thomas' bourbon and apologized to Eveline that the bartender had no bitters.

"That's fine." Eveline smoothed the lace of her slate-blue sleeve over her wrist. "I'll just have a glass of white wine."

Camille felt as if she were standing outside a window watching the party within as Eveline and Alicia babbled on about fashionable drinks, hats, and cars and the men discussed their grading loads and class plans for the fall semester. She watched as Faye Rittenhauer floated into the room on Adolph's arm wearing her sleek beige jacquard hobble dress. She sighed as they took seats across the room before Alicia noticed they had arrived. Charles and Maribel Barrington were in attendance, as were Milton and Edna Williamson. Renfrow and Jewel blew in after everyone else was seated, and Jewel bustled over to give Brooks her congratulations and demand a signed copy of the first run. Grabbing him up before he had the chance to completely rise out of his chair, she embraced him within the ample bosom of her bronze and silver lamé dress. Thomas checked a smirk as Brooks' arms flailed in the attack. "Thank you," Brooks gasped as she released her grasp. He pulled himself up over his feet as he straightened his coat and tie. Renfrow shook his hand before he spun around to locate the waiter.

Jewel hugged Eveline and Alicia and looked across the table. "Camille, darling, how nice to see you out and about."

"Thank you," Camille replied, "I . . ."

"Your dress is ravishing," Jewel went on. "I've never seen that design before. Did you find it in town?"

"No, I . . ."

"Where on earth did you get that stunning lamé ensemble?" Eveline asked Jewel.

"This is a Poiret," she answered as she did a full turn. "Isn't it scrumptious? I ordered it in Manhattan on our trip to our Esmerelda's home over the Christmas holiday. It arrived yesterday." Renfrow had flagged down the waiter, ordering bourbon for himself and a glass of brandy for Jewel. Oscar urged them to find seats so he could start his presentation on time.

Once everyone was settled, Oscar rose, stepped into the floodlight on the small stage, and adjusted the microphone on the lectern. "Good evening," he said and waited while the professors and their wives hushed one another. "We have come together this evening to honor our esteemed associate professor of philosophy, Brooks Abernathy." The room broke open in applause while Brooks smiled discreetly and nodded politely. Merriweather continued, "The academic world was already buzzing with the success of his first book, *The Dichotomy of Human Nature*, when he arrived in our midst from Seattle, Washington, thirteen years ago. Since then, not only has he proven to be an invaluable asset to our scholastic community in the classroom and on several committees, but he has devoted himself to the research and writing of another volume of work, which is sure to enlighten and enrich mankind for generations to come." Merriweather held up a large, thick book. "Universities throughout the country and, in time, perhaps even the world, will no doubt teach the history of philosophical inquiry with the guidance of our own Abernathy's *History of Philosophy,* published by the Yale University Press." He stretched out a hand toward their table. "With great pleasure and pride on behalf of myself and the rest of the administration, I present to you, Doctor Brooks Abernathy."

Brooks stood slowly and grinned his appreciation of the thundering applause and occasional shouts from his colleagues. He made his way into the limelight and accepted a congenial handshake and hug from his dean before stepping up to the lectern. He waited and waved until the applause subsided and allowed the room to stand in silence for several long seconds before he began. "John Stuart Mill once wrote, 'Liberty consists in doing what one desires.' I'm blessed to be a part of a community that offers the intellectual, financial, and personal support that has afforded me the liberty to pursue my desire to further the understanding of the history of man's thought."

As Brooks continued his perfectly timed, intoned, and memorized speech, Camille hardly heard a word. She noted the admiration of his peers and studied the glowing faces of their wives as they savored his worldly charm and fine features framed by thick dark hair—enhanced in distinction by his recently graying temples. But the most disconcerting aspect of all was the comfort with which he addressed their social circle. Years of disappointment, loneliness, and resentment welled inside her into a flash of unadulterated hate before it dissolved into an indifference as solid dark gray as his silk suit.

While he ran down the list of his acknowledgments, two dark figures entered the room from the foyer. Brooks stopped for a moment while they took seats at a back table. When he commanded full attention of the room once again, he extended his final gratitude to the company in attendance and sat at a table on the stage to autograph copies of his book.

His colleagues lined up to congratulate him and purchase the book. Waiters bustled out of the kitchen to assemble a buffet of finger foods and bite-sized desserts. A champagne glass was set at each place, and Oscar stepped up to the microphone to interrupt the activity long enough to propose a toast and urge everyone to enjoy the refreshments. Eveline turned to Thomas. "Shall we get a plate?"

"Let's wait," he answered as he watched several couples line up at the table. "Look, Jones brought Morgan." Camille looked toward the back of the room where he pointed. Durwood Jones sat back in his chair puffing on his pipe, with an arm on the back of Morgan's chair. She looked lost in a tremendous embroidered shawl and a hat with a wide brim pulled down over the sides of her face.

"Why was he invited?" Eveline sneered.

"He's part of the faculty," Thomas replied. "He couldn't very well be excluded on that basis alone." He folded his hands and glanced over his shoulder at Camille before he looked back at his wife. "Besides, Oscar pressed Brooks to consult with him on several fine historical points. Brooks mentioned him in the acknowledgments, didn't you hear?"

"I suppose my mind wandered a little during the credits," Eveline replied. "Poor Morgan. She looks like a turtle with its head retracted into its shell in that outfit."

Camille excused herself and went to the buffet table. She took a plate, but the sight of the food made her nauseous. She set the plate back and turned around to find Adolph and Faye Rittenhauer had blocked her path. "My wife says your colored help assaulted her in the department store," he thundered.

Several conversations around them stopped. Camille's cheeks grew warm; her legs went weak. "I'd hardly call Coral's defense an assault," she replied and walked back to her seat.

Adolph and Faye followed her. He stood over her and raised his voice. "With all due respect to your husband, Mrs. Abernathy, I'm shocked you allowed your colored maid to presume to reprimand a woman of my wife's social stature. It's incomprehensible. It's inexcusable, and I demand you apologize to her."

Faye glowered from behind him as a deathly silence followed his command. Camille looked up at Brooks behind the table onstage. He set down the book he'd been signing, and the rosy hue in his cheeks yellowed over as he sat mute, waiting for her response. She willed her spine to stay straight and dared herself not to give into the tears that threatened the corners of her eyes. She looked over at Eveline, who watched her with a dreadful fascination, and even Jewel stopped swirling her brandy, took out her lorgnette, and remained speechless.

Thomas cleared his throat. "Look, Rittenhauer, I wasn't there, but I've known Camille since the day she stepped off the train in Austin. I can assure you, I've never known her to be disrespectful or rude in any way."

Professor Rittenhauer turned on Thomas. "Are you calling my wife a liar?"

"Of course not," Thomas replied. "I just . . ."

"Alicia was there," Faye shouted. "Camille's maid assaulted her, too. She called us both vipers."

Alicia shrank back in her chair with a nervous giggle. "It's true," she said as she cast a forlorn glance at Camille and then turned around to face Oscar, who stood behind Brooks at the author's table. "Her maid hollered at us, and Camille didn't reprimand her. She didn't do anything until the department manager made them leave." Oscar's forehead knotted up. He stared back with his mouth open.

"Well," Rittenhauer pressed, "it's an affront not only to Faye and Mrs. Merriweather here, but to the legal establishment of white supremacy for you to allow your colored washwoman to insult God-fearing white women. If you apologize, I won't press charges."

The window Camille had been standing behind rounded out into the mouth of a deep well. She stood at the bottom, and the whole room looked down at her. "Faye," her voice cracked. She swallowed the salty taste in her throat. "Faye and Alicia insulted my daughter," she said.

Faye and Alicia looked at one another, and Faye's shoulders lurched up toward her ears. "We thought you had left," she snapped. "And we certainly didn't say anything that wasn't true."

Dean Merriweather walked toward the table. "Come now, Camille." His voice oozed from the pity on his face. "You know that child should have been institutionalized from the start. You can hardly blame . . ."

"I'm not the one laying blame," Camille said.

Maribel moved in behind Eveline. "Camille, darling," she crooned, "we all understand how difficult all of this has been for you, but you can't dismiss the wisdom of the trained psychologist. Tell her, Professor Leighton, from a professional perspective. Explain to her how much better off it would be for everyone if she stopped flouting the system."

Thomas took off his glasses, pulled a handkerchief out of his pocket, and polished the lenses. "Well," he glanced at Camille with a weak smile before he addressed the group that had gathered around their table. "Generally speaking, in cases of mongoloid idiocy, it's prudent to commit the individual to an asylum before he becomes violent and so difficult to handle that the whole family suffers."

"You see, dear?" Maribel interjected.

"But," Thomas put a hand over Camille's. Eveline sat up straighter. "From what I have observed of Margery Rose, she hasn't exhibited any violent tendencies to date and actually seems to be flourishing under her mother's care." He gave Camille's hand a squeeze before he released it.

Durwood Jones stepped up beside Oscar Merriweather and took his pipe from his mouth. "That's all very noble, Leighton," he roared, "but we all know these violent tendencies can manifest themselves at any time." He turned his attention to Camille. "And Mrs. Abernathy, aside from your presumption that you know better than the medical professionals at the hospital or the asylum, you've also taken it upon yourself to administer healthcare to my wife. Since we all know you've had no formal medical training, I ask you, Madam, who the hell do you think you are?"

Camille put her hands to her cheeks and looked at the tight circle of opposition that had suddenly formed around her. Eveline's eyes softened, Jewel looked dumbstruck, and Brooks sat mute—now white as a specter. Camille felt one tear trace the curve of her cheek to her neck. She stood up, squared her shoulders, and looked Jones in the eye. "I am Elisabet Ney."

She heard Eveline catch her breath. Jewel tucked her lorgnette in her sash and took out her fan and a handkerchief.

"I told you she's possessed!" Jones turned to Brooks. "She used her pagan potions on my wife, which left her in such a state of tortured frenzy, I had to take her to the hospital. I was afraid in the end I'd have to have her committed to the lunatic asylum. Maybe Camille's the one who belonged there in the first place."

The room started to spin. She couldn't make out the myriad of voices around her, so she sank back into her chair while watching Eveline's face lengthen and pale. The room grew louder and closer. Camille's vision hazed over, and her head dropped. She felt as if she were about to faint when a horrendous squeal filled the room. The after silence was so sharp, she felt as if her eardrums had been pierced. The faces around her had turned toward the center of the room. Camille took in a deep breath and sat up straight. Morgan's shrouded figure stood in the spotlight hunched over the microphone. She struck the microphone with a thin white finger until someone moved the cord and the squealing stopped. "Excuse, me," she said in a voice just above a whisper, "but I have something to say." Jones lurched toward the stage and stopped himself. Morgan gave him a doleful look as she took off her hat and let her shawl drop around her shoulders. Gasps filled the room at the deep bruises that ran from Morgan's hairline down her face and neck and over her right shoulder. "Durwood beats me," she said. "He beats me at least once a day."

She waited until all the reactions of disbelief had abated. "Camille and Jewel came by one day on a suffrage call after he had punched a gash in my forehead and bruised my neck and shoulder much like this. Camille gave me a salve for my wounds and an herbal tincture that eased the pain a great deal. Any hysteria Durwood observed from me was due to my own sense of self and resistance after Camille and Jewel had expressed concern for me. He did take me to the hospital recently because he'd beaten me until I miscarried and dislocated my hip, but it certainly wasn't because of anything Camille did. She's never been anything but gentle and kind to me."

Jewel rushed forward. "You're coming home with me," she announced with a reproving look at Professor Jones. "We'll get you the best domestic attorney available."

Jones raised a fist and cursed Morgan and Jewel. He lowered it and assessed several of the shocked faces staring back at him before he stormed out of the club.

The crowd that had amassed around Camille broke up, and Brooks glared down at her from his table with a blank face. As everyone had rallied around Morgan, he had no one waiting to discuss his work, so he autographed a few books, placed them in a neat stack at the front of the table, and went to the buffet. In a few moments, he sat down next to Camille and set a plate in front of her. She nibbled on a chocolate strawberry. As he poured her more champagne, she tried to engage his eyes. "I thought your book was about desire."

Brooks took a swig of bourbon and looked down at his lap. "No. I had to give up on that years ago. My research kept leading me round in circles, so when I had trouble finding a good text for my History of Philosophy class, Oscar suggested I write one. It seemed so much easier than wrestling with another universal. I gave in."

The children were asleep when they arrived home. While Brooks drove Coral back to the east side of town, Camille put on her gown and curled up in bed with quill and rose-scented stationery. When he returned, he washed up and lay beside her. "What are you doing?" he asked.

"I'm writing a letter."

"To whom?"

"To Mother."

Brooks waited while she folded up the letter, put it in an envelope, addressed it, and placed it and her quill in the nightstand. He turned off the lamp. "Perhaps it's time we took a trip to Washington," he said.

"I'd love to take the children to the sound," she replied as she closed her eyes.

"I'll arrange for rail passage tomorrow." He kissed her forehead before he turned toward the wall and started snoring.

37. Home

Two weeks after their train left Austin, the Abernathys took a steamer from the Seattle–Belltown dock to Bainbridge Island on Puget Sound. Camille was anxious to show her children where their grandfather had worked. They watched crewmen cut and shape wood for the huge trading ships for over an hour as Camille related to her sons what little she remembered of her father and how the supports of one of the great cedar masts gave way and caused his untimely death. At a general store on the waterfront, Camille selected items for a picnic lunch and Brooks bought each of the children a shiny pail with a shovel and a bag of saltwater taffy. They hiked up the shoreline until they found a secluded stretch of sandy beach.

Brooks, Alexander, and Andrew ran into the low tide, splashing one another until they grew tired. Brooks found a stick and drew a perimeter circle for a castle and demonstrated the fundamentals of packing and shaping sand into walls and towers. Camille walked Margery Rose slowly to the water's edge until their feet were submerged. Margery Rose squealed with delight as the receding waves pulled the sand from under her heels. They looked for seashells until Margery Rose's pail was half full.

Camille spread a blanket in the sand and made ham and cheese sandwiches as she kept close watch on her daughter, who continued to hunt for bigger and more colorful shells. Camille took delight in the way she leaned over to inspect each one and turned it over in her hand several times before running it over to the boys for use in decorating their castle. Brooks wiped his hands and lay down next to his wife to revel in the Pacific sun. After a few minutes, he turned on his side. "It doesn't seem possible, does it?"

"What?" Camille covered the sandwiches with a cloth.

"Being here with our children." He smiled.

"No." She measured blueberries into five cups. "Are you ready to eat?"

"I'll wait for the children," he sighed. "I thought we might talk for a bit."

"Really?" Camille turned. "What do you want to talk about?"

"Well," Brooks looked out toward the horizon, "I'm glad we came, aren't you?"

"Yes." She tilted her head, stretching her neck.

Brooks sat up. "It gave Dad a lot of pleasure to show the boys around the apple orchard."

"Your parents did seem to enjoy getting to know the boys," she replied as she brushed sand off her shoulder.

He reached out to brush off her back. She started at his touch. He paused for moment before he continued. "Mother commented on how well you've done with Margery Rose more than once."

Margery Rose dumped shells on the beach next to Alexander and waited for his approval before she ran off to look for more. "She did seem particularly impressed with her dexterity at shelling peas for dinner Sunday," Camille answered.

Brooks let out a nervous laugh, lay back down for a few moments, and sat up again. "Let's talk about yesterday—the visit to Belltown and our trip to the cemetery."

"What about the cemetery?" Camille's head spun around.

"How did you feel, I mean . . ."

"What *do* you mean?"

Brooks scratched his ear and stared down at the blanket.
"You see, Thomas said it might be good for you to talk about
it."

"Oh," Camille wiped the sweat from her forehead, "now
I understand. This whole trip was supposed to be some sort
of therapy for me."

"No, I . . ."

"So, you *do* think I've gone mad," she snapped.

"Not at all. Sometimes it just seems you've lost sight of
the line between . . ."

"So, I've crossed another one of your lines." She listened
to the rhythm of his breathing behind her. Margery Rose sat
down in the tide flat several yards from the boys and shoveled
wet sand over her legs.

"All right," Brooks took a long breath, "how many letters
have you written to your mother since we moved to Austin?"

"I don't know." Camille took a bite of a sandwich. "What
difference does it make? You should eat one of these before
the bread gets stale."

"Don't change the subject," Brooks frowned. "About
how many would you say you have written?"

Camille set the sandwich down on a napkin. "Several—
hundreds, I don't know."

"Hundreds!" He moved around in front of her and took
her by the shoulders. "Camille, your mother is dead!"

Over his shoulder the clouds blew open to reveal the
outline of a waxing mid-morning moon. She listened to the
sweet sound of her sons' voices. Margery Rose squawked
with pleasure as she packed the wet sand over her shins. "Of
course my mother's dead," she replied as she looked into his
eyes. They had faded through the years, but their depth was

still inescapable. "I buried her one week before I married you."

"Yes, yes." He stretched out his arms to embrace her. She gently pushed him away and hugged her knees. She counted the waves that washed up on the shore behind her children. Somewhere in the sixties, she heard him whisper.

"Camille? Do you still love me?"

She took her comb out of her hair and pulled back the strands that had blown loose. As she re-secured it, she scanned the hills to the east. Somewhere within them was the home she had lived in before her father died. She imagined him walking between the cedars. He looked a lot like Oscar Merriweather. She closed her eyes and shook her head. "I swear, I don't know any more."

"I suppose you think I could've been a better husband," he sighed. After a few moments he continued. "I'll tell you anything you want to know." She cast him a wry look. "Really," he insisted, "anything at all. I'll tell you the truth. I swear to God—I owe you that much. What do you want to know?"

Alexander's voice rang over the sand. "No! We need four towers and a gate on the ocean side." Andrew refuted in words she couldn't make out.

"Nothing," she replied.

"Nothing?" he exclaimed. "Nothing at all?"

"Nothing at all," she repeated.

He drew his legs up to his chest, rested his forehead on his arms, and spoke into the cave he'd made of himself. "How can you say that?"

"I don't know," she said as the clouds swallowed up the moon again. "I guess somewhere along the way I just unattached myself."

The boys' bickering grew louder. Brooks yelled a sharp reprimand and leaned back on his elbows. "I should have . . ." he said.

"You should have what?" she asked.

"I should have defended you at the reception."

"Yes," she turned to face him, "you certainly should have."

"I'm sorry," he moaned. "I'm truly sorry."

"Boys! Margery Rose!" she called. "Come for . . ."

"Wait," he interrupted. The children looked back at her. The boys hushed over their argument, and Margery Rose shoveled more damp silt over her knees. "Why did you write so many letters?"

"You told me to write to her," she retorted.

"The first time," he answered. "Thomas said it might be healing for you, but I never dreamed you would . . ."

She turned her back to him and wrote her mother's name in the sand with her finger, R-O-S-E D-E-N-N-I-S-O-N. "I was so lonely."

"But you've always had so many friends." He touched her arm.

"Not like that," she sighed. "You wouldn't understand."

"Where are the letters now?" he asked. "Did you post them at all?"

"You still think I'm mad, don't you?" She offered him a weak smile and poured out lemonade. "They're all in hat-boxes up in the attic."

He managed a grin. "Will you continue to write to her?"

"Probably not," she answered. "I've decided to join the workforce."

"Really?" he watched her set places around the blanket and shouted another warning to the boys to stop their bickering. "What will you do?"

"I've decided to be a philosopher," she said as she

watched his eyes widen and narrow. He took a handful of sand and let it sift slowly through his fingers. "You would be a splendid philosopher," he answered.

"Yes, I would." She called the children to lunch again. Margery Rose glanced around at her and continued to pack the sand down on her lap with a wide smile.

"Just a few more minutes, Mother, please!" Andrew called back. "We almost have the walls finished." The boys argued over whether or not they should build a drawbridge before or after they poured water for the moat.

Camille sighed. "But, you already hold the most prestigious philosophy position in Austin, and I'm not heartless enough to deprive you of it."

"I see," Brooks chuckled.

The sun appeared overhead. "Their lunch will spoil," Camille fussed as she checked the sandwiches and covered them again.

"Let them play," Brooks answered. "Who knows when we will be able to come back."

"Who knows if." Camille took up her sandwich and handed one to Brooks.

"What?" He folded it over and bit half of it off.

"What if the nun at the asylum was right," she said. "What if Margery Rose doesn't . . ."

Brooks put a hand on her shoulder. "Now, Camille, we were made aware of the circumstances before we decided to, well, before you decided . . . That's why everyone suggested we leave her."

"It wasn't a decision," she replied.

"Then what would you call it?"

"An instinct—a mother's pure instinct. If my daughter might not make it past her tenth birthday, I just couldn't let her live out her few years without her mother's love."

Brooks hesitated. "I understand how you feel," he said. "But," his face soured as he threw his sandwich on his plate and waved a hand toward his daughter, "just look at her! She's so disturbed she's spent the last hour putting mud on herself and sitting in it."

Camille's mind went blank. Margery Rose smiled sweetly as she patted the mound of sludge piled up to her chest. Andrew was scolding Alexander, who had accidentally knocked over the northern tower as he stood up to get water for the moat. Camille observed the pain in her husband's eyes as he watched their daughter revel in the dank folds of the earth. "No, Brooks," she answered. "Look closer. She's the only one of us who is not disturbed."

He winced, opened a beer, and ate the rest of his sandwich. Camille lay back on the blanket and inhaled the salty air. A gull screamed overhead, and a dark shadow moved over her followed by a cool breeze. The back of her neck prickled as she opened her eyes. "Oh, my God!" Brooks yelled. "Look!" A tremendous wall of water roared toward the shore from the mouth of the sound. "Get the boys!"

Camille sat up and froze as she assessed the weight of the sand Margery Rose had piled over herself. "Now!" Brooks yelled as he sprang off down the beach. "Get the boys!" She found her feet and ran to Alexander first, who was nearest the water's edge, taking him under one arm. She gathered up Andrew with the other. They shouted their protest until they heard the sound of the high tide behind them and ran with her up the bank to the grassy ridge.

Brooks pounded up behind her, covered in wet sand. Margery Rose clung to his breast, laughing hysterically. As they watched the high tide pound the castle to ruins and carry their pails, shovels, and sandwiches back into the depths of the sound, Camille put a hand over her heart to make sure it hadn't stopped. "I can't believe I let myself forget how violent the noon tide can be."

"Our castle!" Andrew shouted.

"It's all right," Brooks exclaimed. Camille had only seen his cheeks glow so ruddy once before in her life. "We're all right now," his voice trembled as he tousled the hair of each of the boys. "We can get cleaned up and have lunch at the café."

"The taffy!" Alexander started down the beach toward a candy left stranded in the sand. Camille caught him. "We'll get more."

Tears welled in Brooks' eyes as Margery Rose's laughing grew louder and wilder. He held her close to his chest all the way back to the shipyard.

38. Perennials

So much happened in Austin during the three weeks they were gone on vacation, Camille felt as if she were returning to another life. Thomas picked them up from the train station and told them a violent storm had blown through town the week before with winds so high, the damage had been severe throughout town. He also said oil had been struck on the university's West Texas holdings where Renfrow Kimbrough had calculated. The Santa Rita Number One well had already produced so many barrels of oil that the University of Texas was predicted to become the richest college in the world within the next year.

When they arrived home, Thomas helped them carry their baggage and inspect their home for storm damage. The house itself was fine, but high winds had razed some of the backyard. The trellis had been lifted out of the ground, blown across the lawn, and smashed against the back fence. The Madame George Staechelin roses were severely damaged, and the Kathryn Morley English rose bush had been completely uprooted. Brooks said he'd arrange to have another trellis made, but after looking around the yard as the sun fell behind the trees, Camille decided she preferred the way the yard looked without the extra clutter.

Then Thomas told them the biggest news of all. The week before, Eveline's mother had suffered a severe stroke. Eveline had left to travel up the Atlantic Seaboard to help care for her. Camille expressed her concern and extended an open dinner invitation to Thomas. He came over almost every night for a month; then she didn't see him at all for about a week. When he came back one evening in midsummer, he confided to her that Eveline had sent him a letter to report her mother's condition had improved, but she had decided to stay in Boston permanently. Though he was upset, he didn't seem surprised. Things hadn't been the same between them since he'd suggested they adopt a child.

Her husband's new fame didn't deter Jewel Kimbrough from accomplishing her latest civic goal. She prevailed upon her son's influence in St. Louis to contract a nationally known attorney. A month after he arrived in Austin, Durwood Jones was tried and convicted on several accounts of assault. After Morgan's testimony and several of Durwood's untimely outbreaks throughout the legal process, the judge pronounced him violently insane. He finally gained admittance to the crossroom at the lunatic asylum and never came out again.

Morgan sold the smelly old mansion between the university and the capitol and bought a charming new home in Tarrytown. Camille, Coral, Brooks, and Thomas helped her move and get settled, after which Thomas had dinner at Morgan's house almost every night.

For the rest of the summer, Camille and Coral helped Morgan decorate her new home and start a cutting garden in her backyard. Morgan developed an interest in making scented candles, so they spent several days experimenting with wax melting methods and different combinations of additives, including flower petals, leaves, oils, and extracts. Camille taught Morgan to drive Durwood's sports coupe. They took several outings each week for lunch, shopping, and to research their business plan.

Brooks decided it wouldn't do for Morgan to have her own car while Camille didn't, so he announced his plans to buy himself a sporty new 1924 Renault Torpedo and to give her the Cadillac. She explained to him the Cadillac wasn't really her style and how much she had admired the looks of the new 1924 Chryslers. After much discussion, they took several trips to the Chrysler dealership and ordered one to be delivered on Camille's thirty-third birthday.

Daisy started the first grade. Margery Rose's days were long without her, but they picked Daisy up in Morgan's car every afternoon, and after she finished her spelling and sums, she spent the remainder of the afternoon working in the gardens and playing with Margery Rose. Daisy manifested a natural talent in floral arranging and took to making small wreaths and garlands. As she worked, she taught Margery Rose to trim stems and braid ribbon. Margery Rose also took pride in her ability to dust furniture and sweep floors with her toy broom. She fussed around the house while Camille and Coral worked around the clock portioning out tinctures and salves; concocting lotions, toilette waters, and bath soaks; steeping fresh vinegars and oils; mixing potpourris; and stitching up lace bags for sachets.

By the time the first leaves of autumn yellowed, Brooks helped Camille, Morgan, and Coral obtain a lease on the Wheatville Bar from Samuel's former owner. Brooks hired contractors, and by Thanksgiving the site was remodeled, freshly painted, and ready for business. The women spent three days and nights baking a variety of holiday pies, tea breads, and cookies before Brooks, Andrew, Alexander, Samuel, Thomas, and several other curious faculty members helped them move everything in and set up shop. On the first day of December 1923, they opened the doors of *Rose's Herb Emporium*.

They were overwhelmed with customers from the first day. Camille couldn't keep enough comfrey salve or feverfew tincture on the shelves, Morgan sold out her stock of candles within a few hours, and Coral rang up so many holiday wreaths and garlands that Camille, Daisy, and Margery Rose spent every extra second they could find in the back working on more. Jewel came in the first afternoon and bought the last tray of cookies and tea breads. She heartily suggested they add on a tearoom as Camille, Coral, and Morgan exchanged desperate looks.

They slept very little those first few weeks. Camille spent more than one night baking until dawn, but every day they learned ways to streamline their production of goods and services, and before long they achieved a comfortable work rhythm. By Christmas Eve they had already turned a handsome profit.

Though she was completely exhausted, it turned out to be the best Christmas day Camille had ever known. As soon as the dinner dishes were cleared, the boys excused themselves and went out back to play with their new croquet set. Margery Rose took Daisy by the hand to show off her new dollhouse. Brooks opened champagne and proposed a toast to the women and their success. Samuel served mincemeat pie, and Thomas ran upstairs to get the Victrola while Camille brought down her forget-me-not scented stationery and quill. As the men washed the dishes, she wound up the Victrola, put on Chopin's *op. 10, no. 3,* and sat down with Coral and Morgan to begin drafting plans for their new tearoom.

39. Comfort

January 3, 1924
Dear Tess,

Thank you for not crossing me off your Christmas card list! I appreciate that you've kept me in your holiday thoughts despite the fact I haven't sent out cards in the past few years. The truth is, my world felt as if it was falling apart five years ago when I gave birth to my daughter, Margery Rose. She was diagnosed with mongoloid idiocy, and despite the doctor's warnings to have her institutionalized, I just couldn't. While I can't pretend it hasn't been a strain on all of us, she's grown to be such a loving and integral part of our family. Now we couldn't imagine what our lives would be like without her.

I'm delighted you and your girls will have a stopover in Austin on your way out west this spring. You didn't say how long you expect to be here, but I hope it will be long enough for us to visit. I can pick you up at the train station, and if time permits, I'd love to show you the herb shop I've opened with two of my dearest friends. By then we plan to have the tearoom fully operational. If you'll be here for more than one day, Brooks and I insist you stay with us. We have plenty of room.

I thought about you last summer when we took the children for a trip back up to Washington. We spent a few days with Brooks' parents in Tacoma and over a week in the Seattle area. It's the first time I've been to the cemetery since my mother's funeral. She died a cou-

ple of weeks before I met you on the train. I know it sounds odd, but as I put fresh roses on her grave, I felt as if she passed some of her leftover life energy into me. Nothing's been the same since.

I've been thinking a lot about the last fourteen years since Brooks and I started out from the West Coast and began our lives in the heart of Texas. We had such grand plans for ourselves, for our home, and for our family. I've come to the conclusion there are two ways in which one can assess success. So many things didn't turn out the way I'd dreamed; still—everything turned out exactly the way it was supposed to. Do you know what I mean?

Best wishes for the happiest New Year yet—
Camille Dennison Abernathy